Jesus is the one who provides the dreams. I just write them down.

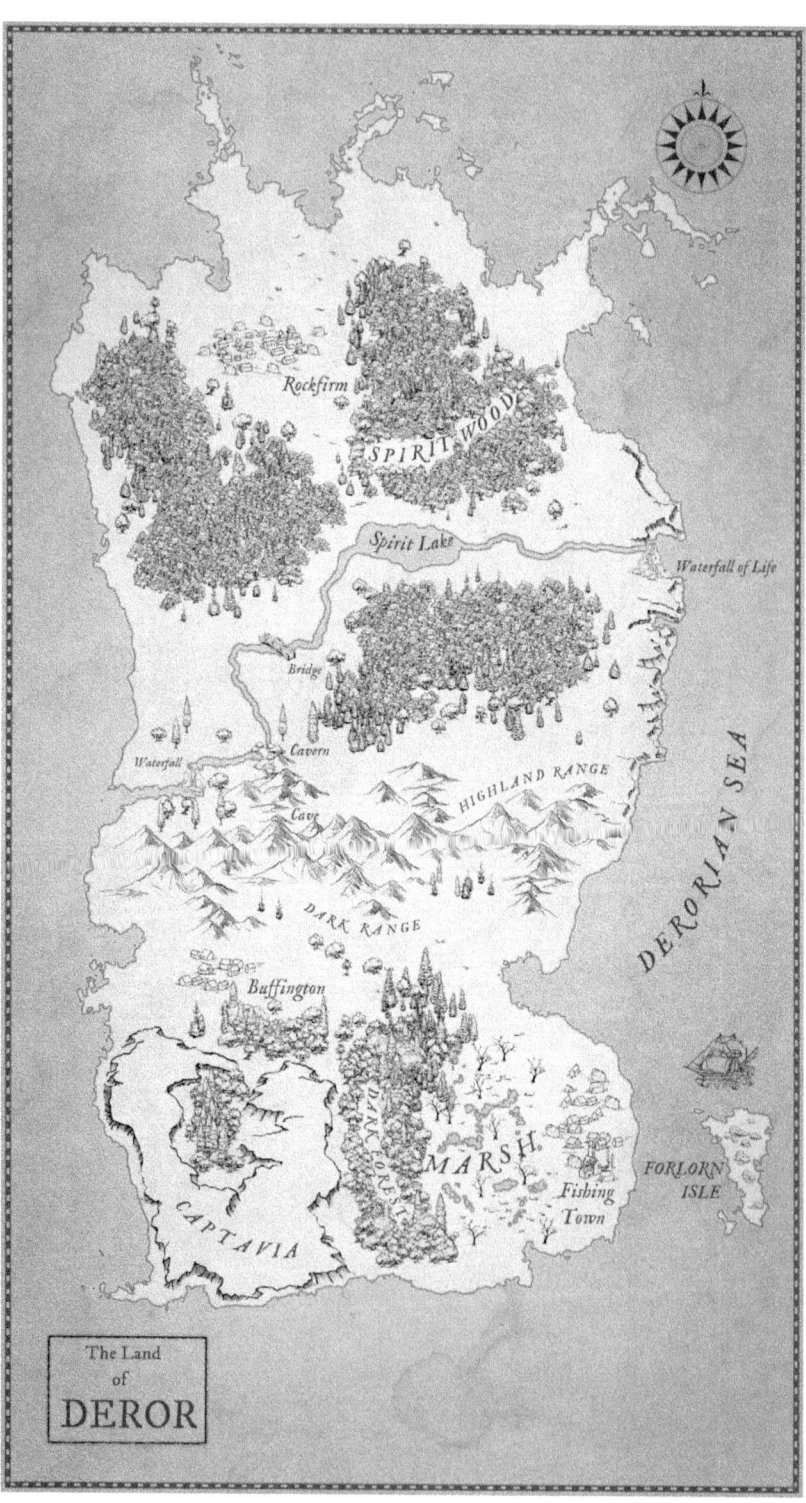

Rockfirm

SPIRIT WOOD

Spirit Lake

Waterfall of Life

Bridge

Waterfall

Cavern

Cave

HIGHLAND RANGE

DARK RANGE

DERORIAN SEA

Buffington

DARK FOREST

MARSH

Fishing Town

FORLORN ISLE

CAPTAVIA

The Land
of
DEROR

4

ISBN: 979-8-9946517-0-4 (Paperback)
ISBN: 979-8-9946517-1-1 (ebook)

Cover design by: Sienna Arts
Library of Congress Control Number: 2026901807
Printed in the United States of America

Published by Purple Wisteria Press

The Vision of Spirit Eyes

Written by Lauren Stanfill

Purple Wisteria Press

Psalms 107

V 10 — Some sat in darkness and in the shadow of death, prisoners in affliction and in irons,

V 11 — They had rebelled against the words of God, and spurned the counsel of the Most High.

V 12 — So he bowed their hearts down with hard labor; they fell down, with none to help.

V 13 — Then they cried to the Lord in their trouble, and he delivered them from their distress.

V 14 — He brought them out of darkness and the shadow of death, and burst their bonds apart.

V 15 — Let them thank the Lord for his steadfast love, for his wondrous works to the children of man!

V 16 — For he shatters the doors of bronze and cuts in two the bars of iron.

V 23 — Some went down to the sea in ships, doing business on the great waters;

V 24 — They saw the deeds of the Lord, his wondrous works in the deep.

V 25 — For he commanded and raised the stormy wind, which lifted up the waves of the sea.

V 26 — They mounted up to heaven; they went down to the depths; their courage melted away in their evil plight;

V 27 — They reeled and staggered like drunken men and were at their wits end.

V 28 — Then they cried to the Lord in their trouble, and he delivered them from their distress.

V 29 — He made the storm be still, and the waves of the sea were hushed.

V 30 — Then they were glad that the waters were quiet, and he brought them to their desired haven.

Note from the Author

For the reader's sake, there is a sun , ☀ , symbol with the chapter number at the beginning of the chapters that show Keeper is dreaming. The *italicized* portions show when someone is dreaming. Also, when someone is thinking words to themselves it is represented with 'apostrophes' around the words.

Chapter 1
Spirit Eyes

Spirit Eyes—they are eyes that have been opened. They can see, but not merely the common world around them, but the one above. Seeing through these eyes is what makes us different. What sets us apart; what gives us our purpose while living on earth.

This is a story of how Keeper's eyes were once opened into new life, so that you may believe and see for yourself the hope of the calling. Surely, it is placed on those who are called!

Thus, this story begins with a dream. Yes, a realization that started it all, thus catalyzing the journey of one's life.

There was darkness and there was light, there was nothing and then there was everything. For the life of her, it was the beginning of the end but, if she looked at it truly, it was more like the end of the beginning. The world had changed from many years ago, its population was futile, but there still was hope. In this, the people of the world would cry out and believe. As Keeper stood by the Waterfall of Life she would say as she dreamed of the change the Holy One could bring, imaging herself flying:

As I stood on that lonely peak
I thought of what could have caused that fate
So as I gathered all my breath
I closed my eyes and began to fall
Down I fell through the cloudy walls
And what could have caused it all
To that I thought, 'is this the end?'
And that is what I tell you friend

I thought it could have ended then
But, as I thought of this fate
I began to think it could wait
So as I thought about this, friend
'This is not the end,' I thought at once
With a change of mind and heart
I was going to live my life, make it art
So I stretched out my new wings and began to glide
Fly I did, away from loss
Up I flew through the cloudy walls
And I thought about my new fate
I knew for sure I could not wait
For a life to be forever more.

For everyone there is a gift and for every pupil there is a teacher. And to the wise there is wisdom and to the ones of understanding there is knowledge. Keeper asked herself: What if not everyone has a gift and what if your gift is not of any help to you? Who is the teacher? Who is wise or understanding? She didn't know the Holy One's brilliant ways then, so she did not have those answers then and there.

To each one of us the Holy One gave a gift. To some he gave a sharp understanding mind and to others he gave a gift what he called a spiritual gift—to her he gave the gift of Spiritual Eyes. She chose to accept her differences from the start but, after some time she began to think that there was something off-beam.

Keeper was unusual to the other beings that had received their gifts. In the beginning, she was not very positive nor was she like a typical person you would come in contact with. Keeper constantly lived in her own miniature world—it was lonely and shrouded in discharged thoughts of how she of all people was unusual. And she thought why did it have to be her, a different, cast off, unneeded, unwanted, misfit? She felt like she was stuck in a glass cube—she could see the world, but she was not a part of it.

Still, Keeper would get up for the day for doing her own will apart from the Holy One's will—never changing her thinking and never changing the way she looked at others and herself. The days she had lived in were cold, dark, unforgiving, and unloving. For the life of her, it was the beginning of the end but, if she looked at it, it was more like the end of the beginning. Every thought that came into her head was what she wished to happen, what she knew could not happen, but begged to be true. Somewhere in her heart and soul she was begging the Holy One to change her life. And she had faith she would have a future but, to what type of future she did not know.

"Father," Keeper cried unto the Holy One in heaven, "I need your guidance. I am stuck in a world without hope. Please change my life, Father." And he answered saying, "To change your life, young one, you need to come to the end of yourself. When you are at the end you will encounter change."

There was dark and then there was light, there was nothing and then there was everything. For the life of her, it was the beginning of the end but, if she looked, it was more like the end of the beginning. The love and mercy and power of the Holy One was strong and full until it brimmed over. The world was new and increasing with its populace. For all she knew she was alone and in solitude for the rest of what she knew to be life.

"Father," Keeper would cry, "I need your guidance. I have no way of knowing the truth. Teach me. Please teach me Father." And always the answer would be "You will know in time, young one." And that went on for as long as she could remember. And for her life it was what she called the end of the beginning.

And so was the beginning of the end.

Chapter 2

The stones were stacked high, forming the wall that stood underneath Keeper's feet as she carried out her position of Spirit Keeper. The length of the wall was built to surround the inhabitants of Rockfirm. Looking out to see the horizon of trees that barred the inner part of the forest, Keeper continued to scan for any movement. The eyes were always seeing, the mind almost spotting something that was not seen physically. The sight of the wall gate swiveled open for a traveler to come through the gate. The city stood in the northern part of the archaic land of Deror.

Blinking steadily, Keeper stood with one hand resting on the rock face. The people of Rockfirm moved steadily beneath her. The midday sun had ascended and began to make its descent in the late sky. For many hours a day, she would stand looking outward without paying much attention to activity inside of the city.

In her mind, though, it felt open. She could see as though a vision and also a sleeping mist of night enveloped her. The life she lived alone, enveloped in the importance of her position, but as she saw what was formed in front of her then her eyelids fluttered to close. Time formed the movement she believed helped her feel alive.

Keeper was dressed in layers, with long sleeves under a sleeveless shirt with castle wall shaped hems at the end. She wore a skirt with a piece of triangular chain mail hanging on the side. She had thick leggings and leather shoes. It was a plainly looking outfit, though comfortable. She wore her brown hair up in a braid down the back of her head with the end pulled to one shoulder while the side of her face was framed with wispy side bangs. Her eyes were hazel, but mostly green.

An eagle soared over the heights of the trees that surrounded the walls of the city. In many situations, a bird like that may warn of someone who may have come along the narrow path that wound its way through the forest. Keeper studied this bird as the tips of its wings skimmed the bristles of the pines. She had been able to sense certain visitors before they came; she had seen them in a vision.

Countless visitors came through these gates at many hours of the day. Looking up, she saw the bird who had just alighted in the underbrush of the forest away from sight. It reminded Keeper of her duty to stay atop the wall, as the bird could see from such height. Standing down below were two soldiers who kept a strict record of who came in and out, sometimes turned some away because of their certain business that did not have a clear benefit for the city in which they entered. The role of the guards consisted of manually allowing the city the protection it needed from down at the ground level. The difference became clear between their job and Keeper's, where one could alert for far away attackers that found themselves miles away. Not much could be done if an opposing group already descended in a dark shadow from the mountains through the trees. The call would have to go out first before they reached the gate in order to prepare. There once was a battle that was fought long ago.

Rockfirm boasted a powerful exterior, while there was much that rotted away at the inside.

From the inside wall, someone began to call out Keeper's name, with a satchel strapped around his side.

"What do you have to say?" Keeper, who stood and watched on the walls, turned and cocked her head back slightly to address the person. Keeper was also looking back to scan the area that the bird had alighted.

"The Mayor has called to meet with you." Messenger continued to be incessant in his speech.

"I am needed in this position; there may be someone who is coming to the gate soon. I need to continue watching, but I will listen to his request anyway," Keeper answered.

"There is need of you in town. Please come to talk with him," Messenger replied.

Keeper reluctantly agreed with Messenger, stepping along the stones on the wall, she reached a hand out toward the ridge of the wall to steady herself as she stepped down a wooden ladder that leaned up against the structure. Carrying herself, she felt the weight of the moment as she swung side to side making careful steps downward.

Messenger held out a hand to steady Keeper as she made her final step to the ground. Adjusting his satchel again to the opposite side, he continued to press Keeper with his words, "We must be going quickly," so that Keeper headed directly after him, moving toward the center of town.

Keeper followed attentively behind him as he gave comments about the situation of the city. Many people found themselves roaming around town at the many stands that sold items from many lands.

The smells of the foreign spices filled Keeper's lungs as they passed a herbalist shop. Along either side stood stands with fruits that could be found nearby and close to the city in a plentiful forest. Much of the growth of the area came from other regions that did not have these imports. The system served as one where much buying and selling took place of commodities and valuable goods. Some of the seemingly hard working people of the town made their living in this way, though at night they did evil while many others slept. Keeper stopped to feel the deeply smooth satin and soft pieces of clothing folded in a neat pile reflecting the light from the sun and from a hanging lantern. The strange

13

thing was that no one stood at this stall as the items had been displayed from the day before. She remembered this vendor, but where was she? Keeper looked to see the next stall in which she found books, old texts, and the scriptures. Keeper, concern lacing her voice, asked the vendor, "Have you seen the vendor who sells the linen?"

The man shook his head and replied, "No, the woman went missing, and no one has seen her. People have searched her house, and they found this lantern standing lit in the corner. Even if she is not here, I set up her stand with the linens in order for people to buy. The money we gain we will most likely use to find her."

Keeper shook her head and a deep sense of fear began to creep in at the thought of someone going missing. Messenger stood by watching, and offered a strange sentiment. "I believe she will be back soon."

"You know where she is?" The man at the book vendor's stall lit up with the delightful news.

"No, but she may be in the 'Great Place'. I believe she would not go far. She would have to come by. She will be returned." This was strange wording, but it lightened the mood of those present. Messenger at once grabbed Keeper's arm. "I said it is time that we must be going." Keeper agreed and without offering another word was pulled away back into the crowded street.

Farther along, she could hear the sounds of neighing from stables in which horses were bought and sold, while being sheltered for the time being. Much of the money made in this town was from these many shops and tradesmen.

Hearing a handful of coins clatter upon a measuring scale, someone asked, "What price do you desire for this creature?" This type of trade was normal. On most occasions there would be an auction, but in this case the seller believed that they should sell in the present to this buyer. They must have seen him to be important.

"It is 80 shekels."

A hazelnut brown horse pranced around the circle proudly. The sound of its neighing deeply came out until it became loud enough to be distracting. The incessant noise made the buyer want to hurry up the process.

"It is a deal." The seller handed a piece of paper with a contract of buying the steed. A rope was thrown over the horse's neck, opening widely, as one then pulled tightly as it tried to move away. With leather gloves, the assistant reined the horse to the outside gate and pulled down to keep the horse from careening away from the stable yard and off into the crowded street. The assistant's voice gruffly commanded the horse to calm itself. The horse continued to neigh loudly as he was handed over to his new owner. Holding onto the reins, the buyer took the rope and tied it to the back of a cart. At this point, the horse had enough and lifted his head high as to tower over his new owner. Quickly securing his new purchase, the buyer moved around to the front where two horses had been attached to a carriage.

Messenger, who had gone up ahead for a moment, began to realize that Keeper was concentrating on this activity so that she had stopped to watch. "It is so sad to see him sold," Keeper said, her gaze fixed on the horse. "If only he had a way to be free."

Messenger had just reached Keeper and pulled her away so that she could follow the way he was going. "Come along quickly. The Mayor will not tolerate you being late to see him." Keeper listened, coming to walk behind him as the crowd formed around them. The stark, white walls set a barrier on two sides of the street, rising above the noise. The walls stood tall causing a looming shadow to cast itself halfway across the dirt, shading the corner at which both turned. Soon after they saw a building standing in the middle of the square. Shutters bared the windows as tinted wood covered the rim of the door from which held a sign that read, "Public Office" in official lettering. In the middle of the square there stood a wooden platform in which a person could make a speech to an unsuspecting crowd, sometimes bringing forward important news to the inhabitants of the city. It was for that very reason that it stood. Another noteworthy part was the bell tower that stood high above the public office where it was attached to the building. It would always chime out the hour and it did just that with melodic notes as the two drew closer.

"See, we are late!" Messenger grabbed Keeper forcibly by the hand, and he dragged her to the front door. It flung open easily and they continued into a foyer with a glittering chandelier and tiles underneath. The room was connected to several hallways that led to different offices of the leaders of the city. Leading Keeper down a dimly lit hallway with a yellowish glow, Keeper scanned the walls and saw the succession of leaders, important days, and the opening of a new building. Keeper saw her name listed as she had signed a document for the city's peace. Her signature was placed on a document of her duty to keep Rockfirm safe from invaders. Further down the list could be seen several members of powerful groups from surrounding areas who had come together in peace. Though many different types of people lived on this oblong island of Deror there stood widely different systems. They did not bother after the battles they had faced in the past. In this case the protection was very strict, keeping everything under management. Most of those who caused trouble were gone in the present time.

Many of these meetings served as a report to the Mayor of the condition of the wall's security. Turning another corner, they were confronted by a steep set of stairs. Lifting their knees high, they put an arm on a hand rest set beside them. They both came to the top ledge and stopped. Messenger who knew of the rush they were in, still hesitated a moment before knocking.

As though he heard them standing there, the Mayor's gruff "come in" was the only reply. Messenger quickly grasped the door latch and allowed the door to open itself. Coming forward into the room, Messenger bent over and motioned behind toward Keeper who stepped into the low hanging doorway. The room was set with bookshelves lining the walls and contained many thick volumes, some even stacked in piles on the floor. Two wide windows allowed light to open into the room and gave a great view of the city to gaze out upon. The light was limited as the Mayor took the massive, hanging curtain, untying the material and allowing the fabric to swing in front of the panes. Outside of the window pane were shutters that could be shut closed. Sitting back at his desk, the Mayor raised his head to meet them. His intense stare lengthened as he asked for Keeper to take a seat. His tall hat that he wore most times was set aside on the table in front of him. Tied in a mismatch of fabric was a self-made collar up his neck that contrasted the red tie that slung across his chest with a crest in military style. The brass buttons of his navy coat came up the middle in precise fashion. Keeper sat in anticipation of the questions he may ask next.

"What is the news you have found from overseeing the wall?"

Keeper handed over a detailed list of the people and activity listed by date and time in order.

"It has been rather quiet; no real disturbance to count as anything worth mentioning." Keeper explained the present situation.

"Have you seen any recurring visitors, any unusual patterns?" The Mayor inquired.

"The traders usually are followed by a procession of commodities. People from other lands are not as frequent. I am not anticipating any change, any sign of trouble, but anything can prove to change that trend," Keeper answered back.

"Good, good," the Mayor heartily replied though in a discontented way and then trailed into a sigh. "Could you tell me if you have seen anything in your mind's eye?"

This came as a surprise to Keeper, who had told the Mayor of her ability to see things, but was never asked for the specifics. In previous days, she had many dreams that made her concerned. It was hard to know which ones were telling of something real or relaying a subconscious thought to her mind. Not knowing of either being important, she decided to relay a disturbing sight.

"I dreamed of people digging. It was deep and up to their eyes. I am unaware of who those people are, nor did I know that they existed."

"Do you have any ideas why this happened?" Mayor's furrowed brow drew as he listened intently.

"No, I have been having these dreams as though there is much danger, as if there were Pullings." Keeper was able to explain what she thought.

"Pullings? You mean something is trying to get a hold of you?" The Mayor was confused at the thought.

"Yes, but somehow I am able to ward them off as if the Holy One was helping me."

There was silence in the room. Keeper had forgotten that these people did not believe in the Holy One. They had lived their own way, living in their own direction.

"The Holy One?"

"Yes, sir." Keeper couldn't help but swallow.

"You know my position of you talking of such a being as him in my presence."

Looking toward him, Keeper still respectfully said, "Yes, sir," while adding, "but it will still be my belief."

The Mayor, not wanting to say more, waved both Keeper and Messenger out of the room. "That is all—for now," he said, blinking. "I always need an extra pair of eyes," stopping a moment he relayed.

Keeper, receiving this information, raised a hand and motioned while going down the stairs. Closing the door behind her, the Mayor pulled his Messenger aside, "What in the world did she see? I know of none under bondage."

"Yes, sir. I am unaware of such dealings."

"It is your job to find out. Keep your ears open. Be on the lookout for anything."

"Yes, sir," Messenger replied before returning down the stairs.

"I believe she may be seeing much more than most," Mayor said to himself, returning his hand to the pen as he continued to write and sign some important papers stacked high on the table. His eye flickered with light as it turned in his head as though he was having a vision. Sometimes there was more that could be seen than when it first appeared.

As Keeper looked she saw that before her a vision of what was and what was to come. As though the Holy One was guiding her, she could fully see what she had been blinded to before. From above the world he loved, for every hint of life, there still was life. From a point of view of the world of the land of Deror was the one who created it and was creating in it more and more each day.

Deror was a land located a distance from other larger

lands. There were many islands around it. It was surrounded by the Derorian Sea. It was in a warmer part of the world, with a moderate climate. To the north there were colder regions. The islands and other larger lands were where a lot of goods would be transported to Deror. On the island there were two cities of Rockfirm and Buffington that had a war, many years before, but there was peace so that they did not war against each other anymore. It was a peaceful place, despite the fact that the Pursuer continued to capture those in sin with chains with hypnotizing Pullings, and keep them in strongholds. This was not readily talked about, but some discovered what was occurring and wanted to do something about it. The people were sinful from the beginning because they had sinned against God the Father in the garden of Eden so that the Pursuer had control over their souls because of their sinfulness so that they were in chains. The Pursuer would capture the people and put them into strongholds. Because of those who were captured, God the Father sent his Son, the Holy One, to free those in chains. In ancient times the Pursuer and the Holy One, who was the Son of God, had a war with each other, but the Holy One died. The Holy One rose again because he was without sin, taking the keys of sin and death in Hell and freeing those who would believe in him. It was now at the point that those freed, would free others in the Holy One's strength. Those who knew the Holy One worshiped him for his great and mighty power.

Above the world so small, the Holy One watched the yellow and pink hues of clouds as they floated over the western sky. She had walked from the city of Rockfirm to the Waterfall of Life where she would go to reflect and be alone. Looking across, she saw the edge of the great cliffs as the Waterfall of Life flowed forth from the Spirit Lake. Falling over the cliffs, through the wall of clouds and atmosphere, it descended into the depths of the unknown. The wind swirled, spun, and came floating up to seek his face. The green grass moved gracefully in its powerful current across the meadows and fields.

Keeper had once stood by the cliffs of the Waterfall of Life and looked off into the distance for something more, some freedom from darkness.

The current of the Waterfall of Life flowed into the vast water of the Derorian Sea that surrounded the whole of the land of Deror.

In the inner part of the land, Keeper would walk around the area near the forest to enjoy the field on some days.

A spark of light reached the ground as the first morning hours began to chirp with life. The Sun, which had always and will always be the object and person of him, the one who is and is to come, rose in its course across the sky. His radiant beams, ever present, consumed the world in which he loved so dearly. In the world he loved so dearly, he planted a forest. In the western part of the wood there he planted great shady oaks, weeping willows, tall pines, wide maples and strong sycamores. There he planted them for shade and protection from the untamed wind and rain.

And in the very center of the Spirit Wood there was the lake.

Out of the Spirit Lake there grew herbs. The sick and afflicted would be healed with its very touch. Spiritual, mental, physical problems—they were all healed by its heavenly power.

Close by the people had built a town, calling it Rockfirm.

The town, seemingly small, contained most of the population of the world. Buildings, containing two stories, were connected closely so that one walking down the road could only see the sun in the middle of the day. With many layers of light paint, the buildings had an air of being fairly new, but inside there was filth. The light did not come to meet them, for they spent most of their time in the darkness of night. Their hearts equally showed of darkness: these consisting of hatred, fear, and greed. Their souls, tainted by their own filth, were not ashamed of the darkness that spread across the town.

They knew not the light that would shine in the day, neither did they desire to become acquainted with its ways. Seeing in the dark proved to be the only way they knew how to live. As the night fell, so did the evil rise. As each one, knowing only of their own will and deep desires, indulged in the very being of sins. It came as a shadow in which their souls welcomed hardly for each other's approval of their sinfulness. Woe, the cost they would pay for their actions.

As the town system stood, there was no way to make money except to do the bidding of their master. The people of the town bowed down to every will of the master, succumbing to his will in order that he would give them the freedom to follow in their allotted path. As some have seen by experience, the lives of those who had hard heads and thick mouths, were put into the chains of his imprisonment and taken away in the very depths the moment their spirits left their body. As a slave trader, the Pursuer would agreeably take away those who he thought deserved this punishment, assuring them that they would never see the light again. It was a punishment for those who hate the light already and are more than willing to be rid of it. Thus, each person at a certain point would have to go unto the Forlorn Isle where they would spend the rest of their days digging in the pit, which was filled with fire and ash.

Moreover, there stood one among the group that saw a

light, not knowing what it may be, in fact. Seeing the world in its truth, one stood watching the way to the Forlorn Isle. This being was the Spirit Keeper, a messenger of the northern town of Rockfirm. There was still hope on his part for the Holy One had sent a guardian not a few hours before to answer to the lonely Spirit Keeper's aid. He had chosen this one to represent the Holy One, who was coming soon. Yes, sooner than what the Spirit Keeper could have known. This Spirit Keeper did not know him, thus she did not know why she had been called. Surely, it was the Spirit of the Holy One who had stirred her heart into wanting to know the truth. Eventually, it seemed that she would know him deeply, and then see him face to face, but for now she was confused and needed guidance. If indeed the Holy One could have mercy on this one, who would soon be called Spirit Keeper, surely he would have mercy on the rest of its populace. This sign that he pursued a mere human, showed that he wanted her to come to himself. Yes, even the rest of the world which he had created, he wanted to show his love. Praying, hoping, that they would one day see the light and follow after him. But still, they did not want to believe for their hearts were darkened and their mouths were thirsty for sin. Turning her eyes away, she could see the sight of the Forlorn Isle, which mirrored the lives of the inhabitants of Rockfirm.

From the Forlorn Isle, surrounded by the Derorian Sea, fire arose and came from the depths to devour the cries that had been and were always to be heard. "From the west comes your leading brethren," the Holy One, the Sun, said in a loud voice, "for it is coming soon. Do not become anxious or become weak for I am coming in order to lead you from your enemies." The earth quaked and shook at his voice so that the fire ceased its wrath for the time being, for the Forlorn Isle quaked with pain. The land was, has been, and will be destroyed. Woe to them who were enslaved in those parts.

Through Keeper's mind's eye, she could see what awaited the inhabitants of the town of Rockfirm to their detriment and dismay. There were ones that had already disappeared for the Pursuer still had the ability to enslave those who were not freed and were not the Holy One's. The Pursuer still used the hypnotizing Pullings to enslave their minds in order to capture and bring them to the Forlorn Isle. The Forlorn Isle was a stronghold for those living who were still in chains. They were captive since Eden and needed saving, or worse they would die in their sin. They still had chains, but the Holy One had the keys of sin and death so that those alive could be freed of those chains. The Pursuer still enslaved those who still had chains. What awaited them was the stronghold of the Forlorn Isle which Keeper saw in a vision while standing looking out at the landscape of the land of Deror.

Keeper began to have a vision, like many times before. She was able to see it through her Spirit Eyes. It was a vision of those captured by the Pursuer in the stronghold of the Forlorn Isle.

"Dig, dig, faster! Back to where you were created, back into the ground is where you seek your inhabitants." The faster the captives dug, the quicker they descended in the ground. Faster still they dug for they had no clue of what awaited them– it was but darkness. Deeper with their hands they dug until the dirt reached their elbows, it engulfed them completely.

Think, think, brethren. What do you think will await

you? Where are all your minds? It happened to be so, they were all but one mind. One, it was to be a clock to control all their heart beats and the rhythms as they dug. Fear, fear brethren? Do you fear the fire to come? Do you not have fear? And it also happened so that they had no conscience, no consciousness of fear, of fire, of darkness. So deeper they dug. Woe, to those who were enslaved in those parts.

Even in their blindness their spirits still wept for their condition, so that they would still cry out, "Woe, woe, to those whose life is in the parts of darkness. Woe, to those who live in the utter Isle. Let our tears flow out like a stream, as a stream of unquenchable water that it may quench their thirst." But still they were consumed by their own appetites. What they hated became exactly what they longed to do. As they stumbled forward, feeding on the rubble left of the earth. In an immeasurable amount of voices there was heard the mournful chant, "Stretch out your hands for more, more, more! More to which it falters. Falter soon young ones that you may not see the wrath to come. For the earth quakes with destruction."

In their own mind they had become desperate as one who lives in a desert. They sought for the water in a puddle; they found it and drank. Their mouths were filled with its delight only for the slightest of moments. Withering, becoming tasteless, their lips began to chap and their voices became raspy from the dryness. Thus they drank ravenously of the droplets cupped in their hand. While a bright, clean feeling filled their throat, they began to feel that the dry, cracking sand around them had spread inside them. Their eyes started to shut and their feet under them began to sway. As they toppled over, they saw a slight glimpse of the water. "I need it or surely, I will not survive."

Surely the inhabitants would surely perish if no one stopped them. The hole the captives dug made a bite like a *gash in the Forlorn Isle, making the earth quake with destruction. The earth groaned for they were captives who not only caused destruction, but had become destruction. A word they feared second most to darkness, and their darkness is what Pursuer wanted the most. For the creation waits with eager longing for the revealing of the sons of the Holy One. Woe, to those who live in the land of darkness. The Forlorn Isle was a stronghold that needed to be destroyed.*

Seeing this vision, Keeper knew she in some way needed to help these hurting people, but how?

In the city of Rockfirm, all the streets held the filth of the world. Some sat on the ground motionless in the cold, and others sat there almost thought to be too far gone. Yes, there was sin surrounding; there was wrong they had done in the night. In their eyes could be seen a fiery glint that only one who was of the light could recognize or even move away from. The evil one, who had enslaved them, still enslaved them in their sin. Yes, these beings were consumed by their own flesh, whose desire was only for evil. Continually they did the deeds of the flesh unto darkness. Yes, their place was among the captives of the Forlorn Isle. As was Keeper, until he touched her. In that moment she knew everything would change. The once darkened self would become the one bearing light. And in him, she knew she would see amazing, shocking things. He would give her Spirit Eyes in which to see what the spirit of the Holy One saw. All that was hidden would come to light, and all that was once thought to be covered, were dug up in order for light to invade every place. So that no sin would be beyond the Holy One, beyond the hand that reached out to save the sons of his people. Surely, to them was found the greatest joy. To the ones who believed in the death and payment of those sins unto the resurrection and life. The forgiveness, the hope that came when all was washed away, when all shame was put away with and replaced with confidence in a new life to come.

Yes, as she looked at that alley she felt confident in some way. The Holy One had appointed her to show them the truth, to give them a taste of the hope that they could experience. If they should receive this gift, they would be set free. The darkness that so firmly clung to them would dissipate into the light that shone into the heart and revealed the secrets that one hid, so that they could be free of the troubles that plagued them and did live a new life, one that would last forever. This was the plan for those who believed in his name so that they could have life everlasting.

Chapter 3

Keeper, after she would work her position as Spirit Keeper, would go back to her house to rest. She had a small boxed house in the middle of town, with only a bed, table, chair, wash basin, and few shelves where she stored food. She had lived there for many years alone since her parents had been taken by the Pursuer as her house lit into flames. She had rebuilt her house after it had been burnt down. She wondered if she would dream of the memories of that night again. Growing up alone, she decided to get a job as a Spirit Keeper as her only way to support herself. She already knew she had Spirit Eyes which was important to have dreams in the night to be able to see for upcoming attackers, so she became the Spirit Keeper of the town. She would have dreams and visions with her Spirit Eyes which would show what was to come, and Spirit Eyes were essential to being a Spirit Keeper. While on the other hand, the dreams would torture her in her sleep so their was always a sense of dread with the Spirit Eyes she had. She worked during the day on the wall. Many people would come in and out on her watch. She would also report back to the Mayor to tell of what had happened during her watch. At night, she came home exhausted, but she would have dreams, making sleep few and far between. Her dreams constantly took up her mind. For her Spirit Eyes were a blessing and a curse. She was always tired.

In her dreams she would see the Holy One who she knew of, but did not know personally most vividly and she would see the evil Pursuer who was always after her. There was a spiritual war occurring.

She got ready for bed and as she laid down to close her eyes she knew that the dreams would come, though she was scared of them. She opened her eyes back open to see the small room around her, but in a moment she knew she would feel like she was in her dreams. She finally closed her eyes and braced herself for what was to come.

Keeper had a dream while in her bed.

She felt as though she was standing in a forest. She looked at the tall trees, looking at the branches reaching outward. Looking at the mossy ground and pine needles. There was a dark green mustiness around her, with a little bit of fog. There was a bird that came whirling past with a red ribbon tied on one foot. The bird went up into a tree, to rest its wings, curling up into a nest.

Suddenly she felt a darkness from behind her, as the light dimmed. Her heart began to speed up. She knew what was happening. She turned around to find the Pursuer in a dark hood, his red eyes glowing. His snake tongue slithering from his mouth. He held a sword in his hand. He was coming closer quickly. At once Keeper started tripping, but still she started running.

All around was the darkness of the forest. The trees seemed to not grow branches and wither, compared to the dark branches she had previously seen. Keeper weaved in and out between the trees, finding a path through the forest. She was losing her breath.

The Pursuer began to taunt, "I am coming to get you. Then you will be no more."

Keeper did not say anything, but continued to run.

She in a moment tripped over a tree log, but it was too late because the Pursuer was already close to her.

The Pursuer, slashed his blade at Keeper as she lay on the ground, but she rolled away from where the sword struck. At that moment, the Pursuer bent down and pulled Keeper up by the neck so that she was lifted from the ground.

"I do not like you very much, There is no one to help you." The Pursuer said into her face. His face was almost like a skeleton, with red eyes, and the snake tongue that slithered out. The dark cloak with the hood, covered most of the features of his face. He held her neck tightly. These were the Pullings of the Pursuer used to hypnotize her and control her, bringing her to him.

"Why do you always chase me?" Keeper cried, as she was being choked.

"Because believe it or not, because of your weak form, and your weak gift." The Pursuer paused, "you know I remember when your house was burning down and I took your parents, but I could not find you. Maybe now I can end you and your gift."

"Go away," Keeper spoke. "Leave me be, Pursuer." Keeper lashed back despite his taunting voice, choking in her response.

"You have no gift. You are worthless." The Pursuer continued to taunt her.

"I may not have a gift, you may be right. The gift torments me, but you will not have power over me." Keeper had a forceful tone.

"I have power over you. You cannot get away from me." The Pursuer sounded like he was hissing. He tightened the grip around her neck.

"I will be free of you. Do not torment me," Keeper said as she thrashed in her bed.

"How will you be free from me?" The Pursuer sneered.

"I will fight. I will fight against you until there is no breath in me." Keeper stated firmly.

"Perhaps, but you will never be free of me. Never." Pursuer continued to squeeze her neck.

Keeper could not speak at this moment, but only mumbled the words, "I will fight with everything in me. Leave me alone. Help me Holy One."

The Holy One was the name of a savior she had heard of. He was supposed to be the Son of God the Father, who was the ruler of all. She had heard the power of his name, but did not know him personally.

As the Pursuer heard this name he lost his balance. Keeper said this, kicking the Pursuer in the stomach and Keeper broke free from him. She dashed as fast as she could. She moved through the darker part of the woods until it became lighter. Keeper was then able to make it out of the woods into a clearing. She was able to see as the Holy One and his troops were standing for battle. She ran out toward them, so that maybe now she could be safe.

The sky had turned black as soot from a coal fire. Smoke was the only thing that could be found in Keeper's lungs.

Waving in the wind, the flag and banner, Nissi flew high above the cold rocks which we had just stepped upon. Red it was and it stood firm in front of our troops as a symbol of being—victory.

Jehovah Sabaoth—leader of heavenly hosts, troops too many to number for the Holy One—led them to where they could battle against everything not pure, lovely or right.

They fought against the things unseen by the bare eye—things unseen but harmful to life. Overall, Jehovah Sabaoth was under the Holy One's command.

The troops had trekked to a group of high plateaus, Keeper had just joined them. From the point where they stood they could see the whole woody landscape was covered with dark clouds and smoke.

"See there, over on that hill," El Roi rang out, "there is something on it." We looked and saw for El Roi, the lookout, who saw all things. Just as El Roi had said, there among the greenery of the hill was a black smudge of shadows coming over the peak of the hill toward them. El Roi, Jehovah Sabaoth, and Jehovah Rapha were among the troops who fought for the Holy One.

"Jehovah Sabaoth," said one of the troops who spoke, "it is the Pursuer. I see that the banner wears the emblem of darkness."

"Sire," said El Roi, "There seems to be many of the enemy marching this way." A gasp was let out in the realm. There was only about half that size of their troops standing on the plateaus.

"Truly, truly I say to you," Jehovah Sabaoth said at once, "in the name of the living Holy One we shall defeat our enemies. We will stand our ground, stand fast, and hold together."

Smoke and ashes came as a whirlwind of fury. The untamed wind could not be tamed as the light.

The sun had fallen to the west and darkness had brought its sorrows of the day with it. Volleys of arrows from the infantry had brought them to retreat. Behind their

barracks, the leaders discussed what was to be done. As a result of the moment, Keeper felt like she was suddenly slipping away. She was falling through what—she was not sure of. The space around her was dark and void. There was no light, no sound, and no one else there. Keeper's head was spinning and unstable with fear and negative thoughts about her life in her small world of doubts and hopelessness.

She was barely even sure if what was happening to her was real for she had had such vivid and lifelike dreams. She scarcely knew what was true and what part was her imagination. The dreams she was experiencing were more like nightmares—like her life. Keeper just did not know if she was safe or floating out in the middle of nowhere.

And then there was a whisper—a small whisper barely noticeable to a human ear. "For everyone there is a gift," The voice whispered. "And for every pupil a teacher. And to the wise there shall be given wisdom and to the understanding there shall be given knowledge. All will be given to you, if you come to the end of you." This voice seemed to want to help her in some way.

And it was how the Holy One intended that Keeper would jerk up and was in her small home in the city of Rockfirm, in her room, under sheets and in her bed. She took a long miserable sigh and sank back onto her pillow which was drenched in anxious perspiration from the panic of the nightmare. She lay awake with apprehension for her next move, her next breath, her next moment fearing that she would have not made it in her sleep if she had not woken up sooner. But the Holy One would not allow that.

At that moment, her world was a mix of fear and sadness that doubled every night as her dreams became more real to her. She feared to doze off into a slumber—even a light snooze would bring the dreams to her.

Fear enveloped Keeper. It was the one thing that held her back. It clung onto her everywhere she went. It made her heavy and weighed on her soul. The fearful dreams she had only swirled around into the darkness. There was no hope. There was the empty longing for she did not know what.

The fear chased her, it pursued her mind, plagued her thoughts.

Keeper continued to try to fight it, with no weapon, with no one to help.

She continued to feel the sense of emptiness, and how she longed for something. The darkness only enveloped her more. She had strolled along in her life in meaningless sadness. Living her own life. Alone, but still in her own way.

She always felt like the Pursuer was chasing her, like her mind was being pulled into the darkness, almost joining it. She knew not of who she served. She longed for something tangible to aid her. She reached out to touch anything in her dreams, but nothing was there.

She had felt the grip of the Pursuer around her neck.

He had taken her family. The fear of him plagued her and she knew her fear stemmed from something caused from within.

Then it dawned on her who had spoken to her. It was the Holy One. Who else could have spoken to her? With dreadful change in thoughts she asked herself, 'Why did the Pursuer want me?' She questioned herself, 'Did he almost have me?' Then with a realization of what had just happened she asked herself with a miserable sigh, 'Why did the Holy One not save me?'

In recent days before that Keeper had spoken with the Holy One and he told her that she would have to come to "the end of her".

The light poured in and swirled around her window of her small box shaped house. The separate beams of light colored in every shade of yellow. The morning was beautiful and like a fresh breath of air. And then as she lifted her eyelids open she saw what was to be the most beautiful sight of the morning light.

To her delight, it was just what she needed to keep her life going, as she had almost given up and let the Pursuer have her. "Thank you," she said aloud with a small bit of hope to be detected. How she wished she could be one of those holy beams of light swirling and landing where it pleased.

And to what she thought came an important thing to question: fear. As she experienced the night before—the Pursuer had almost had her in his grip on her—as well as the fear that gripped her life. She asked one question: was this real or was it all in her mind?

It was too hard for her to begin to fully contemplate all at once, but she did take it to a deep and contemplative consideration. Maybe it was all in her mind. So with that she flung herself out of bed and out the door to the outside. She stood there in the grass outside of the town of Rockfirm looking at the clouds that were so close she could touch them. In a world of newness it was marvelous, but her joy did not stay long—like always it would slip away like the untamed wind away as she thought about reality.

Going back to her home, Keeper got ready for her position on the wall, washing her face, straightening the chain mail that hung from her skirt. She grabbed her spyglass from the table used to see at far distances.

She knew that as she worked she could forget her

dreams.

Chapter 4

The day was slow so that she could hear those in town moving about. And looking out at the forest from the place at the wall, she could see those traveling with packs of goods to bring to the market. She took out her spyglass and scanned the area outside of Rockfirm.

That night, Keeper came home from a long day of being on watch. She made herself some porridge and sat at her table while she looked at her vase of wilted yellow daisies. She had picked them in the field outside of Rockfirm, and they had once been beautiful, but now the flowers had a faded gray tint. She also opened her journal and began to scribble in words and pictures of her thoughts. She then cleaned up the table and continued to get ready for bed by washing her face. She again laid in her bed, afraid to sleep, but eventually becoming tired enough to close her eyes. She again dreamed about the spiritual war.

"Jehovah Sabaoth, it has become apparent, the sky has become darker." The battle raged on.

"Yes, truly I say to you, it will become darker with smoke and ash before you will see morning light." The day before had seemed futile. Many lay dead and wounded in a grassy field. What a battle it was. The Pursuer had won the battle, but the Holy One had won the war. Smoke had been blown by the untamed wind in all directions. It created a bowlish cloud that surrounded everything.

Nissi, though worn, was still flapping in the wind. All the legion looked on in horror at the sight in front of them.

The darkness had brought its sorrows. The dead were just now being buried. The wounded were just now being treated by Jehovah Rapha the healer. He used the herbs from the Spirit Lake that would heal any sickness.

Woe to the ones who lived in the place of death who had brought sorrow and destruction to the chosen brethren. For their eyes were closed, since Eden, the garden where the first humans sinned. Now that they suffered in knowing good from evil. Surely, their eyes had been blinded as a fog covered the waters of a lake. It is the army of the light that hopefully prayed that the fog would be penetrated so that the light of life would shine itself through. Thus beginning the new era, the era of peace. One with no war or sorrow, sure this was not the first time before, but surely it was almost to the end of the time.

Until the completion of that time there must have been much more travesty to come, so that life itself would no longer feel real. So that everything would be brought down, every tree, every mountain swallowed up into the ocean. And those who follow after evil went into the Abyss. Surely this would take place, but just before there needed to be a remnant. A chosen race who would shine like stars in the heavens. Knowing the wisdom of the Holy One, their minds enlightened to the battle raging around them. They would be given Spirit Eyes, to test all things that are not of the Holy One. They would see and they would be seen. Not only by this world, but also by the Holy One. The last are the ones that are to stand, they are to be persecuted, but nevertheless, stand for the Holy One they serve. Thus, there would be an army of the Light, it would shine brightly, so that the darkness would hate it and would hide. Surely, this was the time to wage war.

They were like stars, shining in the expanse of heaven, even when the darkness surrounded it on all sides. But look, its light was growing brighter as the expense around it widened. Hope, dear ones for the future. Surely, their light would not be extinguished for its source was everlasting, the source of all. The hope that could bring one to redemption. Surely, the light was shining even now into their own heart, beaming from their eyes. Yes, even now they could see it coming, over the horizon, into their bones, so they were floating weightlessly in the light. Space surrounded them, but the stars were so close that they could touch them with their fingertips. To grasp them would light a fire from within, filling one's whole frame, the heart, the soul, and the mind would be changed completely. Were they ready for this change, but more importantly did they want to be changed? This hope for the future would be the catalyst for change. The light has been surely shining and it wanted to penetrate them if they allowed it to.

El Roi, with his spyglass near his eye, shouted out: "It is not finished, look in the distance. They have returned with more men...I can see horses, chariots...spears!" In front of them in the valley stood a stone cold wall of the enemy, facing them in full force. Dark painted horses pulled in unison the chariots of the men who showed the dark gleam of armor and weapons. As they looked across they could hear the enemy's deafening wail.

"Jehovah Sabaoth," said El Roi, "there are too many of them. What shall we do?"

"You of little faith, let you only put your trust in the power of the Holy One who has sent you. Let not your trust be in numbers and weapons." With one sweeping hand motion, all who had weapons were made ready. "Hold to the power of the Holy One! Let him fight through you in this time of need."

The Holy One stood tall and declared, "This enemy has no power that heaven cannot destroy."

Then the army with its troops upon troops rushed forward, swords flashing, helmets blinding, and spears lowered. Then when the Pursuer was so close that we could see the whites of his eyes—or rather the red of his eyes—there came a yell, "Charge!" Raining full force on their infantry, who were upon them. Archers shot from behind, swordsmen in front.

The Pursuer, eyes glowing with hatred, used skillful strokes with his sword. A black cape streamed from behind, as the dark robe surrounded him ominously. Smiling, you could see his fangs and split tongue slithered in and out. Oh, what a sight it was.

Looking around to those who stood by their side, they seemed to be brothers and sisters. Somehow each felt closer than any brother, doing what the other could not. They stayed together. One of the tactics they began to use that proved to be successful, was a system of spears. Considering a spear can reach a person from a farther distance, when one using a sword would have to be of a closer, more vulnerable proximity. They had surely paid their toll of many wounded.

"Sabaoth! There are too many for us." El Roi yelled out to Jehovah Sabaoth, the army commander for the Holy One.

"Yes, but stand firm. Keep standing. Can you see the shadow forming in front of us?" The Holy One's voice was sure.

"It must become darker before we will see the morning light." Sabaoth said these words.

"Aye, Sabaoth, you are always right." Jehovah Rapha responded.

It was true. Half their regiment was gone. Then the snake, for he knew that they were vulnerable, began to close in on the army. The Pursuer, eyes flashing, tongue *slithering, came steadily forward. His sword was raised, as he lowered his eyes on a victim. This one was very small, but none the less powerful.*

"You. Being, why have you come?" He snorted, irritated at the sight of this being before him. This being was meant to be one of his own slaves. How could she be seeking the side of light? The being hearing these words, shook inside. "Survival of the fittest. No then, on these grounds I will destroy you! Let now, on you, the skies pour forth my furry!" The being did not say a word, but mouthed something inaudible.

El Roi, a swift and keen watcher, saw the Pursuer and the being in which he was so set on taunting. "Sabaoth, the Spirit Keeper! Hurry."

"Sire," El Roi exclaimed, "If you go, won't you be killed?"

"No, truly I was before. Never to die again. But I must fight for his evil reign to end. It will come a day when the powers of darkness will not hold these bonds that have so long enslaved my people. Surely, I will deliver them, and in me there will be life forever more." The Holy One responded.

"Sire, then I trust you to complete the task before you." Jehovah Rapha responded.

"Sssshh." The Pursuer stood rigid, "Do not say such things." The Pursuer spat on the ground.

"Let nothing come from your mouth." He pointed his sword at the being's throat, who could feel the heated metal begin to warm her skin. "Do not utter a sound or I will, by my power, defeat you all." The main problem in this statement was that the being was Keeper.

In her defense, she thought it best to speak, "I am here to fight against you." She paused and added "I am here on behalf of the Holy One, I tell of the light that is coming." She said this not truly knowing the Holy One, but wanting this to be true.

He let out a loud yell. "Raah! Today you will breathe your last." Fire roasting in his eyes, he slashed at her throat. Although, she felt the swoosh of the blade as it went past her, and all went black. She felt peace, there was no denying it, and she did not fight back.

There was another one who had died for a righteous cause and had come back.

Keeper blacked out and then came back to her senses.

Standing there in the field so that Keeper could see the enemy that had backed away but started to come back, she began to become troubled. As if she felt like there was one behind her, she decided to draw her own sword with her hand by her skirt. The moment that came rushing back in her brain was when she had run away as the Pursuer had chased. That moment of weakness bothered her so that she was scared into the thought that it might happen again. She had seen what he was capable of so that she saw her own fear still instilled inside of her.

Keeper would die. She had to die to her own self, but even so another one had died so that all may live. Her life was one of pure joy to spend in eternity with the Holy One who truly loved her. It is in his sacrifice, in his death those that chose him could now live forever.

In the darkness of that moment was when she opened her eyes, and she could see. The events that had only a few moments before plagued her, where now only a shadow. But, in her mind's eye she could still see everything so vividly. As though it foreshadowed a world to come, her future in a way. What did it mean? She pondered these questions for a moment and then waited for an answer to come. Surely, someone was trying to tell her something.

It was morning and a steady stream of light fell upon her face and she heard their words, "Dear child, I have sent you into this world to be a light, though the darkness seems to be prevailing all around you. Though your hope has almost dried out. I have chosen you for this that you may follow me, and doing that you may die so that you may live." Though the words rang in her ears, she did not fully understand what they meant. She was young and of the world that surrounded her. But faintly, she believed what he said could be so. So she asked him. "Could you help me follow you?" And with a faint sound she heard him reply. "Just a little bit of faith will grow a mustard tree. What you have seen today will change you for the rest of your life so that you will become my own."

She ran away from what she had to face: the flashing blade. Away she did in her mind she ran so far that she fell. She was falling, smelling smoke and hearing the yells of the Pursuer and the Holy One. Not just falling, but she was spinning and landing on her bed, she fell. The ceiling shook so that the floor rattled as she made her entry, crashing onto her bed.

What a horrid thing to run, abandoning the Holy One's army. In her mind she had run away from fear.

"What has happened?" She spouted out the words including, "but why had I been so scared? Scared of fear?" Then she remembered the orders; do not speak to the enemy for the Lord's words will defeat them, not your's. For a long while she sat in bed in the dark hours of the morning, but sleep did not come. How could she have done something so senseless? The questions came to question her. "Questions, questions, why so many? I did not think. I did not listen. I did what I thought best." So the question was: why?

Thick clouds came with the wind. What a sight it was. All the clouds were darkened and most familiar. Questions still questioning came to ask. "Why, why did you run away from fear, the sword? It was all right there for you to own. Did you take it? No, you had the chance to live without fear, but you ran away. You fell to the earth."

"Do not torment me," she sneered. "Stop saying things." she fell to the floor and looked up at the dark ceiling. All was quiet for the voices had fled. Her heart was full, but some accusing thought would fill her head.

She looked up and saw a crack beginning to form in the ceiling. The world was saddened. It made a creaking sound and she could hear it clearly. Though she was troubled on the inside, it also felt like her life was spinning around her.

Seeing this, she got up swiftly and walked to the door. She slowly turned the knob. It creaked under the weight of her hand. When it came undone she cautiously inched it open and then all at once she threw it open. The sight before her was dark and dismal. Being a very gray day and questionable she edged out slowly. The clouds which had been pink and yellow yesterday were now dark and gray today.

Keeper again went back inside to get ready for work, she went out the door and spent the rest of the day standing in the intense heat, as many new travelers came into the town. There did not cease to be an intense murmur of what was to come.

Chapter 5

Keeper came back home to rest, this time horrified to see anything else. She hoped that this time would be better, but somehow the darkness continued to envelop her.

As Keeper slipped into sleep that night she could hear cheering as though thousands made up the sound of rolling thunder. It was as if she was ducking and dodging some invisible threat.

"Spirit Keeper, be wary of the sword."

Keeper ducked and skipped away in a mad escape, but the farther she ran, the closer she felt the blade at her heels. Then with a flash she saw the blade and the one brandishing it. Soon it became clear that she had come back to confront the Pursuer. With a quick stroke he slashed it at her neck—like he intended to do yesterday. This time she did not run. She dodged, for she had no time to think. With every dodge she saw that she was being pushed farther off the field, onto a ledge, she had not noticed before.

"Fight, it is all in your head." Hearing these words, she realized it was true. It was a trap that would lead her to certain defeat. She knew that the Holy One was the One for whom she fought so she should not be afraid of these attempts to lead her away from her call. In that moment her eyes were opened. She could see there was a large stick scattered among a pile of smaller twigs on the ground. She was able to make her way over and grasping the stick by the middle, it became a two-sided weapon used as a shield.

"That is it; give him what you are worth!" Keeper

could hear the voice of the Holy One, as he said these words they encouraged her soul to keep going. "Yes, I am with you. Even though evil may seem to win the battle, the Holy One is the One who ultimately wins the war." Hearing this, Keeper swung wildly hoping to keep him off guard. She used her beginner's luck to keep him from backing her to the edge.

As Keeper fought, time began to still. She saw that the one who had been chasing her, the Pursuer, had grown taller since the last time they had fought. She noticed a scar slashed across the left of his mouth. 'Had he been cut? He neither spoke nor even breathed.' She thought.

As soon as she saw these things, with a slash of his sword she had seen what was awaiting her. She swung more widely than before, making a clatter.

"That is the way—press for the goal." The voice yelled from afar. Though she had been quite discouraged before, now she felt some type of revitalizing power penetrate her being. It was a power, that as she looked up, she saw the face of the One she was talking to: the Holy One.

Presently, she did not only think about how she fought her way from the edge, but how she would get him down in order to defeat him, for she knew Who was on her side. Up until this moment, the Pursuer's eyes had been like dark, unfeeling orbs, but now they showed a red tinged glow. His tongue, until now, had been still, but now it rushed and out in a fury.

"I am very disappointed," his tone was menacing, as it resorted to a low, gravelly response, "You've come back to test me. Now you will find my blade at your throat." They went at each other with forceful mighty blows, poking and stabbing each other's weakest places, Keeper's being at her right arm. It seemed as though he sensed this, and purposely thrust his sword at her right with the objective of weakening her to a point of defeat. This second blow rendered her helpless as she held her arm to her chest.

Suddenly, with no warning, she felt herself become dizzy and vision blurred. She stumbled haphazardly backwards, almost close enough to feel the wind as it rushed down the cliff face. But as though she had lost all ability to control her movement, she was suddenly revitalized by a new strength, which allowed her to make a jab using her other arm, slashing his heel. Both his viperish hisses and curses filled the air, as well as her feeling of pain.

She was able, for the moment was right, to make a quick escape from the abyss that had seemed to await her. She could see that in this dream they were running out of time. It happened to be disappearing one second at a time. Mottled with spots of blue and red, then orange and yellow, everything lost its shape and became blurred. Life then seemed to stop; the sound dimmed to quietness. These dreams continued to show her visions of emptiness and need for help, as though the Forlorn Isle awaited her if something did not change.

The last of these terrible dreams was not a dream at all but a fearful memory of the past. One that would haunt her, because it was not only a dream, but a living nightmare.

She could still feel the scorching heat that intensified in the furnace like an entrapment of her house, though it had been many years before.

Keeper woke up with sweat falling from her brow in her dream. She felt as it dripped down her face and her eyes fluttered and squinted at the droplets that stung her eyes.

At that moment, Keeper could see the image of her

mother and father and seemed dazed, but the one who stood in front of them scared her most of all, who stood shrouded in a hood. Keeper peaked around the corner as she dodged swiftly so as to not be seen.

"We will not go." Keeper's father replied in response to something the man that stood in black said.

"We will not," Keeper's mother agreed heartily, but for some reason it felt as though their words had been cut off as she began to stare blankly.

"You will," From the man's mouth came a slithering tongue. The abruptness of the figure's words scared Keeper. For some reason they seemed to follow after him through the door frame, into the street even though they specifically said they would not. They could not resist, it pulled them along as the rafters of the house caught flames. The wafting smoke filled the room so Keeper could not breathe. Keeper had been afraid to call after her parents so as to not become enslaved by the Pursuer. At this point, the room had become too dangerous in order to stay any longer. She went to the window at the rear part of the house. She climbed onto the blanketed bed, latched open the panes of the window, and pulled herself through, but a piece of jagged wood injured her upper arm as she found herself in the narrow walkway between stark white homes. She held her arm as it hurt. She tested it and could not lift her right arm all the way up. Despite this, she immediately turned the corner toward the street where she saw a carriage pulled by a set of dark horses. From inside of the carriage she could see her parents were being pulled away by the Pullings, chains around their wrists as they peered out like they were dazed and could not comprehend what was outside the window.

Keeper felt afraid to call out, but she thought, 'where are they being taken?'

Keeper's heart felt like it had a heavy burden

weighing it down. She looked back at her house that had been burned down by fire as the ash filled the air. She let out a sob of pain. There was nothing or no one left. She felt extremely heavy in heart as though it was a great burden that held her down. She did not know where her parents and family went. She had an idea of what the Pursuer could do. She would run, thinking that the family she had once known were taken and there was a possibility that she would too.

From then on she would run, run from the fear of being captured.

This thought would haunt her most nights.

Chapter 6

Keeper walked haphazardly through the streets. It was her day off from her position, so she decided to get up in the early hours to make the best of the day, though she still had not been able to sleep. The sky was dark; she could recognize swirling clouds that had once been in her dreams. Keeper walked through the town, but the sing-song sound of the market and a particular market stall caught her attention. Taking down the stall for the day, the shop owner, Burman, packed up many of the items into a cart so they could be transported into an inner room, furnished with relaxing chairs and shelves of books. The shopkeeper had opened the door and Keeper peered in after him.

"You want something, miss?" Seeing the full view of her distressed face he exclaimed, "Oh, you do not look so good. Do you need to sit down?"

Keeper nodded without a word, but then added soon after. "I need something to read. I have nightmares."

"Well, it is a dark and dreary day. It fits the mood. Anyway, you need something adventurous or filled with facts…" Burman stopped as he reached for a large leather book tethered together with scarlett string binding. It had golden pages that glowed from the reflection of the lantern in the shop. He picked it up as though it carried much weight both physically and spiritually.

A table stood in front of Keeper and he slid the thick leather book in front of her.

"It is called *The Bread of Life*. It sources as our food. The book called the *Bread of Life* tells real stories in ancient times of those who followed the Holy One. People still continue to read it because of the salvation that is brought through the Holy One who is the Son of God. It tells of the

Holy One who defeated death and sin, and who can set people free." He stopped for a moment. "It looks like you need something to eat and drink. Let me bring you something."

Keeper agreed with an approving nod and a, "yes, I do need that."

He said this as Keeper began to open up the paper thin pages as they glided as she turned them. "In the beginning…"

Keeper read it like she would any other book.

The shopkeeper, Burman, came back out with a slice of loaf bread and a thick porcelain mug, warm with the heat of the herbal tea leaves turning the water green.

"Everyone who drinks of this water will thirst again, but whoever drinks of the water he will give them will not thirst again." Burman explained.

Keeper held the mug lightly and sipped it for a moment of calm. She breathed slowly, pulling her knees up. With no premise Keeper blurted out. "I had a dream that I fought against someone, that I fought and could not win so I ran. Will I ever defeat him?"

Flipping through the pages the man guided her to the pages deeply wrinkled and with blotches where moisture had fallen, probably tears.

He seemed serious as he looked around, but still shared.

"Yes, you will." He answered calmly.

"If you do not know who is in this book, I will tell you. He came to defeat what you are facing. He came to let you know it is only through his sacrifice that we can live.

"You know you cannot do it on your own. There is nothing that can be done for his sacrifice. We are all condemned, but he gives freedom.

"Everyone who calls on the name of the Holy One

will be saved. How are they to hear without someone preaching?

"He helps us to see the truth. He dispels the lies and fear. He helps us to battle what we cannot. Oh, the Holy One is the one to help you live life and share hope.

"Do you know the Holy One?"

Keeper responded with, "I do not know him, though I know about him." Keeper answered truthfully, 'But I want to know you, Holy One. Please show me.' Her eyes were fixed to the sky as she spoke in her mind.

The shopkeeper looked at Keeper and gave her the words. "Well, he is the only way to be righteous." He did not give her any more words, but in Keeper's heart it stirred deeply. As if he was in front of her, she looked at this Holy One and what he did for her.

Keeper kept reading and she came upon a book called Romans. She sat there and it began to soak up, but she still knew something was missing.

The shopkeeper, Burman, had shared what he could and as Keeper absorbed this information she still felt far away from the source. She felt like she was beginning to understand. She loved the book on the table.

"Can I read this sometime later?" Keeper asked this question to the shopkeeper.

Burman responded, holding it in both hands. "You can read it anytime you come."

Keeper turned and walked out and began to see something different. It seemed as though she was realizing something important.

She looked down and saw something around her wrist. She moved her hands and she could see them move. They were translucent and she could see that they hung down beside her. She then looked around at others passing by on the street who also carried these chains.

She could see that these chains were entrapping her and those of the town. They walked around doing their own business out in the market, but knew not of the chains that hung down beside them.

They needed to be free. She remembered the words of being slaves to sin. How people are in need of a savior to set them free. 'Is this what Burman was talking about?'

From deep within her Keeper again cried out, "I want to be free. I want to be free of those fearful dreams and chains."

At this point was truly the beginning of the end.

Chapter 7

Keeper was scared of the dreams she had, but talking to Burman and reading the book, *The Bread of Life* that he had shown her gave her hope. It had talked of this Holy One and what he had come to do. Who was this Holy One?

She came out of her home carefully and something was different. She felt like she could see something with her Spirit Eyes. Her lungs were filled with ash from the streets. She saw the thickly painted white walls and the dark alleyways. There was great clamor and quarreling she could hear from those in the city, doing their bidding. What she saw shocked her. With the vision of Spirit Eyes she looked at those who walked the streets and on their arms were heavy chains that weighed them down. They walked along not knowing of the burden that they carried. It was like a sheet that covered their eyes and they did not know how to remove it.

'Do I have chains?' Keeper thought this and looked down at her own wrists. She moved her arms around and the translucent chains became clear to her. She felt the heaviness of what this meant so that she knew that there were not only chains on her wrists, but a weight on the inside of her. She could feel the darkness only grow. She realized she was empty within herself and there was no way to get rid of them on her own. She realized that this deep darkness that trapped her was the same that trapped those in her town and those digging in the Forlorn Isle she had seen in her dreams. She had come to the end of herself. She could feel the pain of it all and desired to be free.

She got on her knees in the middle of the street, while crying.

"Why are you crying? What is wrong?" The people on

the street said to her, since it was annoying them.

"We have chains. I have seen them on the wrists of the people of the town."

They laughed hysterically, "Chains on the people of Rockfirm? That is ridiculous. You are crazy." They said this walking away. Many people still lined in the alley ways in the filth, not accepting the spirit state of captivity they were in.

Keeper continued to cry while on her knees while looking to heaven. She knew she needed help.

"How did this all happen? How can I be set free?"

"Who the Son sets free is free indeed." Keeper looked up to see a man dressed in linen. Those around seemed to shy away as they saw the light emitted from him, while she felt drawn to his pureness. There was a profound difference in him, as though he was not of this world. There was a sense of kindness in his face; when he said these words, he extended his hand. It was then that she saw that he desired her to take it and follow where he was leading. She looked back at those standing around, who inhabited this town of Rockfirm, and then toward the stranger, whose image was fully illuminated by the light of the sun as it peaked through the cloud cover.

With a sudden moment of clarity she thought that this person had been sent as response to the prayer she had prayed so recently. If she could suddenly see, he must have been the One who had suddenly cleared her eyesight so only she saw things that angels wish to see. There surely was a reason for him being here, especially with one such as herself, a Spirit Keeper who guarded the city. Formulating what she was to say to him, she realized only few could understand what she had just seen since their eyes were blinded to the light.

Looking upward, Keeper asked him. "Sir, do you know how I can be set free?"

"Your faith has made you well, but soon you shall surely be set free. For now you know in part, but soon you will know fully. The life that you live now is but a testimony of my glory that you see and will continue to see until all is completed. In you he has been pleased in allowing you to see the unseen, even beyond the living. I am the Holy One, but my Father has sent me to guide you as your very life spreads the light of life you have experienced to this ever darkening world. Though the darkness has come, there is still hope for morning. Surely, there is still hope." He, the Holy One, motioned as though asking Keeper. "Will you come follow me?"

Looking beyond, Keeper's eyes focused on the horizon as the morning's lights seemed to fill her soul. This world that she had lived in was one of empty longings for more. Looking at the haggard faces of those few who dared to look her way, she could see their fear in coming forward. This fear was not easily admitted. Some attributed it to weakness of the mind, but was it one thing that was unavoidable as they tried to sleep at night while feeling the pangs of loneliness and depression envelope their being. "This, my friend, is the fear of fear, and this is what drives them to find more and more to satisfy them in life, maybe even to gain life." The Holy One explained. Oh, how Keeper desired that they too could feel this warmth and wholeness that she was now only beginning to feel, but she knew was for certain. Even so, the last of them sunk away in the darkness of their homes to sleep, while the early morning hours illuminated the streets. If only they would come to the light, instead of hiding in the darkness, where they could keep their ways from being exposed. If only she could share this with them.

The man in linen expressed his concern. "The light has come into the world, but they neither see nor believe. Those who were not my own do not receive me, but it shall not be like that with you." Feeling the disappointment at his words, he lifted her chin and with a gentleness explained, "I came that I may give testimony of my Father who is in heaven so also you will tell of my glory, but first, you must come so that I can cleanse you."

"I am not worth that you would even do such a thing." Keeper's self pity shone through miserably.

"This must be done, so they know that it was I that sent you. And so that soon, the fullness will be completed. Go into the wilderness, preach of what is to come. I have come to set the captives free."

In the presence of the people of Rockfirm, Keeper left without a thought of what she was leaving behind or what she was going towards. In her heart, there was a deep gladness that sprang so that the more she followed, the more peace she felt in her tread.

Keeper looked down at the chains that illuminated around her arms. As she looked around she had seen those who walked down the street and all around her. The realization of seeing these chains began to give her a knowledge of what was occuring. Here she stood in the darkness of the city of Rockfirm, carrying the same weight that all the others had. She began to pull apart the links and they felt as if they would not break away. How would she get rid of something like this? Was she trapped? She had never seen this before. Though she admitted to herself that Spirit Keeper's had eyes and wished to see what may come, she was not aware that with these deadly chains on her heart.

They could see the things that were in front of them, maybe what others could not. She again tried to pull them apart and could not. In this sense of desperation she began to take a road out of the town with the Holy One beside her. She went to an open area with grass stretched out wide before her. She would walk here on days where the dream she had been having became too much for her to handle. She looked up to the sky and realized that the Holy One was with her so she said these words.

"Holy One, please help me. I am trapped in my own way. I am like everyone else in the city of Rockfirm. Will you please help me?" Keeper said these words in desperation and with much meaning. She felt her knees fall to the ground.

"I will do anything… Yes, anything." Keeper's words seemed to cut off as she heard an audible voice as though speaking clearly through her as a person.

"There is nothing you can do…" the Holy One's voice trailed off as he said these words and Keeper's thoughts turned dismal at the impossibility of the idea. "But I can." A silver breeze of cool air, as a thought that had become understandable, Keeper raised up her head.

"Please, will you do that for me?" Keeper asked pleadingly as she could see in her mind's eye that from behind him the Holy One pulled out a sword.

The Holy spoke in kind tones, "With answering your previous cries, I have come to free you. Stretch out your arms in front of you." Keeper did as he had instructed all the while closing her eyes and maybe peeking out from one eye anxiously. In that moment the Holy One let down such a blow from the sheer glorious blade of a sword, that the chains that she had seen almost translucently all at once broke apart and disintegrated so that they hung loose from the cuffs off her hands, hanging down and then disappeared as with a flash of light. Keeper looked up to see that the Holy One retracted the blade, slipping it into a sash with a holder.

Keeper moved her arms covered with long sleeves and could notice the lightness that had come and at the same moment knew she had been freed. Keeper, although noticing this for the first time, realized that though she thought the Holy One was a vision, but was in fact standing before her. Seeing him standing there she came up quickly and drawing near to him, he stretched out his arms and they both hugged each other tightly, droplets of water falling from her eyes.

"You may have fearful dreams, but I have freed you. What will happen is beyond your knowing, but what I have done for you I also want you to do for others."

"I have sent one in order to guide you on your journey," the Holy One explained.

"Journey?" Keeper seemed confused.

"Yes, in order to save those who are captive. Only know you will be provided with all you need."

Keeper heard these words as an encouragement, while at the same moment the Holy One began to disappear. Keeper reached out, but realized that he had already gone, but in an image in her mind she saw the sword that the Holy One had used to save her as if it clattered on a hard floor.

"Only know my words and know that I will be there in the thick of it all." Seeing these images, the sword too disappeared and Keeper found herself seeing the tall grass of the overgrown field.

She spun around and on several sides she could see the woods rising with greenish growth for it felt like summer. The breeze blew quickly and fully pulled back the hair from her face. In this moment she was reminded of the sweetness of the Holy One, who she knew had created all of this and the joy that she felt immersing her. She lifted up her knees and began to run a considerable distance of the field, dodging some tree stumps that presented themselves. She felt herself turn around as a lively tune accompanied the movement of her feet in a dance that she had never seen.

Keeper was looking over the edge next to the Waterfall of Life. The waterfall was a long walk from Rockfirm as Keeper made her way through the Spirit Wood filled with many green trees. It was located on the east part of the Island Deror, connected to the Derorian Sea. The water was connected so that it flowed in a river to the Spirit Lake. It was a place she went to think. The waterfall seemed to go on for an eternity, she still felt there was some loss in it. Losing this world to gain the next. As she looked on, she asked herself if this leap would be worth the effort on the way down. Now that she thought of it, she was not looking down, but straight into the sky where the clouds had parted and all she could see was the brilliant light of day. One that does not come from this world, but only from the next. Now in her amazement, she felt as if she had already reached out toward this light, without knowing what she had done. Taking hold of its beams, the world she knew disappeared around her. In a moment the light surrounded her being and she was enveloped in its glory, never to lose the feeling of that light.

The light pierced through her. The beams, made of purest gold and silk, went into her being. Nothing she could say could explain what happened next, but as she was filled with a song that rose within her and a hope. The darkness around and within fled, for where there is light, no darkness can hide from its power. Truly, no darkness was left hidden. As the light filled her being, her eyes became brighter so that her sight became pure so then she saw for whom her life was meant. The day had come; the darkness had fled. As she looked around she realized that life had changed, there was change ahead. She did not know where this life would lead, but as she pondered she deeply heard a small voice say. "You will know me better as you follow. While you do there are many trials, but now, I am with you, even to the end of the age."

Tears filled her eyes as her knees hit the ground and she cried aloud. "Thank you, Father. You have done what I could not. You have done it all. Now I will follow." With this she raised herself to find that she was on a mountain on which sunlight shone down. Looking down she saw that fog filled a valley where a path stretched across the earth. "There you must go," she heard him say, "for where I have called you, there I will lead you by my righteous right hand."

Keeper was overjoyed at how the Holy One had saved her. She felt peace like she never had before. It was something that she could not feel fully. The Holy One had broken her chains, the sin and bondage that kept her captured. She was overjoyed at the thought. She could feel the Holy One close to her.

She continued to feel the hope that he gave her. All at once her world made sense and everything had been made right.

Her eyesight became clear, and she was able to see for the first time, as though she had been blind all her life and now found that she was healed. His love, his mercy fell upon her. She was covered with his love, she could feel it flowing from within her for the Spirit of the Holy One now abided within her.

She knew that her life would never be the same. For all she knew, she reached the end, but now there was a new beginning.

Chapter 8

Keeper stood in the middle of the marketplace in Rockfirm. She knew that she needed someone in order to replace her duties. She had been having these dreams of those who were suffering. They were in need of help in their plight. She knew that something was pulling her away towards these beings in the Forlorn Isle.

Foolishly standing in the middle of the road, a horse just about bumped into her and she moved away quickly. A voice said, "You must watch where you are going. The horses are not able to be controlled sometimes." Keeper saw that he walked beside a horse with a rope, leading it along to a wooden stable tucked into a corner of the street.

Keeper followed, watching as he tied up the horse to a post. He let it drink from a trough as he brushed its coat. The horse did not notice that Keeper had come forward, but the attendant did and raised his head.

"Do you need anything, miss, by chance?" The attendant asked Keeper without faltering from brushing the horse's hair.

"You are just good at taking care of these horses." Keeper commented, as she saw that the attendant was already committed to something. The horse seemed to enjoy the treatment he gave to it. The attendant seemed young in age so there was not much time to learn.

"Well, that was acquired." He answered as though reminiscing over a time gone by. Keeper kept pondering the question she meant to ask so that she could word it correctly.

Her hesitation caused him to ask, "Why are you over here?"

Keeper answered with, "I am curious because it seems like you are good at what you do. This makes me think you would be good at something else where you take care of others."

"What might that be?"

"Would you be willing to become a Spirit Keeper?" Keeper asked, trying to sound convincing.

"You mean one of those who watch over the wall for intruders?"

"Yes, that is what they do. I am one actually."

Squinting at Keeper he asked, "I have heard one like you has to have dreams in order to help you know what will happen."

"Dreams are a part of it, but I am willing to train one on how to watch for intruders. Most of it is just done with the spyglass." Keeper explained all of this in detail.

"How do you know that I cannot have dreams about what will happen?"

"Well, that is true. So I will ask, who will come a day after tomorrow to the city? Report back to me who comes. Then I will truly know—"

The attendant cut Keeper off to answer as though he already knew. "There is one dressed in white coming up a long path from the southern land. He will want to talk to you and for you to come on a journey with him."

Keeper, who had not even had a dream like this herself, felt astonished by all that he was able to articulate.

"You dreamt this?" Keeper stammered.

"Yes, a few days ago. I was unsure of the meaning because the visitors seemed to be looking for the Spirit Keeper. I had no understanding of how it related to me, but now I know for whom it is meant." This person seemed wise beyond their years.

"You still do not know if it is reality," Keeper reminded him of this fact, "It is only real if it occurs as you say it would. Then I will know if you are right for the job, if you accept."

The attendant seemed happy at the news, "Yes, if it comes true just let me know. Several others work here at the stable so there is enough to take care of the rest of the horses." He surprisingly came up and hugged Keeper around the waist and this is when Keeper realized how much shorter he was compared to her, and then drew away.

"I will let you know on the sunset of the day after tomorrow what happens."

Since the attendant had a dream that made him capable of being a Spirit Keeper he felt like he needed to help her. "Thank you for considering me for this opportunity." The attendant waved and Keeper waved back as she made her way down the street. He then went back to taking care of the horses in the stable.

Keeper made her way to the main town hall where the Messenger and Mayor worked. Coming into the upstairs where the Mayor's office was located, Keeper clearly stated what was on her mind though it could prove to be dangerous to say what she was thinking.

"I feel like I need to do something important, so I am considering stepping down from my position as a Spirit Keeper."

The Mayor seemed disgusted and surprised as she said this to him, "Keeper, who will take your position?"

"I have found someone." Keeper responded back to him.

"They must be able to be a good watcher, as well as have dreams of insight." He scoffed as Keeper had talked about the dreams that she had that proved to be real.

"Yes, I have asked them about a dream and if it comes true they will be qualified as a Spirit Keeper."

"Not without my permission," The Mayor slammed his fist on the desk so that some paper fell off. He felt

Keeper was taking over so as to control the situation.

"Yes, I completely agree." Keeper tried not to go against what he wanted, so she was compliant with what he said.

"Well, you should. Just tell me if what he dreamed is as he says and maybe we could allow him the position. It is sad to hear you will be leaving. Where will you go?"

"I am not sure where. I am just feeling a pulling toward helping those who are hurting. I sense it more and more. I will definitely train him."

"Yes, but we will see. It still may not be enough. As one on the board you need to tell us definitively of where you were going as a Spirit Keeper." The Mayor had secretly tried to get rid of the Spirit Keeper from Rockfirm because he did not agree with her speaking of the Holy One, but it was now happening. Even so, he needed to know what she was doing in order for her to not spread her thinking to others elsewhere.

"Yes, I will." The conversation ended and Keeper walked from the room.

The clouds which had been pink and yellow yesterday were now a different sight. The wind was not moving. No tree stirred, no bush quivered. She looked along the earth in its station then looked at the sky in its place. She saw in the sky the clouds moving downward, swirling around and round as they came. Then a breeze picked up in a rush. Such a force of energy pushed everything around, this and that. As it lifted up, it became a great turning cloud in the sky.

"It looks dark, but above the clouds there's always light from the sun." She heard a voice and turned her head swiftly for as he said this, she believed that he was one who spoke truth. Standing there was a tall man in white robes by the name of Gabriel. His face was serious, but there were lines at the edges of his mouth leaning upwards that seemed as though had smiled in days past. There were better days then these for she could see that he held in his hand the hilt of his sword.

"What's happened?" She asked with confusion.

"It's all falling." His face was pointed toward the sky. He did not move, but his eyes did as he looked back into her face. These very words awakened a great feeling inside. She fell silent with fear. 'Had the Pursuer come to the world?'

"It is time to go." Gabriel replied, sensing Keeper's fear, "To the Forlorn Isle."

She looked at him with horror as her heart fell to her feet. The darkness was too great a power, as the world is controlled by its evil. Now, looking at him, she realized that the good of the world had sent her to the evil. She heard the seriousness in his words. She asked herself, "Is this what the Holy One has sent me to do? Why, I am not old enough." She protested in her fear.

He looked at her shrewdly, "This is not the time to ask questions. It is time to obey." And there was no questioning him. He instructed her to bring all the food and water she could carry. She also brought a blanket, journal, and charcoal pencil. Besides that, there was nothing else she would take. Even though he was a stranger she felt that he had the authority to be obeyed.

In an eager tone, he said that she would leave as soon as they had rested. It would be on the next afternoon that they would start walking down the wide path to the Forlorn Isle. And why, she was not told, but she listened intently as he spoke for answers. To go to the place that had been described as the very pit of darkness was a dangerous action. Why would one such as Gabriel take her to such a horrid place? The question remained all afternoon. In all of this, her peace had given way to fear. She felt horrified. Could the Pursuer be coming or could she be traveling to where he lay?

The clouds still circled like a strained ship in tidal waters. In every shifting movement, no light is shown from the darkness. All in this moment she looked toward the sky, feeling the longing of the heavens above.

"What is the matter?" Gabriel asked this in a way that seemed like he did not sense the danger lurking before, above, and around them. Though in his eyes Keeper could see a great sorrow and pain for the world, but maybe not this one.

"The sky seems closer," Keeper replied. "Is there something wrong with it all?" With this statement Gabriel's eyes lifted toward the heavens as he said.

"The work I have been sent to do is harder than you may see, but there is also an aspect of the world that still contains hope. There is hope as we walk along this road. The wind comes and goes, but you do not know where it comes from or where it is going. Though you cannot see it as a physical being, it is still at work." He looked at Keeper with stern eyes, "All that is required is to keep walking this road, though it leads to destruction, for there is a time when there will be no one left to stop the evil one."

Far to the north, far from the Forlorn Isle, far from the cries of the brethren, who were captured and farther still farther from the unquenchable fire there were two of which stood in the Spirit Wood. One of which was more knowledgeable than the other, while the other, being younger in spirit and inexperienced in the world. Though she was young, she had seen a new light which illuminated her sight in that she was now able to see the world. For this reason, there was a purpose for the Holy One to send a helper in order to complete the task before her. This younger soul had not yet taken the journey of the hills, a test of resistance among those who are trained as a Spirit Keeper.

As the quietness of the wind blew past, they drew their attention to the face of the Spirit Lake, which looked like a finely polished piece of glass. As the Spirit Keeper stood, looking on, the other, Gabriel, spoke in a voice of stern silver. "See what is real and right, young one." Stepping toward the lake, he took from his cloak a piece of white linen and let his hand drop into the water, dropping the piece of linen on the surface of the water. As it sank into the depths of the lake, to Keepers amazement, rays of light formed from underneath the water so that it touched her face. It was a light of such purity, that it blind one to look straight into its brilliance.

"What is this light?" looking at the one with more knowledge than she.

"This light, it is beyond the light that any man has seen. His light has come. He will be the light to all men, for though they walk in the darkness of their ways, they will see Him in a glorious life. Like this cloth, he shall be pure, ever purer still, for he will be laid down as into water and lifted again as a servant of the Holy One." The being, lifting the white linen cloth, showed that its brilliance was much like the sun as it shone brightly in the afternoon sky. "Soon, he will not only be laid down into water, but to death." These words stirred his spirit for he knew that a price must be paid for the darkness that the world, in which the Spirit Keeper lived, and how it's very existence. "He must come so that this reign of evil is put to death. Yes, death must be killed so in turn, this world may live."

Looking on, the Spirit Keeper did not entirely know the meaning of his words for light did not shine so as to overcome the night. As the dusk turned into night, so did its power rest. All around the light shone, replacing the shadows of dusk with the brilliance of the heavens. Could this be heaven on earth or could heaven be coming to earth to die? Whichever it was, the world could never blot out this brilliant light.

The one holding the white linen looked down toward the Keeper, he gave a nudging glance, "The light is coming, and this is the reason why I have come, so that you could be appointed as the one who makes a way for the King. His light is coming and is already evident in our midst. Now, for the time being, He has chosen you to be the one to send this message to the world." At that moment, what seemed to be a dismal cloudy day was broken into by the rays of light that tumbled onto the face of the Spirit Keeper. Looking around at the trees and grass, the forest began to sway as if, at this very moment, it came alive. But as it began to move, Keeper could also feel the sadness that came with it. Though the Holy One had created the world in beauty, it was now beginning to decay, even in the hearts of men. Their minds had turned from good so now, even the creation was paying for their recompenses. How must this healing come about, what will happen until then, or will it ever recover?

Gabriel, the one who stood beside her, smiled, "The Holy One will send a remnant, for even if this world hates Him, He will come for them so that in turn they may live, and live abundantly. There is a reason why I have come." With a short pause, he put his hands on the shoulder of the younger one, Spirit Keeper, and looked into her eyes, past every fear and past. "The Holy One said, 'I, the Holy One, have chosen you to carry out this message.' You must be on guard and vigilant of what will happen after this point. He has also appointed me to be a helper to you so that you may be able to fulfill all that he has planned. But, surely, he is the one who is always with you. He will be the One who guides you. Listen to him in the quiet places—even in your dreams he will be speaking to you. So listen and see. Yes, you will be able to see much more clearly these days than you have ever before. Glad you thought it over. Now. Rest as we have a long journey ahead of us."

Keeper reflected that when she was able to see Gabriel, the messenger sent from the Holy One, as he asked her to come on a journey with him, as her mouth went wide open. He had asked her to come and journey just as the attendant at the stable had said and she remembered that she needed to tell the attendant that Gabriel had come. Running toward the street on which she knew that the stable was located, she came close to the area tucked in the side of the road where she could hear the neighing horses. She came to the lot and saw that the attendant led one of the horses by a rope toward the road. There was a client waiting who had let the attendant take care of their horse while staying in the inn.

The attendant handed the rope of the horse to the client, which in exchange handed the attendant some coins. Leading the horse away to the cart that carried his goods of the one who stayed at the inn the night before, he harnessed the horse securely to the front and climbed on a high chair. The sound of the words "walk on," caused the horse to carry him away toward the gate. The attendant turned his head to see that the Spirit Keeper stood there and he greeted her with a wave and asked, "Did it happen the way that I said?"

Keeper nodded and did not answer until she got close, "It was the same and more. The visitor also talked about the dream that I had."

"So two confirmations in one about your journey that you will take with him. Do you know of who else is coming?"

"I am not sure of that fact. Gabriel has only said he would go himself. The fact is, you receive the job. I will train you—"

"Do you think I need training?" The attendant laughed, feeling a little confident as Keeper said what she would do. "Did I not pass the dream test? I think that the watching part would be the easier or more straightforward part."

Keeper laughed at his confident forwardness. "While you are right, let me allow you a quick run through. Can you follow me? It will only take a few minutes."

The attendant yelled back to one of the other workers in the horse stable, "I will be back soon. I am needed."

"Yes, be right back. We are expecting a lot of travelers tonight and their horses will need to be taken care of. Is that right, miss?" One of the workers in the stables said back.

Keeper nodded her head in reply.

The attendant turned to the man in the stables and replied with, "It is understood." The attendant waved and began walking with Keeper.

"When will you tell them you are leaving your job?" Keeper asked.

"Probably when I get back. I have been a helpful stable worker for them, but they will not object."

They continued walking the streets until they came to the gate of the city. A ladder stood against the wall leading up to the walkway at the top. Keeper went up the ladder first and the attendant followed, grabbing the rungs on the way up. They both reached the platform and they were able to gain a view of all the surrounding area. The breeze also blew on their faces and through their hair.

Pulling out a small metal cylinder, she lengthened it so that it fully formed into a spyglass.

"Take this, it will help you." Keeper handed the spyglass to the attendant so that he could hold it to his right eye. With it he could see all the way through and get a glimpse of the far reaches around the city.

"What do you see?"

"The forest."

"Have you ever been there?"

"Yes, I have," he said hesitantly, as though he did not want to talk about the subject.

"Well, if you remember, the forest has many types of trees. In the middle there is something called the Spirit Lake."

"I remember. What about those dark shadows in the distance?"

"Well, those are the mountains that separate the northern area of this world from the other," Keeper explained.

"Have you ever been there?" The attendant seemed intrigued.

"No, to get there I would need the help of those who had gone along that journey before. Would you like to meet him, the man in white robes who will go on the journey with me?" Keeper explained.

"I do not think I should," the attendant said this with conviction.

"Why is that?" Keeper asked.

"I just do not think I should." The attendant said back.

Keep nodded and agreed with him without

understanding fully. "I do trust you after these things happened. Just continue to report to the main hall to the Mayor. I will leave a note explaining everything about your new post. I have told them and they will understand." Keeper did just that and slid a note between the door of the Mayor's office later on.

Keeper led the attendant back through the streets and into the town hall, where Keeper went swiftly into the Mayor's office. Keeper could hear the voice of the Mayor as he said for them to come into his office. He immediately noticed the attendant with Keeper, while he sorted through piles of papers on his desk. "Who is this?" He paused and gasped, "You cannot say that you have already found someone to take your position. I know that the watching portion can be the easiest part." The attendant nodded in agreement. "Well, the dreaming part can tell if you are fit for the job and proves you are a true Spirit Keeper, as they say. How would he fare?"

Keeper raised an arm toward the attendant, "he was able to tell me of a dream that not only came true, but also aligned with my dream." Keeper had left out the fact that the person named Gabriel was coming with her.

Raising an eyebrow in suspicion, the Mayor rose from his desk extending one arm to shake the attendant's hand and the other to pat his shoulder. The Mayor seemed strangely more optimistic than normal. "Good, well, you will be here early tomorrow morning for me to give a list of who is expected to enter the city and then you will be straight off to watching on the wall. If you can handle that?"

"Yes, I think I can, sir. The former Spirit Keeper gave me a run-through of what I will be doing."

The Mayor turned away disapprovingly and thought, 'Keeper going through all the procedures before being granted permission is a little presumptuous.' He gritted his teeth and said a farewell, "Well, see you tomorrow then." The attendant nodded his head and walked out of the office as well as Keeper. 'I wonder why the Spirit Keeper has to leave so urgently. Spirit Keepers are usually loyal to their city. I must find out—'

At that moment, Messenger came through the door.

"Close the door quickly," The Mayor commanded. "You just missed me as I allowed some new fellow to be the next Spirit Keeper of the town. It does not make sense why she is to leave so suddenly. We must figure out what is happening. It may even be a threat to our city, compromising our town's morals or lack thereof. So we must be eyes and ears for now on what Keeper is doing."

After Keeper had gone to the Spirit Lake with Gabriel and told the attendant that Gabriel had come while introducing him to the Mayor, she went back to her home to rest for the journey ahead. Soon morning came and the wind was not moving. No tree stirred; no bird chirped. Then, in the sky she saw the clouds moving downward toward her, swirling as they came. The breeze began to pick up. Such a force of wind pushed everything around, this way and that. It had become a great torrent of turning clouds in the sky.

There are times when a person may feel like they want to hide, but they know that they should step into the light. Although there was so much ahead in life, it was easy for one to retract and go backwards from who and where they were supposed to be. In that moment it was a place to hide from what they believed were their worst problems.

There was this fog that came over the Spirit Keeper's eyelids so that she felt she was sinking deeper into something she could not escape. Her thoughts became irritable as she mulled over the set situation bothering her brain. The fear had passed, the storm had calmed, but she still felt like she could not get out of her panic. She heard that she must let it go because it had ended. Everything had calmed, though the trouble may still be there in the end. She was tired of the fight she had experienced and had taken time away to recover. In a muddled, deluded moment she started to turn to look back.

"Wake up, Keeper. Wake up." Her eyes opened at once to see the clear blue sky out her window. She could see Gabriel standing in the doorway of her home. "It's only forward from here. It's over, you can live now. Step into what the Holy One has called you to do. Did you not think the Holy One would deliver you and bring you out, so that he could accomplish in you what you could only imagine? Wake up!" Gabriel tried to get Keeper's attention, "It looks dark, but above the clouds there is always sunshine." Again she heard a voice and turned her head swiftly. Standing there was a tall man in white robes, holding the hilt of a sword.

Seeing him, Keeper exclaimed, as she sat up in bed. "It is you, Gabriel." She continued with the question that bothered her. "What has happened?" she asked with confusion. She stood up at once. "Where am I to go next?" she said pleadingly.

"Home," was the simple reply. The answers he gave were usually short, but it was exactly what needed to be done. "They need you there. Your family needs to see you. It's imperative that you listen and obey. Do not abandon those who need saving. Go and love them as the Holy One has loved you. Some of their broken hearts may be mended as the Holy One will use you to help them." Gabriel continued.

"The Holy One has come to free the captives. He has

given you the keys, and allowed you to unlock doors and chains all in the Holy One's name. Know the authority and power that he has given to you. Be wise and in all you do for he will instruct you in the night. Ask for wisdom and he will give it to you. Have peace in knowing he is with you always." The afternoon clouds were sinking in the west. The orange and pink hue of the light shown, reminding her of a promise in her time of greatest need. The day had wasted away, so that she had awakened drowsy.

"Think of others more than yourself. Your time is a gift from the Holy One; use it wisely." Keeper knew that it would be dark soon so she decided to go back to sleep and awake early the next morning to travel home. "No," She heard his stern voice. "You need to start now. Do not waste this time for all you have is today."

With a nod, Keeper agreed with his instruction. She packed up the items for the journey, and flung them over her shoulder. After Keeper had packed her bags she left a note for the Mayor with instructions for the new Spirit Keeper who would take her place. When she did this, she continued to walk.

She left through the gates of Rockfirm and began walking out into the grassy field. At that moment she realized the pressing feelings inside of her. Though in her head she asked, "Keep going, to fear and the sword? This is not the time." She said this looking at the sky, "I cannot face fear." Her heart on the other hand realized that disobedience was futile, only causing more destruction. As all the corners of the earth quaked, Keeper realized that there was a need for the light of day to destroy the darkness of this world. And this all started with obedience.

Keeper and Gabriel walked under a blotch of trees as they sat in silence both their eyes wandered toward black splotches of darkness floating on the grim horizon.

"See the mountains? Those are the ones leading toward the Forlorn Isle," pointing them out, Gabriel turned to Keeper, "We will climb them on the 'morrow. That is the main reason why we have stopped here tonight, to get enough rest for the journey to come. As soon as there is light we will follow suit." Keeper nodded in unconscious agreement as she turned to face the base of a tree. The clouds, which were making her nauseated just looking at them, were coming still.

"It is all in your mind," Gabriel said, sensing her fear.

She sat up, looking into his honest face, "Gabriel, I see them. They're there and even if what you said is true I still see them."

"Aye, seeing is different then sensing. Do you see that they are falling?" Gabriel continued on, "You need to know that now that things are falling and the world is quaking, this is the time for change. Changing the way you think. Changing the way you see."

"Changing the way I think and see. What difference does that make?" Keeper asked with real understanding.

"The way you view the world shapes your world. It has become your fears and dreams." They both then silently contemplated, as though the choice that they made at this very moment would impact the rest of their lives. As Keeper sat there she wondered at the reason why the Holy One had sent her on this mission, and why she was the one which was one of the most pressing of those questions. This was a very important task he had laid in front of her. She knew that she was incapable, but she was the one he had chosen to grant her all of his eyesight. Ever since that moment she had seen the oppression of those who believe that they were free to do anything, but in reality had become captive to its every whim. Thus, there was no way out, unless there was a hand that reached out to save their soul. There was one, he had come, and he had touched her. It was her belief that he would touch those who he chose. Those who only received would be saved.

"Sir, sir." Messenger knocked his fist against a door, "I have good news."

"Yes, Messenger," The one inside called out, "come in from that horrid weather."

The man who stepped inside had a wild expression as though he desired to cause harm. His hair was heaped untidily upon his head, seeming like he had been awake all night, and had not the time to prepare to present himself. He wore an outfit which seemed disheveled, tilted at an angle around him so his coat collar was up. He moved his coat collar in the correct position to better represent his important station. "Sir, the news I have just been told—" He was immediately interrupted by his superior.

"Who has told you?" His eyes had a glint of fire that could rise up at any given moment.

"Ah, well, one of the ladies of the well told me they saw…" He stopped, trying to gather the words to express what he had to say, "uhm, the, the Spirit Keeper."

As the words poured from his mouth he could see the fire rising up in the Mayor's eyes, as his face turned a dangerous color of red. He grit his teeth and ground out, "Spirit Keeper? She is up to it again? Surely, she must be punished. She must be plucked out, as an eye from a socket so she cannot see. All that nonsense that she goes on about, who would even believe the words that she says? She puts her will above others; her opinion is dangerous to our way of life. Surely, all she says is filled with hate."

"Aye, but what Keeper did was most certainly odd."

"Out with it!" The Mayor was not accustomed to waiting.

Seeing his master dissatisfied, a fearful look spread across Messenger's face. "Yes, but, you will not hear much more of this hate directed toward Rockfirm's people. The Spirit Keeper has indeed left, it seems, on a long journey to the Forlorn Isle. Her departure was quick."

The Mayor smiled in a way that showed his deep pleasure at the news. He had tried several attempts in ridding the town of this pest. He would cut down the plant, but never the root, so that it would grow and spread to others. Otherwise, he wanted to keep an eye on her in order to make sure she did not spread any more of her beliefs to others outside of Rockfirm.

The ideas that were circulated by this group of people who believed in the Holy One were quite unpopular. Their message seemed to pierce the very soul each time they spoke to those who did not believe. Those who were of the Holy One said it was good news, but for the others it was foolishness for their eyes had not yet been open to it.

Keeper had prayed they would see the truth, that they were in bondage. She walked so lightly, yet with a heavy heart for those she saw suffering from a condition they could never cure, unless they had a physician. At this point they were unwilling to take the only remedy, but for now there was hope.

"Is it true, sir," Messenger continued, "but they told me something more odd."

"For goodness sakes, out with it." The Mayor snapped as he commanded.

"Yes, the Keeper was accompanied by one that had a

shining glow about him and wore a linen cloak." He knew that just by mentioning someone such as Keeper's companion, there were reasons to fear. His face tensed as he felt as if a blow was about to be dealt to his brow.

"By the rock, why is one such as he doing with a Spirit Keeper? One described in such a way could only be from the world above, but why would one such as him come to earth?"

"Aye, sir. My same reaction." Messenger shifted, looking quite uncomfortable, as the Mayor began to speak.

"This must be dealt with."

"Aye...but sir, they are already a day's journey away. We would need some of us to travel..."

"To the Forlorn Isle?" A scowl crept over his face. "Spirit Keeper has not been acting normal these last few days."

"No one has seen the Keeper since...no one knows. But now, it has become more important."

"Important?"

"Yes, sir," said Messenger. "Who knows what all will be affected if she goes to the Forlorn Isle."

"Yes, the implications of it are great." The Mayor reflected over this with an inquisitive face. "Yes, from what you heard this could be very bad. Indeed...You are dismissed."

"Aye, sir...have a good day, sir." He said as he headed for the door.

"You too..." Mayor said as though his thoughts gradually withdrew into the shadows. "You too."

Besides the Keeper, the Mayor was also able to have visions, but it was in an evil way to manipulate. He would have these visions in order to stop the Spirit Keeper in her journey to influence others. His visions were different from Keepers so they were not ones where he could be a Spirit Keeper to watch on the wall. They are strange and evil.

The Mayor of the town of Rockfirm could see the journeyer's trek in the forest as there was a moment of pause where all around went silent. All the noises from beyond the trees faded into quietness as it disappeared. Sometimes the Mayor would have the ability to doze off from reality of everything in front of him.

Standing in a room the Mayor could see round, spherical objects floating clearly illuminating as he reached out his hand to touch them. The colors blurred from the inside with images that could almost be recognizable except for the fog that surrounded each. One could have wondered what these images floated like delicate bubbles which could be popped. Gliding by, a bubble began to surface as something he had seen before but at a different stage of time. He saw the same battle that he had seen, but much more smoke covered his field of vision. He reached out to try to manipulate the orb and somehow see what it covered up, feeling a pull of resistance as he reached in, trying to move the contents. Reacting to his hand, it quickly began to spin on its axis away from him, restoring whatever he had just moved. Stepping away he realized these images had another meaning than to be tampered with. He began to see other, more related scenes that he had experienced, some of them more recent and others farther away. Floating in a scrambled order, he could not make sense of it.

There was a battle raging that could be seen. He could see the Holy One and the Pursuer. He had heard of these two beings, but did not have much belief in their existence, but what he was seeing looked real. It was the Holy One's army against the Pursuer's. Although the Mayor did not seem to know either, he had heard about them. It was a vision, just not for good, but for evil.

"What is this place?" Mayor muttered to himself.

Chapter 9

Captavia was a stronghold, a dark dungeon with those in irons. Captavia itself was in the southern region beyond the Dark Range of mountains. It stood with many cliffs that rose tall above the ground and in between was a valley that had trees that dotted the area. It was underneath these cliffs, deep in the dirt, was the domain of Captavia. It was composed of a Court where many were condemned by a judge and then sent to the Prison where many were chained up. Initially the Pursuer would capture individuals with Pullings and take them to the Forlorn Isle, which was an island on the Derorian Sea, but if they rebelled against the system of the Forlorn Isle they were then sent to Captavia where a judge would condemn them in the Court and they would be thrown in Captavia's Prison for their rebellion. In the deep dirt inside of Captavia was where some new people came into the story.

The ground was the crust of civilization for some and for others it was what separated them from the world. Before someone came below its dirt they were willing. After they were placed in the sediment they were disagreeing whether they should have come at all. Though if a person was one of those that wanted all the details—for this was not enough for them—it would be explained. In the world under the soil of Captavia there were ones that worked as captives— without pay but their own lives as ones that have already been encountered.

This was to say that they were forced to do this digging. All around was darkness, all one could see and hear was emptiness. It lasted for but a moment when the scuff of rock upon rock was heard and the place where one was standing became illuminated. The area was located now in a cavern beneath the earth. One saw an unidentifiable silhouette in the torchlight. One would notice that it was moving in stiff, quick movements.

His gate then became wide and he stood still for a moment before he collapsed on the rock floor. The lantern he was holding fell to the floor, and its light was smothered. One might be wondering what had become of this unfortunate being. If only one could have seen the unfortunate expression on his face as he fell.

The being, only seven minutes before, had to rendezvous with an unknown being, but to do so would require absolute secrecy.

Until then, there had been messages that had been passed between the two. Some perceivable, some physical. It had been tedious to pass the many messages between each other without the prison guards becoming suspicious and deciding to make an end to the whole ordeal. The guards did not know of these notes. Those in the prison waited on the day when they would receive the next interception, just hoping that the day that they were found out was far from soon.

The scene was abruptly interrupted as one could hear a scuffle of human feet. With a new light someone rushed forward to support the limp arms of a person. The newcomer then struck a light for a lantern and was left on the cold floor. "Sir, sir, are you well? This is not the time to fall out on me—" The man with a round monocle saw a new breath forming in the struggling young man's throat and exclaimed, "What! What! You are breathing, now up and down with it. That's the way—calmly if you can." He rested his hand on the other's chest, feeling his breathing increase slightly.

The one who had just fallen on the floor opened his eyes, blinking to adjust to the dark room and the figure crouched by his side. In a most relieved tone he addressed the man, "You are here Percy." Though Asher had never seen this person, it was apparent that he was one who was sent to rescue him, whose help had allowed him to come this far. Percy had heard that Asher was a revolutionary that was captured in Captavia and Percy wanted to free him so Asher began receiving letters from Percy on a way to escape. Asher knew that he could trust Percy since he knew Percy was a part of the League who rescues captives and so Asher responded to the letters that showed him how to get out.

"Good to see that you made it out safely. With no harm, I suppose." Percy's look showed that he was more hopeful than sarcastic.

"If you could say that being fed poison is no harm. Then, yes, I do say that I am feeling quite fine. Now that you are here, of course." Asher did not reserve any sarcasm, even though he was thankful that he was alive at all. Taking a quick glance at Percy's calm expression, he closed his eyes, recalling all that had occurred in the last few hours.

"Preferably, it is for the best that we were able to find each other in this time of need." Percy let out empathetically.

The one laying on the ground shot Percy a glance, "—everyone is in need in these times."

"Us specifically. Now do let me feel your head." Feeling the heat of fever as it rose up in red splotches on Asher's face, Percy asked, "How were you, exactly, fed poison?"

"Perhaps it was my frequent requests for charcoal that made the jailor eye me suspiciously…soon afterwards I stopped asking for charcoal. It was on your request that I should leave at the time we previously discussed."

"I see you have completed that task. What next, sir?" Percy inquired.

"Well, I guess that I had been very quiet the whole

day when they attempted to do something against me. I reflected on the days I had been busy working in the mines, always continuing to dig deeper into the dirt. For some that he saw as ones of suspicion, we were then put into the prisons. That is where I sat at night. That is when it happened." Asher tried to explain.

"He did what? We do not have much time."

"He placed poison in my food, I suspected that he knew I would try to escape tonight." Asher recalled the details.

"So what happened, exactly? I mean after that."

"Well, from that time on I felt ill. I waited until the jailer had fallen into a loud snore. Then, when I knew it was time, I inserted the toothpick into the lock, which you most generously provided. Turning the key, I opened the door with conscious awareness. It was a very stiff lock indeed, but when it was ready it gave way. The door easily moved on its hinges, opened, and then carefully closed."

"Did the jailer ever stir?"

"Yes," Asher elaborated further, "right as I closed the cell, he gave a sudden wince. I stood just a stone's throw away from him. His beard moved as he grunted, then hesitated as he fell back to sleep."

"That's amazing; how did you get away?"

"As the situation was, I slowly walked through the passages and changed directions on the thrice before I found myself another set of guards." Asher began to shift slightly in an attempt to picture the situation to tell his companion, but the conversation was set in another direction.

Percy interjected, believing this point of the story would play an appropriate point to educate his friend on new whereabouts. "Have you heard what is happening in the court?"

"Was there a meeting for swearing of alliance?"

"Aye," Percy nodded in agreement, "someone refused, I heard. It pertained to one who escaped in the night. They say he is already in the North."

"It seems I have already been found out." Asher sarcastically replied.

Speaking to his partner, Percy continued, "It seems they talked of your escape from Captavia Court. It is good that you have gotten away, without those in Captavia interfering."

"Yes, and the journey to the North." Asher laughed, "Quite interesting. Gossip goes around fast."

"Even though we have taken to talking, there still is no time," Percy instructed.

Placing the palm of his hand on his temple, Asher commented on his condition, "My head has recovered. I think it best that we were off."

Just as Asher said these things they heard muffled yells and footsteps of some creatures clawing at the ground. "We must be off, at once." Percy whispered as he took Asher's hand. Percy led him to the place he had come. Through the tunnel they made their way to a small opening in the wall. As they dug themselves through the gray dome sediment they found themselves in the floor of the large cavern. Echoes of these beings could still be heard as the two escapees approached the hole, seeing that the beings turned out to not be beings at all, but scaly creatures of the lowlands. Eyes glowing with a red tinge, their fangs sharply protruding as their tongues slithered out like snakes.

As they approached, they seemed to not see the hole which had been dug out of the wall. These scaly creatures were as blind as any human, though possessing twice the sense of smell.

The Digstons made their way up to the entrance. The

leader of the pack, sniffing the soil, smelled humans. Without a second thought, he scurried up the hole, claws reaching deep into the dirt as the others followed his lead.

Asher cried out to his companion, "Sir, I hear something approaching rapidly."

"Aye," Percy said, "Quickly now...to the other side of the cavern." He said in large puffs of air. They ran over the stones and found themselves another hole. Percy heaved himself through the opening of the hole and pulled Asher out as well. The above cavern that they had just stumbled upon had no light and the floor felt wet to the touch as though puddles of water gathered. "Up and out—that is all it takes."

"Is this where you came through?" Asher questioned.

"Aye, down a hole and into this cavern." Percy said while lifting his friend up. They had in a small amount of time almost scaled two levels of ground. They both lifted themselves upward. The Digstons could no longer be heard below them.

Down in the cavern the Digstons took in gulps of air, bursting forth through the dirt. They had only just started to sniff around when they picked up the scent of the one who escaped. Tongues flicking, they raced across the floor toward the scent.

When they reached the other side where the hole lay there seemed to be a scuffle on who should go through the ground first. The leader started biting and clawing its way through the pile, but the others kept him away from the entrance, becoming stuck in a tangle of thrashing.

Meanwhile, the two beings continued to put their hands upward, pulling dirt down the sides of the tunnel they created upward. They could now hear the fight that had broken out below them, digging faster still.

"Here it is...we are almost through." And sure

enough, the sun broke through the tunnel and a gust blew past into the dark cavern below. Coming out, they found themselves on a sandy ledge.

"Sir, we are here…we made it." Asher choked out a response as he received in the air.

"Aye, we are out. Still, we must not stop now while the beings are bound to be at our tails at any moment now." Seeing a stone nearby, he motioned to Asher as they pushed it over the top of the entrance. The wind that had blown through the tunnel had stopped, and the cavern became enveloped in complete darkness.

Gabriel and Keeper traveled along the dirt path on their way to save those in the Forlorn Isle.

If one listened with open ears, though there was no sound that could be heard, one could hear the majestic melody of heaven. Their voice was heard throughout the earth for those who would listen. There was no excuse, in the human heart of hearts, they knew the reason for these sounds.

Though these sights filled Keeper's eyes, darkened thoughts dissuaded her from the peace that could have been felt in the moment. She then saw the darkened clouds that had come from the south, which covered the sky above the distant mountain range. In her mind, there loomed some sort of doom if she dared to move forward, though her mind quickly checked itself as the fear was displaced with the peace of the thought that the Holy One was always with her. Yes, she could sense him even in this moment. She thought about the fight that had raged between darkness and light. She could see that along the range of the hills, they started to glow as an ember from beyond the horizon. It then turned the clouds a lighter, cool color, even those that had shown a darker gray before now, were penetrated with the beams so that they disintegrated as puffs of dust. Just then she heard Gabriel behind her. He said suddenly, "They will be here soon enough. Up, we must go to the Forlorn Isle." As though suggesting the idea, the sun peeped over the horizon to reveal the sorrows of yesterday. "Look no more on the past, but on the present. What more could the future hold if we lived without sorrow or shame?" He paused as though allowing her to remember something important before concluding. "And the cuts and bruises are all that you can remember. Cheer, there's better times to think about in the future. Look forward; press forward for the goal." Saying this, he drew his outer coat over his shoulders and they continued their long walk toward the Forlorn Isle.

The clouds still came closer to the world. Keeper had been thinking about what Gabriel had said about looking at the present. What more could one expect from the past anyway? One could only remember the hurts and attempts to succeed, but where they miserably failed. One could always see the scars, instead of looking at the good things and be thankful. Keeper thought, "When have I been thankful and lifted my eyes off myself and seen the bigger picture?"

Usually, it all seemed to be good and satisfying at the time, looking at her own needs. Now, in this time of need it was the time to look up. Now was the time to see.

"Gabriel, why are we going so quickly?" Keeper asked, while picking up her pace so as to catch up.

"Do you see the danger awaiting? It is coming and it is time to act. He is leading and we are to follow." He then added with a smile, "But there is no reason to worry, for he is with us and will never leave us. Let us keep our eyes on him for our strength and decisions." The day was windy and went by slowly. The grass along the road in which they traveled seemed to lose its green tinge and rather took on a gray, dead look. All the fields of grass seemed to be filled with pain and sorrow as the breeze slipped through the decaying blades. Water soaked the ground as though it weeped for the ones of the lowlands to the Forlorn Isle who had fallen away from their set purpose.

As the two walked, a mountain range came into view that Gabriel had informed Keeper to be the Highland Range. There on the bases of the range stood thick woods of lofty pine trees and oaks. As one peered close, a few clear rivers could be spotted that flowed from the rocks. Above the frothy snow clouds, one could almost spot the snow peaks of ice.

It all seemed so wonderful, yet dreadful. For when one saw closer they could spot a dark mountain range behind the snowy ones, just looming with the stench of darkness. "Whatever are those?" Keeper raised a finger, pointing upward.

"That is the Dark Range, which is the beginning of the lowlands territory to the south and on toward the Forlorn Isle."

"Why do they call it that?" Keeper asked in a reluctant tone.

"It is because of who owns the Forlorn Isle and its territory. The snake, the lizard. Some even say he is a dragon, seeking whom he may devour in this world. I have most commonly heard him called the Pursuer. He is the father of lies, who has lied to the minds in order to drag them into bondage."

"It is all a hoax then, is it?" Keeper asked, "the gossip of the 'Great Place' has just been a lie?" For many years she had heard of this place in the lowlands that some people may go to, many who had disappeared suddenly in the night without as much as a farewell. Even though they had gone missing, no one searched for them. They said that they had physically gone to the 'Great Place' where they lived safely and securely for the rest of their days. 'Could the night that I felt like I was being strangled be when the Pursuer tried to lure me in with Pullings?' Keeper acknowledged that she had fought with much strength through the night. 'Something must be connected,' Keeper concluded, 'but how did this snake not get me?' Keeper felt that though she had never encountered this being while he had somehow confronted her, via her dreams.

"In most cases it has worked too. Beings are not as wary as they used to be. Having become captured, what does that have to do with anything? While we hold fast to him; everything is possible." As though his words played a part of a prophecy, Gabriel spotted two travelers up ahead. "Speaking of possibilities," he said with a smile of expectancy, "here are some that could be of great help to us."

After a few moments one cried out from afar, "It is you again, old friend. So glad to see you here."

"Blessed that you made it as well," Gabriel replied in a sing-song type manner. "Who is your companion traveling with you?" Coming up to them, Gabriel reached his hand out, shaking the young man's hand.

"Eh, you mean Asher?" Percy pushed his monocle to his eye and continued to reply with, "Well, I picked him up on the way. I had heard of his imprisonment in Captavia and decided to hear his side of the story, seeing that he proved a revolutionary." Percy replied jovially, giving Gabriel a proper, gentlemanly handshake.

"He acted as a deliverer for me from Captavia Prison," Asher replied thankfully, "He even planned an escape route for us. We continued to dig our way out of that place, and the dirt settled under our fingernails and sweat ran down our faces. When we finally reached the light… I was overjoyed." Asher wore a leather sailor's coat. He had dark, short, and messy hair. He laughed a bit and turned to look at the smaller figure standing beside Gabriel.

"Seeing that we are all here together, let us talk of what is to come." Percy, being eager about the engagement of the mission, had overlooked one other member of the group who had not spoken up yet.

"Speaking of companions, this is Spirit Keeper who is coming with us as well." Gabriel put a firm hand on her shoulder. "I have brought this one along because the Holy One has chosen ones as these for His Kingdom, the ones with a pure heart."

"Glad to meet you. It is always an eventful moment to find others who think just like you in the way this world should unfold," Asher hesitated and then grabbed Keeper's hand in greeting.

"Very nice to make your acquaintance," Percy said, bending over to respond while looking at Keeper in a belittling way since she seemed inexperienced. "We know you will be a great part of the cause."

"Nice to meet you both," Keeper replied, "I am glad you have both come."

Turning away from her presence and taking Gabriel to the side, Percy spoke in a concerned voice. "Why did you bring an inexperienced person, sir? Concerning what we are about in the present, there is much urgency in what is happening. It is for the cause." Keeper stiffened, but listened on.

"Do you realize that the cause is best fought by a being who is still young in their faith. Many like her are falling away from the trust. Many of those around her already believe in the lowlands and what it brings. This is one of the few that have not succumbed to the mind-leading tactics of the Pursuer. For this reason the Holy One has found this one to be of a good heart, one ready to fight."

"Of course! Why did we not think of it? Spirit Keepers are separate from all else and that means they do not listen to the others around them who may have a negative influence on them. Many like her have not bought into the lies. At least, not at the moment." Percy had been on this side of the fighting and knew that what Gabriel said was of the truest meaning.

Gabriel continued enthusiastically, "This is why I think that if we can relate the cause to the innocents while they are inexperienced, we could stand a chance against the Pursuer and those of the lowlands."

"Aye Gabriel, this is worth carrying out. It could change if everything began to fall through." All those who stood around looked at each other, evaluating the strength between them in order to fulfill this task.

"Percy," Gabriel looked at his friend in anticipation of the process that would follow after. "We might need to discuss the plan to Asher and specifically to Keeper. It is valuable that everyone understands what we are doing on this trip."

"Relate it to your heart's content." Percy waved a hand in a motion for his friend to begin when ready and then adjusted his monocle to see better. They stood around each other in a moment of anticipation of what Gabriel would relay. In the meantime, both Keeper and Asher had a discussion as well.

"It must have been exceptionally risky to escape from that place that was essentially a prison," Keeper said.

"I know it was extremely risky, almost to the point of madness I would say. Moreover, Percy wrote to me on how to escape, describing in detail that this seemed like a normal greeting with much more of a meaning because of its importance to the mission." Asher explained.

"Had you ever met before your meeting in the caverns?" Keeper asked.

"Well, no, but I heard others that had tried to free prisoners. I took a chance by just answering the note he had written to my cell." Asher replied.

"How did you get the notes to him?" Keeper asked, curious about his answer.

"A set of receivers were set up in the prison so that the note went from one jail cell to the other. Finally, when it reaches a certain League member's cell on the outer banks of the dungeon he slips it through a small hole which drops off to where the Assembly meets. The Assembly is when the League has meetings together on how to rescue captives. At the League's Assembly they read the news of the ones who desperately need to escape and they reply. After the fact, the process is started all over again until it reaches the specific correspondent they desire to set loose. This is how I got the message from Percy. In this sense the assembly is one to help us compared to the Captavia Court, which is not well trusted in making a fair judgment. If one receives a letter from them with the official seal it means that they are truly cleared of their crimes and are able to leave, but without the notice of the prison guards. The letter is proof enough on the surface of the land, if one is questioned. No one can touch them."

Despite the explanation of his correspondence with Percy, Keeper still had a concern with what Asher had brought forward. "Why did you trust him? It could have been anyone who corresponded to you, leading you into much more trouble. Maybe even a longer sentence and much more evidence against you."

"I had to take a chance on that. Sometimes there are

faulty letters, but most are trustworthy. Besides, I had heard of such a group of receivers, who call themselves the Rocklings. They try to help many folk escape from Captavia and are members with the League that meet regularly which is a group who rescues prisoners. The Rocklings are the ones of the League who are assigned to do the manual work after the members in the Assembly meetings have responded so that they give the envelope. I have heard of such notes that they placed in the prisoner's food and drink of choice. In passing these messages along so that news spreads quickly even when under lock and key. They seem to be skilled in their secrecy, for I had not even known of the communication between the cells. As I have explained before, I was actually unaware of their existence until I received this letter." Asher waved the letter that he received with a red wax seal with the symbol of a chain imprinted on the substance. "This group of the League is one that Percy has been a part of for years, one of their finest Rockling members. A risk-taking type that undertakes these types of missions. He would have to be, I imagine. I will have to ask him more about his involvement. He proves to be a great story teller." Asher laughed in thought of his adventurous friend.

"Aye, he did have to trust a bit. The system is one of secrecy in Captavia." Percy chimed in, guiding the conversation to what was at hand. "If you are done talking, it is time for a meeting...Under the trees, I must say." They all sat under a patch of oak trees, located only a few feet from where they stood. The branches provided a shade from the bright beams from the afternoon sun. They sat patiently waiting until Gabriel and Percy were able to begin. Finally, after a few moments of silence, Gabriel spoke.

"We have brought two more that we may start to bring many more. It is much greater to gather with two or more. We have done just that and gathered more, may he be among us."

"Aye, in this time he will be." As Percy concluded his opening, Gabriel lifted his eyes to heaven and said a prayer. "Help us as we make this quest. Much is to come and we need your protection and guidance. May our fruits multiply as long as we are on your path of righteousness. Lead us not into temptation but deliver us from evil, for yours is the kingdom and the power and the glory forever." Echoing his prayer, they all said, "Amen." Gabirel continued as he brought forth any anticipated information needed. "As you know, it has become important that we come together, for the League is restless of the changes that have occurred."

"We have come to tell you our plans since we have found trust in you both," he said, gesturing to Asher and Keeper in reference, "You shall trust him here after. It is time that we are to act, as the League has ordered us as spies to the lowlands. We are to find a way to free the ones first at Captavia since they have fought against the system. This will be our first point of defense in creating a group strong enough to ultimately free those who live in the Forlorn Isle where the prisoners who are digging the earth have become captives."

"Excuse me," Keeper begged pardon suddenly so as to say something that had come into her mind that she thought to be important. "If they are in jail for doing wrong, should we let them have their sentence in Captavia?" Keeper did not understand who these people were who had been put into cells.

"That depends on what you call wrong," Percy relayed the words to his friend, explaining specifically what he meant to say, "They have done nothing wrong in the sight of heaven but have surely done good."

"But what good did they do?" Keeper felt confused at

the statement.

"We were the ones who would not listen to those in charge who forced us into digging and the nipping of the Digstons. Those there were convinced for the time that the snake had planted the thoughts into the hearts of man. A group of us tried to escape from that place of the Forlorn." Asher Callaghan sighed regretfully, thinking of the situation, "If only we had not gone on strike and done it in secret. If we had known of the Rocklings and the system of the League, we could have appealed to the League members who meet in the Assembly meetings for them to help us and something may have been done. After hearing of our actions, a court meeting was held in Captavia. The jury sentenced every being who refused to dig and said that it led to death, throwing them into the prison of Captavia."

"Anyway, the League came through and Asher was blessed to get past the guards and to the surface alive. Though we stand here talking of this system, many more need someone to help them to escape. Still more need to understand that they are not captives at all." Percy thankfully responded and decided to continue to discuss their importance in this mission.

"That is why we have called you all to this consensus, so that we might find a way to revolt against the Forlorn Isle with the prisoners of Captavia behind us." Gabriel explained, seeing the face of his companions light up at the mention of the hope for the lowlands and the Forlorn Isle.

"So where do we start?" Asher showed eagerness in his tone and the question was directed at Percy.

"With all who we find to be a part of our allegiance, we will head to Captavia first. There is no time to waste." Everyone rose suddenly in agreement of the forward plan. Knowing that this was the moment of beginning, Keeper took in a deep breath to keep her composure. Much would happen to bring them to the place they needed to end up, but she knew that every step would be guided by the Holy One since he had called her and provided the people needed to help in the mission.

Green and yellow light shafts fell onto the leaves as Keeper stared at all of its radiance. Light had come to greet them on this gloomy day. By the grace of the Holy One, the light had that very effect. Though being only a small bit of glitter, it could have filled a well to its brim. The others looked up, all seeming to see different signs: war, danger, peace, hope, a new day. With one glance it had dispersed behind the blackened clouds. A small drop of sunshine could do a great deal.

"Aye, it is a sign from heaven above. He is saying, 'Go to the Forlorn Isle and free them for me,'" Percy sighed suddenly and raised a hand to reach out toward the sky. "If I may translate into meaningful terms from the natural ones."

"Now on with our pledges," Gabriel started with words of what to come, "I, Gabriel, guardian, do pledge upon my oath as a follower and worker of the Holy One that I do as he has commanded and follow him in his path, for my life," Pausing a moment he indicated for the group to follow, "Now, after me everyone."

With one hand raised they all pledged with cheerful hearts for they had been chosen to carry out the plan of the Holy One. They thought of the pain leading to sorrow of those who still lived in the lowlands to the Forlorn Isle. They hoped that the Holy One would lead them down paths of righteousness, praying that they may not fall astray from the narrow. Lightly they traveled on, carrying heavy hearts that had a small amount of knowledge of the darkness that may befall them. Into the dust they must stumble, through the darkness and deepest gloom they must find there still stood a light that still dimly shone.

"The light of the type from the Holy One was inside those who were no more slaves to sin, but to righteousness. Doing what good he may to persuade the hold of the underground that they would know what better they could possess. Their fathers and their father's fathers had done the same as they, having been slaves to sin.

Initially, they succumbed to the Pullings of the Pursuer to the Forlorn Isle, but as they slaved away in their own way they realized that they did not have to surrender to this fate and fought against it. Their minds had somehow been released as they dreamed of deliverance. As they realized this, they fought to escape, ending up in a place where they could be watched and secured. It was positive sometimes to go against what they know to be wrong. As they realized they helped to build the Pursuer's kingdom, they decided to build another. Moreover, they have become partial toward our cause." Pointing upward, Percy smiled softly and studied Keeper's expression to see if she understood.

It had been a long day, and the sun was beginning to set up over the horizon before them. Earlier they had entered into a deep wood. Its branches became thick so the path that they traveled on began to become very narrow. They had not planned to have gotten stuck in the middle of a wood, since they thought that their pace was quick enough to get them to the other side. The screeching of a night creature came from somewhere in the distance.

"Who knows what is out here." Asher hesitantly

remarked to the others around him.

"With as many people as with us, they would not think of getting in our way." Percy laughingly joked, slapping his partner on the shoulder.

"I am serious…" Asher's voice trailed. "Something more powerful is bound to be here."

"And that only means we will have to stand up and fight them." Gabriel instructed him, seeing if the way Asher answered was out of fear or his own character.

"But what if they overpower us, what if we are not strong enough and we fall?" Asher showed true concern in his voice.

"Then we have done our best and what was meant to happen did, in reality, happen." Keeper at last replied.

Having a surety around the group continued to bring out the fear that she also felt about going forward. Much of Asher's comments stemmed from fear, but Keeper often wondered if he had any other motives. There was the importance to keep everyone in the resolution of the same spirit and of the same purpose. When they traveled together in this way, each one's reasoning began to come out. Gabriel led most of the time; there was no need for them to worry in which direction he led them. Honestly, Keeper trusted his leadership even if they did not know where they were going. He had proved himself enough times that Keeper realized there was no need to thwart him. Although in this moment, she felt like the words expressed by Asher held a grain of salt.

Around she could hear that the sounds drew closer. No stopping them. She began to experience the same amount of fear expressed.

"We should take camp here." Gabriel said suddenly as he could say it at any better time. There was a gasp heard from the group as they shuffled to a halt. What Keeper did know was that this thought was an absurd one. And for her to speak out next was unlike the way she had acted previously.

"We cannot, we must go on further before stopping. This part of the forest is too narrow for us to stay." While she said this, she really meant what Asher had expressed: that there was something out in the forest lurking to come after them.

"Yes, please Gabriel. Have some sense." Asher did not usually talk to Gabriel while they had been together. When they were all together his thoughts came as one that were for the ears of all to hear so that the others could comment and respond.

Gabriel was always the one to have the final word on these matters. Moving his bag from around his shoulder to the ground, the group saw his action and the others followed despite the previous disagreement. Around they placed their belongings. One gathered branches off in the bushes, while the rest laid out the stones needed to make a circle to enclose the fire.

Gabriel pulled out a blanket from the bag and some few other items.

"How much do you have in there?" Asher laughed.

"This is my never ending bag. It can carry whatever I put into it." Gabriel put a rock into the bag. "Now carry it," he handed it to Asher.

"I cannot even feel it! Where is it?" Asher dug around and found a plethora of knick knacks.

Gabriel laughed, "That is why it is called the never ending bag."

Asher sat down first on the blanket laid out, lowering his head down so that he looked toward his feet. All the while he twirled a piece of grass between his fingers. Gabriel sat on the opposite side of the camp, bringing out the parchment map which he had been given in order to aid their travels. Both Keeper and Percy were content in keeping quiet and raising their eyes momentarily to meet the blaze of the flames which spurted up in a smooth flow of orange and yellow. Licking up the remains, the wood continued to fuel its ascent. The warmth was felt and in each of their faces could be seen a flicker and a glow which served enough to enlighten their features.

No one asked about the map until Keeper thought to understand what they should do for the next day. Coming alongside Gabriel, he pointed to an area on the map covered in trees. This area stretched out around most of the mid north part of the map surrounding the area of Rockfirm and coming along the side of the Spirit Lake. In his explanation, Gabriel set his finger in a straight line toward a spread out range of mountains and hills that seemed to split the terrain of the northern and southern region into parts. A portion of the mountains were covered in snow while the other parts were covered in fire. Much of the land on the northern side seemed to have much more internal growth than the south, producing a brighter shade of green compared to the reddish brown of the lowlands. The stark difference would soon be seen. Out to the east could be seen the form of the desolate island of the Forlorn Isle.

"There are a few days until we reach the mountain range. This area has a covering of trees and will be much easier to travel then the steep terrain that the hills will provide. I say go slowly and rest these few days before we take on this endeavor." Keeper followed Gabriel's finger as he traced the way.

She nodded in agreement and added, "Do you think we are ready for this part of the journey?"

Replying back to Keeper in a laughable but serious manner. "Ready? I believe that many of us have been waiting our whole lives to be able to battle against such obstacles. Remember both Asher and Percy just recently made this journey upwards towards Rockfirm and I have known my way. I guess all that leaves is you. It is like we are escorting you to this place. Just know that you will be able to face anything when it comes the right moment to do so." The folds of the map rolled into a scroll that Gabriel placed in one of the bags.

In a moment Keeper felt like she needed to say something. Keeper voiced her concern for her parents to Gabriel, "I once had parents, but now they are gone."

"Do you have any idea of where they would be?" Gabriel's expression was sorrowful.

"No, I do not, but perhaps in the Forlorn Isle."

"Yes, is it a possibility," Gabriel sighed and looked around.

"I will search for them. There is a possibility that is why I have so many dreams." Keeper voiced her pain.

"Yes, that could be true." Gabriel was serious and searching, "but that is why we are searching. We will look for them."

"Thank you," The creases on Keeper's eyes raised as she nodded his way. Scanning around Keeper saw Percy who had laid his head down, and his deep breathing could be heard. He seemed to be trying to talk so that a mumbled conversation could be heard as if he bartered the price of an item at the market as he bickered with an attendant. "What! What!" With this, his monocle moved up and down.

Deciding that he truly slept, Keeper scanned the area to see Asher who had his knees toward him with his head hunched over, while resting his head on his knees. He then sat upright with his back against a tree. He had a short breath as though he could be woken up at any moment and start

105

walking on their trip.

Keeper got out the charcoal pencil and journal and jotted down a few words and drew a few pictures describing her dreams and their beginning on the journey.

Gabriel had also stopped conversing with Keeper and had already rested his head down upon a rock that sat flatly protruding out of the ground. Keeper also decided to put her head down as she stared toward the flickering fire as it began to fade in her vision and go out completely. What a sight to see the many bright lights glimmering, placed in their specific arrangement in the sky. Keeper's mind wandered in these moments and sometimes with more clarity than if she had been awake.

Chapter 10

Keeper struggled on. How could she still be following the Holy One and still have this fear? This inescapable fear that no matter what she did that she would always fall, always struggle, as feeling like she was being chased through the forest. That the Pursuer always stepped not far after her heels. She almost felt that it had become her burden to carry.

"Put on your new self," She heard the Holy One clearly speak this to her mind. He repeated in completion, "Put off your old self and put on your new self. This act is the only way the old man will not dominate who you are. You have been made new in me, but now you must walk in it. If you know you are righteous then you will walk righteously in who you know that you are. Who you have been made to be."

"How can I walk righteously? I feel like the old man so easily clings on to me." Keeper answered back.

"It is only through me. I will give you the righteousness to walk in the manner I have called you. Walk in the Spirit."

Keeper still almost looked away and stomped her foot in determination. 'I can do this,' she thought, 'I will give myself one more chance.' She looked away from the Holy One and envisioned her problems with the solutions she had formed. As she went through everything one by one. None. Had. Worked. She looked up again, beginning to want to receive this help.

"Perfect love casts out fear. My perfect love." The Holy One seemed to grow larger in size as the anxiety and fear diminished. It still seemed to be nagging at the corners of her mind, but it had loosened with the thought of his words.

Keeper seemed to wake up in the dreams of her mind in an old house. It felt like long strands of sticky spider webs grew in a part of her mind as she walked with a sword. She began to try to remove darkness in the edges of her mind. For this was her mind anyway. This, too, was where she saw important things.

She said in that moment in the heaviness of the stage in which she sat. She felt as if the lights had gone out. She at once tried to bring the light to her mind.

She could see a centralized light shining, but as she looked around everything seemed cluttered. She went around trying to dust off everything as though it had been mahogany furniture that sat in a room for ages.

As she saw before, there needed to be someone to dust everything.

In a corner, she could see something hidden in a box, shut tight. Keeper went over to look at its contents. She applied a hand to open the box in order to pry the hinges. The wood creaked, but the lid would not open. This was a dark corner, away from the light.

Keeper at once grabbed the box and pulled it into the brighter area in the middle where she could shed light onto the item.

Keep knew what was inside of the box. It had to be. "He said to bring things to the light."

It was a thinking problem that had plagued her for a

long time, but she would not release it. Like jumping in water and it would be removed as far as the east is from the west.

With her fear she thought she could not trust the Holy One to free her, but yes he could do it.

"He said to tear down every lofty thing that puts itself against the knowledge of the Holy One.

"So far has he removed our transgressions from us."

Keeper slashed down on the locked opening, but she would not release it. She felt like she had to have it. It had become part of her for a long time.

"Let it go." The Spirit said.

"I cannot." Keeper cried out.

The Spirit would open the box up. "Maybe you have kept it sealed and chained up for so long that you do not know what to do with it. Let me have it so I can heal you and you can walk in the fullness of what I have for you."

"Let me keep it. I can hide it. I can find my way around it. I can deny it. I will find my way to live with it, but still follow you."

"I am afraid you cannot serve two masters, for you will serve one and hate the other. Would you want to serve me, the one who can for you? You know who you are. I have made you new. Overall, it is not about cleaning your sin up, it is about coming to salvation and finding redemption, and I will start to refine you.

"I want you to walk in the true freedom that I can give. I know you will struggle, but would it be better to run the race and throw off what hinders you so it does not drag you down and keep you from helping others?"

Keeper agreed with him and thought. 'How can I help others when I cannot help myself?'

"You cannot help yourself." The Holy One replied in a peace-giving tone. "That is what sanctification is about, in *order to be righteous. It is about pruning. It is about taking away the dead branches in your life until there is only new growth." Keeper could literally see a tree in her mind with a farmer with clippers snapping off branches. "I am taking away the old. Abide in me because I am the vine and you are the branches. You will grow when you abide in me."*

Keeper felt like she had walked out of the dark hole. She now walked into a brightly-lit meadow. It had the vibrant colors of spring as the petals of the flowers flourished. She saw the sights of the moment with the birds flying about. She felt like she recognized this moment. She looked backward as she had just walked in the door frame of a darkened room of what her mind used to be. The wooden edges seemed to splinter and the paint began the peel at the embellished swirls meant to be colored brightly.

The Holy Spirit made his abode in Keeper's heart. It was a seal of promise. The Holy Spirit used the keys of sin and death to be able to open up the door to the house of her heart.

The creaking sound of the door caused her to realize that her life and the way it had been had closed up tightly. She could see, and it revealed everything, as she looked through the door frame. There was someone who had lit the lights from a lantern and the room revealed everything. There was a mist as though someone sprayed to clean the walls and floor. The dirt and grime came out as the person rubbed with a sponge and soapy water. They used a broom in order to swipe away all the spider webs that had hung stretched out by the spider's own making. They came down and in wads, wound around the tip of the broom's straw bristles. When this was done, the person began beating the rug with an iron instrument as it hung by a wire. The dust sprayed up almost making a person cough, but they backed away and did not. The person then took the sheets off the furniture to reveal red velvet couches and mahogany tables engraved with lion paws at the legs. In a corner, there revealed a wardrobe with an oval mirror covered in a thick layer of dust so that the person wrote the word 'new' to reveal part of his reflection as he then wiped from the top to the bottom of the glass. With a polish, he rubbed on the mahogany wood of the pieces of furniture until there was a clean reflection.

He then again swept through the room with a wash rag and towel and cleaned every inch of the room until everything gleamed. It was spotless as one would have a guest over to stay and live to make a permanent residence.

Keeper saw the person looking at her through the open door. "You have been made new, behold the old has passed away and the new has come. Take care of the room where the Holy Spirit has cleaned and made an abode. Let not anything come in, not of the Holy One and fill this place."

Keeper looked back and knew it was true. She felt like she was beginning to understand.

The Holy One came up beside her as he began to discuss these things. "The old has become new. You are a new creation." He explained simply.

"How do I walk?" Keeper asked this question hoping to understand.

"You walk righteously through the power of the Holy Spirit."

"That makes sense." Keeper joyfully ran across the field feeling the grass move beneath her as if she could fly.

She could not describe this feeling. To her it felt like freedom. To her it felt like something had lifted off of her.

Keeper had been running through the grass. There was so much freedom that accompanied this decision. The realness and the emotion of it enveloped her.

Gabriel had a conversation with her about her mind and not trusting everything as if it was a fact. Keeper wanted what she was hearing to be true, but she needed to rely on the Holy One most of all. Keeper, as though she felt she had not talked to the Holy One in a while, came running up to him and they both hugged. The Holy One rubbed her head and patted her on the back.

"How are you doing, my daughter?"

Keeper closed her eyes for a moment and looked back up at him. "I am confused about how these Spirit Eyes work if I am a Spirit Keeper."

"You do know that you need to rely on me more than on the ability to have foresight about the future?"

"Yes, do you give me these dreams?"

"Yes, but as Gabriel said, some things may start to come that bombard your mind. You are going to have to gain the skill to fight and to discern what is true."

At this moment, Keeper could feel something creeping from the forest as though it were one of the Pursuer's own. The darkness and fear welled up creating much distress. *'How will I fight it? I feel like it comes so easily.'* Keeper thought.

The Holy One could discern her thoughts and knew what was occurring. "You will need to discern what is true and fight for it."

"But how?" Keeper's voice felt concerned, but she

knew that the Holy One had a plan to help her.

Chapter 11

Messenger came to a halt before he reached the door handle of the Mayor's office. With a quick, deliberate pull, the door handle already swung open. Mayor glared down at him. Even if Messenger had gotten there in the middle of the night, the Mayor would have believed that his Messenger was late and deliberated on any information to him.

"What have you to say?" Mayor asked shortly.

Pausing, Messenger tried to find the words to explain the situation.

"You are late." The Mayor cut in.

"I have not even told you the news, sir," Messenger explained.

"Well, you do not have to. There are some who have already given ear to me." The Mayor continued to interrupt Messenger every time that he tried to talk. From the Mayor's right eye there could be seen a spark, as it began to glow with light. Messenger stepped back slightly for he had never seen his superior in this way. Though the Mayor had power, Messenger was unsure on how he had been given his authority. It maybe came from some sources, which his eye continued to glow for a moment then dimmed. "I still see Keeper and where they have traveled, but there is something…" he banged his fist against the table. The Mayor pulled out a map and placed a X on where he believed they were located. "There is something hidden, that I do not think even Keeper is able to see. I saw the world falling in swirls. There is smoke coming down over the horizon. I think something stands in the way of seeing. It must be removed." Wheeling his gaze over to Messenger, he searched his face. "Why will you not answer?"

Messenger replied in an honest way. "I was unaware

that I should answer you."

"You should be ever-active in answering what I say to you. You should anticipate what I will say so you will be ready at any moment to act." The Major's strange absurd words were ridiculous.

Messenger inquisitively looked up and asked. "How will I know what you will say before you say it?"

"You just will." The Mayor impatiently sighed at Messenger's incompetent understanding, but still there was more to be said. "Those bubbles I saw in flashes recently in the night..." The Mayor trailed off in his words.

Bubbles could pop; memories could be distorted. Who knew what would really happen in regards to the future? One could always guess by using sources and plan ahead. Something seemed to have shifted, something in the atmosphere. The wind flung open the windows and the Mayor strode to close them. Close behind him, Messenger observed. "Do you think that the clouds seem to be coming closer?"

"That depends on the way that you see it," the Mayor tried to explain. "Time will always seem to be cut short. The question is how long you can hold onto what is changing as it begins to affect you. Much is starting to happen in that regard. How much more until everything is turned in a different direction all together. Much of what we have decided to do can in some way be swayed. Then resistance comes when you choose to keep the ground that you have gained. It all depends on what you see as the enemy. Perception may change the direction in which you turn." Returning from the furnished office with a cluttered table which was piled with many scrolls laid out to be seen.

Out of the windows there was a wall of clouds that billowed far into the sky that shifted in a fine array, beating down as the rain began its torrent against the pane of the windows. The Mayor's hand became wet as he reached out to latch the ajar hinges of the clear pane together. He could feel the pressure pushing the windows inward; he placed a hand up against it to steady the incessant pounding force.

Moving away with a shiver of cold, he muttered. "What a change. Very ghastly today." Pulling a chair up to the table with the many parchments that laid out in the middle of the table, piles of books also surrounded every side of the desk. Signaling for Messenger to come closer, he extended a hand to another chair. Pulling a piece of parchment from the edges of the thick pile, he glided his fingers to a spot on the sheet. He asked Messenger to take note. "This is where those who have left our sides are gathering a party against us. This Keeper has chosen to follow a path that though she did not admit a purpose has an underlying desire to undermine this place. They have decided to commit to service instead of roaming the land to find someone. The Keeper was meant to stay in the place they are assigned to stand guard, to be the one who sees what may happen. This Keeper perhaps has seen too deeply. Seen something creeping underneath the surface. We are a free people of the city of Rockfirm. We live here peacefully in our own ways."

Messenger agreed with a nod and an approving, "We do not desire to be any other way. We do not want to change."

A snicker came from the Mayor, combined with his agreement."How might we rid ourselves from this?" The Mayor asked, imagining what Keeper was doing to the clouds that came billowing up, but the darkness reflected another.

A rumble of thunder could be heard booming through the town as though it was a carriage with wooden wheels. From the window of the house where the two conversed,

116

they sensed nothing different with the low rumbling. Many of the nights there could be heard the exchange of noises as they bounced off the walls of the paint-covered homes and into the hearts of men. The Mayor paused before saying, "It is time to go."

There came from the mouth of the horse who pulled the carriage, neighing and the sound of another. The rocky road of the opening of the forest made the wheels jostle as the rumble of the carriage wheels thundered as numerous roots of trees reached up to grab at the wheels of the carriage. Rounding a bend, there came from the outside the appearance of a man carrying the reins. The whipping crack of the leather against the horse's skin, producing a high pitched whiny. A heavily hooded figure, whose face was hidden from view, could be seen scanning the area of the town in which he traveled through. Much of the noise that was made did not reach the ears of ones who slept and had become accustomed to night, while others heard and there was nothing they could do to escape it. Many, of whom were the freest, came unwillingly and became captured. Those came as they abruptly awakened. Without their hats or coats girded they came out as if they were not ready for the cold and to leave in a hurry. The noise that came from the carriage only reached those whose ears were attuned to the sound, the rhythmic motion of the wheels against the road.

The carriage came to an abrupt stop near a raised platform set in the middle of the city. Jumping off his seat he handed the reins of his carriage with the horses to a Porter standing outside of an inn. "When they come, let them go." The glow of a lantern accompanied his tread as he strolled into the crowded area. One side housed a bar with stools where the clink of glass could be heard as many came out to enjoy a night to themselves.

The man at a desk immediately raised his head up as

he greeted the new guest. He was dressed neatly in a navy uniform clean pressed that denoted he worked there at the inn. "Do you have reservations?" Came from the host's mouth.

Meeting the lowered stare of the visitor, accompanied with a gruff, "Yes," begged the question of who. The figure raised a finger and through a split tongue slithered out of his mouth.

The host's eyes widened and he hurriedly penned down the name. "Yes, we have room for you tonight." As he studied the retreating figure, he studied the markings of his cape and allowed himself to wonder of the darkness that shrouded over this figure's face. The figure had just sat down at a corner table in the room and raised his eyes to see the host still staring, who hurriedly turned away to make himself seem busy.

A deep hush prevailed over the place, even if conversation could still be heard coming from the banter of two who sat in the middle area, filled with round wooden tables. With an intense look to one another, the two conversing members decided to enjoy themselves. The night had dragged on as they had decided to be available, waiting for some important news.

Their eyes also followed the host so they had noticed the man in the corner, though they had been loudly bantering and talking before. Leaning over to his companion, Messenger commented, "Who is that, sir?" Lowering his foamy drink down, the Mayor also viewed the man shrouded in black sipping something strong, unmovingly not making any sign of action. A ruby red glow pierced through the glass pitcher, giving the contents the appearance of dark red.

Looking over at the figure, neither could make out clearly the dark outlines of his face which were mostly covered by the oversized hood hanging over his face.

Nudging the other, they both turned away as a waiter came to ask if they needed some more food and the Mayor raised his hand in affirmation. The Mayor did not answer all at once but kept quiet as he raised the glass to his lips and studied the figure. Something about him was intriguing in the Mayor's mind despite the initial terror as the first glance would suggest. He still needed to be wary. "Yes, who is that?" Then for another moment, he stood silent. Raising his head to meet Messenger's, he made a sweeping gesture. "He seems as though he has come a long way. Look at the way he is gilded; his cape seems old." A silver sparkle came from his belt as his cloak swung out of the way to reveal a round metal loop, attached to many keys. With a sudden drop, the man put down his glass and rose to leave. Both of the conversing men lower their heads. The Mayor commented, "He looks serious," which he commented on the abrupt way he left money on the table and glided past the head host into the streets.

"Did you see those keys..." Messenger commented with a gulp of liquid as he wiped his mouth with his sleeve.

"Oh, yes. I saw them. What could one do with so many doors?" The Mayor speculated about the use of the objects. Pushing his chair under the table, the Mayor motioned for Messenger to accompany him in order to catch up to the visitor.

Deep mist had accompanied his cape and left the room seeming to be filled with smoke. Emerging directly from the inn, they both noticed there was a light further down the road that was illuminated on the panes of the windows. The same mist that entrenched the inn followed the stranger down the road so that one could see it from the light of the open doorway of the inn. The silence of the moment became suddenly interrupted. A latch handle of a door unbolted, and a person came out to accompany him.

Others from across the street began to respond and trickled outside to meet the glowing light of a lantern. A crowd gathered around him but there were only a select few for some of the faces that the Mayor would recognize did not appear.

Coming up slowly behind, the two observers held behind some houses as the figure turned the corner. Once he had rounded the corner they came after in intervals sometimes slowly and sometimes quickly. They continued to follow through the streets in the city.

People continued to find their way outside, silently pacing behind the figure. Standing beside a door frame they saw as someone came out near them, deep seriousness clouding their features. They watched as this person went past to the other side of the road. Messenger asked, "What is he doing?" Messenger came up close to ask the person. "Are you alright?"

Without an answer, they could immediately hear the wheels of a carriage as the horses had been untied from the reins for their great uneasiness and the response of "When they come, let them go," which the mysterious man had commanded the Porter.

A sudden neighing and shrill sound could be heard, but somehow it did not awaken the others who still slept inside their homes. Wheeling around the group standing around the figure, the sight of him made the horses halt, grabbing the reins. He then took the lock that secured the back of the carriage and with one of his many keys unlocked it from the chain that held the wooden door with metal bars shut. It creaked open and with a motion of his lantern, the group of unresponsive people climbed into the back of the barred carriage with no second thought.

"Where is he taking them?" The Mayor finally asked. "Maybe that helps explain those who have gone missing." One could almost hear the invisible chains clanking as they came up the stairs into the door. The Mayor stepped out in the open with Messenger coming behind. Coming close to the figures going into the carriage, the Mayor yelled, "Sir, what are you doing?"

The figure, who prepared himself to presently slip the key into the lock of the door, turned around suddenly and with an intense look made both men step back in the same fear they had experienced as when he had turned to see them at the inn. With a quivering speech, the Mayor declared, "I am the mayor of this town and any dealings that come from interacting with the people here is my business. There have been many that have come in and out that I watch carefully."

The Pursuer made a disengaged response. "Oh yes, I did need to talk to you. I feel like that would make my dealings here much simpler." Looking at the group of people close together on the seats alongside the inside of the carriage, the Mayor could hear the click of the lock as the Pursuer intersected the key into the lock.

"What are you going to do to these people?" Messenger quickly responded as it seemed like these people would be taken away soon if they did not intervene.

"I need willing workers." This was the Pursuer's quick response without an explanation.

"These are my people," The Mayor said with an exaggerated tone that was meant to cover his lack of interest. The Pursuer presently alighted up onto the front of the seat near the horses.

"Would knowing that they were going to be doing something beneficial suffice?" The Pursuer let out.

The Mayor looked at the townspeople that were now unsafe since they had been captured and scoffed, "Yes, just do what you need."

Seeing the map that Mayor held in his belt, the Pursuer pointed a boney finger his way. "A map? May I see?" Although hesitant, lifting it from his belt, the Mayor unscrolled the map with his hands so that the light of the eyes of the Pursuer lit up the parchment paper. He studied it for a moment. He stopped on an "X" marked somewhere near the mountain range. "You said that you kept the dealings with the people here but it looks like one has escaped you."

The Mayor was enraged at the Pursuer's words but steadied himself, "Yes, very recently one of the leaders here left without warning. We were suspicious and concerned."

"Why?" the Pursuer asked, but the Mayor was unsure if the Pursuer already knew and was just playing with his words.

"Because someone in white linen accompanied her," A sudden silence pervaded and a quick movement of the map as the Mayor put it away.

"And you need someone to find this—" The Pursuer got cut off with the answer.

"Keeper." The Mayor replied.

"Yes," The Pursuer replied while adding, "It is best that we stop her." Moving his hood further on his head, both the Mayor and Messenger saw as a thin tongue split on the end came out suddenly from his mouth and then returned. "I will find them for you, if you allow me to come back." This figure did not seem the type to ask permission, but he would use the opportunity all he could.

Giving an approving nod in agreement, the Mayor backed away as the carriage made a circle to turn around. The lantern hung, swinging on the side of the carriage and illuminating the blank faces of the people who were being escorted to who knows where. Although it had been an understood statement, both had gotten what they wanted out of the deal. For the Mayor and Messenger, the carriage proved more danger than what they realized. Still, those who were captives had their minds influenced by the Pullings from the Pursuer. They followed without question.

Chapter 12

The day felt new and the birds began to chirp above the group of travelers. They had slept soundly through the night and several of them were only beginning to stir. Gabriel, who had been up for at least an hour, had walked around the area listening to the breeze, praying in a quiet tone. He now prepared a fire with a breakfast of fish that he had caught in the stream nearby.

The musty smell of smoke drifted through the camp so that it penetrated their blankets and clothes. It began to fill their noses and Keeper began to cough awake from her dream. Regaining her equilibrium, a brisk breeze ruffled her hair. The smoke blinded her for a moment as it went through the camp. She looked to see that Gabriel bent over the fire, cooking fish. He did not see her for a moment. Taking a stick to bring the fish away from the flames, he slid it onto a rock to cool. None but Keeper had gotten up to eat the now-simmering fish. She came up close as Gabriel turned to grab a pole and began to walk through a path of trees. "Can I have some fish?" Keeper asked. "Where are you going?" Keeper again called out and Gabriel turned, hearing Keeper's voice from behind.

Swinging the pole to one of his shoulders, "I have found a river nearby with some fish. That is where I have been and am about to return for more before the morning gets away from us." He motioned forward, so that Keeper decided to accompany him.

The thick wood seemed impenetrable by night. Even in daylight one could get lost if they had not been there before. The great oaks whispered with their bright green leaves moving to brush up against the sky. Both figures traveled on the narrow path until Gabriel decided to go through a deep patch of bushes. Both continued to move the branches away as they still were blinded and their motions were stifled. After much navigating, they reached the other side, both gasping. Keeper, though being winded, gasped for another reason. In front stretched a river, rippling over rocks and underneath a fallen tree. Gabriel sat propped up on a wedged rock that jutted out from the bank. His line landed quietly as it splashed into the moving stream. Looking down into the green tinted water, Keeper could see several fish, their scales shimmering as they reflected the faint sun coming through the forest canopy. Skirting away quickly from the moving lure, Gabriel sat back, anticipating the long wait before them.

Keeper, still marveling at the stream, took in moments like these as a reminder of who she served. She remembered the stories of how the world had come into being and how the Holy One had, out of nothing, created all that she could see and even things that she could not. Her mind was open in wonder, reflective yet excited that he had gotten ahold of her and prepared others with her to carry out this journey. She bent down from the rock, untying the long laces of her leather shoes and placing them on the bank. She pulled up her leggings so that she stood in the middle of the stream. The water that she had cupped in her hands dropped a bit as she lifted it to her mouth to drink. The water in this area of the wood was clean and pure tasting, much better than the more brackish water from Rockfirm. Everything was so natural out in this area. She had always hoped to have traveled this far. She had seen much of this land from her post on the wall, but the forest always proved too thick to know who traversed its grounds.

Keeper spun around to see Gabriel already tugging on the line, lifting a notably sized fish from the stream. Its tail flapped as he struggled against the line but Gabriel had more strength. Gabriel, with the fish in both hands, tried not to get stuck by the barbs on its sides. He removed the hook gently from the fish's numbed mouth, but not without getting nicked by the fish's barbs on his hand. First setting the fish down on the grass, he held his hand for a moment and then reaching down into the water, he squeezed his injured thumb.

"Are you alright? Looks like it got you!"

Looking up at Keeper, he replied, "I will be fine. It was just a knick. I just needed to squeeze it to make sure everything is out."

"Can I look at it?" Keeper said, making her way back across the river to her friend. He offered her his hand. Seeing something still in there, she squeezed it to remove a small barb that Gabriel was unable to remove before.

"Thanks," he said. Taking a piece of material from a blanket he used to carry the fish, he wrapped his thumb.

"Will you be catching any more fish?" Keeper inquired while considering his condition.

"Maybe not," Gabriel then reached over to grab the pole and handed it to Keeper, "But we still need some more. Would you mind?"

Keeper grasped the pole and eyed the river, throwing the line in as she remembered how she had been contemplating her life. "Yes, definitely. I am sorry. I was thinking about the Holy One." Looking down at Gabriel's hand, Keeper remarked, "I was unsure whether you even could get hurt or not."

"Just because one seems like that they are on a good path does not mean there will not be struggles on the way. There is not a way to measure who is better in the fight. He is not a respecter of persons. 'Blessed, rather, are those who hear the Word of God and keep it.'"

Keeper looked at Gabriel and though he had seemed

very wise, almost other-worldly, he had become to her as a friend that was extremely trustworthy. It was as if they could talk about anything. Still, she had questions of who he was, "So, you did come from the Holy One?"

"Yes, I am one of his messengers. As I have said, he sent me for you. I believe he was talking to you."

"Yes," Keeper had not told him about her dreams that she had—some horrifying, some enlightening. "May I tell you some of my dreams?"

Gabriel, who knew she must have had them often, seemed eager to hear what exactly she had seen. "In his world things are different. I am here because he needs me here for now. Everything is attacked more than you think."

Keeper closed her eyes as she envisioned what she would say. She was unaware of what she should actually convey. In a moment of solace, she decided to continue.

"I have seen things that I would not have known unless I was told." Keeper's head lowered and she looked back up at Gabriel. "I saw the Forlorn Isle. Not the prison that Asher had escaped from, but our final destination where many are forced to dig. They are held in captivity despite them not knowing why. They do what they do not want. They think that their desires would cause freedom."

"Those are the ones that are summoned by the Pullings," Gabriel confirmed.

"Yes, the Pullings," Keeper had speculated this before, and Gabriel had just confirmed her questions. "I felt like I was being suffocated one of those days before I had this dream. So, did the Pursuer think I was following my own way and would come with him?"

Gabriel's face was unmoved, like he was unsurprised at this. "He thought that you were a threat. Even so, he wanted to take control of your mind when you were vulnerable."

"Why was I vulnerable?" Keeper questioned.

"You have not been sleeping." Gabriel looked in her eyes.

"I sleep just fine." Keeper rebutted his words quickly.

"You have mostly been dreaming," Gabriel said concerningly.

"How can I keep from dreaming?" Keeper's eyes grew wide. It was as if Gabriel expected her to control something that occurred naturally. "How can I stop myself?"

Gabriel replied with a surprised, "I do not know." He paused and then collected himself. What Keeper said was concerning to Gabriel. "It is not bad to dream, but you cannot allow these dreams to consume what is real before you. They may feel like you perceive things from them, like you are reading some of the future, but a person is to live by faith."

"Is it wrong?"

"No, you have the gift of prophecy. Specifically, you are able to see things that most people cannot see. Maybe sometimes even physically."

"Yes, I saw people in my village in chains. I do not want to seem too important because I have this gift. I want to do it for the Holy One." She raised her arms as though she was trying to pull away.

"I know what you are saying and, yes, you need to continue to commit this gift to the Holy One for his use. You know that you were chosen not because of your gift. I think he is more interested in your heart. He sees it and sees your love for him."

"How can you know that?" Keeper was unsure of what to think.

"I could see the way you were jumping from rock to rock as you crossed the stream. I could tell by the smile on your face that you were talking to him. It's not just a religion to you; it's a relationship. He will guide you in the way you should go, but keep me aware of what you are seeing so we can work through it together."

Keeper looked away for a moment, her hands shifting on the pole as she watched the line flow down the stream. When she turned back to face Gabriel, some tears watered her eyes. "I see him in you too, Gabriel. Just the kindness in your voice, the way you respect and treat others and regard them so highly. I am thankful for that. Thank you for following him. It is truly encouraging to be able to talk about these things with you." With an arm stretched out, Keeper gave her friend a hug of gratitude for his company. He also extended an arm, hugging her and they both resumed looking at the river. There was a sudden pull as Keeper exclaimed, "I think I just got one!" Overjoyed, she yanked the fish up out of the river, dangling it above the water. Pulling the fish on to the shore and off the hook, she readied the rod and cast it back into the stream.

"You know your mind needs to be guarded. You have to be careful with what you let influence you. Not everything that you think is true. You must first test it to see if it really is true. You must learn that the weapons of our warfare are not physical but spiritual. I think that you may have experienced that. The battle is not an actual battle but one in your mind." Keeper believed there would actually be a battle, but she now knew the Holy One had already won the war.

Adding to his comments, Keeper said, "I did dream of a battle."

"You did?" Gabriel was surprised that her dreams had been so literal.

"I thought you would know that."

"For some reason you have gotten me wrong. I am

only a messenger. I am not a mind reader. Anyone with that type of power is a manipulator. That is not right, but some may use it for their own gain."

"So do you think the Holy One wants me to use my gift?"

"It is whatever lines up with his *Book of Old*. Have you read it?"

"Yes, I have a copy that I have learned from one of the town's scribes. I have enjoyed learning everything that the Holy One taught. He is very wise. I believe it to be true all the way up to the beginning as he created the world. The creation just speaks his name."

"Yes, and he is sovereign over it all, over you and me, over nature. Creation just speaks his name." Gabriel paused for a moment, "I do not want you to be afraid of your gift. He will use it."

She yanked another fish up out of the river. The fish began to flap wildly as she swung the rod to the bank and put the fish down beside the two others. Keeper, taking her hand, adjusted it so as to not get stuck by the barbs that Gabriel had and carefully removed the hook from its mouth, safely tucking the fish away in the never ending bag. Still feeling the bag flap around with the fish inside, Keeper was unable to hold it as it fell to the ground.

Gabriel again brought the cloth material close so Keeper could secure the fish.

As the moisture began to thicken, a low rumbling could be heard overhead. They could hear the ripple of water behind them as the beating of fins continued. Keeper threw the bag over her shoulder. Gabriel, still holding the rod, swatted the pole like a bug came to fly around him. Resting the pole toward his neck, he began to whistle a whimsical tune that Keeper had never heard. It started in high-pitched, shrill notes and ended with low, deep hums. His voice was steady, causing slight inflection to highlight certain sounds. He continued all the way, wordless through the branches in which they had made their way. Keeper, bending over slightly and with a hand to cover her face, came up from behind. She decided to mimic his humming in a higher octave, but she could only get out a few notes quickly before he moved onto the next set.

The sound of the whistling burst drowned out by a crack of thunder and a flash of light. Gabriel, who had reached an area where there was room to move between the trees, looked back at Keeper and beckoned for her to move quickly.

"Come."

It did not look like he was afraid of the storm, but only that the sudden downpour may hinder their travel. Gabriel rushed to the group stationed farther in. Keeper started to walk swiftly and almost lost her friend as he rounded a bend. As she also turned, she saw him up ahead and dashed to be able to reach his heels. The branches of a tree parted ways as they followed their way to the clearing while the rest were at peace resting. None had stirred since they had left. The fish that Gabriel had cooked earlier was still sitting on a rock by the fire and though it was much cooler, it was still able to be eaten.

Another peal of thunder rattled the camp, waking both who were still sleeping before Gabriel and Keeper had time to shake them. Both started upward, one after another in wide eyed shock, accompanied by Gabriel's charge, "Come quickly. We must leave and get to higher ground." Although he seemed to be talking about the rain, the pure concern in his voice suggested something more serious. "We must get back to the main road."

The group both stared at each other. "I thought we were on the only road." Keeper commented.

Gabriel replied, "We must keep going." The group, folding their blankets and placing them neatly in their bags, slung them onto their backs. The fish that they had just caught were quickly roasted by the fire, and as soon as they were done, they ate the food hastily. This did not minimize how good the fish tasted as the meat fell off the bone. They all enjoyed it immensely.

"Very good, I must say. Who might I give thanks to?" Percy asked, and Gabriel pointed to Keeper.

"Gabriel was the one who did most of it." Keeper wanted to give credit where it was due instead of receiving it all.

"Well," Percy remarked comically, "I guess he just wanted to build you up a bit." Keeper smiled at the thought and looked at the others, almost not hearing the conversation at hand. Keeper saw Asher looking off slightly into the Spirit Wood. It was broad daylight, but it still seemed as though he was seeing something.

"What are you looking at, Asher?" Keeper abruptly commented. The worried, deep look in his eyes was elevated by his comment, "I miss the sea."

"The sea?" Keeper asked. "We are nowhere near the sea. Why are you looking around as if you can view it?"

Percy gave the answer for Asher, "He used to be a sailor, you know. Much of his time was spent on the waves before he was brought to the Forlorn Isle and then rebelled so he was taken to Captavia."

Asher, though hearing this, did not explain. He sat quietly, still glancing over. It was strange, Keeper thought, but as the moments lengthened, he began to open his mouth. Peals of thunder rumbled as he seemed to gauge what he needed to say at that moment.

"Where did you sail?" Keeper was unsure if he would answer. He cleared his throat but didn't answer, studying

Keeper's expression.

The peals of thunder continued until they were right upon them as the dark clouds filled with liquid began to drop down. It was good for the group that they had started off because the slight rain could cause a deluge. The cracks deepened and the light flashed, causing the shadows of the trees to land down in front of their way on the path. Something screeched in the distance making the group jump in fear, but not without hearing the noise that accompanied it. Rumbling came from behind in a deep rattling force unlike thunder. Another high pitched shriek and this time the sound became recognizable as a horse whining under the crack of a whip.

Something inside of Keeper dropped as she felt an uneasiness only recognizable in her recurring dreams. Something was after them, maybe even for her.

Asher had paused for a long while, so Keeper decided to ask again about the subject. "Where did you sail?" Keeper was unsure if he would answer. Instead he cleared his throat, continuing to walk swiftly and looked over to study Keeper's expression before he would begin thinking of what he should say.

Recalling this to him seemed a ways away in another more favorable time in life.

"I sailed around the cape of the world. Not only near Deror, but in the vast unknown. There are islands far off to the horizon, and many have not been discovered. The waves become rough as sudden gales come to batter up against the ship, threatening to take my life and the lives of the crew." Turning away from the group a moment, they could hear his tone weaken into a miserable sounding sigh, and he choked up with tears.

"Are you okay?" Keeper asked, wondering what could have come up to make him act in such a way. There was a silence. Asher looked up, a tear trailing down in his face. It was Percy who was the first to interject, filling the wordlessness of his friend.

"The crew was lost," Percy replied somberly, placing a hand on Asher's shoulder for comfort.

"For many years, I sailed with them," Asher resumed, recalling brighter times on which he traversed the earth. There was something about bondage in which one would feel all of that stripped away completely until what was left was only what a person thought should be important. Whatever they saw as important in their lives, no matter how small and immaculate they kept it before they had arrived as a piece of rock, had become roughly covered and caked in dirt. The glimmer in the rock had left as they tried to wipe away the smudges in order to see their reflection. If they could, they would remember what they looked like, maybe see themselves in that way, but it seemed like it was too late in the moment to see what they meant. Sometimes they would never see it clearly. Remembering these thoughts, Asher's mind blurred in what was exciting and adventurous instead of those which were deeply seated in failure.

His eyes widened as he began to recall the crew's faces and some he could not. The waves of memories continued to crash to the forefront, but his tumultuous mind made it hard to visualize. The pain of it had a call to choose whether to weep or to take action.

Asher remembered the memory of several years before.

The wind swept past the sails along the placid waters of the ocean.

Asher pointed a spyglass toward an island stretched at

a long distance so it showed as a pale blue dot on the horizon. The quietness became interrupted by the squawking of the sea birds overhead.

From beside Asher came the Cabin Boy named Cephas who came to help with the orders of the day.

"I mopped the deck this morning. What else do you have for me to do?" The Cabin Boy named Cephas relayed this and Asher stopped for a moment going over a list of tasks formed in his head.

"Well, you can untangle the rigging and the ropes. You know how the knots in the rope on the anchor always get jammed when we are lowering it." The boy turned to skip away, happily going to do the tasks assigned to him when Asher abruptly called out, "Hey, I have something for you." Cephas turned around as Asher produced from his leather sailor's coat a golden compass dangling from a carved chain. He motioned for Cephas to hold out his hand, and Asher placed it into his palm.

"You are giving this to me?" Cephas moved his finger along the dome-like surface covered in intricate four pronged stars that raised off the surface. Cephas pressed a round button at the base of the lid so it popped open to reveal the coordinates of north, south, east, and west with a needle adjusted to the magnetic north.

Asher pointed up at the sky. "This compass points north. It is best used at night when it aligns with the North Star, the brightest one in the sky." Asher tried to school his Cabin Boy with some science, "It is the truest form of north. It will guide you when you are unsure of the correct way."

Cephas nodded a reply with a cheerful, "Thank you, this is very nice, Captain. You did not have to. I will use this. I will."

"Yes, one day you will be the head of the ship, but for now you practice."

"The sailors are all gone. Many of our trips led us to the utter ends of the world. There are many lands to discover, and so many that we have already seen. But as you understand, the sea has its own intentions. One such time in late autumn, the tides shifted in response to the increased amount of wind so that it began to churn up a fierce gale." Closing his eyes, he could feel the warmth of the breeze of the air. The water that splashed up against the sides of the boat was surprisingly, almost dangerously, warm for that time of year. The boat called *Atticus* had its main sails filled with air as the red and white striped flag fluttered against the breeze. Dipping down into the crest of the wave, the water crashed up at a considerable amount against the front. It came over the side and proved to be concerning.

"The men who worked at the rigging cried out as the waves became too high and made the ship turn to its side in a precariously dangerous position. The waves began to crash upon the deck of the ship so it threatened to pull the sailors out to sea and meet their end."

A rumble of thunder continued to come to interrupt Asher as if the group could hear the storm Asher described. The thunder also carried some weight as they saw Asher narrow his brow as they experienced the thunder around them and in the story being told.

"But there was a more dangerous threat looming to overtake them," he said, raising his eyes as though searching for something behind on the path.

"Then everything changed," he said.

"This is important. Is this where amid the storm, you see another ship?" Percy, who had been told the tale once before, asked.

"Yes." A flash of light shot down from overhead and ended in a close sounding boom. The rain had been held off for the moment by the moisture still hanging heavy in the air.

"The boat, being much bigger than mine, came up from the starboard side. I had not seen it coming up because I was concentrating on steering the ship through the waves. It had also gotten much darker, so I was only able to see the silhouette of the boat." Asher paused once again remembering every moment clearly of his memory.

"The ship came up beside us quickly. I could see that it was advancing aggressively, as if it was going to attack. The men were already battling the storms, but I ordered them to prepare to attack the ship instead. Looking closely at the ship, I could see that the flag was raised. It was the sign of a snake with red eyes."

There was a collective gasp among the group at the thought of the encounter with the Pursuer. Even Percy, who had already heard as much as Asher would say, still found horror in the statement. Asher tensed as he said, "The Pursuer wanted my ability of my talent to sail on the sea; that is why he was after me. Coming alongside the boat, his men began to throw the anchor onto the railing of our ship. Despite attempts to blast through the side of his boat with our ammunition, his men began to ride down the ropes jumping onto the deck to fight my men. My men fought relentlessly to guard themselves against these attackers but the invaders proved to be ruthless. Many men were surrounded, pinning them to the ground.

"One of my closest men came up to the steering platform where I stood and urged me to come and fight. I crammed a wooden instrument into the wheel, and I was able to keep the boat on a steady course. I picked up a long, curved sword, which was thicker near the base and tapered off into a jagged tip. The Cabin Boy had been along with me for the moment only to hurry to help the others. We could not save them but we can save the present group." He could not prevent the ship from sinking.

The ship, staying a steady course, was far from land, and Asher had a responsibility to keep the rest of the crew safe as they made their way back to port. In the event of something such as an attack, there was no one to make the correct directional decisions. Cephas, though he was trustworthy, Asher was unsure of his ability to steer. Calling out for him, suddenly, Asher realized that he may be in need of his assistance as he depended heavily on him at this moment. There was no return answer.

Asher, rushing down from the top of the deck, entered into the fray against invaders who fiercely fought against the ones on board. A burly-looking creature spun two daggers simultaneously as he slit through the throat of one of Asher's men nearby, causing Asher to gasp in pain of seeing this. The men who came aboard were heavily clad with sharp weapons, usually wielding one and keeping the other in the sheath on their belts. Though this was not always the case for those who swung sharp, spiked balls hanging by chains. Whipping one in a full circle, it crashed down, splintering the wood of the deck. It just missed the left of the defenders who had skipped away fast enough. Asher was confronted as a man raised his head from over the railing and saw him. Coming up to his face, he swung a blade that intersected with Asher's in a steady position, but the weight of the other caused the blade to slide down toward his feet causing sparks and a sharp shift. They both unlocked for a moment, Asher jabbing toward his chest swiftly. Though seemingly very trained, the attacker was not able to defend this quick move. In a moment of time, he collapsed on the ground as Asher turned around to find many more attackers around him.

At this moment, his thought of survival was centered on another individual. Cephas stood a few feet away, also occupied with attackers. Asher needed him to reach the front to steer. Cephas was very young and his limbs quaked from the strength of his attacker's sword. A tall figure stared darkly at the boy. The boy fought fearlessly, using all his strength and ability. Asher knew it could only be moments before he was overtaken. Asher, rushing and forcing himself through the group, was confronted several times as a new opponent reverted his efforts to reach Cephas. The boy, sweat dripping from his brow, had stepped back suddenly as the larger figure threatened to make a blow that would end him.

"Stop!" Asher yelled. Asher's crew was trained to resist the mind control of the Pullings of the enemy. The ship came close and saw the guns in Asher's ship were ready.

When he had pulled out from the control of the Pullings, Asher was exhibiting the same amount of resistance which he had instilled in the Cabin Boy and the crew. He would have fought to the end, but with lack of strength, he was unable to follow through.

The slice of the blade lashed out as Asher raised his own up against this tall figure. A crack sounded as the wooden support in the steering wheel broke, followed by a jostle as a wave came up over the suddenly tilting ship. Asher managed to get in front of Cephas in defense. He saw in the fearful stares of his sailors and the intense red glare of the Pursuer. He felt it was too late.

"Your crew resists me," The Pursuer's words bit at Asher.

"They have been trained against men such as you.

Your control on people's minds is horrifying. I have informed them of your ways."

"So you know who I am," the figure replied, his dark cape caught up in the wind whipping behind. Despite the imminent sinking of the ship, he still stood steadily, boots firm on the wooden panels. He let his sword come down to his side. The intense fear showed on his face of encountering this being of whom he only heard people talk about from word of mouth. With a glint in his eye, he responded with, "I am the Pursuer." His tongue slithered out from his teeth, producing a low hissing noise to accompany the intimidation of his tone. He was truly the enemy that Asher had known before.

Asher winced as the Pursuer's blade landed on the tip of Asher's sword, forcing him to quickly propel it away. Cephas, who stood behind Asher, looked stunned standing completely still because of the shock of being so close by.

"Get further back." Asher quickly asked for him to move further away but Cephas sat still. The Pursuer continued to batter Asher with the sword so that Asher's footing was shaky from the sudden jerking of the boat. The water sprayed out of the sea and damaged the front prow of the boat, as they prayed for help. Stumbling backwards, Asher felt the back of his heel catch the figure of the hidden Cephas, finding himself tripping over him and falling further along the deck. Exposing Cephas, the Pursuer and the boy saw each other and a strike of fear filled Cephas' soul. The Pursuer, sensing this feeling, yanked the boy up, sliding the long sword in front of the boy's throat. Asher looked up and saw that they had been trapped.

"Turn this ship around, or this one will be gone." The water started to build up around their ankles as the ship began to tilt. "Come with us, and this one will survive." The boy let out a hasty cry of panic, though he did not move a muscle because of the close proximity of the sword. The rest of the men hung onto the rails of the ship as they almost fell into the sea.

The ship was at the point of capsizing. Asher hung onto a mast that had tilted down to meet the horizontal waves. The Pursuer's cape whipped out in front of Cephas' face.

"Set him free!" Asher yelled above the wind.

The Pursuer gestured toward the boat he had come from. "Come with us, and I will." The Pursuer's words remained firm as the boy now had been covered by a cape, still at knife point.

The men that had stood strongly with Asher clung to the boat as the waves came as an undercurrent, suddenly pulling them out into the sea. Asher, knowing that he had put lives on the line. He only hesitated for a moment before nodding in the Pursuer's direction. He knew he should have found a better way to save his friend, but what other option did he have? As the Pursuer gestured for him to walk forward, Asher let go of the mast and let the torrent of water and the tilt of the deck act as gravity as his feet hit the railing of the ship. Grabbing hold of the side, he saw Cephas sitting in the water still waiting for Asher to preserve his life. "Doing wrong for good," Asher muttered in justification.

The Pursuer began leading the Cabin Boy closer, but at a few paces he called out, "Get on the boat," One of the Pursuer's men looking at Asher looked toward a rope that held a pulley system that could help him back to the ship.

Asher was told to hang on tightly as a leather harness was secured around him. The man below him crossed to the other ship and called orders for the men on the other side to start to manually crank a leaver. The waves underneath splashed up, making the ropes stiff so that the pulling process was drudgery. The metal rigging swung while Asher continued to ascend toward the boat. It was at this moment that he heard a cry come from the boy who was still veiled by darkness, "Do not do it captain!" They had hoisted Asher unto the boat, releasing him from the harness, but immediately fastened him in irons. From behind he heard a shriek, as the boy's face had been uncovered to see what had happened. This momentary vision of duty morphed into regret. The water splashed as Cephas was plunged into the ocean. Cephas was then put into a row boat to seem to Asher as though Cephas was safe and got away. Asher, falling to his knees, was pulled away from the edge and forced into an opening in the deck that held countless prisoners. He was led down the dark hall. Looking at the other prisoners in chains, Asher felt that he deserved as much punishment as each and every one of them. Though the ones that gathered on board had most likely come there by the manipulation of the Pursuer, they still innately deserved it. They still believed that they had done something so terrible that they deserved the sentence. Asher, not able to contain the feelings of what he had allowed to happen, began to weep.

"My crew has perished at my unwatchful eye and in trying to save the last one, I allowed him to perish as well. It is such a vast, dangerous sea for him to survive." Sadness and anger both found its place as he realized what trust he had put in the one with such a dark spirit.

Though Asher had thought he could fight against the Pullings of the minds and persuade others to do the same, the unveiling of the circumstances made disaster unavoidable.

Asher was shoved on a rough wooden seat near the back row next to a burly gentleman whose tattoos displayed an intricate design of a wave of the sea. The picture became interrupted by a scar that came across his arm, probably as a result of the scuffle before he had been captured. There was a long wooden oar that jutted out through a hole in the wall into the rough water of the outside. Throwing it into Asher's hands, the tall taskmaster who had put him into chains commanded him to start rowing with the other members. The dim lighting of the hull faded the shapes of the figures so details of their profile could not be made out.

It seemed a long while before there came a loud thump from above them and a shout to pull up the anchor. The Pursuer, whose laugh could be heard from down in the hull, made Asher's brow furrow in anger, but also cast a sense of fear of how he had the ability to manipulate calamity.

The Pursuer wiped his face, tongue slithering outward, as he hissed as he watched the mast of Asher's ship sink into the sea. He shivered as he stood chilled and soaked to the bone. There was a type of military power to defeat the others and build what he desired to create.

If he could allow the fear of any number of things to control them, it was an open gateway for allowing him to work. Looking toward those of whom were the ones who did his bidding, he looked at their grimy faces and eyes glowing as red as his.

"Set a course to the Isle. Our ship is ready to drop off what we have found today." Avoiding the remains of Asher's ship, the Pursuer's eye went toward the Forlorn Isle, where those captive are imprisoned.

"Yes, but first, we must drop off." Looking again at his worker, he made up his mind on Asher who was an insurrectionist. To the Forlorn Isle. "That is out of the way with the storm still brewing." The Pursuer stopped his crew member and shot him a contemptuous glance. "Captivity is not far away for anyone." The worker's mouth closed and, ducking his head, hurried to the front of the boat to change the course.

"Yes, you resisted me. You will be punished." The flag, embellished with the symbol of the snake, continued to flap wildly as the storm lingered still.

Asher had not seen from the deck what happened to Cephas. The Pursuer had let Cephas go, and he rowed a single person row boat. The Pursuer did this so Asher could see that Cephas was safe in the row boat, but the Pursuer did not truly let him go. Deep down, Asher knew that Cephas was still in danger.

Going back to the moment as Asher walked down underneath the deck, there was a moment when the Pursuer himself swiftly boarded another row boat. The speed of his rowing intensified in pursuit of Cephas' vessel. The Pursuer hooked an anchor to Cephas' ship so that they became attached. In a swift movement, the Pursuer boarded, pushing past Cephas' attack with his own oar. The Pursuer wrestled the boy, and he pulled out some iron cuffs. Cephas punched the Pursuer in the face so that he held his nose.

Cephas at once sat up, grabbing the oar tightly and swinging it so that it hit the shoulder of the Pursuer. He toppled into the rough waters, on the opposite side of the Pursuer's own boat.

Cephas undid the hook that attached the two boats and kicked it out to sea. In this moment, he took both oars and whacked the Pursuer again, this time in the head. This time, he sank deep into the water and when he came back up, the Cabin Boy was not anywhere in sight.

Chapter 13

There was a deep rumble that seemed to feed into the waves in the story Asher had been telling. There came a sudden break in his speech as he and the others suddenly looked back. They had been traveling through the woods, but the way had opened up revealing a path that came jutting from one side. The deep sound became much louder, creating a sudden fear among the group. Keeper's heart felt a sense of being chased. As the object came around the corner, carriage wheels pummeled the dirt. Gabriel was the first to say, "Run, quickly!"

The Pursuer, who sat on top of the seat of the carriage pulled by horses, had seen them. In front of them, the tree line began to thin so that there was not a way to hide in the woods. The group ran fiercely down the path as it opened out into a field. They were out in the open. The horses whinnied in response to their fears and each turned around frantically with not knowing what to do. It was Gabriel that pulled Asher's sleeve and called to the others, "Hurry, we can still find shelter!" They darted across the grass toward a river in which a wooden bridge stood arched over. The group hurried down the steep slope of the bank and stepped across stones arrayed across the river. Making their way to the opposite side of the river, they hid behind stones that held the bridge in place. Their feet padded on the sandy bank. From above them, they could hear carriage wheels as they hit the rocks found in the path. Asher, rising up, was suddenly pulled back by Percy as the carriage wheels stopped on the wooden panels above their heads. They were deathly silent, and Asher began to shake. Everything seemed too familiar to the horrid memories of the past. Keeper, too, felt that somehow she had been followed there, that the one who had been distorting her dreams was at her doorstep.

Footsteps sounded as the Pursuer walked the edge of the bridge overlooking the water. The Pursuer's breathing could be heard as he scanned the area. It seemed as though he thought the party had somehow hidden themselves in the woods before he had the chance to overtake them. The group, lodged up against the rocks, were partially hidden by a boulder that jutted out from the base.

Moving away from the edge of the platform, the group could hear the figure step back into his high seat and with a clicking and the crack of the whip, the horses' hooves were heard cantering across the bridge.

Keeper sighed slightly and pushed on the rock boulder as she tried to raise herself up. Several rocks were loose and threatened to crush her feet. This only caused more to slide from the upper part of the pile until it created an opening in the rock face.

Percy backed up exclaiming, "Why, see what you were able to do! You opened up some new path." A cold wind blew out from the inside of the deep tunnel. For Asher, who was now only thinking of the underground that he and Percy had arisen from, took the sight as a warning.

Keeper, looking in, felt still a little shocked at what had just occurred, but was extremely curious of what had come out of it.

Gabriel, peering in, raised the thought, "I think this tunnel leads somewhere," as the cool breeze coming out from the opening suggested.

Percy, latching onto the idea, suggested, "Maybe we will be able to hide. I am sure there are myriads of tunnels to make us disappear." Percy was more eager than Asher to plunge himself into a dark pit. Asher was not wishing he could return there now.

Gabriel, looking at Keeper as though to ask for her

opinion, was met with an approving glance. There was just something about this passage that made Keeper curious. She had never been underneath the earth and the thought of escaping the face of the Pursuer was a comfort to her.

"Yes, let's go. I'll go first." Keeper said, but was abruptly stopped.

Asher's hand shot out in front of her, shocking Keeper at the force. "No, I should go. I have become accustomed to the darkness of night." Although one could see that he was still a bit hesitant, he suddenly became protective in the moment. "There could be anyone down there. I do not know what we will be walking into. The Digstons could even be this far north; their caverns are endless and nothing would stop them from capturing us. I say we still go, but we must be careful!"

"Agreed," was the consensus of the group. Asher, grabbing a piece of wood from the shore close to the river bank, constructed a makeshift torch, and the others did the same. Asher still shook, though he was fully sure of the decision. Being careful not to dislodge any more rocks, he made his way into the shallow tunnel. Walking a few paces, he was able to straighten up, and he looked down the pathway. He could see the light from the torch, proving there were several passages up ahead.

"It looks surprisingly promising. It is a bit small at the opening. Watch your step," Asher suggested as Keeper made her way into the entrance. "It gets wider down the way with many more tunnels. Seems a promising day of exploration. Much different than that chase." Keeper's eyes met his in an agreeing nod.

There was something about Keeper's voice that made him sense a bit of uncertainty, not willingness. There was something that happened as though there was a flash of a vision as though it was Keeper's point of view. He knew that

Keeper had mentioned that she had the ability to see things.
At this time, he thought he saw something about her, as if
the sound of the sea had returned and he was surrounded by
the men whose lives he had caused to perish. In front of him,
he saw the eyes billowing with tears as a knife was pinned
against Cephas, the Cabin Boy's throat. It was mirrored in
Keeper's face. As though he was pulled under a wave, he
pulled back out to the cool air of the cavern around them.
He blinked hesitantly and took a step back.

Keeper moved her hand out as though to steady him,
"Are you doing all right? You seem a bit shaky."

Asher felt unsure how to tell Keeper that he may have
seen something spiritual.

"I am doing fine," he said, pulling his arm away from
her, not wanting to scare her with some type of fearful
vision such as this. Asher turned around and faced toward a
tunnel.

Percy filed beside Asher with a slight comment.
"What! What! What kind of place have we here?"

Keeper looked up at Percy concerningly as she was
still worried about what just occurred.

"You seem like you have seen something
frightening."

Keeper looked away, seeing that Percy was beginning
to question as she thought. 'Although what was weird, I do
not think that Percy would understand. Does Asher have
Spirit Eyes?' She was unsure of who but knew others may
also share this gift. 'What did he see?' It seemed that most
of these visions were declaring ones of something ahead, but
sometimes there were pleasant ones about the Holy One. It
was only after Keeper had been drawn to the light of the
Holy One, that there was a sense of peace. Yes, he brought
some purpose and meaning; though there were unsolved
troubles in the world, there was still a being who was

availing in peace and continuing to guide.

Through the fear of that moment, she felt something like a voice reach her in this moment assuring her, "I am still here." Keeper was looking up in her mind's eye to see the reassuring gaze of the Holy One. She was beginning to see him more clearly than she had before, but the more there was trouble, the more she had to talk to him about, for her to trust him with. In that moment, she felt the same as when she had run away from the Pursuer's blade. Somehow in the moment, she was reminded that there was someone greater, someone who was more powerful than the fear that the Pursuer caused.

She looked to find that Gabriel and Percy had already gone ahead. Keeper's hand trailed against the rubble of the dirt wall, and she found her way by torchlight. The tunnel continued to stretch out before her, stooping as she went so as to not scrape off the dirt from the top of the tunnel. She went along, almost seeing the figure of the Holy One in front of her, a torch in his hand. "I am leading you." His words instilled a sense that this was the right direction. On his side was a sword that ensured if anything came against them, he was ready to protect their very lives.

"Keeper," Gabriel called as he had just disappeared beyond the bend. Keeper's heart swelled as though she felt the Holy One's hand holding on to hers. She ran ahead, stumbling along as the light of the torch ahead began to disappear. Gabriel's voice again called out as Keeper rounded the bend which widened into a cavern. The group stood looking at the unveiling crystals protruding from the walls and floor of the cavern. The internal growth of the diamond facets reflected a fractured mirror up against the wall from the firelight. Each of their faces reflected the cool blue tone of the pretty objects. Going up toward one, Asher moved his hand along the shaft of the diamond stalactites, still reflecting the concern of before.

All around Keeper turned, studying all the facets of the room. Though there was no light, the room glowed because of the light streaming through the gems reflected from the torch light. Gabriel was the first to utter, "We have found ourselves a crystal laden cavern."

"Not one I have seen before," was the reply of Percy who had adventured many of these underground tunnels as he aided the rescue of those from Captavia with the League. "There is nothing quite like this in the southern region. Mostly red boulders of clay and rudimentary stalactites. They are impressive, but nothing compares to all this." Percy's arm gestured around to the glittering rocks. "There must be a source of water close by to cause such growth." His voice trailed off as he looked about to see a wide opening among several others leading its way to the sound of the drip of water. He turned and walked toward the entrance, gesturing for the others to follow. Gabriel nodded and looked around, following Percy, who seemed to have a good idea of what should happen next. Coming into the opening of the new tunnel, Keeper saw a myriad of different paths before her. It was overwhelming. Percy had already gone ahead, so all she could see was the light fading down one of the tunnels. She took a running stance and raced after them.

"You can become lost quite easily," Keeper mused.

Asher stepped around a corner to the left and raised a hand toward Percy who had already filed his way past. Going down a slight slope, he found himself inside of a deeper part of the cavern. Laid out before him was a still pool of water. Trickling from a small opening was a stream that came from overhead and formed in the pool. There were several passages leading in directions, but Asher was unsure that they would lead to anywhere pleasurable. He still remembered the moment he and Percy had arisen into the light, free from harm of anything down below. He could hear Percy's voice down one of the passages, reassuring him that the others were not far away and he could still reach them.

Asher called out that he had found a stream of water. He was silenced by the presence of one who called out from behind him, "You are alone down here." Asher's heart stopped, recognizing the familiar tone. He wheeled around to see in the same way he had confronted him on his own ship.

The face of the being was not like he had seen it before. His eyebrows raised as the sound of his voice still pierced the inner workings of Asher's soul. "I have been found out."

"You know that it is impossible to hide from me." Asher's eyes bounced around the cavern in panic. The Pursuer's words were what haunted him. "You are trapped. You are alone."

Chapter 14

Keeper began to dream about the stories from the *Bread of Life* that Burman, the book shop owner, had shown her. It was in a time many years before in a land where the *Bread of Life* was written. Though it being old writings, their implications were true and real in the world of Deror. They helped explain what was occurring in Keeper's present world. It helped her understand how the trouble of sin started that kept those captive in chains and the one who would bring redemption to their souls. It all started at the beginning.

The garden in which the Holy One had created perfectly replicated what he wanted for the world, which was how the world was first created. It had many fruit trees growing lusciously in Eden. The Holy One had created everything that could be seen. He placed animals, all different and unique. He also placed humans there. Those of whom would have a relationship with the Holy One as they walked with him in the cool of the day.

It was one of the commands that he gave that these humans saw a way to follow otherwise. The woman strolled through the garden alone, pulling a branch out of the way to see and became startled at the sight of a serpent hissing.

The serpent asked, "Did the Holy One actually say, 'You shall not eat of any tree in the garden?'" He motioned to a vibrantly growing tree filled with fruit.

The woman began by adding to what the Holy One had said.

"The Holy One said, 'You shall not eat of the fruit of the tree that is in the midst of the garden, neither shall you touch it, lest you die.'"

A serpent replied, "For the Holy One knows that when you eat of it your eyes will be opened, and you will be like the Holy One, knowing good and evil."

The woman saw that the tree was good for food. She took it and gave it to her husband.

The sweet juice oozed out of the fruit, but they both knew something had changed as the fruit fell to the ground.

They at once hid themselves from the presence of the Holy One.

The Holy One then asked where they were.

They said they were afraid so they hid themselves. They relayed how the serpent had deceived them, but knew that they had disobeyed.

They were then banished from the garden.

The serpent who was the Pursuer now had authority over them so that they had invisible chains upon their wrists unless they had faith in the Holy one's power to save them.

The Pursuer gained the keys of sin and death in order to keep them captives in chains to their sin. They became captive unless there was one to free them...

There was a man in the archaic days in the past who lived in the midst of a dark generation, but he knew faith in the Holy One. He followed the Holy One in many ways, he even took everything he owned and moved to a distant land. Abraham was obedient in many areas of his life, but when it came time to wait on a promise, he decided to take action in his own way.

Gleaming from a distance, there was a silhouette that

could be seen standing there.

Opening his eyes, he saw the brightly sparkling gems woven into the fabric of the night sky. "Isn't it beautiful," The Holy One looked down from heaven to this man standing in a desert land. "See their infinite number; they are too numerous to count." Looking at the myriads of twinkling spheres spread across the chilled atmosphere, there was no place to look but up.

"Surely, you have made even the night to be penetrated by your light," The man on the ground marveled.

"You are to have as many descendants as the stars that you see above you and the grains of sand under your feet. So is my righteousness toward you, that there will be a promise, surely a promise for salvation. There will be many saved, you can't even count them.

"Only if you have faith in Me, will this happen, but then I promise that you will be the father of these. They will be more than you can imagine..."

Keeper dreamed as she lay on the couch in the room in her visions after contemplating these stories from the book, the Bread of Life and specifically within the book of Habakkuk. She saw the Holy One ready for battle with a horde of others alongside him. The battle was gruesome, and the flag of Nissi flew in the air. Horses neighed in the midst of the fight. Archers fired arrows from their bows, sending them raining down on the enemy. The clash of armor upon armor echoed in the valley, and many cried out as they fell. The enemy drew closer to the Holy One sitting upon a white horse. The Holy One's eyes blazed with fire, and his tongue was like a sword.

Have justice upon the earth. He heard the cry of many

who were captive. *"How long, O Lord, will I call for help, and you will not hear?*

"I cry out to thee, 'violence!' Yet you will not save.

"Therefore, the law is ignored and justice is never upheld, for the wicked surround the righteous."

The Holy One replied with, "Look among the nations! I am doing something in your days—you would not believe if you were told."

Keeper saw she had been standing on a guard post, and she stationed herself to keep watch. The Holy One was speaking with Keeper.

"But the righteous will live by his faith." The Holy One spoke.

The Lord allowed a fierce people to seize dwelling places which were not theirs.

"Woe to him who gets evil gain for his house to put his nest on high to be delivered from the hand of calamity." The Holy One explained.

As Keeper saw these things, she also began to understand deep things.

The Holy One comes with His splendor that covers the heavens, and the earth is full of his praise. His radiance is like the sunlight; there is no hiding his power.

The Holy One stood and surveyed the earth; he looked and startled the nations. Yes, the perpetual mountains were shattered, and the ancient hills collapsed. His ways have been everlasting.

Keeper saw these events and realized what the Holy One sacrificed: himself. He came up close to the ranks of the Pursuer, with not a sword raised. Keeper was standing on the field behind him. A human had joined the fight, and the

Pursuer was about to destroy him. The Holy One, fully dressed in armor, took the blow that was meant for the man standing there. The person could represent all of mankind.

The Holy One fell to the ground, and Keeper could not do anything. Keeper had heard of the battle that the Holy One had fought. The Pursuer stood there over his body.

The Pursuer dropped the keys that were meant to lock up the prisoners, but picked them back up. "I have control, and I've had it since Eden. They have been under my control. Each has gone their own way."

The Holy One lay on the ground of the battlefield as the Pursuer walked away in triumph. He believed he had defeated the Holy One as he lay lifeless, pierced by the wound of a sword. Those who served the Holy One put him into a worthy grave as the banner of Nissi flew. The procession on that day was solemn as they bore the rustic dark brown box on their shoulders. Many that knew him cried desperately as their friend had been put to rest. They lowered him into a stone tomb.

They mourned over the Holy One, and some even ran and hid without him behind closed doors. Their master had been killed.

What they did not know was that even Abraham had faith that his son would be the heir of many nations, like the stars, and that he would live. Even so, the Holy One would not see death, but would live.

The Holy One led a host of captives free.

He marched to the depths of Hell, wielding a mighty sword, but His power evidenced the fact that he had power over sin and death.

The Pursuer's eyes became wide as he realized what had occurred. The Holy One came into his ruling dominion over those who had sinned.

Raising a sword, the Pursuer could not resist him as the Holy One ripped a round ring of keys from his hands. The keys of sin and death.

The Pursuer, knowing he had been defeated, stepped back as the Holy One began to unlock the shackles that entrapped the prisoners. He took the keys as he walked back in the direction in which he came—toward the light of the morning.

It was only three days that the Holy One stayed dead, but then he rose.

"Those who believe in me will live spiritually even though he dies," he walked up to a woman in a garden.

"I am looking for my Lord," she replied. It was at this moment that he replied with her name so that she knew it was he who had died. "Go tell the others," He instructed.

He truly was alive. For a moment, there was a glimpse of somewhere better. A place after life where those who had faith in him for salvation would go. For once, there seemed to be hope from their depraved state.

Now once he lived, those living were able to be free those from the stronghold where they were entrapped in their own ways.

The Pursuer walked away as though the battle had been won, but then the Holy One came back to defeat him.

He had actually died, but he could not stay dead since he defeated death. His sacrifice for humankind was to die *for the sins of all humans since he was sinless. He rose from the dead and defeated sin and death. With a foot raised up, he stood steady upon the ground. He raised his sword at the Pursuer, who at once realized what was occurring. The Holy One was able to take the keys that the Pursuer held on a ring. The Pursuer knew he had no way of stopping him.*

The Holy One brought all those who would come back to him.

"I have taken away the debt that they owe." The Holy One declared.

The keys were lifted up and there was not any power left to take them away.

The captives were made free, but they would have to choose to receive the gift of freedom that the Holy One gave. For those to come they would have to proclaim this freedom.

From that point on, he was able to set a host of captives free who believed in him.

He walked from death, from the Pursuer's grasp and rose up into life, never to die again.

They realized they were free, but they realized they had to tear down the strongholds of the Pursuer.

As Keeper saw these things, she looked at the Holy One and bowed her head.

"Thank you."

"There is nothing you can do to repay me, but only by giving yourself. I fought for your freedom. I fought for you." The Holy One said this, lifting her head up. Keeper could see the hope in his eyes. "The war is won. Now we free others. We are tearing down strongholds where people are stuck in their original state, and we tear off their chains. They need hope, and that is what we can give them. Like

holding onto what you do not see, but onto what you hope for."

It was like the morning sun shone on him, making his face glow. It was magnificent to behold. The Holy One and Keeper hugged, and there was peace in the world—no matter what would happen.

Chapter 15

Pulling his sword from its sheath, Asher pointed it at the Pursuer.

"You would not want to do that," was the Pursuer's reply. Asher, in spite of this, steadily made his way forward. The Pursuer whipped out a chain that he had been carrying. Its links rattled as he jerked it up in the air like a whip.

Asher realized what type of pain he was capable of inflicting, but continued forward.

"Again, you know you should not do this. You know what you have coming to you."

Asher suddenly stopped, not knowing whether to continue on or make a quick escape. The Pursuer had found him, but his only comfort was that he had not found the others. The unwanted sound of Percy uttering, "What! What! We have found something," created such a great fear that he stood in between the Pursuer and the passage with their echoing voices.

"I see that others have followed you in this cause against me. Do they know you are still bound to me?" He turned and walked toward the distant voices. Asher also pivoted, watching every slight movement that the Pursuer made.

Although Asher knew the Pursuer was threatening, there was something in his voice that produced a numbness as Asher began to become drowsy and off-guard.

"You are free now, but you and the others are moments away from a signal that will summon the Digstons who would drag you all away." Asher stayed silent, standing in a rigid stance. From the direction at which he had just come gathered a pack of Digstons, with their teeth sharply serrated and their throats creating the low rumble of a growl. They looked ready to pounce on him, but they were somehow held back. The Pursuer, almost as if he held Asher in the position that he wanted, began to grin while keeping his eyes fixed on his prey.

"You know, I have them under my control. Your friends will be safe, and it could just be you that has to face me. This whole mission could be dismantled." His eyes began to glow a reddish tint. "And your friend Keeper." Asher's mind at once reverted back to the vision that he had seen; it was as if Keeper had been the replacement of Cephas. The Cabin Boy had been allowed to escape while Asher never saw what occurred to him, while he was dragged away for Cephas' safety.

"If you want me, then you can take me. Leave them be. I have experienced Captavia and will do it again if it means they are safe." Even in his verbal surrender, the tip of Asher's sword slightly raised toward the Pursuer, who he knew was not in any way trustworthy.

"You could listen to me, and they would be safe," he again said, looking toward Asher. He continued, "I have seen your way of fighting yourself free from me, but you have surely failed in the attempt." Asher knew what he was risking by standing against him and knew it would be a better idea if he were to run. "I have an offer that could be of interest to you." The hissing sound of the Pursuer's tongue could be heard gliding across his teeth.

"Why are you waiting?" Asher was not entirely sure what the Pursuer was talking about.

"I want to spare the time you and those with you will have to spend in chains. If…" He purposely let his voice trail. "If you will help me."

Asher's eyes shot up in shock, but as he looked at the Pursuer's face, he knew he was not joking. The Pursuer was trying to make him an offer. "No," Asher shot back. He had followed the Pursuer before, and he did not intend to make the same mistake twice.

"What about Keeper?" The Pursuer's words once again called Asher's mind to when he had seen Keeper in Cephas' place. This caused him to tremble as though the Pursuer had put his finger directly on Asher's heart. He had seen a vision of imminent events and understood that it may have been pointing to something. A thought struck Asher. Had he the ability to see with Spirit Eyes?

It was not to Asher's knowledge that the type of "Spirit Eyes" that he received may not have been out of faith but of fear.

In the vision, Keeper's face was marred with terror.

Asher, in that moment, became a pawn in the Pursuer's hand. Even more, he knew that somehow that was a connection that he felt protective of Keeper and like he felt protective of Cephas. That pain was excruciating. Asher was one to protect his own; he endeavored to save as many as he could. He had only saved one.

"Do you know that I know where Cephas is? He is still alive," The Pursuer taunted. Asher jaw slackened. There was an ability to find him again.

"What have you done to him?" Asher's temper rose thinking about his friend and imagining what could have happened to him.

"This Cabin Boy is still alive, but I have the ability to crush him." The sole of his heel ground against the dirt.

Asher felt as though he had methodically been pinned against the wall with the Pursuer's words. Asher had been strong in refuting his demand, but he felt like his choice to resist had become futile. The more that he tried to escape, the more he felt entangled.

Asher felt like there was no choice if the safety of those he knew was on the line.

"This is your nature, you know. To serve me because it is the only thing you know how to do. What type of thing could break that?" The Pursuer raised a finger, giving Asher a look as if testing if he would run. "I want you to lead your group to the island first. It is where the captives are imprisoned. But your friend, he is on the Forlorn Isle. He has been rotting away for these years while you have been dragged away to Captavia for your insurrection. You know, he never fought back."

"It is because he was young. He did not know how."

"Yes, but everyone has the ability to choose. And your friend Keeper—find out what she is thinking. Her visions are being tampered with. Find out what is to happen with this," The Pursuer's hand rested on Asher's head, feeling a voltage jostle in his skull which immediately made him close his eyes. He saw something like a vision.

He opened his eyes with fright.

"What was that?"

"I just gave you a sort of way to help me communicate with you. Nevermind that. What did you see?"

Asher did not answer for a moment, but the Pursuer's sword was a threat that did not need to be verbalized.

"I saw a vision of seven people walking onto a battlefield."

"Seven, only four are here now. That must mean there are others."

"Asher—" The call from Keeper from another corridor of the cavern frightened Asher as he turned around to protect his friend. He was not sure of what to do. Keeper appeared from a tunnel further ahead. "There you are." Asher looked back to where the Pursuer had been standing but there only showed quiet nothingness leading into the dark. The Digstons had also retreated on the demand of the Pursuer.

Keeper was unaware of what had just occurred, but as she drew closer she stopped and looked at Asher's arm.

"What is the matter," Asher could see the paleness of her face reflected in his own.

Keeper, reserved a certain thought and reflected whether it would be better left unsaid. Keeper had seen Asher as he moved his arm heavily weighed down. It moved as he did, without having an end that she could see. It was almost translucent, but the closer she had gotten as though inspecting his life they were undeniably real. She had seen these same chains binding those who lived in the town of Rockfirm. She did not know for what reason Asher had become weighed down, but she continued to wonder what proved actually true. Looking at his past enslavement, Asher should have been one who had reason to fight against such a way. He was in a group that was meant to set others free, but would be unable to see if he had his own chains from some unseen slavery to sin.

"We are in the cavern up ahead," Keeper continued, not pointing the chains out. She did not know if it was her place to intercede and talk about such things. This did not sit well with her, but she was afraid that he would think that she was being judgemental. She did not realize how not saying anything would hurt him.

Putting on the best front she could, she smiled and continued to speak courteously to his replies.

"Yes, I was about to come over that way." Asher's response became terse as though he felt Keeper told him what he already knew.

Keeper looked at him, still questioning what could have happened. Keeper led him to the opening of the tunnel, but the puddles of water suggested that they were nowhere near the entrance. "I see you found water, but I do not think it is what we are looking for."

Asher nodded, "We will keep looking," Asher, filing into the tunnel, took the lead. Keeper, standing at the opening, looked back into the cavern. 'I wonder what could have caused a change in him?' Keeper thought as she turned in the direction where Asher had gone through the passage. The Pursuer stood watching, with a pack of Digstons huddled behind him. It was that first time he had seen Keeper, but he had known her to be a threat. She could see important pieces of information of what would happen, much different than the ability that he had given Asher, one of knowing others' minds in order to sway them. Asher had fought, but the Pursuer had made sure he could read Asher's mind and communicate with him.

Although at this point Keeper saw nothing, she felt uneasy. "Now I have seen you, there will be more in your mind than what you have seen. Though we have never seen each other, we have met in the dreams of your mind," the Holy One reminded her.

Keeper prayed for Asher, looking up to Heaven and whispering, "Holy One, please reveal yourself to Asher. He needs to know who you are, and I know it is possible through you. Please give me the words to say to encourage him because I know only you can change hearts."

Asher and Keeper went down several winding passages, some opening up into wide caverns that hung down with stalactites. The light of the flame that Keeper carried was beginning to dim when they saw light coming from one of the openings. They began to run as they traveled up an incline. Their hands moved against the side of the walls as they staggered toward the daylight and the voices of the other two members of the group.

"I did not know we were that far away from everyone," Asher said between gulps of air.

"I know. When we could not find you, I told the others I would go searching for you while they found water sources that could lead to the outside," Keeper replied.

They stumbled into the largest cavern they had seen yet, gasping when they saw a river rushing through it. Glancing around the cavern, Keeper and Asher shouted with joy when they saw Gabriel and Percy.

"We have found a way. What! What! I knew that finding a water source would eventually lead us to a way out." Percy laughed while cupping some water in his hand and gulping it up.

Glancing around the room, Keeper saw something written on the wall. "Look what I have found," she shouted.

Gabriel, coming over, began to read out what it said:

"To those who seek to save what is lost must place burdens down, stepping into the light so all is seen. You cannot do it alone. Only one is worthy of such a call."

The group considered the words as their brows knit in confusion.

"What can that mean, I say?" wondered Percy.

"I think it could be taken as a personal truth to help one's life, but those words could also be a guide to lead us one step closer to where we are meant to go." Gabriel explained.

"Who do you think put this here?" Keeper asked.

"For all we know, it could be the Holy One himself. We have his truths written on tablets of our hearts, sometimes written out in text to see in the scriptures." Percy interjected.

"What does it mean?" Asher's tone reflected the thought that the Holy One had a plan in guiding them clearly. Despite the fact that he could not stop thinking about the path he was ultimately choosing.

There was a beam of light shining from the opening, but as he got closer he hesitated to touch it, keeping himself in the darkness.

"Into the light. If we walk in the light as the Holy One is in the light, we have fellowship with one another. If we confess our sins, he is faithful and righteous and he cleanses us from all unrighteousness." Keeper mused.

"Does that mean we must go directly toward the Forlorn Isle where the captives are placed?" Asher questioned.

"Why would we do that first?" Percy questioned, remembering they had discussed a different plan. "Did we not agree upon Captavia in order to go into the prison of where there are those that are kept for their insurrection against the ways of the Pursuer. I guess in their own way they wanted to be free in their ability but needed help. We are going there first because they are the most ready to fight with us as we free the Forlorn Isle."

Asher knew that the group was being swayed to go in a direction he knew the Pursuer did not want them to go. Asher knew what the Pursuer wanted.

He had to get them to go to the Forlorn Isle first; it was quicker anyway to the goal that they were ultimately trying to achieve. The fear of losing everyone close to him rested on his shoulders. He was the guard of their safety.

"No," Asher abruptly stated. Keeper looked over at him. She could see that his eyes were mixed with tumultuous fear that covered his features in addition to sudden forcefulness. This fear was familiar to her, as she had run from the Pursuer in her dreams. She did not blame him, and instead felt more connected in knowing how he felt. The only difference was that she felt comfortable in the light.

The others considered him as well. They had already agreed upon what they were to do. "I thought we all agreed that this would be the right decision to make." Percy's fail-proof idea was set out as a plan for the group, but was being disrupted. His impatience showed.

"You know, the saying on the wall may be leading us a different way," Asher reasoned. "We are here to help free those who are lost. What better way than to go directly to those who are captive?"

Keeper found herself agreeing, "He is right. We need to get to them as soon as possible."

Percy rebutted her statement, saying, "We are not doing this alone; we need others where we can count on to help us in this fight, for it truly is a fight."

"Why so harsh?" Asher did not like Percy's use of words. "No one is getting hurt. It will be a clean break, so to speak. We will get them out of there so that will be it. They are in need of us the most."

"How about those whom you may have known from Captavia? There are ones just as valiant as you." Asher saw Percy's point, though he did not want to admit it.

Asher quarreled, "Yes...but we must." The group became silent as they listened to these friends argue about the direction to go. Gabriel joined in the conversation.

"I am not sure of the real reason I feel like we need to go to Captavia first, but there may be something along that path that is important for us to do, something imperative to our mission together. I do see the point in both." Gabriel gazed at Asher and remarked, "I do say that our friend Asher is adamant about his opinion to go to the Forlorn Isle."

Percy jerked as he began to open his mouth, but closed it suddenly in respect for the speaker. "I know this is not what we originally planned for ourselves, but we may be the specific messengers the Holy One has called in order to fulfill this task. Moreover, we may meet other willing travelers along the way who could help us in this way. Even so, the very sight of Captavia may bring back dark memories of the past for some." Gabriel remarked as Asher's eyes reverted downward.

Percy was still confused that Asher was not wanting to rescue some of the people he had spent years with, but he did not pursue the point. Both Asher and Gabriel had stated the meaning of their quest, each focusing on different aspects. For Asher it was the safety of others, and for Gabriel it was for a purpose laid out that later the meaning would be unveiled. Weighing the options he could see the good in both, and Percy believed himself to be leaning Asher's way. He was just unsure of one thing when Asher was speaking on saving others. He seemed urgent like lives depended on it, like the life that depended on it was his own. He seemed like he was carrying something, like some weight on him created tension of where to turn.

Gabriel was the first to speak, "Who is in favor of revising our plan to go first to the Forlorn Isle?"

"Aye," Percy approvingly raised a hand.

Keeper followed in agreement, while surprisingly seeing Asher raise his hand up last.

"There is no need for ceremony. We may find a better way and have to revise. To the Forlorn Isle it is." Gabriel announced.

Gabriel glanced over at the river flowing through the cavern that they were standing in. The river opened up into the sunlight. "Now, what should we do? We found the opening because of the river—now we just need to find a way to get out."

"We could use a boat." Percy suggested.

Asher was the first to offer, "I could build at least a small one if I had the materials." There was a veiled darkness on the other side of the river, where there was a dark shadow.

"What is that over there?" Keeper asked. Its structure was shrouded in the shadows.

"What are you saying?" Percy asked.

"I think I see what she is trying to say," Gabriel replied.

"I think I do as well," Asher remarked.

"I am going to try to get across," Percy asserted, finally catching on. He waded into the river, shuffling his feet across the stones on the floor, the water rushing past him. There were crystals that glowed from below the water. Rising up out of the other side, he made his way toward the object that Keeper had seen in the corner. His hand moved along its edge. "It's wooden." Percy commented. Going around behind, he was able to push up against it so he could move it into a more suitable light. It scraped across the pebbles on the cavern floor.

"It actually is a boat!" Asher exclaimed.

"I wonder who would have put it there," Keeper wondered, coming up to the edge of the water. Gabriel came beside Keeper and dipped his hand into the river. Rising back up, he commented, "I believe that there are some who work for the Pursuer who may have used it in a way of transportation, maybe even this far toward Rockfirm." The sides of the boat were covered with something that looked close to a carving along the side.

Asher shouted, "That is one of my life boats! I had that design carved into the railing. How could it have gotten here?" Asher's eyes widened as the memory of Cephas rowing out away from the boat into the sea came into his mind. 'But he could not have survived in that storm,' Asher thought. 'Was he here?' Percy pulled the boat out further from the darkness. There were two oars that were laid down inside, with two seats in which several could row.

The group watched as Asher waded across and helped Percy pull the boat close to the riverside.

"We will hold the boat still while you get inside," Percy said to Keeper. "Then Gabriel will be able to step in. Asher will then get in and I will be the last."

At Percy's word both he and Asher lowered the boat into the river so that the water began to billow up behind it. Keeper swiftly made her way into the front seat, taking hold of the oars. With her knees braced, she felt as Gabriel stepped into the front seat beside her. The boat was heavier now and Asher made his way quickly into the farthest backseat. Almost losing his grip, Percy ran along the side and jumped into the last available seat. The river rushed behind them, and Keeper handed the oars to Gabriel and Asher. The darkness that had enveloped them for a long while suddenly faded as they sailed through the low-hanging entrance of the cavern.

The moisture of the splashing water came up against the sides and sprayed into their faces. The rocks in the river jutted out so that it became a concern that they might be battered up against them if they were unable to maneuver around them. Deep swells turned so that the boat sped up and barely missed the adjacent rocks. They continued to dip down into the current and were forcibly launched upward further down the river.

The oars that they were holding were lifeless in their laps without the knowledge of what to do with them. The end of the oar jutted out as they skidded across the water and were caught up in some of the spray. Asher, who saw that none of them had the knowledge of how to maneuver the small craft they were riding inside, took an oar and plunged it into the water. He gave a sudden instruction to Gabriel who had the other oar, which was unusual for Asher to give instruction to him. In this case, Asher knew he needed to help due to his expertise in this area. It was for his welfare as well as their own. Gabriel nodded in agreement and listened as Asher yelled out over the roar of the water, "Sharp forward paddle...now!" Asher, at the same time, dug into the water with backwards paddles to move against the current. The boat tilted backwards and then swiveled forward as it swerved in the direction that Gabriel had thrusted his oar into the water. This movement sent the boat out of the way of a pile of stones that protruded from the riverbed.

Asher asked that both Keeper and Percy would lean to the left to increase the amount of space that they could move. Rocks began to spike up all around them as Asher again directed Gabriel as they continued to make their way past one obstacle and then find themselves confronted by another. The full strokes sent the boat skidding away to escape from demise. The spray continued to lap up against the boat and splash into their faces, dangerously blinding their eyesight for a moment.

Rubbing a sleeve against her eyes, Keeper tried to open her eyes fully without them stinging. She recognized a mist rising up ahead of them. As she focused her eyes intently, there came a loud rumbling that resonated from the river in front of them straight into her heart.

It took the others a few more moments for them to notice what Keeper had just seen. It was not until Percy raised his head that he realized what the others feared. "There's a waterfall up ahead." Immediately Asher began to take control of the situation, as he and the others frantically looked to the side of the bank in order to search for anything close to grab onto. The only hopeful resource that could be seen was the branch of a tree hanging on the left side nearest to Gabriel and Percy.

Gabriel's tone was steady when he remarked, "Have peace. Despite this, we will be safe in order to continue the journey set before us." Even though his tone was there to comfort them, there was still a hesitant twinge of fear. Asher jammed an oar into the river in order to lodge it in between the two rocks. It slowed the speed of the boat down ever so slightly without bringing any hope of rescue. With both oars carving out paths in the water, the boat began to make its way over so slightly to the left shoulder of the river. With much deliberation, the speed of the strokes increased, knowing with every moment their time dwindled until they would meet the edge.

A hand reached out toward the overhanging tree limb that overshadowed a shallow bit of water before the boat sailed into the blustering foam that reached out to grab them. Percy's hand grasped the limb with a grip that made the passengers jerk forward and then backward as the momentum slowed. The river still rushed and the weight that pulled upon his arms made his hands clench into fists. His hand began to slip as he yelled, "What! What! My hands are loosening their grip!" With a sudden move, Gabriel came alongside him and was able to secure his hand also on the oak branch. At the weight of both Gabriel and Percy as well as the boat, the branch began to bend ever so slightly as though it would break. "How are we going to get to the shore?" The boat still stood a few feet away from the dirt of the shore. Asher's chains felt heavy; it was drawing him toward being enslaved to the darkness so that he could not hold them up.

Percy, who was continuing to lose his grip on the branch, called to Keeper, "Grab hold of my hand so I can pull you out! Then you can swim the rest of the way!" The bank was close enough to reach if one made their way holding on to one rock and then another. Keeper was immediately scared that once she jumped in, the current would be too strong for her and it would pull her down the river. Although she had this fear, she knew that Percy and Gabriel could only hang on to the branch for so long in order to steady the boat. She decided to take the risk. Reaching for Percy's outstretched hand, she was pulled up toward the side of the boat and with the weight of his push, plunged directly into the river. Her head went under the swift water and she opened her eyes to see the uneasiness of the swirling around and above her. She quickly raised herself to the surface, shivering and reaching her arms out in strokes as she proceeded toward a large stone. The river had already pushed her toward the waterfall, so that the fear of not taking hold of a rock propelled her forward. In one quick movement, she was able to grab onto a stone securely as the water built up around her, the current flowing strongly underneath her. There was yet another boulder that she could reach that was close by. Gathering her thoughts and her breath, she thrust herself forward to the next rock with her legs kicking and arms extended. The current continued to create an obstacle as it began to change her course. Though she was nearing the bank, there was still a force that continued to pull her.

"Keeper," Asher yelled as he saw that she was floating away rapidly. Gabriel also seeing what was occurring saw that she was in danger, but he also saw something else.

"Asher no—" Gabriel yelled out. A splash drowned out his voice.

"Keep going toward the island without me." Asher shouted, urgency in his voice.

Percy, who also saw what was occurring urgently, raised his oar out toward Asher, "We will lose both of you if you do not hang on." With a sudden realization, Gabriel asked Percy to let go of the branch and swim toward the bank. If they could reach the bank, they may be able to extend something to both Keeper and Asher.

Percy was able to grab onto the branch, and he jumped out toward the water with the branch still in hand, hearing it crack as it came also with him. The length of the branch allowed it to lodge between two rocks, steadying Percy and keeping him from floating down stream. Gabriel, who had let go of the branch right before Percy, grabbed onto it with all his weight and made it crack. He exited the boat swiftly as it went along past those struggling and careened over the edge of the waterfall. Its intricate designs shattered up against the stones at the base where the water launched itself over the edge.

Gabriel grabbed the stick from in between the two rocks. He and Percy were able to make their way swiftly to some boulders by the shore. Pulling the large stick between them, Gabriel was able to swing it over to Percy, who was able to pull Gabriel onto the shore. Their quick maneuver was imperative in order to reach Asher and Keeper downstream. Each holding one end of the stick on their sopping wet shoulders, they ran along the bank.

Keeper had finally grabbed securely to a rock so as to prevent her from moving any further. She had to maneuver away as the boat careened downstream and threatened to knock her unconscious. It was Asher that had grabbed ahold of her and pulled her away before being hit.

"Watch out," he warned. Asher was suddenly picked up by the current and found himself further down the stream that he anticipated, leaving Keeper still firmly grabbing a rock.

Percy was soon there to comfort her by extending a stick in rescue. Keeper said a prayer of praise for their quick exit from the mouth of the river. She let go of the rock and was securely brought close to the bank. Gabriel extended a hand and she emerged from the water, freezing and breathing hard.

"Hurry, we must meet our friend before he meets an end." Percy's words were rushed as they all grabbed the stick, hoisting it to their shoulders to carry.

"We must hurry!" Gabriel warned. Keeper did not know how much Gabriel knew or whether he had Spirit Eyes, but she knew he was concerned for Asher's well being. Asher's hand was close to taking hold of a stone, almost losing hold, but then was able to climb on top of it since it was large enough. He was only a few feet from being pulled over the edge of the water as the moisture rose up in bubbles and splashes. The rest of the group felt relieved that he had rested his knees upon the last available rock, but nevertheless extended the branch in order to bring him to shore. Asher's arms were just the right length as he was plunged back into the current this time with the ability to get to shore. He arose crawling on his hands and knees and then raising his head up to look at the others standing before him. He laid on his back and smiled at the sky and covered his face, rubbing his face with his hands. He continued to laugh. Despite his joy, he still felt guilt from his underlying scheming.

"Are you okay?" Percy was almost winded as he sighed slowly, but continued to speak. "You really should have not plunged in. It could have caused both of you to go over."

"You are not thankful?" Asher's eyebrows went up, as

he stood up.

"Yes. You were brave though." Gabriel responded. Asher, who honestly was not concerned about how they thought of him, was more concerned for the well-being of Keeper.

"That water could have pulled you all the way over." Asher raised himself and put a hand on Keeper's shoulder, "Most importantly, you are okay."

Keeper who was more in shock than anyone else, responded with a simple, "Yes, I feel fine. Yet I am relieved. Thank you for coming out into the river."

"Definitely, you were about to go over." Gabriel, who had been concerned with the well-being of Asher, seemed scared to let Asher out of the boat. It was as if he wanted to have a special protection over him, as if he could have gone to Keeper first. "I am just glad both of you are safe. Especially that the stick we were able to carry was able to reach you. I know we could have gotten there in time, but I am thankful you were able to pull Keeper away from the boat. Every second is important in those types of moments. I am going to keep this handy stick." Gabriel grabbed it, holding the wooden rod like a walking stick.

Percy too was relieved and took the free hands of both Gabriel and Asher, and lifted them up slightly and replied, "We are blessed to be alive. Thank the Holy One."

Gabriel's head at once bowed as did the others, and he prayed, "Holy One, surely you have saved us from a possible end." His words were reverent and full of gratitude.

"Holy One, if not your hand protecting us, we would not be standing right now." Percy continued, merging into the prayer.

"I thank you for giving me a way out and a way to live." Keeper's eyes were closed with her face raised.

"Yes—" Asher was unsure on what to say, "I am

thankful that we are all standing here right now. I feel like you sparing us must mean we are completing the rest of our journey. Yes, our journey to the island." Asher raised his head and opened his eyes.

Gabriel looked at him. Asher was leading the prayer as if he was trying to tell the others what he wanted to have happen.

Percy was catching on, "Aye...The island first." There was no other reason why it was wrong, but he felt like Asher was saying this forcefully. Percy began by asking the next appropriate question: "How are we going to get to this island?" It was what they had agreed on beforehand, but being tossed along a river after just arriving from an underground tunnel was disorienting to his sense of navigation. Percy, who was fairly good at telling what way in which to go, was truly in need of a little prompting.

"Southeast," Asher directed, "that is where the island would be, a few miles off the coast." Percy replied with a quick affirmation of "Aye," and turned away from the bank of the shore toward a large incline.

Percy stared up the mountain range and before he could say their name, Keeper offered, "This is the Highland Range, and beyond this is the Dark Range. We must get over those." Gabriel nodded in agreement in what he had told several days before. "I know that despite not going to the Captavia Prison, for reasons I do not understand." Keeper was showing her distaste. "If we decide to go to Captavia first to get the fellow revolutionists free, I would not mind, but since we are going to the Forlorn Isle, to set the captives free, we will still be going the same way over the mountain." She looked to Percy and Gabriel to see if this was correct.

They both nodded. The fruit tree stood at the base of the mountain, and Gabriel went by picking some fruit from the branches with their help.

Percy added, "We will still go over both the Highland Range and Dark Range, but we will go east instead of west towards Captavia. Nevertheless, we will have to go through some of the same territory, including Buffington and the Dark Forest and the like. It will get a bit dangerous from here. Not that we have not been through enough for today. There is an opening in the mountains that leads in that direction."

The snow that capped off the mountain seemed to rise before the group, creating a stark contrast in color from the stone side of the mountain and the powdery white covering above. Keeper had no time to notice the wellbeing of the sky above. Here it was again, the clouds continued to lower themselves down toward them, not like a tornado or hurricane, but threatening to look like one. This seemed to be the constant state of the weather. The world continued to ache as it had done since the fall. It only made Keeper think of their own state without him, the Holy one, as she had read he was there to set them free. Sometimes she felt that she was only a mistake away from also finding herself in chains. She heard that it was only through faith that she was even set free, but sometimes she felt like it required more. Her mind went back to the chains that hung from Asher's arms. Keeper's fear of the same made her raise up both of her hands as she turned them in observation. Did someone else see the chains that hung from her hands, if she had them? She jostled her arms up and down for a moment to see if she was able to visually see the chains and she might be able to hear the heavy clanking.

'Was the heaviness of the chains pulling him under and farther, making it hard to swim and even more possible to go over the edge to another unknown end?' This thought led her to the next, 'Am I the only one who is seeing this event of being captive or even my own position?'

Gabriel's voice interjected, interrupting Keeper's thoughts, "We are getting closer to our destination and then freedom."

In a moment of wrestling over her own thoughts, she decided to ask him as they continued to walk up a steep terrain of the mountain, "What is freedom? How does one know that they are free? I have seen this from the village where I lived where they did not see they were captive." Asher looked over in fear as though she was referring to him and the fear that he harbored.

"Yes," Gabriel paused, "If you remember in the *Old Text* that it talked about how one knows a tree by its fruits. A fig tree bears good fruit, with its figs, while a thorn bush only produces thistles. You see by a person's fruit that they are free or not, but that is only a sign that you are free. That is not how someone becomes free, that is another way altogether. It has already been done."

"So is it what someone else has done?" Keeper continued to understand what Gabriel was trying to convey.

"Yes, what the Holy One did. He became a sacrifice for us to set us free. It is not as much dependent on what you do that saves you, it is more dependent on one's acceptance of that sacrifice." Gabriel continued to explain.

"What if one feels like they have gone too far or they are not in need of him?" Keeper posed a question for Gabriel.

"Well, it is for them to know that no one is able to be free on their own and even sometimes people struggle with the idea even after they have been freed." Keeper's eyes went down for a moment. "Even so, they are dependent on him. It is only for us to accept it. Once one has accepted it, they are sealed with the Spirit. No one can go against his loving hand reaching out for all of us, for us to receive him on the inside."

Keeper's Spirit Eyes begin to sparkle and open up some new realization. 'One has a choice, choose to stay in captivity or they can choose freedom.' she thought summatively.

"So it is by grace you have been saved through faith, not of yourselves, it is a gift of the Holy One," Gabriel continued.

"What is grace?" Asher asked after listening a while to the conversation that both Keeper and Gabriel were having between each other.

Gabirel said these words, "By one man there was a free gift given. Through one man sin came into the world. Much more can through one man there be righteousness. 'For if, because of one man's trespass, death reigned through one man, much more will those who receive the abundance of grace and the free gift of righteousness reign in life through the one man. For as by the one man's disobedience the many were made sinners, so by the one man's obedience many will be made righteous.'"

Gabriel's words were sure. "It is a sacrifice from the Holy One, bestowed as a free gift that is given to us."

Asher did not say a word; he was actually astonished that the Holy One would give something like freedom as a gift, but the thought of the path he desired to trek, and that it was too far away, made him doubt. "It is freedom."

"Yes, but one must have faith in the Holy One. That is the only way to raise one from who they used to be into who he wants us to be." Gabriel knew that even those on their journey needed the understanding of what the Holy One had done for them—without already assuming that they knew.

181

He, too, needed this knowledge renewed and needed to have something that they continued to think on.

"Not as a result of works, that no one should boast. For we are his workmanship, created for good works, which the Holy One prepared beforehand, that we should walk in them." Gabriel continued, "So you see that it is not by what you do that brings the freedom, but by having faith and receiving the Holy One's grace. That is the key.

"The Holy One gave his life for us. Since man sinned the graden called Eden at the beginning of time, they were enslaved to the Pursuer because of their sin. They were captive. That is why the Holy One came to live a sinless life on Earth. Near the end of his time on Earth, there was a war between the Holy One and the Pursuer. The Holy One was killed by the Pursuer, but the Holy One did not stay dead because he was sinless. He went to Hell and took the keys of sin and death so that he had access to break the chains of those who would choose him. He then rose again, conquering death. That is how we have the freedom we have." Gabriel continued.

They stood around him and marveled at what Gabriel had said of the Holy One. It made sense to all of them that the story of the Holy One came to save them. They were all amazed.

"That is how we have freedom. Thank the Holy One." Keeper said.

"That is quite amazing. It makes sense." Asher replied.

"Thank you, Gabriel," Percy, "that is the real reason we are here on this mission. It is only through his sacrifice we have hope."

Keeper was always glad to have these conversations as they walked along the way toward the head of the mountain. It was definitely needed. She would pray that it would help her and the group to see what their mission was before them. Secretly she hoped that Asher would also know it clearly. She wished with everything in her that he would understand as well, but she knew that it was something that he had to contemplate and accept himself.

Chapter 16

She was beginning to see things at every moment. She wondered what was the true meaning of the Spirit Eyes. It was a guide to seeing chains on others, but she felt unsure of a way to not be invasive and judgmental of their lives. She wondered if having them was even good at all. She closed her eyes and, as if she was dreaming for a moment, saw a chess board with two kings playing against each other. They took a hold of different pieces and as if a hand went around her, she felt like she was being picked up as if she were one of the chess pieces. She was moved to a light square further along the battle of the board. She landed in front of a pawn that was then taken off the board and captured. She then saw as the other king took up one of his own pawns. She looked back behind her to see both Gabriel and Percy standing as one of the other pieces. 'But where was Asher?' In front of her, Asher landed close as he moved straight across as a rook. Keeper herself was also a rook. Percy and Gabriel were both knight pieces. The king that was controlling Asher was trying to knock Keeper out. She could tell. "Was he on the other side? Was there a way he could anticipate their movements?"

It felt similar to when she had been picked up before she had met the Holy One. She knew it was not her, but something else. She knew that she knew him for freedom, but nevertheless there was something coming after her on this chess battlefield. She could see the angry brow of the king sitting across from them. She, too, looked up and it seemed like evil was on every side. Even so, she knew that was not the case. Gabriel had warned her not to take everything she thought of as pure fact. She knew she was still lacking sleep and her thoughts could be affected by that fact alone. She did not know at that close proximity that Asher was able to change, as the Pursuer used him.

Keeper felt like she sat in a room that represented her heart that had been swept and cleaned with a sponge and soapy water. She sat looking at a water basin rimmed with blue birds flying about. She asked the person taking residence there for some clean water so she could wash her face. The person gladly fetched a pitcher of water freshly bubbling up. He at once handed it to Keeper who poured the basin full so it was up to the tip of the rim. Keeper plunged her hands down into the cool water as it bubbled as she cupped her hand and brought it to her face. With drops of water trailing down her face, she took a washcloth and dabbed her face dry. She looked into the mirror and saw her green hazel eyes, braided hair with wispy side bangs, her long sleeved shirt and sleeveless tunic on top, and her skirt with chain mail on the side. As she tried to clean her face, she saw that there was a dark spot creeping up into the corner of the wall reflected into the mirror.

'Oh no,' Keeper thought as she looked backwards, picking up the movable basin and the towel wrapped around her arm.

She steadily walked over to the other side of the room, trying not to spill the water, but unsuccessfully sloshing some on the hard wooden floor.

The dark spot was high up on the wall and it looked like dirt and dust had built up. Keeper at once lowered the

185

cloth into the water of the basin, wringing it out with her hands. She intended to fling the cloth at the spot hoping it would take it away, but instead she grabbed the velvety couch and, with difficulty, moved it until the couch rested beneath the spot of decay.

At this moment the person in the room watched, not saying a word.

Keeper took the wet cloth that had been scrunched up and began rubbing up and down and spinning the rag. Keeper lifted up the rag, but could see no progress. She once again knelt down to soak the rag into the basin of water. She then wrung it out over the basin, and she felt her forehead dripping with perspiration. She rubbed at the location of the dark spot with more force, as to rub every dust particle, and she raised it again to find that the rag had collected some remaining dirt, but there was still some left. It had once been a spotless wall cleaned by the Holy Spirit.

She looked around to see the Spirit watching as she rubbed frantically.

"I cannot get rid of this dark spot on the wall." Keeper cried with tears in her eyes. The fear of so many visions came up to envelop her. She dropped the rag into the basin and the dirt filled the water.

The Spirit looked at the basin and then at Keeper. "Do you know that...You are already clean. Who can say, 'I have cleansed my heart, I am pure from my sin.' If you walk in the light as he himself is in the light, we have fellowship with one another, and the blood of the Holy One the son cleanses us from all sin. If we confess our sins, he is faithful and righteous to forgive us our sins and to cleanse us from all unrighteousness. You are already clean because of the word which I spoke to you. Will you confess it?"

The Holy Spirit that lived within her said this. The

Holy Spirit lived within those who received the Holy One's salvation. The Holy Spirit explained what must be done.

"I am sorry. I confess. Please cleanse me because I know I am cleansed in the Holy One." Keeper entreated.

The Holy Spirit that lived within the temple of each believer cleansed the spot. Drawing a new pitcher of water and grabbing a sponge, he climbed the couch and rubbed in a specific manner so it seemed easy. As he lifted the sponge, there was no spot to soil the wall.

"Since you abide in the Holy One, you know you are cleansed." Keeper sobbed and her eyes wouldn't stop filling with tears. As though zooming from inside the closed room, Keeper again found herself staring in at the cleansed room on the outside.

Keeper walked up to the Holy One who again greeted her with a smile so deep and kind.

"Someone wrote, 'I am writing these things to you so that you may not sin. If anyone sins, we have an advocate through the Holy One. I am the propitiation for your sin.'

"It also says, 'Abide in me and I in you, as a branch cannot bear fruit of itself, unless it abides in the vine. So neither can you, unless you abide in me.'"

Keeper asked a question to be able to understand what the Holy One meant, "What is abiding?"

"I am the vine, you are the branches; he who abides in me and I in him, he bears much fruit. For apart from me you can do nothing."

"So I will have fruit?"

"Yes, you will have fruit. If my words abide in you. If you keep my commandments, you will abide in my love."

"How do I keep your commandments?"

The Holy One replied, "Obey the commandments and so that they are not burdensome. That is done through the Holy Spirit."

The Holy One said this sitting down upon the grass and Keeper sat beside him as they continued to talk about abiding, about being cleansed, and about obeying his commandments. Keeper continued to have her ears opened to these words of the Holy One as he began uncovering these truths.

"Do you have faith?" The Holy One was trying to see her heart, though he knew her.

Keeper replied, "Yes."

"Yes, that is enough." The Holy One went on, "The story of the man Abraham was written in the Bread of Life. Abraham had faith and it was reckoned to him as righteousness."

Chapter 17

As though someone was listening. she heard a voice come from outside of her mind. Her eyes refocused to see as Asher was saying "Yes," though she had not asked him any questions. "Yes?" he repeated this time as a question.

"Yes, what—" Keeper was confused.

"Do you need help getting up?" She saw now as he reached out his hand to help her onto a ledge. Somehow she had continued to move up the hill and climb while still daydreaming as she had done often with her Spirit Eyes.

Keeper looked up at Asher and blinked for a moment and chose not to connect what she had just seen with the present. It was better that she did not, connecting one occurrence with an insignificant one. Doing this would make everything confusing and make everything seem like it had a significant deeper meaning. Surprisingly, Keeper did not think this way, even if she had this type of ability. It would be exhausting to make everything confusing, so she stood away, considering what type of manipulation that the Pursuer was capable of as explained by Gabriel.

Keeper received the hand that he extended as she firmly secured her feet and used the pull of his hand to hoist her legs to the edge and she was able to rest her knees. This ledge steadily went up the mountain side. Both Gabriel and Percy were already on the ledge beside them. Gabriel used his wooden rod to help pull himself up the steep incline.

"I guess we can take this way up the side of the mountain," Percy said while grabbing onto the side of the rock face. The ledge was narrow, and they grabbed along the rocks in order to keep their balance.

Keeper's thoughts dangerously went back to the chess

board where she was almost captured by the other side. Gabriel was captured as he was sitting on the sidelines with Percy on the side where the other king sat upon the throne. As Keeper looked, she saw as the crown that sat on his head merged into a hood and his eyes glowed. The hissing noise of his tongue could be heard as he used the rook—Asher to fly both over Keeper and the king piece of the chessboard, declaring, "Checkmate."

'How am I going to get out of this? I am through. How would someone save me as I have gone against them? I am stuck. I am headed in the wrong way, but I am doing it to save what I have lost.' It seemed to be Asher's voice as he reasoned against himself.

Somehow Keeper was still walking along the ledge, holding on to the side of the wall. 'Why was there an enemy in our lines when we all took an oath?' Keeper continued to stretch her arms out to reach the sides of the ledge.

The wind began to sweep past Keeper. She could feel the coolness begin to make the temperature drop. A white speck fell beside her and landed on the stone beneath her. Several more flakes descended beside her as she looked back out toward the area that they had traversed. She could see below them the river as it dropped off a cliff into a lower level. Further back she could also see the edge of the tree line of the forest they had traveled through. 'We have already gone so far,' Keeper thought.

Keeper raised her head to see the snow gathered on the mountains above. Further along the rock face, the way became much more narrow. They came to a point where there was an open gash and then the ledge continued upward. Percy, who was at the front, yelled back to the others over the loud bluster of wind, "What! What! There is a blockage out ahead." Percy was the first to reach the ledge. "I am going to try to jump." Without the response of anyone else he was already on the other side of the surmountable space. Percy grabbed onto the side with a tight grip. Keeper also went across as a wind whipped past her, and she grabbed the hand of Percy to steady herself. Gabriel went across and so did Asher right after him. A few stones gave way in landing.

The place where Asher's foot landed last crumbled and a portion of the rock which fell down the incline. Despite this, all were on the other side, not realizing how fragile the ground was. Suddenly, they realized that they also were on dangerous footing.

"Run! It is about to give out!" Gabriel yelled. Just as he had thought they could feel the unsteadiness of the rock below them, a few small pieces of rock began to gradually fall away from the footing making the ground unstable. The group sprinted along as the way had widened out. As they rushed away from where they had stood, the rock fell away completely. With Keeper's hand moving along the rock wall, she followed after Percy. They were running up a steep incline, nearing an opening in the hard surface of the wall. Debris fell around them from above. "This must have not been created by us. There must have been an earthquake." Gabriel tried to explain the phenomenon.

Percy, being more concerned with a hopeful escape up ahead yelled, "We are nearing an opening! We may be able to find shelter before the ledge completely gives way!"

Asher asked, "How far away is it?"

Percy called, his voice tense, "Only a few feet." Percy soon disappeared in the wide carved opening.

Keeper was also able to reach the opening and climb inside. The stones began to fall away around Gabriel and

Asher, sending Gabriel to the ground. Asher, who had been behind him, came around Gabriel to help him up. "Are you okay, Gabriel?" His unexpected concern had grown from the time he had already spent with the group, especially toward Gabriel.

"I am all right," Gabriel replied, patting Asher on the back since he felt thankful for Asher's help.

Asher pulled Gabriel's arm over his shoulder as they hobbled along. They were only moments away from the opening when they both felt the rocks underneath them give way. Percy and Keeper reached out their hands as they held onto both Gabriel and Asher. The weight of both proved hard to hold, but as they shifted their weight back, they were able to pull them inside of the mouth of the opening. As they all sat on the floor of the opening they breathed hard, thankful that they had evaded the many obstacles. 'Yet another cave. Why so dark?' Keeper remarked to herself in a thought.

They had entered into yet another cave and Keeper knew that it would not be the last on their journey.

The walls absorbed the breeze as it filtered in snow flakes from the outside. A thin powdery outline settled on the edge of the opening. Keeper went close to the edge to look at the space where the ledge would have been. She could see as a bit of rock had fallen off, but it seemed not to extend its way toward the opening, stopping as though they were all on an invisible line not to pass. Keeper was relieved. 'I cannot believe we have made it this far,' she thought to herself. The orange and red hues of a sunset showed on the horizon.

Keeper turned around to find that the members of the group were now busying themselves by taking two rocks and striking them together. They did this near a bit of moss, and white flecks of light jumping off the rocks flashed for a moment as the repeated movements continued to cause airy smoke to rise up. These mosses housed small bugs that nested themselves inside and fed off the plant. The flies buzzed around as Percy applied the heat to the plant.

Percy was a legalistic sort and the way that things had been done was the way it should be. Good for the sake of it. Not much grace and forgiveness. He wanted to follow the rules and for it to be the way it had always been. Asher gulped looking his way. A flame spurted up from the moss after Percy continued to strike two stones against each other.

The moss burned quickly, making the fire lick up and rise from the patch of moss. Gabriel, who had wrapped up a few pieces of fish in brown parchment from his never ending bag, unveiled it now to the sound of the group's mouths watering. The couple of fish were placed on a hard surface beside the heated moss. Each watched until the fish was beginning to sear and then they flipped them over to cook them all the way through. Gabriel then removed the pieces of fish from the heat and served it to each guest, using rocks as plates to set the fish down between bites. Since they had not eaten much since that morning they ate rather quickly despite it being hot. Picking apart the pieces, they continued to pull meat from the bone until there was none left. Those who finished first laid back and rested on their supporting hands.

"That was some wonderful fish. Aye?" Percy remarked.

Asher answered with a resounding, "Yes."

'I wonder how we are going to get out of here?' Keeper thought about the situation as she jotted down her thoughts of the mission in her journal. There had been much that had been seen that day and she wanted to remember everything.

After this remark the group was silent for a while as

each member collectively started to lay themselves down and began to rest. No one talked to each other, for each nodded and sleep overtook them.

Chapter 18

The troops that had been gathered had grown to a larger size, despite the correspondence that they had received. A sign of fear was beginning to show among the men. Despite the flag Nissi still waving high, it had grown ragged from the whipping of the wind. El Roi still continued to look at the plans and discussed with the Holy One, "Despite the setbacks we face, there is no changing what is able to happen. To freedom, I say." Sabaoth looked up at him, "You have heard the trouble of the spy. Do you think he is far too gone?" Jehovah Rapha looked at his supplies of herbs in his bag, making sure he would be prepared if anything happened.

"No, he is already turning his heart back; he is healing it." Jehovah Rapha responded graciously.

"What must he do to bring him back?" Sabaoth knit his brow with concern.

El Roi's voice was strongly serious. "There is actually nothing that can be done. Despite anything he could do there is nothing to put forward."

"Then why do we even fight this battle?" Sabaoth was confused.

"Why do we fight? None are good, none want right, but as we fight we do it in order to do what they cannot. They cannot save themselves. You have heard it said that the enemy may have won the battle, but the Holy One will win the war. I and the Father are the same. The sacrifice that I desire to give is only done from myself and cannot be given

any other way. It is for the sinners and not for the righteous. Even if someone was good, how can one save their own life? Surely, all their works do not match up to the wholeness of the Holy One."

Sabaoth was still confused and asked, "So what about those who are striving in a good direction. How might they be helped? Do they need less intervention for the portion they compensated for?"

"Do you not understand? There are none that are right. If there were, the sacrifice that I give will be for naught. Sometimes those who are striving are the ones who need my help the most. No, they are all in need of help." The Holy One replied.

They both looked over and saw the figure, Keeper, who was looking onward toward the enemy. She saw the terror to come and turned back. She brandished her frail sword as if she was practicing to fight off the enemy.

"Does it seem as though she feels that she will have to eventually fight off the enemy in her own strength?"

Sabaoth replied, "Yes, her fear of what will happen may be blinding her from how the Holy One is able to change every one of us. How, despite her fear that Asher is too far gone, he may be closer to the truth than any one of them. With his heart for saving others, he fell captive to evil. He cannot save others, and neither can she. Even so, the Holy One will be able to resolve their hopes until they understand."

Both Keeper and Asher had been listening to this conversation of El Roi and the Sabaoth as if they had been standing close by.

Asher felt shocked that these beings knew about him in the situation.

"They are both in need of help, while one thinks that they can overcome their fears by themselves, the other thinks

196

they are too far gone. Do you see that it is about their ability? Looking down on the plight of others does not help oneself. Maybe they have a fear that faith in the Holy One's grace is not enough." El Roi replied to Sabaoth.

"Even those who show care for others understand that they have been set free, that good comes out of knowing what the Holy One has done. I hope that they understand this. Even so, the Holy One is that one who can defeat their fears and make everything right. Only he can set people free from their fear and the past. He gives grace and makes them understand it was not through their works, but through what the Holy One can do. You cannot free yourself." Sabaoth replied.

Asher began to think. The question came down to: "How do you get free without the works?"

He could hear, "Trust in the work he has already done because he does it through you. Trust in his righteousness to save you." Jehovah Rapha answered back.

Asher responded while thinking, but the Holy One heard what he said, 'But you do not understand how I am stuck, how if I do not follow in the way that the Pursuer has set that I might not find Cephas. If I follow the Pursuer there is a way he could be safe, but if I do not, my Cabin Boy will surely be lost.'

The Holy One responded, 'How do you know that he is under the Pursuer's grasp? Do you think that the Holy One is not capable of keeping him safe?'

Asher was unsure, 'But what if he's on the Forlorn Isle. The quicker we get there, the faster we could save him and we could remove him from the Pursuer's grasp.'

'Do you not have trust that the Holy One, who you first knew when you were released, will make a way? Were there not provided for you those such as Percy who allowed you to be freed physically. You could not save yourself even so, you cannot save him, I will have to.' Asher then realized that it was the Holy One who was speaking to him.

The Holy One also had the troops of Jehovah Sabaoth, El Roi, and Jehovah Rapha, who represented the Holy One. Sabaoth came up to Asher, handing him a sword. Keeper was standing a few spaces behind him also with a sword. For a moment they both recognized each other in the dream.

They could hear the Holy One who said, "You will also need to fight."

Keeper continued to think about Asher's chains. She could hear this and seeing the chains on Asher's arms interrupted, "How can he?"

"You do not understand now, but you will," El Roi knew the reason because of what Keeper was seeing.

"Please help us." Asher was scared and did not know what Keeper meant.

"You will both be trained," the Holy One answered. "Iron sharpens iron." The Holy One's arm extended and he instructed, "You need to learn to fight." Asher's head was lowered for he knew he had pledged with his mouth, but his allegiance was elsewhere. "Your training will come in time."

"How do you know who is with you?" Keeper asked, confused.

"Those who stay beside you," El Roi assured.

Raising a sword that was within his sheath, he began by swinging it gently towards Keeper as she was able to easily defend herself. He really was just training her for what was to come. Her mind was still being attacked by the enemy so she needed to be on the defense. The swords swooshed back and forth as both Keeper and El Roi almost playfully clashed the iron blades together. She was still a beginner though. Asher was standing close beside them *watching as though he was in the same dream with Keeper, having the same thoughts and living them out.*

"Now it is time for you to try," El Roi pointed to Asher, who had the sword hanging down in the grasp of his hand. He was hesitant and did not move, but as El Roi came forward and swung his sword, Asher's blade instantly felt as if it was drawn by a magnet in order to block it. Asher's brows lowered as he looked at El Roi's face, but El Roi understood what he felt. Asher pulled away as if Asher had seen the kindness in El Roi's eyes as he swung his sword against him. As he did this in fear that he could not do what he promised, the thought of, 'why?' came to his head. Asher began to have a conversation with El Roi without Keeper hearing.

'Cephas is under the clutches of the Pursuer. Following him is the only way to get my partner back.' Asher's words echoed into the deepness of his hopelessness.

El Roi smiled as he moved back towards Asher and they held a firm stance, becoming much closer as they leaned in. 'Yes, but as I said: do you have faith?'

Asher huffed angrily with much frustration and moved back. He was trying his best to understand. 'I have to find him myself. I know my own way. I have gained much deeper ideas and know much more than I originally knew. When I was in prison, I learned more than just the hopeless mind blinding and eye closing understanding of faith. I can find a way to find him without your help.'

El Roi also stepped back and said, 'I will still help you. Please trust me. I am here to give you new life and help you understand your life. You are conflicted, but I can help you. You think you can be good and find your own way. I will help you find him—I promise.'

'I do not believe you.' Asher said through tears. "And

199

that is why I will do it on my own," Keeper could hear these words out loud. "Why would you keep me in prison all that time?"

"But did you not become free?" The Holy One replied.

"Yes, but somehow I still feel like I am back behind those bars."

"That is why you need help," the Holy One suggested, but Asher was offended.

"Yes, we could help you," Keeper interrupted the conversation trying to console, "Asher, you do understand how you need to be on the same mission with us. We need you. You probably help us more than anyone else, but for some reason you are going another way."

Asher snapped back, "You do not need to tell me what to do. I know what I am doing," Even so, he hung his head in fear.

"I saw you had—" Keeper was almost going to mention the shackles that hung down from his arms, but did not feel like it was the appropriate time.

Asher had no idea that he was carrying chains.

"I saw you had what?" Asher asked, drawing closer and raising his sword, but Keeper had enough time to meet it as she had done with El Roi. The strain was heavy, but Keeper was able to keep it off and dash a few feet away. It reminded her of the dream that she had run away from the blade of the Pursuer.

"Asher, please turn around. We need you," Keeper's voice was desperate as Asher came up close with a slash of a sword. El Roi was watching the whole of the day's events, and now came up to stop both of them. Running up toward both of them he placed a blade in between them.

"You cannot make me do anything." Asher asserted. Keeper moved back and the blade slashed up against it, but she spun back blocking it and Asher's remarks.

"Why are you saving people one moment and then upset at them the next?" Keeper questioned.

"Maybe I feel pressured logistically with my moral duty. Maybe I care about your well being so much, but it comes off wrong so I do not know how to say it." Asher said this in a way that hurt Keeper.

"You cannot change him," El Roi confronted both of them.

The clink of her sword was heard as she put it back into the sheath. She began to walk away when El Roi patted her back. "You know everyone has a choice."

Asher began to walk away, but El Roi did not stop him except with the words, "You do have the choice, but I pray that when you do, you will choose me."

Asher's heart was not ready to accept it, and Keeper's mind was not able to understand grace when trying to help others. Keeper's words, though it was in the spirit of helpfulness, had tried to push something on him even though he was not at a place to receive the words. Asher held onto Keeper's words and turned them over in his head, defensively going against them.

'She does not understand why I do what I do. She does not understand me.' Asher thought.

The Holy One motioned to his men, "They are here to help. From ages ago, they have been fighting with me."

"We are here to serve the Holy One." They looked at Keeper and she knew they had the same hope that she had.

"He can help you," Sabaoth was able to say to Asher, but Asher did not seem responsive.

Sabaoth continued, "We are all in training for whatever there may be in the future. There may be many battles." Sabaoth brandished his sword. Sabaoth offered sword practice, and Keeper continued to fight against him, slashing again and again. Sabaoth was quicker and Keeper's sword went flying.

"Checkmate," Sabaoth said comically.

Keeper just laughed and stood back up.

"There are also many hearts that need to be healed." Jehovah Rapha pulled out the pouch filled with the ground-up herbs. He was able to include some liquid and mix it together for them to drink.

Chapter 19

Asher, after having a dream, woke with fuming anger.

Keeper heard the sound of someone getting up in the night. She opened her eyes and saw Asher on the other side of the room. She decided to get up and ask him what was going on. Asher suddenly raised up a sword in defense so it seemed like he was almost frightened and yet angry.

Asher rushed at Keeper. Keeper ran and grabbed Gabriel's sword that was left on the ground from the never ending bag.

"Why were you angry at me in the dream?" Asher demanded. "You were treating me as though I was an enemy."

"Are you an enemy?" Keeper said, raising her sword, but at that moment Asher jabbed at her so she flinched backwards.

Asher made another strike toward Keeper, but she fought back.

They shuffled as Keeper could feel the weight of Asher's sword against her own as she extended it in front of her. They could see the strain in each other's faces. Asher had a defensive, aggressive look that scared Keeper. They looked into each other's determined eyes as they strained against the weight of each other's swords. They could see something unrecognizable come from the inside as they looked at each other. She had never seen this side of him, though she knew she did not know everything about him. Asher could also see Keeper's face, with her firm determination for the importance of the mission.

"I am an enemy to you, Keeper. I do not like what you are doing here. You think you know everything."

"I am not trying to do anything. I am sorry for whatever you feel like I did wrong. Despite that, I feel like you are trying to undermine this mission." Keeper said as she lost her strength and pulled her sword back, Asher following suit.

"Keeper, you do not understand what I do. You do not understand." He sliced his sword and Keeper defended herself with a swipe.

"Well, we do not have to be enemies," Keeper said, trying to smooth over the situation.

"Your dream revealed we are against each other. I am your enemy. This is where we are at." Asher gruffly repeated back, gritting his teeth and telling what he knew to be true. Asher swiped with a heavy clash along Keeper's sword so that Keeper also forcefully fought back. Keeper backed up a few paces away from his sword.

"Despite that, are you willing to still go on this mission with us?" Keeper asked him, not knowing his answer. Keeper was hoping he would at least agree.

Asher breathed and let himself calm down for a minute. After a while, he lowered his sword. Anger steamed from inside him, but he suppressed it, allowing it to subside. "Yes, I will still go on the mission." Asher replied to her request.

"I will have to trust you for now." Keeper said lowering her sword, despite knowing that she really did not know what Asher would do. She was risking everything by doing this.

Asher also lowered his sword.

They could hear the others waking up. Keeper put Gabriel's sword back to where it was previously.

They both went back to the side of the cave where the others were and slumbered for a while.

Keeper opened her eyes to find that the light of the sun was shining in glowing streaks. The clouds had moved in order to show a majority of the sky as she looked out the opening of the cave.

Her mind immediately reverted back to the dream that she had that night and her sword fight with Asher. She wondered why Asher was in her dream and if they had the same conversations. Somehow he had gone into the dream where she saw images and acted with her Spirit Eyes. 'Why was he the only one who could see these? He had never been in one of them before. He had been there, but never talked to me.' Keeper thought, feeling apprehensive at the realization. She had sensed something following her. Maybe it was all part of the Pursuer's plan to go against them. She needed to be wary of what she said or did while she dreamed. She had no idea of how it would affect reality.

Gabriel, who just then stirred, had suddenly moved and sat up and saw Keeper who had just stood and curiously looked out the opening of the cave. He came and stood beside her silently as they meticulously scanned the skyline in search of an enemy.

"Did you see anything last night?" Gabriel knew that she could see many things with her Spirit Eyes that could be helpful on their journey.

"Why do people walk away?" The question rose up before she had answered Gabriel's original question. Gabriel assumed it had something to do with the thought of what she had seen that night.

"It depends on what you mean by 'walk away.' Away from what?" Gabriel asked.

Keeper lowered her voice so that no one could hear.

"Away from a belief once held."

Gabriel let out an understanding sigh, "Oh, I see what you are saying. Well, it is not your responsibility to put their choice on your shoulders."

"Yes, but what if you know they are in trouble? If they continue the way they are going they may become stuck, worse than what they were before?"

Gabriel's eyes rose. "That is terrifying to think about, but how do you know something is going to happen to them?"

Keeper tried to phrase her words in a way that would not allude to whom she mentioned, "I can see it somehow. There is something wrong." Keeper did not know Asher was following the Pursuer since Asher had spoken of it privately in a conversation with the Holy One. Keeper believed that Asher calling her an enemy was more of some personal beef he had against her.

Gabriel continued, "But you do not know what. You know this person is in trouble, but you do not know why."

"Or how to bring them back," Keeper seemed apprehensive.

Gabriel could understand her concern, praying that the Holy One would reveal his love to her. They all needed to know the kindness of the Savior.

"You know, there is no way to keep someone from making the choices they do. You can encourage them and pray for them. If they do not believe, it is not your fault."

Keeper replied, "Sometimes I pray that they will turn back. Is that wrong to ask?"

"You know that manipulation to do good is as bad as manipulation in order to do evil. Yes, pray, that they would see the Holy One by his kindness that leads to repentance so that they would come back, apart from having to do good. Goodness does not save another." Gabriel continued on with, "He will come when he is ready. Just show kindness from above. That will set someone free. You do not see everything." Keeper nodded in agreement.

The group stirred as they heard the sound of the conversation being had between Gabriel and Keeper. Keeper felt a sense of humility, understanding their place in helping others along this journey. She knew she may have offended him, but all she could do was ask forgiveness and try to rectify the situation with kindness from the Holy One. She resolved in herself that she would not try to go against that person, but instead she would show kindness to them despite her knowledge of their faults.

Asher opened his eyes and found that the fire had gone out in front of him and Percy. He scanned the area to see that Gabriel and Keeper were standing at the opening of the rock cave conversing.

Thinking about Keeper's dream that he had entered into, he shuddered at the thought that he had said his inner intentions to Keeper. He wondered how much of it that Keeper had heard. Most likely they talked about the dream that Keeper experienced. Asher continued to do what was right in order to save Cephas, but she was totally against him in the way that he went about it. Still, he knew he needed to cool down because he knew that this combativeness would be found out. Asher felt shocked as if he had almost given away everything as he thought. 'I will just act the same. It is okay. I am on the mission, but I do not have the same plan.' And as for the sword fight, he remembered the conversation he had with Keeper. He realized he had acted out of a lot of anger, and so did she. Out of the anger, he began to feel something else, though he did not know what. All they knew is that they were on opposing sides, and that made all the difference.

Asher looked around to make sure nothing he said was observable by Keeper or the others. He had sunk into a moment where he felt like he was inside of his brain, and it could communicate with the one he was still on the mission for, namely the Pursuer.

'Yes, I heard yesterday that she suspects that I am on the other side. It was implied in the day dream about a chess board where she saw me on the other side, as well as our sword fight. She might try to go against this mission more than I thought, but I still do not know.'

From somewhere inside of his head he could hear the hissing of a tongue and a low gurgling sound in the Pursuer's throat before he answered with a snappy, 'Good,' and continued with the words, 'You may have given away too much, and for that you may be penalized. Your trip may be harder. Now, did you hear anything else?'

Asher's mind reminisced on what had been said. He remembered what El Roi told him and Keeper about the swords. For a second he asked, 'Why did he train me if he knew I was on the other side?' This thought was heard by Asher alone.

'Well,' Asher continued by describing how El Roi had handed him a sword and trained him to use it in order to fight battles.

'Are you on his side then?' The Pursuer's voice dangerously dragged so that Asher answered within seconds.

'No, you are still the side I am on, even if they paint us in such a negative light.'

'Did they come against you?' The judgmental assumption could be heard.

'Yes, the Spirit Keeper came up against me in this sword fight trying to turn me, but her judgmental remarks did not affect me in my course.' Asher used the tone of his voice and tried his best to convince the Pursuer.

'Like I thought. All they would do in the band that follows the Holy One is become mindlessly blinded and bring others along with them. A prime example of those who try to come against me and my system. They believe they have to be a certain way to be good enough. They go against you. Too many rules.'

Asher nodded his head, agreeing to his statements. He was quite upset at Keeper for going against him, despite what the Pursuer said. The ones closest to the Holy One were the ones to push Asher away the most. They did not understand him or what he was doing.

'Still,' The Pursuer's voice had trailed for a second on the previous subject, 'the Holy One trained you along with Keeper, which means there is going to be a battle. If a lot of what Keeper sees comes true there may be a real war. Still, you are not, so continue to answer to me and bring them to the Forlorn Isle—without wavering in going to Captavia.'

"Where do we go now?" The question came from Percy who was starting to heat up the remaining fish. Gabriel brought out some fruit that he had picked from a fruit tree near the base of the mountain. He then handed it out to Keeper, who stood near him. Making his way toward the firewood, he handed it both to Percy and Asher, who took large bites as they chewed it hurriedly. The red fruit was sweet and resembled an apple. An exclamation of "mmm" came out of their mouths, feeling rejuvenated by the taste.

As they enjoyed the fruit, the smell of it drifted through the open air. From somewhere farther inside the cave, something stirred. The group did not move for a moment, too fearful to say anything. "Be careful, there may be something dangerous—" Percy's voice cut off as they once again heard something. Asher grew closer as he walked deeper into the darkness. With a hand stretched out, he felt his way around. Keeper came up close beside him. Asher shot an aggressive glance, but Keeper also came close to help.

Asher winced as he felt the hair of a creature with its head bent over as it was curled up sleeping. Asher stepped back as if his movement was a warning.

The creature raised its head and its eyes opened in a glowing green ember, eyes staring at Asher straight in the face. It seemed wise, but dangerous so Asher stepped back a few paces. It ran forward rapidly, seeming as though it would run into him. Asher could only see its eyes, but as it came out into the blaring light cast by the opening of the cave, Asher could see that it was a horse that shone with shining blue fur. On its back were a pair of feathered wings. It stopped short just shy of Asher's face. The animal flew upward as its wings unfolded by its sides and it strained against the long chain secured to a rock that had been attached to one of its legs.

It neighed as it tried to escape, frightened from being stuck in the dark cave.

"I wonder how this could have happened?" Keeper asked.

"How else?" Asher, though being on the other side, still seemed to have more of an understanding of these things. "It had to have been the Pursuer."

Percy agreed, "Aye, the Pursuer continues to ensnare those of whom he wills. He has all of them unless the people trust the Holy One to set them free. They are enslaved to something that they cannot change in themselves, a sin-nature, depravity. They are in the same cycle that they used to be from the beginning. He has even chained up this horse for some reason, maybe as a way to travel if he came up this way. What did it do? I know that humans are inherently deprived, but what would a horse do to be under such enslavement? I was reminiscing on the verse that came to mind that the world is tired because of the bondage of sin. How does he even stay alive?" The horse bowed his head and ate some moss growing on the cave floor. He also licked up shimmering pools of water that dropped from the ceiling.

Looking around the cave for something to break this creature free all Percy saw was a rock nearby, but knew that dropping it on the base of the chains would not do well in freeing this horse. Unexpectedly, Percy saw a stick sitting near the far side of the cave and went back to retrieve it. He suddenly heard movement as a pair of wings unfolded and yet another flying horse lifted its head to reveal itself.

"What! What! Yet another pegasus." Percy exclaimed. This horse rose up slowly and Percy could hear the sliding of chains as they stretched across the floor, "And this one, too, is chained." Percy went back toward the base of where the chains were located, dragging the stick. A metal handle drilled into the ground held the chains. The members crowded around the base of the chain. Percy instinctively moved the stick into the link of the chain.

"What might you propose?" Gabriel asked, trying to understand what Percy was trying to do.

Silently, Percy went over to the rock he had seen, and gestured to the others, asking, "Will someone help me to pick up this boulder? I think it will help us by placing its weight on the end of the stick to pull the handle up."

"I think it is heavy enough," Asher commented while trying to push the rock a few inches.

Keeper also tried to move the rock, but it would not

move because she did not have the strength like the others.

"Do you realize that these horses cannot get out without us?" Percy could understand the symbolism behind the occurrence. "We need someone to save us."

"Yes, I know," Asher quickly answered as if he had been targeted. He thought he did not need reminding. "Can we get on with it?"

Keeper could still see the chains that hung down from Asher's wrists, and she could see that it mirrored the struggle and turmoil of these horses. She continued to keep tabs on Asher's condition.

Keeper truly was concerned about him, but decided not to say anything and did not know if she would anytime soon after her conversation with Gabriel.

Gabriel, Asher, and Percy stooped down, putting their arms underneath the rock together in order to lift it. Carrying it a few feet, they put the rock halfway underneath the stick. "Let us get another to weigh it down," Percy insisted. They went together to get another rock nearby, and together they put it on the higher part of the stick. Keeper steadied the stick as they placed the rock on top. Together they kept it balanced on the top as the weight pushed down on the higher end of the stick so it became a lever.

The leverage that this contraption created could be used to pull up the metal drilled into the ground. "Now let's pull down on the rock," Percy tried to instruct. With hands supporting the rock while also pulling it down slowly, the other end began to bend the metal ring attached to the links of the chains. The bending was making progress, but it seemed not enough to move the loop enough to break completely. The members continued to pull down on the stick as they steadied the rock. As they did so, the stick again began to bend.

Asher halted the action. "We need to go slowly, or the

stick will break. Then we cannot do anything to help these creatures." The others agreed, continuing to steady the rock and they went at a less hasty pace.

The metal bent as one side of the handle began to come loose, but still it would not come apart. There was a clinking noise as one of the horses reared up on its hind legs and came toward Percy. The horse tried to ram into him as if it was scared of the sounds and movement. If only the horses could understand what the group tried to do for them. Suddenly, the stick broke and fell as the horse came crashing down. It barely missed Percy while he managed to get out of the way. Stepping back so they would not get hit, a collective gasp carried as they realized that the horse may have ruined their only way of freeing it from its chains.

They needed something to get this creature free. The flying horse snarled at Percy as it clenched its teeth and gurgled out a stifled neigh sound. It flapped its wings wildly, lifting itself from the floor. The chains that were attached to its leg continued to clang and cause the horse to strain as it pulled away. The other horse sat curled up in the corner with its wings folded by its side, and its head tucked underneath. It breathed softly without becoming startled by the movement of the other. It seemed unconcerned about its escape, or had given up in its attempts. It had reason to just sit and sleep, for nothing they could have done would free it because it could not free itself. The area around his leg that stuck out showed to be pink as its raw skin seemed to be an attempt to free itself.

Asher had a moment where he felt the heaviness of something himself, and for some reason the closer he got to the handle the less he could move. For a moment, he felt like he had become attached to the same ring that held the horses' chains, but he was able to move away and feel less.

"Ugh, what will we do?" Looking around the cave in

frustration, Percy said this while he felt unsure what to do next to save these creatures.

Gabriel commented, "If these chains were forged by the Pursuer in a way to enslave these creatures, there must be something powerful about them. Something that a handmade contraption would not be able to break."

Keeper, who had been listening to Gabriel's words, continued to go back into the darkness of the cave. She looked for anything that could free these beasts. Honestly, what was more powerful than a rock in order to cause damage to these chains?

She continued close to the wall, blindly moving along without the knowledge of where she stepped. Even in the darkness, she saw a glint of light that came from close by as if some of the crystals from the cavern that they had traveled through grew in these mountains. Considering their close proximity, it was possible. Still, the light showed as the glint of metallic silver sparkled. Keeper drew closer as the vision of the night before came to her remembrance as El Roi had handed her a sword.

The silhouette of a double-blade sword could be seen as someone lit a torch from the remnants of the stick used to free the horses.

The silver of the sword seemed to be transparent as if it was a clear blue ice. Keeper came up closely toward it. The sword was hanging from the wall by a rope so that it stood suspended. Reaching outward, Keeper grabbed the hilt of the sword, lifting it slightly to remove it from the rope suspension. It seemed hard to carry with the extra blade, but for some reason it fit perfectly in her hands. For a moment as she stared at its clear substance, it seemed as though it glowed. With the two edged sword shown every time she looked at the instrument, she could see visions of the battle that had enveloped her dreams as if it somehow connected to her vision. Her questions remained. What was it made out of? Or what was inside of this sword?

Asher came up close beside Keeper as he held the torch over his head, shining the light through the sword's material.

"What is that?" Asher asked, staring at the sword in wonder. "It looks like the sword is made out of the crystal that we saw back in the cavern when I…" He stopped not wanting to go any further with his point. Keeper did not ask. He continued by remarking, "I wonder how it got here."

Keeper felt like she knew the answer. "Maybe the Holy One himself put this here in order to help us free these beasts."

Asher had not thought about the flying horses, but resoundingly agreed. "Yes, this would break the chains of these creatures. If they would let us help them, that is. We will have to see."

Despite having a disagreement last night, they decided to agree now. It was strange that way. They both still seemed to want the same thing. They both traveled on this quest and these animals entrapped became concerning.

"Can I hold the sword?" Asher asked, looking at it.

Keeper replied, "Yes, you can. I will trust you for now." Taking the sword in his hand, he felt unable to carry it, but was able to steady himself. Somehow it only showed silver in his hands instead of the icy blue. Handing it back to Keeper, they continued back toward the others.

"Look at the sword that Keeper found!" The sound of gasping accompanied their astonishment.

"A sword, what! What! Maybe just what we need to break open these chains off these flying horses which may serve as a way for our escape." Percy suggested. The thought had not come up, but the fact that the ledge had collapsed meant they had no way of continuing. The horses had thick wings so that they could fly easily. They were in chains for good or for bad, but that these winged creatures seemed to serve a positive purpose for them. If only the sword was powerful enough to cut through the heavy spiritual chains—then, it would prove a true victory.

Gabriel motioned for Keeper to come forward, and he pointed to the base where the handle held both the flying horses' chains secure. Keeper, the sword raised above her head, slashed the blade into the metal with a loud clanking sound that once again scared the more skittish horse so that it neighed. However, the horse did not come closer. Keeper saw the sword had not completely broken the handle so that it stood with a dent in the side. Keeper once again thrust the handle with all the force she could muster. Once again, a noisy sound rose as the blade against the steel met each other. The loop started to bend inward as a slight gash could be seen. Keeper continued striking at the handle hoping that it would give way. Then, as if closing her eyes, she saw the vision of the battle scene as she and El Roi prepared to fight the enemy. She asked for strength, "I cannot do this, only one, the Holy One, can do it through me." She could see El Roi nod in approval as she heard the deafening clank of the handle as it was split apart increasing the clanking of the chains. The horses leapt free as both blades moved through the metal.

Keeper opened her eyes to see the sight before her. The handle had been broken in two, and Percy held the chain of the sleeping horse while Asher and Gabriel held the chain of the awake horse in order to keep them from escaping.

"My, that sword did glow icy blue as you made that last strike toward the chains!" Percy exclaimed.

"What?" Keeper did not know exactly what to say,

but knew that somehow the sword did seem to have those capabilities. It was the type of sword that when it glowed it was able to make a blow that could break seemingly impenetrable materials.

'Why did it somehow glow?' Keeper pondered for a moment, not understanding what type of power this instrument possessed. 'I just looked at the Holy One and it worked. Interesting.' Keeper continued to understand slightly as she put the information together, though she still felt unsure.

'Did she have some power over this herself? They had to have something to free them other than themselves.' Keeper looked at the others holding the creatures down and suggested, "Maybe we could ride them?"

Keeper once again thought of the chains attached to their legs and walked up as Asher and Gabriel held tight onto the horse. Keeper once again slashed the sword near the end of the chain, closing her eyes and envisioning the Holy One so that the blade glowed. The blade split into two blades at right angles used to carve, but it did not glow though she had used force. The real power is the power of the Holy One glowed from within. The link detached and the buckle holding on to the leg came loose. Both Asher and Gabriel got a hold of its sides and held onto it so it would not fly away. Keeper then went over to the sleeping horse and with the same amount of concentration she could see that the two blades went through the links as the blade glowed, releasing the leg of the horse and its whole body with it. The horse still did not know that it was free and instead continued its loud snoring. Percy stood by in case the horse suddenly jerked up and started to fly away.

Gabriel was standing in front of the sluggish horse, brushing the front of its lower head. Its shining green eyes were open, but like Gabriel commented, this horse seemed to be more gentle. The horse continued to slow its breathing, blinking off and on as it stared into Gabriel's eyes trustingly. Gabriel led Asher's hand up to the horse's mane and onto the top portion of its head as Gabriel slid beside the horse to keep it tame. The horse continued in the same way to look at Asher as he stood in front of the horse's face. Asher stepped back with a small amount of fear and the horse snarled and backed up.

"I guess he is just trying to get used to you," Gabriel assured Asher, coming closer.

Keeper went back to find the rope that had held the sword and took it down from the wall, finding an additional rope. Using the rope, she put it over her head as she slipped her arm through it while dropping it over one shoulder. Keeper then went over to the material that held the fish they had eaten and wrapped up the end of the sword and found both of the blades could be pushed together into a single thick blade. She folded the material neatly so that she was able to take off the rope tying the light rope tightly around the material so that it made it sheath.

Using the rope she placed it horizontally across her shoulder and the sword hung security across her back. It was heavy, but all she knew was that she could reach back swiftly and could remove the sword from its makeshift sheath. She can easily grab the handle and remove the whole sword in order to use it for protection or even battle. The two edged swords were folded together.

Keeper, being the smallest of the group, seemed the most unlikely to be holding a sword on her person. Others could be more valiant, but somehow she understood how to use the sword the most. The others stood back as if they felt the significance of the sword's power and maybe even the one, yet small, who held it by their side. She spoke and it would fail, but now with this sword she could succeed. It seemed to dispel all fear as if she had a way to go against the evil of the Pursuer which she feared.

Percy rubbed the mane of the dozing horse so that it began to stir, and its movements made it seem to come alive from its slumber. It yawned and lifted itself to its feet.

Percy began to reason through the situation and quoted the riddle they had seen in the old cavern.

"To those who seek to save what is lost must place burdens down. Stepping into the light so all the seen, *you cannot do it alone*. Even only one is worthy for such a call." Percy continued, "Now, with this sword we have the ability to break chains and even bars of prisons. These horses were helpless on their own to save themselves. If we go to Captavia, we will have many more warriors to fight and be able to free the others. The more we have, the more we will free."

Asher, knowing this action was against what the Pursuer wanted, became defensive as he tensed up and then sighed. He knew that he had no way of deterring Percy from going to Captavia. Even the fear that he may be caught was another reason why he did not want to go back to Captavia. The others looked at Asher, knowing he would have complaints in the decision and he sighed letting out an, "Okay, we can. You continue to persist." Asher did not know the real reason why the Pursuer did not want them to go to Captavia, but as Percy had once said, "There may be something along the path that is important for us to do, something important to our mission together." For some reason these words seemed probable.

"Yes, we may understand something important to our mission." Percy's words mirrored the point he had tried to make before, but it might come true on the path toward Captavia.

Asher silently watched as Keeper brushed the side of

the more lively horse, thinking, 'Will they be okay? What will the Pursuer do to them and Cephas in response to my disobedience?' This fear Asher held made him concerned, but he knew he could not argue. 'Do they understand I am trying to protect them?'

"Let us mount these horses and lead them toward Captavia. We should be close once over these mountains." Gabriel gave instructions to the group, "We will be heading toward Captavia and the Dark Forest and will have to pass through, but we'll have to meet someone important in a town first."

Gabriel held on to the side of the more hyper horse as Keeper jumped on. The horse felt the movement and reared up as Keeper held on to its mane. It turned its head back to see the only person on its back was Keeper. Seeing her, it settled itself.

"We are going to let it get used to you. We should let it walk around a little bit with you on its back," Gabriel explained. Keeper did this, allowing the horse to pace around the open cave, while Percy could get onto the least active horse. The flying horse did not move much and allowed Percy to sit comfortably on its bare back. Asher then mounted behind Percy and the horse gave them no trouble. On the other hand, Keeper's horse continued to pace the room feeling quite agitated.

"We are going to have to start going soon." Gabriel said, getting close to the horse.

"I do not think you should get close too quickly, but you could in a moment." Asher seemed to understand these things. "I taught my Cabin Boy how to train horses and the workings of a ship." Explaining as if everyone did not understand, not knowing if anyone needed the words.

Gabriel backed away, listening to Asher's advice. "You can approach them by the side as though you are

220

getting on," Asher instructed further. Gabriel approached the side of the horse as it began to slow down so that the horse saw him as Gabriel pulled himself onto the horse's back. It did not move as Gabriel steadied himself behind Keeper, but then suddenly began running toward the opening of the cave.

"What is it doing? Try to make it halt by saying 'woah'." Asher's voice sounded concerned.

The horse did not listen and continued as it galloped toward the edge of the opening.

"We need to catch them!" Asher yelled.

Percy dug his heels into the sides of the flying horse and it was awakened from its drowsiness and it began darting toward the opening. Both Keeper and Gabriel held tightly as the horse opened its wings and lifted from the remaining part of the rock ledge into the breezy air. The wind made Keeper's hair whip into her face and she had to brush it away as she looked around at the direction they headed. They would need to turn themselves around in order to get over the mountains leading to Captavia and into the Dark Forest. Asher and Percy were soon seen rushing out of the opening on the other winged horse, whooping and hollering from pure excitement and fear of being in the air. The great feathered wings of the horse were soft as they brushed past, causing gusts of air to move from underneath.

"Look at the mountains. We just need to get over the Dark Range and toward the Dark Forest." Gabriel yelled across the expanse of air so both Percy and Asher could hear.

"Should we just turn around and follow you?" Percy asked perceptively.

"Yes, do that." Gabriel answered, agreeing on the plan of action through the wind.

"Aye, we will be right behind you." Percy agreed, and

Asher also nodded his head. He may have been scared of the direction they had chosen. He could see the sea to the east in the far-off shores which he knew they should have gone to first, but now as they turned and held on tightly he looked ahead he saw the dark mountains of the Dark Range with its volcanoes leading to the Dark Forest. The Pursuer could be anywhere at that point; the area they entered was where the Pursuer ruled.

Keeper held tight to the mane of the horse with the sword strapped securely to her back. She moved her hand across the horse's bluish-white coat and through its mane. Gabriel could still reach the flying horse's hair of its mane and use it to steer in the direction that they needed to travel.

The wind continued to flow past as snow flurries enveloped them while they rose upward toward the top of the mountain. The cool air continued to make them shiver, but they continued onward. The patches of thick snow that covered the rock face seemed deep from their vantage point. The horse that Keeper and Gabriel rode upon lowered closer to the snow so that the tip of its wings brushed up against the snowbank, and then it flapped its wings more fiercely so that it rose above the next snow ledge. The other horse Asher and Percy rode upon seemed to follow the other as it went down toward the ground and scooped up some of the snow on its wings, making the feather tips wet. The caked snow broke off into powder as the wind brushed through their feathers. They seemed to enjoy the coolness of the snow as the wind always seemed to understand the way and lead travelers. It blew in the direction that they were meant to go. It always seemed to be that way. Keeper held her hand out as she felt its coolness. Her eyes focused on the top peak of the mountain. She could feel a difference in the air so high up, almost in a way that cleared her mind and made her think better. A thought of hope filled Keeper as she continued to look around and see how far they had come.

The horses began to flap their wings at a quicker pace as their breath could be heard. As they tried their best in order to rise above the mountain, they moved almost gently. They were gentle creatures of the air meant to soar in the sky and graze in the green fields where yellow daisies and dandelions grew. The fact that these creatures could be found in a cave chained up was nearly unfathomable. The Pursuer used horses such as these to drive his cart to the Forlorn Isle. These horses might have been hidden from the Pursuer's grip.

The reason for them being there was still unknown, but there were signs that their steps were being carefully guided. Whether the guidance was from the Holy One himself or he used people who followed him, there seemed to be a plan.

The blizzard-like snow flurries became quite thick. The group could not see where they went, but somehow they believed in the direction the horse took them, even if they could only see the white reflection of the snow.

They knew that they had gone over the mountain peak when they began to see darker shades of the Dark Range ahead of them. The snow created a portrait of white specks against the darker landscape. The snow continued to come down thickly as they flew and it began to stick to their hair and clothes. After a minute, the temperature drastically changed as rock underneath them began to appear, the snow melted on the other side of the mountain, and the valleys sloped downward, attached to other mountains rising up. These mountains looked darker as if they were made of amber stones. A heat wave warmed their previously chilled bones. The jagged rocks radiated as though something boiled from underneath. The horses flapped as if they tried to stay away from this heat. They flew too close to the sun, but in this case it was covered by darker clouds so that the only fear was the heat coming up from the ground that could harm their wings.

The mountains continued to pass underneath them as each seemed to grow as a long shadow from the sunshine.

From up ahead something orange and golden sparked as it gushed up from inside a mountain. The horses flew closer to an open top of a peak and almost got hit by the spray of lava as the force built up from underneath. The heat could be felt passing close. The craters of lava opened up different mountain peaks so that the boiling heat made them afraid of more spewing lava to scorch the horses' wings. They did not like the heat and may have desired to be back in the cold. The snow on their wing tips could have kept the flying horses cool from this bubbling heat.

The horses seemed to be talented at dodging the lava and did not need much leading. They seemed quite independent on their own.

"I didn't know that the Dark Range had volcanoes," Keeper remarked upon seeing the lava coming out of the mountains.

The green eyes of the flying horses flashed at the sight of the heat of the lava and its cooling before the lava reached the lower recesses at the base of the mountain. They began to flap higher away from the spurts. The air began to again drop in temperature. The flying horses tilted their heads upward and their wings pumped, pushing past thin clouds that began to thicken as they plunged upward. The white moisture blinded their eyes as they passed through. Going up higher, they all at once broke from the gray powdery clouds into bright open daylight of the sun above the clouds.

All who rode on horseback blinked their eyes for a moment at the bright light of the sun filling their being. They felt as though they had risen above the darkness from below them in a moment of serenity. They continued flying through billowing clouds as they weaved and flew the relative direction of the Dark Forest and Captavia. From above one could see many miles ahead, with the occasional cloud that they passed through. The air seemed light and the horses seemed to enjoy the coolness.

One could see the clouds that continued to swirl increasingly.

Keeper's eyes grew wider as she saw the mist rise up as she put her hand through the moisture. Asher's mind went to the thought of Cephas and if he could see him from this height. If he had not been captured by the Pursuer he may have been wandering around somewhere, but he had no idea. By the way that the Pursuer had been talking, it seemed as though he had been captured. Asher honestly did not know whether Cephas was alive, but if he was, Asher wished that he would not be in the Forlorn Isle or even Captavia.

Asher looked up and across to the other horse carrying Keeper and Gabriel. He was imagining how he could keep his secrets hidden forever. Even in this serene moment he could not shake it off. Most of all he was afraid that his Cabin Boy may be lost because of their change of course. A sort of darkness hung over him as if the clouds came around him, creating a gray filter over his vision.

Keeper at the same moment could feel that the Holy One felt closer just like the wind that came to seek his face. The sun grew closer and Keeper reached out one of her hands toward the light. Though she had only seen the Holy One in visions and once in real life, she knew that he still was close. She could see a vision of him calling to arms those who were willing to fight. Though only being in her mind, she could see all her party with them and more called out to fight in some physical battle.

Above that she could see his loving gaze as he called

her to himself from the first day she met him. Though for most of the time she felt fearful of what the Pursuer could do to hurt her. Despite this, she could see how much the Holy One had been there helping them. All the different events took place in order to get this far. The riddle on the wall, the boat placed in the cavern at the edge of the river, the tree beside the river, the horses inside of the cave in the mountains, and the sword found on the wall. They all seem to be placed there for a reason.

Chapter 20

Keeper came from the other room in the house of her heart. She stepped into the field outside of the house. She deeply felt the fear she had been sensing about the chains on Asher. She had doubts in her mind because she thought that he had been one of them, walking in truth.

The Holy One handed her the sword that had been found on the wall of the cave as she had seen it during the day. It glowed brightly with the clear blue mist from inside.

The Holy One said, "My precious daughter, I am with you. I am here. Please trust me, know I am with you.

"You have a lot to learn. Give all your hopes and anxieties to me. I will lead you if you follow. I will help you if you are having a hard time. I will bless you if you follow my commandments and make me first. You need to love me first. Let me be more important than other things in your life. Give yourself to me. Let me use you to do great things. I will help you.

"For as high as the heavens are above the Earth, so great is my love and kindness for those who fear me. As far as the east is from the west, so far have I removed your transgressions from you.

"Just as a father has compassion on his children, so the Lord has compassion on those who fear him.

"But the loving-kindness of the Lord is from everlasting to everlasting on those who fear Him. And his righteousness to children's children."

"I definitely have a lot of fear." Keeper replied.

The Holy One corrected her and let her know something important.

"It is different from the fear that comes when you are scared because the Holy One has not given us a spirit of fear but of power and of love and of sound mind." He paused and added. "Perfect love casts out fear."

Keeper straightened up and felt a glimmer of hope creep in.

"We can talk about it." The Holy One's words were sure and steady as he saw that Keeper experienced some difficult situations. He extended a hand and allowed her to hold it as she talked.

"I just feel that the darkness of the Pursuer tries to creep in as I am trying to follow you. With the realization of Asher having chains on his hands makes me doubt everything. I continue to watch him with the chains. Are we even safe if there are those that are not with us?"

"You know the answer. They are following their own path, but you can share the truth and help with life. I will help you to do the rest. Let's pray for him."

Keeper voiced a prayer, "I pray that he knows like the freedom of knowing the Holy One. Amen."

The Holy One replied with, "And this fear.... I will help you dispel it in yourself. It is time."

The Holy One handed her the sword that had been found on the wall of the cave that she had seen during the day and it glowed brightly with the clear blue mist from the inside of the sword wrapped in a cloth. It looked like the same sword that Keeper had seen the Holy One use to set her free when she first came to know him and her chains had fallen to the ground and they sparked brightly.

"You are giving this to me?"

The Holy One nodded before showing her some sideways swings.

Keeper unwrapped the cloth wound around the blade so that the strip fell off and the sword showed brightly.

The Holy One nodded, allowing his hand to rest upon Keeper's hands cusping the underside of the sword. It glowed and from the Holy One's view he could see Keeper's face light up.

"You know it is used in order to fight against fear or anything else that comes against it.

"We are destroying speculations and every lofty thing raised up against the knowledge of the Holy One, and we are taking every thought captive to the obedience of the Holy One."

"So this will help me do that?" Keeper asked.

"Yes, but your mind is a battlefield with what we put in it. For though we walk in the flesh, we do not war against the flesh, for the weapons of our warfare are not of the flesh, but divinely powerful for the destruction of strongholds."

Keeper pulled out her sword and began to swing, but in a haphazard type of way so that it fell to the ground.

The Holy One laughed playfully as he grabbed the metal hilt engraved with intricate swirls. He then handed it toward Keeper who then grabbed it and held it unmoving and steady.

"Let us first pretend I am representing one of those thoughts that might come to bombard your mind with fear. Just start saying things."

The Holy One removed an extra sword that hung from a belt. He extended his arm so that the sword was extended towards Keeper, who at the same time got in the correct position, ready to fight.

"Everything is going to fall apart." Keeper began

with the attack of words.

The Holy One responded, *"In him all things hold together."* At the same time, Keeper's sword was deflected with the power of this truth so she physically could not fight back against the truth of the Holy One.

"Can you think of one against it?" The Holy One asked.

Keeper thought, *"The Holy One makes everything work together for those who are called according to his purpose."*

It felt like the power of the phrase, *"everything is going to fall apart"* lost its control on her in reality.

"See, once you go against that thought with actual truth, you can actually fight it, beyond using a sword against flesh and blood. Try again."

"I cannot fight fear." Keeper confessed.

"This is going to be one you remember. 'For the Holy One has not given us a spirit of fear, but of power, love, a sound mind.'" Keeper's blade swung as she hit the Holy One's sword, but these lies, she told herself, did not match the truth.

"Fear the Holy One and serve him only. Do not fear for I am with you."

"Yes... Yes. You got it." The Holy One congratulated her on this small victory. Seemingly small, but impactfully large.

"Just know the same old recycled thoughts might come back, but if they do, you know what to do." The Holy One paused and wheeled around to the other side of the field where a great stronghold stood. *"Now it is time to storm a stronghold... But first you need the full armor."* The Holy One repeated. *"You need armor."*

"What? I thought I was protected." Keeper added this on.

"I know you only had offense, and not defense. Allow me to show you."

The Holy One stooped down to a cinched bag holding many materials. He lifted them out one by one.

"Do you trust me?" The Holy One asked Keeper as they stood in her dreams.

"You know I do."

Keeper could see the deep eyes of the Holy One. His eyes were deeper than the ocean and he was filled with the knowledge of everything. His long brown hair fell around his face and he had a beard that grew out. He wore a purple sash that hung across his white robe. He wore leather sandals. He had a look that made one know that he cared more than any other.

Keeper heard his words and he extended a hand, and she grabbed it. They turned in a circle as he showed her the field around them with trees in the distance. There were flowers underneath them. He looked back at the house. It was at the first time she had seen it, an old dilapidated house with broken shutters. He went up to the shutter and straightened it. He hammered a nail into the wood to keep it stable. He got a ladder and cleaned the outside, washing it thoroughly and painting it so that it looked new again.

Keeper looked on, sitting on the ground as he did this as she twirled a flower between her fingers. She knew it would take a moment of time.

She saw as he did everything in steps so that it was complete. He was washing away the old and making it new.

It now stood as a fixed up house with a certain sort of golden glow on the inside.

"You know this house represents your heart. And the

field is what represents your mind, where there are battles. Both are a part of you. You feel comfortable here and your mind is filled with these dreams of your Spirit Eyes. This is where you find me, but you will always have me inside of you."

"I feel you in me all the time despite what happens around me."

"Yes, I have chosen you for this mission. Those people are there and I gave you the need to help them from your dreams. I will continue to grow you in strength. Your heart has been made new. It is fixed and clean so that it is new. Your old broken down self that you did not know how to cure is redeemed. Do you see that there used to be only darkness and torment and now there is light?"

"Yes, there was complete darkness right before you met me. There was a deep depression and fight right before I found you, but it is when I lost myself that I found you. It was like I broke through a wall, that the light came in. I had to surrender myself to you, and there you were with your light. Your light enveloped me, and now I am in this beautiful place with you. Even though I struggle, I know you are with me. I know I am learning, but I know when I fail I can always come back to you."

"Yes, I am the one who will heal your hurts, supply all your needs, and keep you protected in my hands." The Holy One walked from the house and gave Keeper a hug. In this moment she knew this was all she needed. "You will learn to need me even more."

Inside of the room there seemed to be more items as though it had become more furnished. There still stood the velvety couch, the wardrobe with an oval mirror, the mahogany table with lion's feet, vanity with another mirror, and basin with a blue bird design.

The Holy Spirit came over, setting a bowl of fruit displayed on the center table. It contained a rustic red apple, a green pear, and dark purple grapes among the other items.

Keeper reached out and began to eat a piece of the grapes.

"Why are you decorating the room?" Keeper asked, referencing a decorative bowl. Keeper also looked up to see the Holy Spirit putting a clump of yellow daisy flowers into a vase with long green stems and dainty petals.

"In the middle you see," The Holy Spirit motioned with his shoulder, "those are the fruits of the Spirit."

"Awe, yes. How did they end up here?"

"Well, as you are abiding and as you are living in the Spirit they are able to grow. They are love, joy, peace, patience, kindness, goodness, faithfulness, and self-control."

"I do not feel like I have these." Keeper admitted, "I thought it took a lot in order to get them."

"Yes it does take a lot, but it has come through walking in the Spirit which has occurred through believing the truth. It comes through knowing the Spirit."

"Where is it? I cannot see it."

"You showed joy when you first came into the Holy One. You showed peace when you were able to say the truth. You are showing patience as you pray for others' freedom."

Chapter 21

The Holy One could see them on this journey and had been helping them. Even so, Keeper kept seeing visions of darkness and did not know what to think about that. This fear drew her away from the truth that she and Gabriel had discussed—that the Holy One was close and that she had drawn closer to him despite her feeling like she had not. The voice of the Holy One came through as hearing it clearly. "You are close to understanding my plan for your journey. Only do not fear the darkness, but instead keep looking ahead and trust in me to make everything right. I will do it through you, even despite you. I have given you the tools to do what I want to accomplish. Do not strive, only believe. No one is good, but in me and I will be that good in you."

Keeper replied with, "But Lord, what have I done to help you? I barely feel like I have gotten over the fear of the enemy, the Pursuer, and surely cannot find a way to overcome. How do I find a way to help those who are enslaved when I feel enslaved myself? I feel like sometimes I am chained up."

"Do you see what is strapped to your back?" Keeper could see that the Holy One was pointing in that direction with his arm.

Keeper answered, "Yes, I see. It is a sword we found in the cave in the mountain."

"Yes, but you do not understand all of it. You will soon learn of how it will help you fight as you want to run away from the flashing blade and what you had to face. You will now be able to face what you fear."

Keeper gained a bit of peace at hearing this and at once closed her eyes, continuing to remember the battlefield that was in her dreams.

"Yes, it will be soon that what you have seen will become reality," The Holy One assured Keeper as she opened her eyes once more. They were flying through a dense cloud. "Just be kind to others for you are not fighting against flesh and blood, but against principalities, against dark forces of the air." The Holy One continued to speak these words as Keeper looked over at Asher "Do not fear him, just show kindness. He is not your enemy, but may prove to be your best of friends."

Keeper nodded as she listened to the Holy One's voice speaking to her.

The final piece of information given was, "You cannot change him, you can only show him the way. Each one has a choice to make. All need freeing, and I am the one to do that. He does not need to get better, he just needs me."

Echoing Gabriel's voice about letting Asher find his own way still did not calm Keeper's fears of seeing the chains on his wrists, but now she knew she must just pray and ask the Holy One to do something. What if the chains were actually real and when he got back to the prison he would be dragged back to the place of bondage? She knew Asher had experienced bondage and asked why he wanted to go back. 'He does not know,' but understanding he did indeed want to go back.

Keeper decided to pray earnestly, "I do not understand, but I know you understand. Protect him, heal him, let him see the truth. Let me see the truth." Keeper sighed. "Holy One, just free my friend somehow and help me not to worry, but instead turn it into prayer for him. Save Asher." Keeper had her eyes closed, but opened them looking down and then back up to the sky. She knew that the Holy One would be present and she trusted him.

The clouds all around them thickened, "Concentrate on what I have to do and I will take care of the others." This was said to both Asher and Keeper. They were both trying to protect the others. Keeper could be captured with fear of this if she was not careful. Asher was sort of a rescue mission and so was Cephas the Cabin Boy to Asher. They were both precious to them so that they would do anything to save them.

A dark cloud began to blind their eyes as the flying horses began to descend down from the open sky into the dense gray clouds filled with moisture. They could not see much of where they flew until they cleared the underside of the clouds and began to see the landscape of the dark wood.

The horses descended from the sky and at once the group could see a small town and the horses went straight toward it. The Dark Forest could also be seen in front of them so that they knew they were close to the area at which the Captavia Prison was located and hidden.

The horses' wings beat harder as they began to steady themselves as they lowered toward the patches of grayish grass in the midst of areas of mud. The horses made their landing in a muddy area in which the mud climbed up the shins of the horses legs. They started lifting their hooves as they walked toward a clump of grass where Keeper and Gabriel slid off the backs of the horses who had their feet covered in mud.

"Eww, this is gross," Keeper exclaimed as she held the mane of the horse using one hand so that it would not fly away. Gabriel also realized this and put his hand over the horse's mane as well because he did not want the horses to escape. Asher and Percy had a harder time landing and the horse had thrown them off despite it seemingly looking like it was the more mild mannered type. The two were thrown into the mud face first. Asher lifted up from the goo with a face smothered in mud. Percy likewise raised up looking the same way while he was completely covered in mud. Seeing this site, Keeper and Gabriel both looked at each other and began to snicker under their breath, but it continued until it was rumbling and they held their sides.

"That is not funny. I cannot see." Asher shot back in response, but could understand how they were laughing at everything at his expense.

"Come to make a laughing stock of us, eh?" Percy said this with a slight smirking smile and all at once they all burst out into a bit of giggles as Percy and Asher raised up from the mud. They came sloshing through the thicker part of the wet dirt until they stepped onto the patch of grass where Keeper and Gabriel stood upon. Gabriel took a piece of his own tunic and handed it to Percy who used it to wipe off his face and tried to get most of the caked dirt off his arms.

Percy handed the piece to Asher who flipped it over to the clean side of the material and used it to wipe away the mud from his eyes since it was located dangerously close to blinding him. Covering his face with the tunic he was able to wipe away everything and started blinking. Handing the tunic back to Gabriel, he took it, whipping it through the air so that the mud came flying off. Some of it splattered Keeper as well as the others who are already covered.

The flying horse that Percy and Asher rode upon now ate some of the crabgrass that grew out of the area raised above the dirt. The plants did not seem to bother the horses. They seemed to enjoy it more than the moss found in the cave and even then it did not compare to the grass in the field of flowers that these types of horses were accustomed to eating.

Despite this, the horse seemed to be enjoying himself with what he had. Gabriel looked toward the darker wood, but somehow the sight of a quaint town surrounded by the landscape of the Dark Range and the Dark Forest still brought peace. It seemed vastly different from the emptiness of the town of Rockfirm whose center was darkened by the people's hearts, but around them were the deceptive fields of grass and lush forests with the Spirit Lake which flowed to make the river that they had traveled upon.

"I remember this town," Asher said, reminding the others that he had been this direction before.

Percy also agreed, putting his arm around Asher, "Aye, it seemed quite hospitable the last time we passed by it when we came this way." Their journey where they had come to travel, seemed to Gabriel and Keeper like an eternity. They had need of Asher and Percy there as much as they needed the protection from being together as a group.

Percy explained in detail, "We passed through that mountain range through a certain path, but was not formidable for what happened with the ledge giving way and finding the horses. I believe that our present journey has been much shorter than the one we went on to find you. Even so, we are all together and our numbers have helped us this far. I pray the people of Buffington treat us well which is what they are known for. They take many a runaway prisoner and give them shelter. You know that this place is protected by laws as a safe haven and the Pursuer is not allowed in. The Holy One himself has placed guards there as a protection. You know, Gabriel."

Gabriel nodded, "Yes, I have been stationed here many times in order to protect the citizens of the city from others who would want to harm them or cause these prisons to hurt. Even so, this is only a restful stop and they must find their way from this place to the Dark Range, and to the snow-capped mountains and into the forest with the Spirit Lake until they get to the road that leads to Rockfirm. The city of Rockfirm, though flawed, has been called the city of freedom or peace to those who only know it to be far away from the darkness of Captavia Prison and the enslavement of the Forlorn Isle. The problem is that they do not know Rockfirm is where most of enslavement begins. The problem is not the location."

"Then where should we take these prisoners once they have been freed?" Percy asked this critical question, putting together that this was the dilemma.

Gabriel continued by assuring Percy, "The problem is not the location, but the influence that the Pursuer has over their minds. If they always return to the same ways or in this place that will destroy them, it is themselves that needs to be changed. See that Keeper was unable to be influenced by the Pursuer's Pullings because she was freed by the only one who can free one from their chains."

At this Asher shuddered for a moment and Gabriel saw that Asher became nervous at any mention of anything that was regarded as something related to captivity. Gabriel, who'd had a conversation with Keeper about Asher, was aware of this fact, but was wisely not willing to let that show. Asher still did not know of the chains, though they seemed to weigh him down. Gabriel now pointed to the sword on Keeper's back. "That will be a help, but never mind, the people will tell us more. Let us now go into the city."

The others each grabbed the mane of the horse that they had flown on. The slower horse felt stubborn when they tried pulling him away from his meal. Gabriel continued, "The mind is pulled because they are enslaved; it may be invisible to their sight, but with the Spirit Sword they are freed. What they are oblivious of and need to be freed of only works on those who are willing to be set free. The power does not work on those who oppose it."

The group walked through areas with mud and also areas of the clumped crabgrass.

"Maybe this is the reason that we have come," Percy said, and Asher knew it to be right. There was some reason why the Pursuer did not want them to come this way. Asher knew that the Pursuer would be furious and threaten to hurt Cephas so that he would never be found.

Asher knew he could not risk it, but accepted that this was the direction that they should go.

Percy still held onto the mane of the horse and gestured for Asher to help as well. The group led the horses over the areas where the grass grew in order to keep from treading through the goo.

In a moment, the horses broke loose and began flapping their wings as they made their way back into the sky. There was not much resisting them because the members knew they were wild and needed to be free.

"Come on dear chap," Percy slapped Asher on the back like he had once done as they both looked into the sky, "Here we go on the next part of our adventure together."

Asher grit his teeth but then relaxed, but this feeling of calm did not stay long so that it at once became enveloped with fear. As though knowing what Asher was thinking, Percy pushed him along, as he walked stiffly, but ended up walking by himself in strides.

They laughed and claimed, "You are kidding, but that will not be a problem, since there is much more to come."

They made their way over the clumps until they found that they stood on a steady bit of ground. It was as though they were protected by a ring of good hope since there was green grass surrounding the town. For a moment, if they only saw this one area they would think this town to be located in another area, even a city that could be located near Rockfirm, instead of near the Dark Forest. Buffington just seemed like that sunshine ironically smiled at the darkness all around.

Coming up to the gate of the city, two guards stood to keep a watch. The Spirit Keeper of the town stood there, for each of the cities needed someone in which to watch and see far off for intruders. With their great insight, they would be able to see what would happen. This is why their great gift was important as a Spirit Keeper so they anticipated what would happen. Someday they all would know who were the true Spirit Keepers when they said something that would happen and it turned out to be the way they said it would be.

Looking up at her fellow Spirit Keepers, Keeper began to remember how she had put the position of her station of Spirit Keeper in the hands of the one she was able to train. He already possessed the ability, and was available and easily trained. The Spirit Keeper stood at the top of the wall and two guards stood at the base of the doors.

In a memory Keeper could see as she pointed out toward the world outside of Rockfirm saying, "You will be able to see what will happen next, even if it is in a dream."

Chapter 22

Through the darkness, rumbling could be heard in the streets of Rockfirm. The watch had retired until the morning light and in the town could be heard the faint rustling of the winds through the streets.

The rider on a carriage with a hood drooped over his head stepped into the inn as he let the helper take the horses so they were tied up to a post on the side of the inn.

"Where are the attendants?" The Pursuer sneered at the lack of help he received. Going into the bright light of the tavern, it continued to prove painful. The Porter stood at the front of the open lobby as his eyes once again turned into the size of saucers. Sitting in one of the first seats, sipping some beverage, both Messenger and the Mayor who had been talking, raised their heads to see the Pursuer enter the tavern as he had the first time they had seen him. Both of them stood simultaneously so that it seemed as if instead of having a good time at the inn they actually were waiting to see if the Pursuer would come back. In actuality, they were right and he did as he came for another trip for those willing to follow him.

As they got close to the Pursuer, he extended an arm to keep them away so that they backed into their seats that they had a few moments before occupied. The Pursuer lowered himself into one of the seats at the table and stared intently, waiting for the Mayor to speak. The darkened hood over his face was positioned to hide any emotions that the Pursuer had displayed on his face.

"Have you heard anything about where the Spirit Keeper may be located?" The Mayor tried to sound firm while also having the feeling of timidity.

"I have heard that they are in Buffington," The

Pursuer sneered. "I have one of which I have swayed named Asher who is with them. Asher, who I specifically told to go straight to the Forlorn Isle, has made his way into Buffington and toward Captavia. Directly opposite of what I instructed him." The hissing sound of his tongue intensified.

"I have not heard of any whereabouts." The Mayor was truthful. He continued to aid the Pursuer even if he did not know of where the Spirit Keeper was located. The Mayor knew he felt too stuck to go back now and the fear of the Pursuer, though he would not admit it, pushed him onward. The Spirit Keeper needed to be stopped.

"And your help to me is waning. You would not be a help if it was not for your vision." The Pursuer said this and watched as the Mayor's gaze glazed over, trying to come up with something of aid.

The Mayor was having a vision of bubbles as they popped and floated before his eyes and of a city with walls that rose and a door being barged opened. "Hmm," He trailed off, "You know the city of Buffington is a city protected by laws. If you were able to attack that city then, there would be no protection."

"Yes, and if they are in Buffington they will be on the inside."

"The only way to attack…" The Mayor continued.

"Yesss," The Pursuer's hissing strengthened. "I will force Asher to open up the city from the inside so that Buffington will be taken down." The Pursuer said this as he left abruptly from the building, with his cape behind him. The Mayor and Messenger watched as he left.

"I wonder what all he is going to do." Messenger inquired.

The Mayor stated his thoughts of what he felt, "Yes, I wonder what will happen next. It cannot be too bad, can it?"

Chapter 23

The city seemed bustling with life as the group came to the gate. The guards came up to the group and with a firm voice one asked, "What business do you have in Buffington?"

Percy answered for the rest of the group, "We have traveled through this town right after returning from Captavia."

Keeper looked at Percy, wondering why he mentioned this sensitive topic. She was surprised that he was willing to mention that they had one from Captavia since anyone could be hearing. Despite this, Percy seemed sure in his words.

The guard stiffened up hearing the statement, but allowed himself to be calmed. "Yes, this is a place for those who are wanting to be safe from Captavia and the Pursuer. This city is always guarded. Please, come inside."

It only took a short moment for the guard to shout out to the gatekeeper and for the doors of the city to be opened. It felt strange that the mention of Captavia was the hidden phrase to get into the city. Anyone could say they came from Captavia, even those who controlled Captavia Prison. It honestly felt unsafe to Keeper, but she knew to trust the advice of the others who had been here before. The town seemed too close to Captavia to even feel safe. She could see from her first sight of the town that it seemed quaint and undaunting. From a Spirit Keeper's standpoint, who would watch for danger at the top of the wall, Keeper could see that this place could get attacked extremely easily and might be able to harbor those that they tried to protect. Keeper felt surprised that it had lasted this long.

Keeper's thoughts continued, 'We really need to get

the captives from Captavia back to Rockfirm, where at least they are far away from danger.' Keeper did not realize that the leader of Rockfirm aided the Pursuer.

The gates opened and the group of travelers walked through. They came down the street and Keeper noticed vendors that sold goods of many kinds on the side of the street. They could hear the voices of the vendors shouting over each other which sounded like Percy had displayed while he slept. The spices smelled fragrant and piles of fruit in one of the stands made them feel hungry. Keeper went up to the vendor, producing a coin in order to pay for the item, but a hand clasped onto the top of hers.

"You do not need to do that." There stood a cheery looking fellow who looked quite round and dressed in vibrant colors.

Keeper looked at the man and asked simply, "Why is that?"

"Well for one, you look like someone who is famished and two," he stopped for a moment adding a flourish to the movement of his hand, "I would like to invite your group of travelers to my house to eat. Besides..." he looked over at the upheaval of Asher and Percy's muddy attire. "They look like they need a bath and a fresh set of clothes."

"I heard that," Asher came closer to reply to the jolly figure with a teasing tone.

"Well," Keeper looked around to the other members, seeing what they would say. Both Percy and Asher nodded despite the round figure's obvious jab at their unkempt appearance.

Gabriel spoke first, "Yes, I think that will be a wonderful gift to us. Thank you for being a blessing."

The man blushed at the kind words. "Well, know that I help people and especially travelers in any way that I can.

It is the only way to protect those who have come from Captavia. Anyway," he said with another flick of his wrist. "Let me lead the way to my home where you can get washed up and fed. Some of you definitely need it." He looked back over at Percy and Asher.

"Hey—" Asher protested.

Keeper retracted the money that she had a few moments before held out for the vendor into her pocket since they would be eating at this man's house.

"What is your name?" Keeper asked.

"My name is Frederick. You will soon meet the rest of my family. They are always eager to have company." The man said this, but he eyed the sword on Keeper's back.

Keeper continued to follow the group as Frederick brought them to an open area in the middle of the village. All around them were streamers that hung up from beams erected as though they were temporary. The decorations caused Keeper to ask the question, "What are all the streamers for exactly?"

"Oh," the man answered, looking around at the display of colors. "That is to celebrate the peace that this town has had for these many years. There are many who would want to take the freedom that is our lives. We made this place a safe haven, even protected by law. For almost a week each year we gather each night to come together and to really experience some fun."

Walking through the center of the village, the man's home was on the side of the open area. It was a small home with a thatched roof and colorful shutters. There also stood ceramic pots with bedded plants near the door.

246

"Welcome to my home," the stout man said, motioning toward the building. "There's sure to be a meal on the table when you come in, since my wife is expecting to cook for the festival."

The group followed as the man opened up the front of his store with their house in the back. They were greeted almost immediately with the sounds of children laughing and suddenly they felt small arms giving them a hug on the level of their knees. Keeper looked down to see a set of twins, one a girl and another a boy.

"These are my little troublemakers," the man said. "Their names are Phoebe and Freddie." The children raised their hands to wave at the group and then both ran away into the small living area with wooden chairs where they played with some blocks. "The boy is named after me," Frederick added. "And here is my beautiful wife, Adrianna." A woman in an apron came up and gave him a hug as he spoke.

"Welcome, guests are always invited in our home," Adrianna smiled brightly. "I never know when Fredrick is going to invite someone new." She laughed.

"Yes, absolutely my dear. You put up with me. The question is how do you do it?" Frederick laughed as well and they both hugged again.

"Easy, you just keep me on my toes." Adrianna turned toward the kitchen.

The group could smell a fragrant scent of something from a pot. Adrianna brought out the pot and in it was roast beef and potatoes. She spooned out the food on one large plate, drizzling gravy over the top of the dish.

Frederick went to grab a few chairs for the visitors and Asher and Percy went to help. All those who were present immediately felt their stomachs begin to growl. Gabriel and Keeper went into the living area and played blocks with the children. Asher and Percy washed up and came back in new clothes. The rest came back with the chairs and put them at the table. The children ran back from the living room into the kitchen. Their father helped each get into the gigantic chairs and push them up to the table. Once seated, the children each grabbed a utensil from each side of the plate and held them up in anticipation for the meal.

Frederick, the host, paused and explained, "In our house, we pray that the Holy One's will be done."

Frederick sat down at the head of the table and bowed his head and said a few words. The rest also followed suit.

"Thank you for all that we have here to eat, for those who have traveled far to come today, and for those who have prepared it. We are blessed by you, Holy One, and want to say our appreciation for every blessing that you give. Continue to guide us in your paths." He said these words in solemn reverence as everyone else listened on.

The meal was one that the travelers had waited for a while to eat. Adrianna continued to bring out more items of food that she had prepared. Rolls and the strawberry preserve to spread were presented as well as carrots to go on the side of the roast beef and potatoes. They poured milk into their cups so that each raised their head with a milk mustache. There could be heard laughter and many jokes were made by the group, especially from Percy who jovially talked with Frederick. In a break of the laughter, Frederick let out the words, "Let us raise a cup of... milk," He said while raising up his glass and the others did the same, "for having this group of travelers with us. It is always a great day when we are able to have travelers from Captavia staying among us."

"Well," Asher stated out loud in order to explain really what that phrase meant. "It is Percy and I who are the ones who have come from Captavia a few weeks ago. We did not stop at this town before since we were in a hurry to meet the others. We made our way through a pass that went straight through the mountains in order to meet the others. We were not able to go that way this time since the ledge broke away and we were stuck in a cave." Asher stopped and thought for a second. "But I wish that we had come this way and we would have enjoyed this well prepared food and such kind hosts."

"Yes, we do thank you for all of this. We have not had a good meal like this in a long while," Gabriel replied after he had just wiped his mouth with a soft beige napkin.

"Well, the night is not over yet. We still have the festivities tonight in the center of town and—" Frederick motioned to the outside.

"Dessert," the little girl Phoebe filled in the word that she desperately wanted to not be forgotten.

"That does come next," Adrianna nodded, rising up from her seat and going over to the counter she brought out some tarts shaped into stars with strawberry filling. She tilted the plate down toward the children and where they could take a few pieces. She placed the dish in the middle and the rest grabbed a few tarts.

There was a collective sigh at the taste of the tarts. "These are delicious," Percy replied for the group.

"Well, my wife does make the best tarts." Frederick looked up at his wife who smiled at the compliment.

Both the children went to play a few moments after they had finished their food. The rest finished their meal and took up the plates from the table into the kitchen and Keeper helped Adrianna with the rest of the cleaning as the rest stayed at the table talking to Frederick. After all the dishes were cleaned and put away, Keeper and Adrianna came to talk and joined in the conversation. They discussed how the people there in Buffington had all their homes open in order to keep those from Captavia. Frederick at once asked a question of how. "Why are the group of you going toward Captavia again?"

Without any hesitation, Gabriel spoke. "Well, it is because of the fact that we are going toward Captavia to help it. That is why we are in fact going back."

"Why?" Frederick looked confused and overly horrified. "You have already been freed from that place! Why would you go back?"

"We are not doing it in order to be captured again, but that we could at least get a group of people in order to free those who are in the Forlorn Isle," Percy explained.

The man's eyes went wide, "That horrid place...that place shades in comparison to Captavia where those who have rebelled against this type of captivity and have their own mind, but are still stuck in their own ways to get out. In comparison, the Forlorn Isle is where the Pursuer takes those who are pulled and already entrapped in their minds. Only those who know that the Holy One is their helper and the one who can free them will be able to be freed from their own ways. How do you presume to free them when their minds are already bent toward that darkness?"

Percy answered, "There is a system of correspondence that I had been a part of for many years who are responsible for getting Asher here out of its clutches," Percy put a hand on Asher's shoulder and Asher visibly seemed to flinch.

"Yes, they have worked closely with us for many years in order to get them safely to this city, but there is only so much you can do. Those in Captavia are willing to escape while those in the Forlorn Isle have not desired to get out." Frederick tilted his hand and Percy could see the ring with a signet engraved as though the shape of a chain went across his finger that represented one who was in the League. "You know there are many of us who are against the way that the Pursuer tries to take over people's minds and keep them from freedom. Many have tried in order to undo the chains that bind these people. We are all susceptible to his ways," He looked at Asher as though he saw the invisible chains that he carried and the tone of his voice shifted. "All of us." He continued explaining exactly what he meant. "Everyone is prone, but it is those who are already going toward darkness that will eventually end up there. It will take something powerful in order to free them, even the Holy One himself. There is none righteous, not one." Frederick quoted a bit of the Holy One's book.

For a moment he looked back at the sword that Keeper held on her back and she could see his interest, "Where did you get that sword?"

Keeper answered with the explanation, "I found it hanging on a wall by a rope in the cave that we found on the side of the snowy mountain."

Frederick made a sound like, "Uhmm" as though he was thinking, but he said not a word. The group realized that it had gotten dark since they had their conversation about Captavia and their mission in order to get to the Forlorn Isle. For some reason, there could be seen a light from the outside that glowed on Frederick's face as he mentioned the name of the Holy One.

"It is time," he said while standing up and pushing his chair in. "Those of the town have started the bonfire in order to light up the middle of the town. I have only just seen it being lit from the window. Shall we go?" The stout man went toward the door and his two children came running in that direction with their mother following behind. The band of travelers came behind them, following Frederick. As they came out into the street there was the sound of a flute and even a string instrument as several individuals began to dance around in circles. The fire stood before them in a high blaze so that it rose up towering above their heads and made the darkness look like the light of the day.

Keeper and Gabriel joined a circle where most of the members held tambourines and the jingling of the tin discs vibrated as they tapped the leather surface. Grabbing each other's hand, both skipped in the circle as they followed the rhythm that those playing the tambourines played out. Those dancing added the words of a cheery type of tune.

"Bless, Bless, Oh we give thanks to you
For Holy One your words are true.
You free the captive,
You break their chains,
You give them new life,
You provide safety,
You give yourself.
Hope, Hope, for we trust in you."

Keeper could tell that many among them were those who had been freed from Captavia. It may have been through the organization of the League that Percy called his own. With the work of him and Frederick many could come to safety, but somehow that was not enough. There still hung in the air some type of fear that in a moment that those who supposedly became safe as they entered the gates of Buffington would no longer feel safe. Keeper's mind reverted to the sword that she carried on her back and wondered how it would allow them to save those in Captavia and eventually those in the Forlorn Isle. There had been many of the group that Percy had been a part of that tried to free those from Captavia. How would one sword make the difference?

As the music began to shift into a more melodic type, the flute became louder as it sang out for the many dancers. Keeper looked over to see that Percy had joined a group of individuals who sat near the fire and Keeper could hear his uplifted voice as he talked with those much like him who desired the freedom of others as a calling and one to continue to work toward. There seemed to be many among this group of villagers that seemed much like the group that Keeper had traveled with already. So many that seemed willing to go against the Pursuer and against what he could do to their minds to keep them captive.

She sadly looked over to see Asher over on the side of the ring of dancers sitting and staring at all those moving to the music without feeling like he could be a part of any of it—feeling like he was outside of this type of world and almost in a way against it because of the way he had chosen. He could feel that Pursuer talked to him, "Go from here, this place is horrid. You have disobeyed my command that you go to the Forlorn Isle." Asher still felt unsure of the real reason why the Purser did not want him to go in this way, but he felt like he began to understand. "See what the Keeper sees in her mind's eye." Asher could see that Keeper came toward him feeling sorrow for his isolation from the rest of those celebrating.

"Are you doing alright, Asher?" Keeper's words reflected that instead of much of the judgment or mistrust that she had first experienced had become replaced with a feeling of wanting to help him. In what way, Keeper had not the knowledge of how. "I know you may not be one to dance with a group of people, but it is always good to talk to someone."

"You do not have to worry about me. I am doing alright. Sometimes I enjoy being by myself and not with others," Asher reflected.

"Well, I hope that I can be that person to talk to. Even if it is unwanted." Keeper felt careful with the way she talked to Asher, not wanting to be invasive of his own personal boundaries and what he felt comfortable talking about.

Suddenly as though changing what he talked about into something else all together. "I know you have talked about the dreams you have where you can see things. What do you see?" Keeper's eyebrows raised and wondered why he suddenly thought of this subject.

"Yes, I do have these dreams quite often. They are sometimes about something in the future. Something that I need to see. Especially for a Spirit Keeper who keeps watch over a city, they need a way in which to anticipate if there is danger to come. Few have the true ability from birth; I have only met one in which I would trust my post to since they had the same ability. Others who are not born with this may acquire it in other ways." Keeper tried to give an explanation of really what a Spirit Keeper could do, but trying not to point any negativity toward Asher in any way. Despite her being sensitive, Asher continued to feel offended at this as though he had been called out. "You have got to stop doing that." Keeper looked at Asher seriously.

"What am I doing?" Asher's voice showed his confusion.

"You are taking everything personally so that every mention of any negative thing makes you seem fidgety as though you have done something wrong. Whether you have done something wrong or not, you have to understand that the Holy One has more forgiveness than that and we can all come back."

"So you are saying that I am too sensitive?" Asher asked to clarify.

"That is kind of what I am saying. You are not responsible for everything wrong with the world. There are many players that are a part of all that is happening. We all have the ability to choose our own way."

"Well, you have got to stop getting into my business." Asher seemed frustrated and Keeper saw this clearly.

254

"Yes, I will try my best to leave you alone. I do feel concern for others for certain reasons." Keeper did admit to this fact without going into detail.

"You have nothing to concern yourself about and you never answered me." Asher's voice trailed and he seemed impatient.

"Oh, I never answered you. Was it on 'what did I dream?'" Asher nodded in order to move the conversation along as Keeper answered back. "Well, that seems a bit invasive, but I guess I trust you." Between her words, Keeper asked herself, *'Can I really trust him?'* Despite this hesitation that she felt, she continued on.

"Well, I keep seeing a battle scene where I am fighting against an enemy and there is always this certain fear that comes over me. There are yet other dreams that I see other things." Keeper quieted herself before she said any more and looked away so that Asher could not read her face. She did manage to say something else, "Did you have a similar dream?"

Asher looked downward and looked back up and scared himself by admitting, "Yes, I did have a dream. I remember being on the battlefield. I saw El Roi and he gave me a sword to fight. It reminds me of the sword that you were given." Asher turned again and admitted, "I am sorry for getting upset. I felt verbally attacked."

"Why did you seem so upset in the dream?" Keeper felt concerned.

Asher's face went hot as his anger rose up. "I felt like El Roi was going against me, as well as you, Keeper."

Seeing his expression, Keeper backed away, allowing him to cool off. "Well, understand no one is saying anything against you which you must believe. All of us are here together on this journey." Remembering the advice that Gabriel had given to her about the way she should treat

Asher, she decided to help him by not being too hard on him. She would do this while also being truthful. "I am concerned for you though. I have nowhere to judge, but there is a certain darkness that seems to be surrounding you in these visions I have."

Asher tensed up again.

Keeper looked at Asher seriously, and he tilted his head. They said all that needed to be. After she had talked to him, she felt a weight fall off.

"I am just concerned for Cephas," This saying was the first bit of honesty that came from Asher's mouth.

"I am concerned for Cephas as well. I pray that we find him," Keeper paused, "Asher, I see that you have these… chains on your arm."

Asher was at once horrified at the thought, "I…do not. Why would I have those? It would mean…"

Keeper was not about to fill in the blank of what she thought he would say. "It does not matter the reason. They just need to come off. If you will let the Holy One help you." Keeper pulled out the sword, similar to the one that the Holy One had carried.

"Keeper, just no. I do not need them to come off. I am one of you. I do not have chains. Why would I even be on this mission?"

"It is because you are called. We are all called. We are all flawed, but that is why we need help."

"I am free, Keeper. I can assure you." He winced.

"Alright, I will leave you alone." Keeper said with sadness in her heart, putting the sword back into its sheath and walking in the direction toward Frederick.

"Is your friend Asher alright? He seemed down."

Frederick inquired after Asher.

"Yes… I think he will be alright." Keeper sighed and sunk down into a seat.

"I saw you pull out that sword. You know it is meant for breaking strongholds and bondages. Although I bet you do not know a lot about it."

Keeper nodded and Frederick continued.

"This sword is made out of crystal found in deep caverns. Its form is transparent so that one can know that there is something inside of it. In fact, the power of the Holy One is inside of it."

"Is that how we were able to cut off those chains on the flying horses in the cavern?"

"Oh, its power is what allows you the ability to even do that compared to a regular sword one would smelt."

"So, if it is made of crystal, how is it made?"

"I saw one before... I saw one carry it through this town."

Keeper grabbed the hilt of the sword that hung from the ropes tying the sheath on her back so that it came before her and Frederick's eyes. The orange flecks of the flames in the center of the town reflected off the clear blue facets of the sword. Keeper could see straight through.

"Do you see?" Fedrick paused and looked from the sword to Keeper's face, "There seems to be something inside of it." Frederick looked at the sword again. "This sword must have been given to that individual by the Holy One himself."

"How is that possible?" Keeper seemed confused. "Did the Holy One physically give it to that person?"

"Yes, the Holy One must have known that they needed it. The person who carried it must have also known that you needed it, Keeper." Frederick's eyes never left the sight of the crystal facets as they glinted with the orange tint of the fire.

"I do not understand all that it can do," Keeper replied, her voice quivering.

"Neither do I," Frederick admitted honestly. "These types of things are extremely hidden until one starts to try it out. Have you used it for anything?"

"Yes, I used the sword in order to cut off the chains that held the two flying horses in the cave located in the mountain. It seemed our only way out. It also seems like whoever placed the sword there on the wall did it for that purpose."

"Well, it may be that they expected you would need the horses. Anyway, is there anything else?" Frederick truly tried to understand the properties of this sword.

"It started glowing." Keeper stated bluntly.

"Glow, eh, I wonder if that is part of the power of the Holy One. You know that chains are unable to be cut apart by a regular sword. Only know you must trust that power and, more importantly, the Holy One."

"That is true," Keeper agreed with the explanation of the sword. Keeper nodded and looked more closely at the blade.

"You know the chains that are in Forlorn Isle will be hard to break, and the Captavia yet harder. It is because of the amount of bondage, the amount that the Pursuer has control over their mind. You may be surprised that those in Captavia may be harder to free than those in the Forlorn Isle. They may yet know the Holy One, but have gone back to their old ways and their strength."

Keeper felt shocked. "I thought they would be the ones to help. Not many are freed and they continue in their own ways. I heard the Holy One say they are those better to be spit out."

"Well, I heard they are ones who have rebelled

against the Pursuer. Yes, it is because they know the Holy One is real, but they are not allowing themselves to be changed. There are many who have fallen in that way. It could be any one of you. Inside they are darkened, but on the outside they are whitewashed walls."

"So what am I to do?" Keeper inquired with a concerned tone.

"Use the sword to free them. Some may go with you after their chains fall off, some may stay, but you must give each a chance to that freedom. How can anyone be free unless one tells them? Yes, this sword gives freedom because the Holy One gives freedom... and good news."

Keeper thought of Asher and the chains that he carried. "Can I free one of my own with this sword?"

Frederick's brow furrowed and he looked past Keeper to the individual he assumed Keeper talked about.

"Him?" Frederick inquired and Keeper nodded.

"Yes."

"If you do, you must say it gracefully. He may not listen to you, but when he enters into these places, he will be in danger of being captured again."

Eyes widening, Keeper became concerned for the well-being of her friend.

"How about you?" Frederick inquired after Keeper.

"What about me?" Keeper felt uneasy with his tone.

"Do you feel like you have chains?" Keeper felt startled at the thought and looked away.

She answered with, "I... I don't know."

"Yes, you never know yourself, the chains you may carry. They are hard to see."

Keeper looked down and began to see the faintness of

her chains. "Can you see them?"

Frederick answered with a no and then continued. "If one is freed by the Holy One, they are free. It may feel like you're going back in your old ways, but those chains cannot come back. There are still struggles though."

"How did this happen?" Keepers concerned showed on her face.

"You must search your heart. Only you and the Holy One can understand that."

Keeper reflected on all the dreams she had that came before her face with this intense feeling of fear. She could feel that the Pursuer was after their group and that she would run away every time she saw his face. For some reason that did not feel like the reason why this occurred. As she thought about how she had mistrusted Asher and kept thinking negatively of him.

"I must talk to someone."

Keeper went back over to Asher, and she said was still concerned for him.

Keeper and Asher continued to talk as the fire began to dwindle and many of those who had laughed and talked went away and decided to sleep. Keeper rose up and looked at Asher.

"I need to tell you something."

"Yes, again. What is it?" Asher seemed serious.

"I am sorry. You may have not known this, but I have thought quite negatively of you."

"Why?" Asher said these words before he could reasonably think.

"I have seen chains around your hands," Keeper admitted truthfully.

Asher looked down at his hands and there could be seen fear in his expression.

"Again, why can I not see them?"

Keeper responded with the words, "I was told that only others could see them. Well... I needed to warn you that if you go back into Captavia with those chains, you may be in danger of being taken prisoner again."

Asher seemed impatient at Keepers words. "Do you not know that even going back there is a risk for me, chains or not?"

"Yes, but this sword is said to help those who have such chains." Keeper tried to offer a solution while saying it in a respectful way, showing a bit of the urgency.

Asher looked down and said in a low tone, "You do not understand what I am under."

"What are you under?" Keeper felt regretful that she had said anything.

Asher did not answer and turned away while thinking, 'If I did not do what I do, you and others would get hurt.'

"So, no?" Keeper said these words hesitantly.

"No, but I wish I could."

"Why can you not?" Keeper questioned.

"Those like me are not able to be helped. Like I said, you would not understand." After hearing this from Asher, Keeper backed away feeling as if he had placed a wall between her and him. The darkness grew cooler around her as she walked.

"We are sinners and we can all receive help. The Holy One loves us and extends forgiveness and freedom."

Keeper was quiet after this and Asher began walking away to the home of Frederick. Many of those who had been celebrating were now in their homes and several individuals with water began to put out the last bits of the fire as it burned away the stacks of logs that had been piled up to burn. Keeper could see a light in the house and could hear as Frederick laughed and the others conversed. As a result of the conversation, Asher stood up and came inside of the house, where in a corner Keeper could see that Asher sat away from those conversing about the events of the night. He seemed graven, and Keeper continued to worry for him. Despite this, she admitted that the conversation that she had with Asher had been one of the best since it had started out well, though it had ended poorly. In thinking about the conversation, she felt that the weight of those chains of being critical toward him became non-existent since she had said everything she could in order to help him. She felt concerned that Asher would be captured again for refusing to get help with removing his chains. She had tried her best and felt assured that the conversation was all she could do.

As Asher sat in the house, the thought of Keeper pointing out his chains increased the guilt that he felt of being involved with the Pursuer. He looked down as the others laughed about the events of the night.

Keeper looked over and prayed. Keeper was able to pray for Asher, "Holy One, please reveal yourself to Asher. He needs to know who you are and I know it is possible through you. Please give me the graceful words to say to encourage him because I know only you can change hearts."

Chapter 24

Asher Callaghan had not been aware of the weight of the chains that he carried, but it began to make sense. In his head, Asher could hear the voice of the Pursuer speaking to him, which had become a frightening occurrence to him, but what more could he do.

'You have not followed what I said, you were in the wrong place. You are still hanging by a string.' In his mind, Asher could see as the Pursuer showed him a vision of the Cephas' arm being grabbed as he was thrown into a cell. Asher could see the Cabin Boy's face as it looked toward him in desperation, but nothing Asher could do really seemed to help. Asher knew that the Pursuer still tried to control him, but his fear of losing Cephas forever still gave him the push to continue to follow the Pursuer.

'She is still dreaming about the battle that seems to have begun,' Asher mused.

'Yes, I will need to start to prepare for that. What does she know of what you are doing?'

'She only mentioned that I have changed and she sees only what she wants to see.'

'How do you know what she is saying is true? Is it true she is quite judgmental toward you?' The Pursuer's voice lightened, but lowered in the mention of Keeper.

'I am still not sure,' Asher explained while also seeming worried in the thought. 'But she has no idea of the plan that you are behind what has happened.'

'Good, but listen carefully, or things may be less than favorable. You should go into the cell that you once were a prisoner. You will find what you need. Let them go on, but you, follow what I am saying. Those in the prison will listen since I am helping you, understand?'

Asher sat quietly and could hear a deep slithering sound come from the Pursuer's tongue since Asher did not answer.

'Do you understand me?'

Asher directed himself toward the sound of the Pursuer's voice. Though he had not allowed Keeper to cut off his chains, he still felt as though the Pursuer had become demanding and controlling of him. How did he even know that the Pursuer even had the Cabin Boy captive? Becoming bold in a moment then feeling regret, Asher replied to the Pursuer talking through his mind. 'I do not want to go on with this.'

At this moment, he felt a certain darkness fall over the room. The group sat at the table so that some turned one to another as though they sensed something, "Did you feel something dark just came over the room, aye?" The attentive voice of Percy reflected the fear that had just come over the members of those present.

'You do not know what awaits or what you really deserve.' The hissing sound that the Pursuer made with letters of his tongue reminded Asher that the Pursuer still was a snake by nature. Being in such close proximity with him made Asher forget how dangerous the Pursuer actually could be.

'I will be free of you.' Asher replied hastily to the Pursuer.

Keeper walked into the room to feel the heaviness that changed the atmosphere which contrasted with the amiable time they seemed to have.

"Is everything okay?" Keeper said, asking those who sat around the table.

"What do you think?" Asher said, feeling as though he needed to cover up for the overall feeling of the room while being quite sensitive. The others still looked at Asher without knowing the reason.

Sensing the mood, Frederick stood up. "I think we are going to head to sleep. There are a few rooms where you can rest."

"Thank you," Gabriel answered with much appreciation. "You are a kind host."

"Anything for guests. Come with me." Frederick led the group to their rooms.

"Come with me, Keeper," Adrianna led Keeper to a room, and made a place on the floor. "You will not mind sleeping on the floor? We just do not have enough beds."

"This will do," Keeper replied, hugging Adrianna. "You and Frederick have been so kind in allowing us to stay here. In what way should we repay you?"

"Your presence is blessing enough." Adrianna had a gentle smile and the sweetness of one who seemed to understand how others felt. Keeper really appreciated all that she had done for them that night. Keeper smiled brightly at Adrianna.

"Well, have a good night." She walked away while holding a candle.

Keeper laid down on the soft mat that had been laid out and covered herself over with the blanket.

That night, Keeper had not dreamed something like she did then. The darkness continued to cover everything and she felt as her mind began to be pulled and influenced by something outward.

"You must allow me, the Pursuer, to come in by talking to the guards and the Spirit Keeper. Maybe by using the powers that I have given you, you will be able to divert them."

Asher heard this spoken to him just as he laid down that night. He knew that the Pursuer wanted him to be an aid in order to do what the Pursuer desired. He added, "And if you do not, your Cabin Boy may be lost to you forever."

The Pursuer waved the compass that Asher had given the Cabin Boy the last time on the boat. Asher had given Cephas a gold compass that could direct toward the north using the guidance of the stars. As one flipped it closed it was covered with some waves, carved into a repeated crescent pattern. Above it showed an array of stars. It was to help his way away from the Pursuer.

Asher reached out his hands in order to grab the item, but his hands fell through since he was only seeing the Pursuer in the image in his mind.

As Asher heard these words, he left the house of Frederick while the others slept.

Moving outside, Asher closed the door steadily without a creaking noise of its hinges.

He looked up to see the glowing moon as a ring of light surrounded its circle. In a few moments, wisps of gray clouds covered over the craters of the moon's surface, creating a dimly-lit sight before him.

The streets had been cleared of people who had been celebrating a few hours before that. They had danced and played instruments before the fire, but at that present moment there still stood embers as the charcoal began to diminish in its heat. Smoke still seemed to rise from the place in which it stood. Pieces of items that still needed to be disposed of were still scattered in areas. Asher bent down to pick up some and put them in a pile for someone to pick up later. Asher's feet shuffled quickly down the road, passing by many homes and still seeing the stalls where merchants had been selling items. Asher looked around to see if anyone remained present, but his hopes were correct. Since no one showed themselves, everyone seemed to be in deep slumber, getting ready to rise early to open up shops and go to their work, which seemed different than those in Rockfirm who stayed out all night doing twisted deeds.

Asher continued down the street, holding his arms because of the cool breeze and looking from one side to the other while looking to see if anyone would be there. None appeared.

'What should I do to divert them?' He thought this as he came closer to the gate in which the Spirit Keepers who guarded the city stood atop the wall. In his mind he could see that the guards' minds seemed nervous about something as though there could be a disturbance either around or inside the city. They may have thought this because there always were risks of letting those who did not belong into the gates. It always proved to be a fear of theirs. Asher saw this as he came near. He decided to start running up to the gate in frantic disarray.

"Please help, please help!" He made sure to emphasize his words without sounding loud and waking up the others in the town. Asher looked up at the guard standing on the wood platform of the wall.

"What is wrong? Is everything all right?" Their voice mirrored the urgent inflection of Asher's words.

"There...There...There is a disturbance deep inside the city. There were some people fighting. They were causing trouble." Asher bluffed since he needed something to say and did not know of what else to divert them.

"We will look into it," one of the guards said while looking at the other, "You stay here."

"You both will need to go." Asher seemed insistent on this point. "There are many who have started trouble, maybe even some from the outside." Asher emphasized the need for both of their assistance.

The guards could see the importance of his words and called down, "Can you watch from the wall and tell us if you see anything?"

"Yes, I can," Asher offered quickly and went up the wooden ladder, grabbing the smooth rungs on his way up to the platform. Asher at once took hold of the last bar and he lifted himself onto the wooden surface. The guards' faces at once became blank and unfeeling.

Asher had used the ability of the Pursuer to put them into a trance. This was used to see what Keeper was thinking, but now it did it automatically as if the Pursuer was controlling Asher. It was almost like the Pullings that the Pursuer would cause those in the city to be under.

Asher looked up to see what the power had really done and caught them as they stood up straight and then fell over to the ground. He went up close to them in order to make sure they were let down gently to the wooden platform.

Asher was not aware that this would be the reaction to the trance because of the Pullings that the Pursuer caused and fear gripped him as he saw their faces. The Pursuer would be soon coming and unbeknownst to Asher, this man would be the first to be taken away. Unknowing of this, Asher ran away after he had laid them on the wood. He then pushed around a wheel with pegs that carried a spool of chains. Asher could see that the chains attached to the door were underneath. In grabbing hold to the pegs he firmly used his weight to pull downwards so that the chain links began to become taunt. The doors of the gate began to open.

How he had seen the town of Buffington and smiled, but at this moment he felt as though he slowly allowed the enemy to snuff out the light of the fire that they had danced around in celebration of freedom. How ironic this moment truly felt. For when he believed he may be protecting another by following the Pursuer, he all at once endangered the freedom of those who stood protected and allowed the likelihood of being captured once more. He felt noble in protecting Cephas, but in fact always being under the power of the Pursuer was the truth. 'When will this be enough? What else will I do if I do not believe the Holy One is protecting my Cabin Boy? I believe I must save him myself.'

The chain links began becoming taunt as the spindle wheel began to wind itself completely. Both of the wooden doors clad with metal smelted pieces spread across the surface. The weight of the moving doors proved to be a two-person job, but Asher seemed able to do the work of both.

The opening became wider as light of the clear moon streamed into the street. Asher looked back to see if the guards had stirred. They had not and neither had any of the town, which Asher seemed scared about because of the creaking sound of the two large wooden doors. Winding up the chains on the spindle type wheel as far as they would go, Asher saw that the doors swung completely open. There then stood a deafening silence that permeated everything. He stood there and waited to see if the Pursuer would come in those doors. He felt frightened that he stood so near where the Pursuer would be present in only a few moments.

As he stood on the platform, the time slipped away so there seemed to be no sound of the carriage that carried the Pursuer and those who had been enslaved. With no sign and no sound of anything for a long while, Asher decided to move from this place that still created a great fear in him. He stepped over the tranced guards and Spirit Keeper lying on the wooden platform as he hung onto the rungs on the ladder down to the ground.

"The Pursuer should be here soon." He felt himself grow colder as he once again drew his leather sea coat closer around his arms. "It is night and there stands no one who will close the gate. I will rest until morning."

Asher's feet ran swiftly through the town, past the fragrant smelling stands of items closed for the night and through the square in which the people of Buffington celebrated their freedom of those from Captavia. Little did the city know that as Asher began to sleep inside of Frederick's home, the Pursuer had made his way into the safe city of Buffington with the doors of the town wide open.

Chapter 25

The Holy One stooped down to a cinched bag, holding many materials. He lifted them out one by one. He first retrieved a dark brown leather belt with a silver clasp. "The belt of truth," He repeated as he handed it to Keeper and she fastened it around her waist.

He then lifted out a solid breastplate that looked as though it could cover the front of a person, in defense. "The breastplate of righteousness." Keeper once again put it on, fastening the clasps that went around her back.

He held out some sandals that were made of leather straps wound around them. "Shoes of the preparation of the gospel of peace." Keeper was able to fit both of the shoes on her feet, strapping the leather pieces with a buckle. She moved her toes around, getting used to the new position.

The Holy One then pulled out a shield that looked like a rectangle, and engraved with etchings of metal. It gleamed brightly and he handed it to Keeper quickly, as a flaming arrow came and clashed up against it, barely missing Keeper's face. "The shield of faith with which you will be able to extinguish the flaming missiles of the evil one." Keeper looked to see that it had been shot from a stronghold across the field.

Keeper became hesitant and scared of the oncoming attack, but the Holy One steadied her with his words. "There are a few more items." He raised out a helmet in which the metal covered the top of the forehead solidly, and came down in a point as it covered Keeper's ears. Keeper slipped this over her head. "This is the helmet of salvation." Keeper felt secure. "And it has come through me." The Holy One pointed down at the sword Keeper carried, still glowing. "And that is a sword of the Spirit, which is the Word of God. Just like the scripture you have been learning to fight with." Keeper breathed deep as she knew she felt protected and ready for action, ready to fight.

The Holy One looked at her and said, "Now you are ready to start." He wheeled around from the direction of where the flaming arrow had flown from behind the stronghold's stone walls.

The Holy One repeated, "Put on the full armor of the Holy One, that you may be able to stand firm against the schemes of the devil." The Holy One then remarked, "It is time to tear down a stronghold." The Holy One said this while also retrieving some armor and put it on himself. With the sword positioned downward and his shield positioned over his face, he and Keeper ran across the field of growing grass as it led to the tall stronghold, built with many centuries on the corners, stationed at the top of the wall.

"Is this real?" Keeper asked, trying to make sense of the reality of what they were doing.

"Yes, it is. What you see in reality is not all there is," The Holy One replied.

"For a struggle is not against flesh and blood, but against the rulers, against the powers, against the world forces of darkness, against the spiritual forces of wickedness in the heavenly places. That is just as real and deadly and must be taken down. Follow me."

The Holy One, knowing that they ran in the open field with no defenses, kept his shield up, instructing Keeper to do *the same. The flaming arrows then came again. "It is for the destruction of strongholds."*

Keeper began to read the scroll that rolled out before her, placed on a dark wooden table.

She read, "A man is not justified by the works of the law but through faith in the Holy One, even we have believed in the Holy One, that we may be justified by faith in the Holy One and not by the works of the law; since by the works of the law still no flesh be justified.

"Did you receive the Spirit by the works of the law, or by hearing with faith? And are you so foolish? Having begun by the Spirit, are now being perfected by the flesh? Does he then, who provides you with the Spirit and works miracles among you do it by the works of the law, or by hearing with faith?"

Keeper stared at the passage and tried to understand what it meant. She understood about not receiving the Spirit by her works. Keeper asked the Holy Spirit, "How is the Spirit perfected?" The Holy One saw what Keeper was reading and answered, "It comes through faith that you receive the Holy Spirit. You started by faith and so do not think you can now live on your own. It is not of works of the law, but through faith.

"Even so Abraham believed the Holy One and it was reckoned to him as righteousness.

"For as many as are of the works of the law are under a curse; for it is written, 'cursed is everyone who does not abide by all things written in the book of the law, to perform them.'

"Now that no one is justified by the law before the

Holy One is evident for, 'the righteous shall live by faith.'"

So Keeper asked more deeply, "With faith we are made righteous? Wow, I did not realize that living under the law is living under a curse."

"Yes, you are made righteous through this faith you have and it is the old way you can live. And yes, you are cursed when you live under the law and underneath human's own works to be righteous. It fails. Only he is righteous, so as we come to him we know we are dependent on his grace."
"Yes, grace."
The Holy Spirit continued, "Receiving what you do not deserve. You do not deserve this freedom, but he has sacrificed himself to give it to you. Since you cannot become righteous through the works of the law you are depending on the grace of the Holy One. Still, you should not mistreat the grace of the Holy One through doing your own way, but trust and know it is through faith that you were saved by the Holy One and it is through faith that you will continue to be sanctified and made more like the Holy One.
"The chains will come off in faith."

The room in which Keeper stood seemed to expand with items displayed about. In a corner there stood a box-shaped wooden piano. The black and white keys twinkled under the fingers of the Holy Spirit who began to play a melodic song as one heard in a symphony. It was not accompanied by any words, but Keeper felt as though they began to well up from inside of her.

"Worthy is the one who saves,
274

Who tears down the enemies' stronghold,
Who will give us freedom,
Who has made my heart to sing,
Who has made a way through the sea,
Who has set my heart ablaze with hope,
Who has made me grow strong in the vine,
Who has crowned me with loving kindness,
Who has shielded me with the full armor,
Who has helped me to bear fruit.
Who has given me grace when I did not deserve it.
Who has lavished me with his peace,
Who has become my redeemer and Lord.
Who is giving me the helper as an assurance.
Who is forgiven me from the east to the west,
Who has called me by name.
Who has called me to be set apart.
Who has destined good plans for me,
Who has given me hope when I am helpless,
Who has not given me a spirit of fear, but of power.

Make melody in your heart to the Lord." Keeper
could hear these words in her mind.

As the song continued, the Holy Spirit stopped the
music, allowing Keeper to sit down on the seat playing a
song coming straight from the heart. "Let's hear you play,"
the Holy Spirit prompted...
"Turn down doubt, fear, strongholds, lies, anxiety,
loathing."
It moved out from the door frame, the music that
wafted out.

With the Spirit Sword, it glowed as Keeper held it out and she and the Holy One began to run quickly toward the stronghold.

The fiery arrows flew down as Keeper raised her shield in defense.

"I have a plan. Follow me." The Holy One drew close to the gates, sealed tightly and the arrows stuck solidly into the wood of their shields so that they could feel the heat of flames.

The Holy One gathered his men against the enemy. A battering ram was put up to the wall by the Holy One's men. The sound was deafening as they rammed it against the door. Arrows came from inside the stronghold, threatening to injure them. No one was injured, but the volley continued and the ram hit the door with increased force. There was one final push and the door splintered as the wood broke open with a hole. At this point the wood that held the doors in place was taken from its hinges and the door itself broke through.

Sabaoth led the men in order to open up the door. "We are on the threshold. Hold fast."

The piece of wood was placed in the opening to keep the doors from shutting with its weight.

"How are we going to get through?" Keeper cried.

The Holy One let down his sword in between the narrow opening between the gate door so that it went through the thickness, pulling apart the wooden secured board on the other side. It became released and the Holy One kicked the gate open so the securing bar cracked. Keeper and the Holy One rushed into the open courtyard with the men beside them.

The Holy One and Keeper came rushing in with shields up as a guard changed their stance firing their *arrows downward into the courtyard, opening with rock paving. One on either side, the barracks were supported by pillars shaped with many leaders dressed in robes with arms outstretched with their wide sleeves hanging from their arms.*

El Roi, Sabaoth, and Jehovah Rapha came up behind them as a rear guard, swords raised and turning this way and that against the attackers that Keeper and the Holy One were able to allude as they made their way into the center of the stronghold. Keeper had stormed into the area with the sword blazing as they found the inner workings of the stronghold. The Holy One's men went against the enemy with full force. With their swords outstretched, they were able to fight some soldiers until they lay on the ground. The swords clanked as the attackers came. The Holy One's men were of a good aim as they deflected the arrows and also grabbed a round shield from those on the ground to guard themselves.

"Hurry, this is not going to last for long," Sabaoth exclaimed as another arrow came to penetrate the shield, but only made a dent.

El Roi looked around to spot the arrows as they came and would defend them off with Jehovah Rapha at his side.

They worked together being one with the Holy One and being one on this mission.

The fiery arrows hit near Keeper's feet, causing the heat to cause redness to the side of her heels as the arrow struck into the space between the stone tiles.

Keeper kept running, and the Holy One secured a firm hand onto the top of Keeper's shield, spinning her around so she faced toward the opening of the stronghold up against the centuries. The Holy One lined up the side of his shield up against hers and they both backed away quickly, raising a sword to defuse the arrows flying near their heads. From above came yells of, "They are far inside!" It was time that the Holy One and Keeper had gotten out of the range of the shots from the barracks. Many of them lowered their weapons momentarily and scampered from the barrack wall into the open courtyard, leaving some to keep their position on the ramparts to keep watch for other intruders.

Keeper and the Holy One took the moment as a chance to run across the cool stone to the door with a large middle building stationed within the walls.

The Holy One motioned to Keeper and she lowered her sword between the opening of the door, just as the Holy One had done previously and Keeper in the same way heard the bar that secured the door cracked as the Spirit Sword lit up as Keeper repeated the words, "Tear down strongholds. Break down doors." The blue inside glowed as the words gave it the strength and it began glowing for it was the very words of the Holy One.

The doors, creaking under the weight of the hinges, reverberated as the sound echoed through the solid stone opening securing the stronghold. The arrows flew and hit the thick wood doors, causing dull thumps as the flames licked at the surface.

They flew past as the Holy One pulled the doors closed swiftly as he and Keeper stepped behind them for protection. "Light the lamps," the Holy One advised, pointing toward the iron rods adjusted on the wall with a bowl-shape opening attached to light a fire. The Holy One handed her two pieces of flint as she sparked them together, stepping up a stone ledge coming out from the wall. The sparks flew out and the wick on the inside caught flame. Keeper grabbed on the iron rod that extended it from the wall so she now walked with the light. The Holy One bolted the door with a long plank of wood as Keeper came along beside him and lit another torch. A great pounding came on the door as a wooden battering ram had been made to break the wooden beam that had once been broken and now was used as a makeshift lock.

And this moment the Holy One's men guarded the door from the outside. The attackers came close so they were not able to overtake them. Their shields held in front of them. Their swords also swatted the stray arrows.

In the stronghold, Keeper's eyes looked to the door and then to the wide-open area in which the light shone several pillars holding up the tall ceiling. In the middle stood stone boxes. Despite the fear felt in the moment, the Holy One continued into the middle of the open area with footsteps creating clicking sounds.

"We must destroy these pillars," The Holy One said and Keeper saw words written on the side of the rounded pillars that seemed to support the whole building.

"Why must we destroy them?" Keeper asked.

The Holy One shined the light from his torch, illuminating the meaning of the words. "These are strongholds in your life that are keeping this physical stronghold securely standing." The light allowed Keeper to see the words clearly. The Holy One read the words aloud. "Fear." He guided his torch toward the next. "Doubt." Once again he included. "Complacency." And finally it said, "Pride."

Keeper at once knew these had become true in her life, even in the process of understanding how to walk alongside of the Holy One. She could see as if the things were what she had been stuck in either knowing or unknowingly. She could see the dark shadows that had been shown up in the room where she abided with the Holy Spirit. How are they still here?

"It is about knowing that you are free of those things, knowing how to fight them with scripture, and allowing their power to be loosened. It is a part of sanctification. You can allow chains that once haunted you to come back, but know that is not you. You are forgiven. You know your mind is being renewed."

"So what do I do?"

"Just ask for my forgiveness and receive his power. Do you want to be free?"

"Yes, I actually do," Keeper replied, but jumped since she had become startled as the loud banging of the battering ram threatened to break the doors down. Fear was seen in her face. The Holy One's men fought the attackers, but were not able to keep them away from the door completely. They set up a battering ram against the door.

"Do you believe I am more powerful than these things?" The Holy One gave a word of encouragement.

"Yes."

The Holy One's sword sliced through the dense stone pillar so that it cracked as a blaze drug through the middle. The stone itself toppled as the support of the building began to give way and stones began to drop.

"Are you afraid that we are going to be trapped under here if we get rid of the supports?" Keeper's tone showed her concern.

The Holy One answered her. "Do you know that once the supports are gone this stronghold will be destroyed and we will find another way out? You of little faith, why do you doubt?"

Keeper agreed with the statement, "Help my unbelief."

"Strike as you believe in my power. Just receive forgiveness." Keeper could see these thoughts in her mind as they haunted her. She continued to visualize them as she handed them to the Holy One, who threw them in the deep ocean, drifting to the floor.

'I receive the forgiveness, and I trust in his power.' Keeper whacked at the pillar labeled "doubt" repeatedly as the cracks broke up the front. She could feel a movement and could hear as stones came loose and crashed beside her causing gashes in the floor. She also beat at "fear" and "pride". At the same time, the Holy One looked at her and then at the pillars of complacency, "Do you believe?" Keeper nodded and truly received the forgiveness as she envisioned the stones of these pillars crashing into the depths of the sea with a weight that made the sand billow up towards the clouds. Keeper again started hitting at other pillars labeled, "self-hatred," "helplessness," "depression," "lack of trust," "judgment."

The Holy One continued to strike the pillars as did Keeper. The sound around her became unbearable, but at that moment the light of the sky opened up before them and a large opening appeared as she saw the light break through the darkness. They both began running because the secured stronghold had lost all of its support and the stone roof came down. The doors opened and the enemy ran inside as the stones came loose from the ceiling and trapped them underneath. The Holy One's men also came crashing through the door and ran toward Keeper and the Holy One. The Holy One grabbed Keeper's hand and he ran quickly before her, trying to drag her out. Stones fell down quickly, almost crushing them several times. Up ahead, a large rock had become loose and tumbled in their direction. The Holy One ran ahead, raising his shield and pulling Keeper underneath as the rock had been deflected though it weighed hundreds of pounds. The rock slid to the ground as the Holy One grabbed on Keeper's hand and as they again began to sprint. Keeper breathed hard with the raspy sounds of a dry throat. They ran through the hole of a broad patch of the rock wall, coming clear of the structure of the stronghold.

The attackers were covered in the rubble as the rest made it outside.

A small falling rock hit Keeper's arm and she winced in pain. Keeper held her injured arm from the rubble. She continued to ache. "This is so painful. I just got hit."

"I will be able to help heal it," Jehovah Rapha said as he came up to Keeper and gave her some healing herbs for the injury. The herbs were soothing, yet stung as he applied them. As the Sabaoth came running after them, their eyes filled with the realization that the stronghold had almost completely fallen down on top of them and they were pulled out just in time.

Keeper felt the healing touch of the medicine and her arm felt much better. She held it and then extended it. El Roi kept a look out for any of the enemy that had survived.

"Thank you. You are most kind." Keeper said, picking back up the Spirit Sword.

"It is time to go onto the next pinnacle," The Holy One said.

Keeper's feet touched the grass and she looked back as all the outside walls had crumbled so that the stronghold became a pile of rubble.

Keeper looked back and could see that there were no signs of the pillars keeping the building secure. It was gone. Keeper was relieved that she had become free of these strongholds, knowing that even if she felt that the pillars *with her struggles written on them had power over her, she had the power to combat them. She knew most of all that they did not have power over her.*

She looked at the Holy One and tears streamed from her eyes as the power of the Holy One was beginning to be revealed. Those chains, she knew, were not hers because she was free and could walk in that way.

They put up the flag called Nissi upon a pole, and made it stand in the place it stood as a monument of the event that just occurred and its importance.

Keeper found herself walking along the bank of a river looking into the water as it quietly moved along. She gazed into the reflection of herself and the Holy One standing there beside her, feeling a sense of comfort and strength in him being with her during this fight. Keeper found a stone along the edge and dropped it into the water so that it created a ripple. The Holy One also took a stone and skipped it along the surface a few times before the stone rested among the pebbles of the riverbed.

Keeper felt the grass beneath her, as the green shoots still held some dew of the morning. Keeper and the Holy One both walked along the edge of the river, feeling the relief of the moment.

The Holy One said, "'For you did not receive the Spirit of slavery to go back into fear, but you have received the Spirit of adoption as sons, for whom we cry, 'Abba! Father!' Do you see that you are adopted? You are no longer a slave, but a son and in this case, a daughter."

Keeper replied in her head, "I do not understand my own actions, for I do not do what I want, but I do the very things I hate."

Keeper reasoned in her head a moment, remembering the Book of Old. "Now if I do what I do not want, I agree with the law, that it is good. So now it is no longer I who do it, but sin that dwells within me. For I know that nothing good dwells in me, that is, in my flesh. For I have the desire to do what is right, but not the ability to carry it out. For I do not do the good that I want, but the evil that I do not want is what I keep on doing. Now if I do what I do not want, it is no longer I who do it, but sin that dwells in me."

Keeper sighed, "Wretched person that I am! Who will deliver me from this body of death? Thanks be to the Holy One! So then, I myself serve the law of the Holy One with my mind, but with myself I serve the law of sin.

"So how should I live?" Keeper asked.

"As if I have freed you." The Holy One stopped and added, "If you walk in the spirit, you will not fulfill the desires of the flesh."

"Like fearing?"

"Yes, it is like you are not trusting that I am powerful enough to help you and lends you to also doubt, but like I said, I have given you power to understand more about the authority you have in me."

"Yes," Keeper nodded, beginning to grasp what he tried to teach her.

It felt like a few moments of peace as they walked along the way.

Chapter 26

Asher too had a dream. Seeing the Pursuer's face as he came closer while riding on a carriage as if he would run over Asher, leaving him broken, someone pulled him aside in a lane by the house. It seemed to be Keeper who still showed up in his dreams.

"What are you doing out here?" Keeper asked, shaking Asher. He slumped over on a wall and sat down. Feeling something tangible, Asher realized this was not a dream.

Asher finally replied in a groggy sort of voice, "I did not know. Why were you following me?"

Keeper felt embarrassed, but explained. "I heard footsteps pass my room and wondered who was walking by. When I saw it was you I did not worry, but then you started to walk out into the street and then *he* came down the road rumbling so loudly and it looked as if you would be hit if he stood there a moment more."

"Why did I walk out like that?" Confusion displayed on Asher's face.

"I am not sure. What could have had that effect?" Keeper seemed confused, but quickly quieted herself because she saw the rider get off and look their way.

"This way," Asher pulled Keeper further down the alley next to Frederick and Adrianna's home. At the same moment, Keeper realized who had come off the cart. "That is the Pursuer! He is still after us!" Keeper had not seen the Pursuer closely the last time, only in dreams.

Coming back up to the edge of the wall, they could see that people began to come out from their homes as if they were being led in a way that they could not help but follow. Many more came to the Pursuer there than in

Rockfirm. Much darkness existed in Rockfirm openly, but with a more friendly place such as Buffington where most seemed to believe, there was even more fear.

Keeper looked out and could see that the person from the cart had a slithering tongue and his eyes glowed red from underneath his hood. Keeper had never seen the Pursuer up close like this. "He looks like a snake," she said, and the Pursuer turned his head their way as though he had heard Keeper speak. Keeper once again went backwards as Asher pulled her away from the view of the Pursuer.

"Please get away from there! He will see you, and then you will get captured." Asher warned Keeper of the danger that the Pursuer could bring.

"You did not mention yourself," Keeper wanted to clarify what Asher had said, since it did not make sense.

"Well, you know that I have faced the Pursuer before and been captured by him." As Asher tried to give an explanation, Keeper caught a whiff of a hidden meaning.

"So, he will not hurt you because he knows you? I do not understand. Are you on good terms?" Keeper tried not to sound facetious. She truly did not understand what he meant.

"No, we are enemies... If he sees you here in association with me, he is more likely to hurt you." Asher tried to cover up the fact that he helped the Pursuer.

Keeper looked at Asher and could feel that he was still hiding something. Though Keeper had seen the translucent chains on Asher, she really did not know about Asher's dealings with the Pursuer. She knew he was opposed to good, but he had never mentioned his allegiance to the Pursuer out loud. It would perhaps take a great many more experiences for Asher to admit this fact. All around Keeper could hear the opening and closing of doors and the shuffle of individuals coming out from their homes in a seemingly random way. Those that really went out to meet the Pursuer had surrendered to the Pullings that he had upon their mind because they all had darkness and the ability to be captive.

"What is happening?" Overwhelmed by the unfamiliar sights, Keeper grabbed Asher's shoulder. Asher himself had never been present while the Pursuer captured those from the town.

A group of them went straight up to the cart in which they voluntarily entered. The barred door still stood open for those left to come in. Recognizing someone that she knew, Keeper began to yell as Asher covered her mouth once again.

"Stop making noise," Asher commanded. Keeper could tell that Asher firmly meant this.

Coming out of Frederick's house, Adrianna entered the square. Asher realized why Keeper was so surprised. Keeper broke free from Asher's grasp and ran toward Adrianna who had walked out into the middle of the street. Keeper came up close to Adrianna, grabbing her arm in order to pull her back between the two houses, away from the view of the Pursuer.

Adrianna stiffened and did not move as Keeper pulled her, but in a few moments Adrianna loosened up and followed Keeper's footsteps to the alleyway. They laid her down on the ground and began to wave a hand over her eyes in order to get her attention to come out of the phase she presently occupied. She did not respond with her eyes wide open and unblinking. Keeper did this for a moment and then decided to shake Adrianna by the shoulders roughly, but Asher stopped her, making Keeper move over.

"Please, do not shake her so quickly." Asher took Adrianna's shoulders and shook them slower. She did not respond so they led her by the hand rather hastily further down the alley between the two houses.

She was not responding to anything they did. "What should we do to help her?" Keeper's voice showed her concern as she responded to Asher.

"We are going to have to let her rest, maybe sleep will help her wake up again the same." Asher did not know what else to say because he had not gotten someone out of the trance that the Pullings of the Pursuer had on their mind. Holding her up by her shoulders, Keeper and Asher supported her on both sides as they walked her to the front of the house. It felt slow and moving her with small steps, but once inside they were able to lay her down on the pallet in a room of the house, not wanting to wake anyone up.

Asher was afraid and paced the floor nervously. The reason for this was that the Pursuer had seen them as they went in through the front, but as the minutes lengthened he saw no sign of him advancing, so he felt relieved.

Asher went back to sleep and Keeper knelt beside Adrianna, making sure she could still breathe and still slept soundly. Keeper then went to sleep on the floor of the sitting area in the middle of the house. Later in the night, there seemed as though there was a hard knock at the door that threatened to wake the whole house. Asher's eyes opened almost automatically as he ran toward the door, not knowing if the Pursuer had come to take them back or that someone pleaded for help.

Asher waited a few moments before opening the door to find that someone had left a note hammered into the wood of their door.

He looked around, but could not see anyone who had put it there. The streets were dark and the houses contained a few less people because they had been taken. Suddenly, the carriage of the Pursuer raced past, down a street far enough to be a good distance away, but close enough to cause a scare. Asher could see the Pursuer as he turned his head in the direction that he stood, while Asher felt like he could not be seen. Asher was once again reminded of the red glowing glint of the Pursuer's eyes and the fear that it left in his soul to submit lest there be consequences.

The carriage rattled out of sight and into the direction that Asher knew went toward the Forlorn Isle.

Looking down at the page that he had ripped off the wooden door, there was in bold red lettering a message that seemed to intensify the declaration of the words.

"BE WARNED. You are getting close to falling off the edge. You are going the wrong way. Do you think I will wait in taking all of those who you hold dear with me into darkness? Closely I have seen that you are toying with freedom from me. I saw you keeping those who were to follow me away from my control. I saw you waiting to be free from me. Do you know that you are serving me? This is your last warning—turn toward the Forlorn Isle or all those with you will meet their demise."

Asher stood there reading the contents of the letter, but a deep shiver and dread had come over him so that he quickly stepped inside and closed the door. He stuffed it into the pocket of his leather jacket. At the table, his fear mounted so that he sat there thinking and saying to himself, "Even if I thought I am free, I was not. He continues to plague me into serving him. How can I escape from his grasp, and even if so how can I escape from the ruins of others?" Asher seemed to stand on the peak of a cliff looking down at the water bashing up against the sides.

He had the sense that if he could jump and that somehow he might be caught up in the wind and float away from the trouble standing behind him on the cliff, but the hand of darkness rested itself on his shoulder. At the same moment, he felt tough shackles being put back onto his hands. He was the same as he always was: an afraid individual being swayed in the way of his master. There seemed to be no helping that.

The sun began to rise with a steady stream of light coming through the windows accompanying a sky painted with red, seeming as though it was a warning.

The light seemed to arouse the rest of the house. Frederick came into the kitchen area where Asher still sat unblinking, sitting at the table.

"Where is Adrianna?" Frederick asked, concern lacing his voice.

"She is on a mat in the other room...There is much to say."

"I want to hear, but let me first check on her." Frederick said, hurrying out of the room.

Frederick went into the room where Adrianna slept on the floor where Keeper was located. He tried to wake Adrianna by shaking her shoulder. He remained quiet for a moment and she responded with a few worried words as she began to awaken.

"What is happening?" She sounded fearful as she came to herself. Waving her arms away from Frederick as though she fought to get away from something that came after her. Keeper became fully awake and came into the room as she watched Adrianna struggle and not become calmed. It reminded her of what it must have looked like as she was running away from the Pursuer in dreams that turned out to be nightmares. Standing up, Adrianna continued to yell, "Get away from me." The rest of the house came in since they had quite abruptly heard the fearful voice of Adrianna.

The children ran to their mother to comfort her, but instead Frederick motioned for them to come by his side saying, "Leave your mommy alone for a moment." They obeyed and Frederick motioned for them to get behind him as he came closer to Adrianna, "Adrianna, Adrianna." he said her name in the calmest way that he could in order to slow down her intense breathing, repeating himself many times.

Adrianna said an imperative statement, "Do not let him get me," as she slumped over toward the door. Frederick ran to catch her and let her lay down gently on the floor before she crashed.

"Take the children into the other room," Frederick instructed the others and Keeper brought the two children away from the others and gave them some toys. As they seemed to calm down and actively play, Keeper went back into the other room to find that Adrianna was lying on the floor, saying a few words. She tried to answer a question that Frederick asked, but Frederick had to repeat it again. "What happened?" Frederick asked her, hoping to understand.

Adrianna's face was pale as she said, "I think I was dreaming."

"You mean when you were sleeping?" Percy asked this in order to clarify.

"I think she means something else," was Gabriel's reply. "I think she is describing the event that happened to her."

"She is," Keeper replied. "We saw her last night walking out of the house—"

"It was something that I have seen before while aboard my ship as I was attacked." Asher broke in the conversation. "My men were strong and they could resist it, but it is easy to succumb to it. It is almost frightening." Asher admitted.

"I see him," Adrianna began again as though connecting to what Asher just described. "He has red eyes and he is looking at me. He is trying to lead me somewhat.

Dig, dig. More to which it falters. Sooner into the ground."

Keeper stepped back as if she had lost her balance. Her mind reverted back to the moment that had gotten her on this journey in the first place.

"I have heard these words before. They were repeated as I had a dream about a place." The shadow of the Forlorn Isle returned in full force.

"She spoke of the Forlorn Isle. They must have been taking her there."

Adrianna let out a scream. "He is coming for us! He has already passed by. It is him!"

"It is the Pursuer," Grabriel finished Adrianna's thought and turned around. "He has come here, into the safe city. It was meant to be protected by laws and fortified walls filled with guards."

Frederick seemed unsteady as though he would fall, but finally straightened up and regained his balance.

"What is it, my dear fellow?" Percy's concern was evident in the tone of his words.

"Permission has been granted for some darkness to come into the city. There may be a person in the city associated with this evil. They may not have understood what they brought." Frederick explained the severity of the situation.

"What may have happened?" Percy asked, but no one was able to see.

Frederick continued to explain, "We may have let in something that allowed for the Pursuer to come and take the people of this town as he has done to other cities."

"That is troubling…" Gabriel said this knowing the news changed their plans, "This is the only safe haven for those who are captives. Where else would they go?"

"What must be driven out?" Asher asked, assuming it was something he did, but he also wanted to know what was to be done.

"What will be done about this?" Keeper asked with concern.

"The one who brought it in must be driven out," Gabriel quickly replied. "There is something that can be done, but I say that this will be extremely hard to reverse now that the walls have fallen, per se, to the enemy. Yes, something must be done."

"What *should* be done?" Frederick showed that worry rose at the thought, repeating the question.

"We must hope to only defeat the Pursuer himself by destroying his strongholds that keep captives trapped in sin." Gabriel replied in the most realistic and truthful way possible.

"We must what? I thought we were only going to free the captives," Keeper replied, surprised at this realization that they must also defeat the Pursuer. "How must we do that?"

"You have a sword?" Frederick replied while harkening back at the conversation that he and Keeper had earlier.

"Yes," Keeper answered.

"You have a group of journeyers?" Gabriel questioned.

"Yes."

"We have the Holy One on our side," Percy interjected rather triumphantly.

"Yes, and that is how." Gabriel finally gave the answer. "The Holy One's power will give us strength."

"Yes, we will continue on." Keeper exclaimed aloud. As they said this, the group noticed Adrianna continued to lay still on the floor.

"But how must we help Adrianna?" Keeper stated the obvious. Frederick seemed worried since there proved not much solution for the moment.

"Her trouble is past," Asher gave him instructions. "Just let her sleep, and she will forget."

"But we must keep her and the others safe from the Pursuer," Frederick's voice trailed. "Doing that will be difficult, but we should pray that he does not come back this way for her or others."

"Hopefully if he follows after us, maybe it will be a diversion to keep them away from everyone else," Keeper offered the word to encourage the others, and perhaps to comfort herself.

The sight of Adrianna's visions reminded Keeper of the night at which she had felt as though the Pursuer came after her in her dreams. They were real, they were vivid, and they were frightening. It was as if something pulled on her brain toward a terrifying darkness. Keeper had not the knowledge if she succumbed to the Pullings of the Pursuer all the way as Asher had mentioned that many on his ship were able to resist the Pullings. He once fought valiantly against the Pursuer, so what happened?

Asher felt such an overwhelming sense of fear for the safety of Cephas that he had seen his face as the Pursuer went by. With the horror that the Pursuer caused while taking people away to the Forlorn Isle, his heart wanted to run, although he still feared. He wanted to be free from the association that he had with the Pursuer, but how?

"Yes, as a diversion the Pursuer may follow us. He may be after us anyway. We definitely felt closer to him because of the run-in." Keeper speculated seriously.

Frederick chimed in, "We better just be prepared if he does. He seems to have control over people's minds.

"You know everyone needs to be wary. For even

some that seem like our own."

Frederick continued on with his thoughts. "Even if someone is good, everyone needs to take off their chains.

"Do you not know that when you present yourselves to someone as slaves of obedience, you are a slave to the one whom you obey, resulting in death, or is obedience resulting in righteousness?

"For the wages of sin is death, but the free gift is eternal life in the Holy One."

"Does this mean that Adrianna was not freed?" Percy offered this explanation trying not to seem offensive to Frederick. He also felt confused on the reason that Adrianna had been drawn out.

Frederick responded, "Well, a lot of the people in Buffington are very good at doing good deeds in order to make it seem that they are a good person. This town is known for people who say they are clean for doing good deeds. Sadly, to say, my wife may have been one of those who had never been freed. You can always assume that they have, but all must be freed with belief and with the help of the Holy One. I still love her. It will have to be her choice.

"The power of the Pursuer needs to be destroyed in order to free them." Frederick continued onward.

"That is right. I think that most of the people throughout the city of Rockfirm rightly show that they are doing what would be evil so it would seem like they deserve it more, but all are in need of freedom." Keeper offered gravely.

"Yes, we will need to talk to her. Maybe the sword will help. Overall, we need to use the power of the Holy One to defeat the Pursuer and to free them all."

Adrianna began to move over and step up. Keeper

lifted the sword from behind her back. The fog began to clear, but Keeper could see the chains on Adrianna's arms.

"Do you want to be freed?" Keeper was able to offer her help to Adrianna. "As the Holy One wants you to be."

Adrianna looked up and though she had been vulnerable to the way she had been, replied, "Yes, I want to."

"Does she understand what is happening?" Percy asked this, concerned.

"I do not see anything capturing her. There is nothing there," Asher replied with a rebuttal.

"Yes, there is. I assume she does. The sword has been talked about and she would have heard of it from me and of the invisible chains." Frederick assured Percy that she understood.

Keeper lowered the sword, asking Adrianna to lift her hands apart. Keeper then lowered the tip of the sword through the chains that Adrianna carried. The sword glowed with its icy impact and all at once the outline of the chains could be seen. The sword came down on them so that the whole of the chains were seen and then as the linking began to break apart. It created a violent clanking noise with sparks as the chains began to break through the middle and then dissolve completely.

Those watching blinked as they began to see that the outline of the chains described the invisible sight that Keeper had been accustomed to and expressed. It gave them a surprise that they had seen something invisible just show itself.

"What was that?" Percy once again asked. "I remembered being freed, but those are the chains that hold onto all." Percy continued with the comforting phrase, "I can never get over the sight of those chains breaking.

"I only felt the effect on them falling off, but I never remembered seeing them so clearly. I could only see the Holy One's face."

This information seemed quite new to the group, but they had joined together in a fight against the Pursuer and the Holy One must have freed them. But maybe not all of them.

"I guess if someone like a Spirit Keeper had seen it before, then others would be able to see it." Gabriel delved into the explanation in order to give the others a clearer view of what they had just seen.

Adrianna began to blink and stood up on her own even when Frederick offered a hand to assist her since she had been so unsteady. At once, she began to talk normally. "Where are the children?"

"They are playing in the other room. Do you want to see them?"

"Yes, I would like to," Adrianna replied as she grabbed onto Frederick's hand, and they walked over into the other room.

The children, who had been playing quietly with some wooden toys, came running over to their mother, hugging her warmly as she bent down to pick up Phoebe. Freddie continued to run around the room carrying a wooden ship.

"So she is alright now?" Keeper confirmed with Frederick, trying to see if the effects of the Pullings had faded.

"She seems to have returned to normal." Frederick paused and then continued to thank Keeper. "Thank you for using that sword. I knew it had the power to help, but did not realize it would be in my own home. Moreover, it has power, but the Pursuer must be stopped to release them from their chains. We have to tear down strongholds where those are captured. He has power over their minds, but soon he will no longer."

Frederick looked at the sword resting in the harness on Keeper's back and once again glanced at Keeper's face.

"I feel there is more to learn, but soon everything will become clear." Frederick's voice filled with hope as he drew his inspiration on what would happen to come. "The Holy One will help reveal what this journey is actually for. Souls, my dear, that is what he is after."

Percy came into the room in which Frederick, Adrianna, and Keeper stood with the children, with the others following soon after.

"There is a band of those who you know, Percy, are the League. They are the ones who free those from Captavia."

Frederick whispered into Percy's ear the plan of the hour as it would unfold. Raising their rings with the chains wound around them, they both clanked them together as they made a fist.

To Asher's dismay, he did not hear what the plan would be in order to free those from Captavia. How would he be of any help to the Pursuer? A bleak image sunk into his mind of Adrianna and how she had fallen to the floor.

Even if she had at once been freed because she asked for it and the chains had dissolved off her hands, he felt as though no one was safe. What was even keeping him from being captured, like many others?

Asher looked away from the group that he had traveled with, but never felt a part of. He felt tired. He could not handle being under the grip of the Pursuer as he tried to threaten him and those around him, including Cephas. He was done for, but as he looked out of the window where the rays of the rising sun met the gaze of those who had stood there so solemnly, he saw how Adrianna had been freed of a bondage that had kept her hostage. Now she was free of the terror of the Pursuer. He watched as the children hugged their mother, relieved that she was well and in her right mind. Still he saw the glowing portrait of those who stood there, and around him still hung darkness. He knew no way of escaping the supposed chains that he carried. 'I will do it later. I will ask later. Maybe then is when I will be freed.'

In his mind, he heard an unfamiliar voice speaking in a direct, but kind way. 'The time is soon. The time is now.' He did not know who spoke, but in his deepest being he knew that this one who called seemed concerned, as though he knew Asher.

'Is this the Holy One?' Asher's fear and curiosity rose, but at a moment there seemed to be the sound of a person knocking on the door loudly with their fist.

"Open up, Frederick. People have gone." The sound only increased. "Open up! Open up!" Frederick came to the door and opened to find the pale face of his neighbor. "Frederick, many people have gone missing. Even some of our dearest. What has happened?"

"Yes, I have almost experienced this in my own household as well. I am sure it must have been the Pursuer." Frederick offered his concerned explanation.

"The Pursuer! In Buffington? I thought with these walls we were safe. Maybe there is a traitor, or maybe the guards mistakenly let him in. Why would a Spirit Keeper allow this?" The way they said this, it looked like it was the Spirit Keepers of the town to blame, but Asher knew the truth.

"It has affected us," Frederick said, motioning to his wife.

The neighbor asked, "Are you okay? How did you escape?"

"I am alright. I wanted to be free. They used a sword to free me." Adrianna assured him of her peaceful wellbeing.

"Is that the Spirit Keeper's sword?" The neighbor spotted the instrument that Keeper carried.

"Yes," Frederick replied.

"Well, I am glad that you have it." The neighbor seemed relieved at this realization. The neighbor continued on with, "It must have been the Spirit Keepers of Buffington, but it is unusual because they are the best among us to keep a guard on the city. I feel as though something has distracted them from their cause, like someone else is responsible. Anyway, we might not find out what happened last night. I wish I could still talk to them. I would have talked to them, but they were actually missing. All I know is that the Pursuer has come into Buffington and our safe, guarded shelter from the outside world may not prove safe anymore." The neighbor's face became deathly pale as he said these words.

"Gone… the Pursuer captured them too? I feel as though everyone seems to be vulnerable to this threat." Frederick's brow furrowed at the thought of so many people that he believed to be safe, that continued to be vulnerable of being taken. The walls that once seemed so secure proved to be just a piece of paper. Still, he knew the Holy One to be his protector.

"All I know is that the Pursuer has come," the neighbor repeated. And as he said this he added, "But we know the Holy One to be the real protector for us in this city. There will still be good, despite this fear." The neighbor and all the others who stood close beside felt the weight of the statement, "There is none righteous, no not one."

He continued on with the words, "What should we do to get them back? How will we protect our city?" The neighbor still showed concern as to what should come about to make everything right.

"I believe our city has been opened and there is not much to do to seal it back up. Still we have heard travelers who have seemed to come for this very reason: to free those who are in chains. In doing that, defeating the Pursuer and the chains on their minds, destroying strongholds. I pray then that our city will be safe," Frederick continued on.

"Yes, I pray that will be enough." Frederick's neighbor nodded his head at the travelers and turned to leave. "I will in the meantime determine that the gates will be closed for now and the doors bolted. Good bye, then."

"Good thinking. Good bye, and take care," Frederick replied, shutting the door behind him and looking around at those spread out in front of him. "Well, you must be off then."

"What about you?" Asher asked seriously.

"All you will need to do is follow what the Holy One has called as we will hold our own here. I pray you will come to see us again," Frederick offered.

"Aye, hopefully we will." Percy agreed.

Frederick opened his arms wide for the group of travelers and his own family to gather around in a large hug. Freddie and Phoebe let out a playful laugh as their mother pulled them closer. As they stood close, Frederick lifted up a prayer.

"Holy One, keep this brave group safe as they continue to follow the path you have laid before them. Protect them from evil and allow them to see you. I pray your strength would be present as you use them to defeat the

Pursuer. Not by their strength alone, but only yours. Thank you."

"We will need a way to alert the League of our arrival to free the prisoners." Percy responded.

Frederick went outside and there was a bird standing on a perch. "I will let the League know that your group of travelers are coming to help in Captavia. They will be ready to meet you." Frederick looked at Percy.

"Yes, that is exactly what we will need for the League to know that we will be there soon." Percy answered back.

Frederick went up to the bird standing on a perch. He attached a red ribbon to the foot of the bird and gave it a piece of food which it grabbed with a claw, as it took flight toward the southern region of Captavia. "The bird with the red ribbon will alert the League. It should get there before you in order to give them enough time to prepare for your arrival."

"Thank you." Percy said as he and Frederick gripped each other's hand with their rings carved with chains on their fingers.

"Anything for a fellow League member. Now go spread freedom." Frederick said enthusiastically.

Chapter 27

Moving through the city, the group passed by a stable in which horses had been put into lodging so that those in town could use them. The Spirit Keepers at this side of the town allowed them entrance through the gates and into the bright morning sun. They squinted their eyes because of the immense light that came upon them all as the light hit the walls of the city. Asher and Gabriel had their old clothes washed so that they now wore them again. They carried many packs of goods loaded upon their back with food in which Adrianna had packaged some of her homemade bread. It was made of wheat and other nourishing ingredients in order to sustain them for at least a little while because they did not know where their next meal would come from. Going into the underground of Captavia, they did not know when they would come up to the surface again. Ahead could be seen the deep forest with dark branches that showed no sign of life. Walking over rolling, grassy mounds, they found themselves walking slower than usual. There stood a field of yellow and purple flowers that stood spread out before them. Gabriel bent down to pick one of the flowers from its stem and held it close to his nose. The others sat down from time to time as the flowers seemed to grow all around where they were. This starkly contrasted to the darkness that stood facing them as if a curtain could be pulled back as they went through so that they once again found themselves in darkness.

They could hear the crickets chirp as they would launch themselves onto long stems of grass. Putting their hands down into the grass, some particles of damp soil could be found as they bunched the tendrils in their hands.

They would get up from a moment of rest and take a few more clumsy steps and then fall down again as a green carpet provided a cushion as they would fall on their sides. Tumbling and getting back up, you can hear the whistle of Gabriel as he cheered a happy, wistful tune of the land in which they traveled. The sound almost resembled a bird's chirp and some even did seem to find their way, sweeping past the visitors as they chased each other across the terrain. Everyone savored the sight and feeling of the moment before them.

As they drew near to the wood, the grass became gray and seemed to wither under their footfalls. The wood itself seemed to drain all light out of everything so that all the brightness of the beautiful day disappeared. They found these walking under deadly growing trees while below there grew thick patches of thistles that began to become dense hedges in the area in which they trudged. At many moments, Keeper had to use the sword that they had found in order to slash their way to make it passable.

Percy and Asher knew the area in which they traversed with its twisted paths and were not completely confused on their way to Captavia.

Percy's voice still trembled because he knew that every time one would travel in these parts, the way always would grow smaller since the thorns would begin to sharpen their talons in defense of the entrance of Captavia.

As they would pass by gingerly, one after another, they could feel the punch of the prickly thorns breaking off so that they could find them sticking to their clothes. Stopping periodically, they would have to pull the thorns from their tunics, not without nicking their fingers in the process. It proved to be an almost impossible task to remove all of them so they contented themselves in continuing to trudge along and let them fall out by themselves. Keeper swung against the brambles and they came to smack her in the arm. She let out a yell, holding her arm. The others looked toward her and asked her if she was going to be alright and she assured them she would be soon enough. The area in which they walked began to become narrower so that the dense oak trees that dotted the area became wider around the trunk, pushing the area in which the thorns grew so it became closer together. They all halted together as they had reached an area covered with mounds of boulders. The spot in which they traveled went down lower into a valley as there were created rock walls on either side threatening to come together and crush those who traveled there. The trees grew thick in the pass, and so did the thorns. It had become much closer and thorns did not grow here. As they went down, the towering rock began to grow taller. The humid air began to stick to their skin as they seemed as though they began to sweat profusely. Percy and Asher directed them forward as they assured the others that the area in which they traversed deeper into would lead into the prison of Captavia.

"This is a common way to go to Captavia, much like many have, but the opening is difficult to find. I have been through this way many times." Percy assured those with them of the direction in which they took.

"Not to be confused with the other way we took that ended up higher on the cliffs where we escaped the first time." Asher included this detail.

"Yes, we are going further underneath which will lead us much closer to the area in which we need to be... Near the prison side of the area where the judge's room is stationed."

The length to the valley between the rock face continued to grow longer and the other openings began to appear. The sides of the rock cliffs began to open up so that as they traveled down in one direction, Percy observed the side of the cliffs toward the base, but could not see anything. Looking upward, they could see a bird's nest perched on a crevice on the side of the rock hedge that rose on both sides. The feather tips of a young hawk could be seen flapping as it received food from one of its parents that had come from a ways away in order to find sustenance. It was the bird with the red ribbon that Frederick tied on its leg as an alert to the League. The League would know they were soon to arrive. On the top of the hedge could be seen the dry, parched land of the arid land closer to the exposed area of the sky. The trees that they had seen growing as they entered into this valley area had dwindled so that only the thorny bushes could be seen spread out so that Keeper assumed they grew up above. As Keeper looked at the surrounding area and at the hawk that circled around for its nest, she began to see a flash before her eyes and a vision of clear blue and in the Spirit Eyes. *She saw a fully green tree growing out of the stark rock surface of the ground. As she saw this, she stepped inquisitively toward the tree and instinctively lengthened her arm toward the bark as it circled to a knob on the wood's face. There were some other trees that refused to grow beyond it. Applying pressure on the position of the tree, she felt as the wood revolved as though it had a hinge made of metal that allowed it to clamp open. From inside Keeper was surprised to see a bright light and a dense glow inside instead of the dark, spider infested space found if one could look into the opening of a tree trunk. It was as if there were a crack from the strike of lightning as the tree blocked its pathway to the ground. Even so, termites had worn down the rings of the wood so one could spy straight through the center.*

Keeper reasoned through the strangeness of the light compared to what she expected to see flat out. She decided to step through the opening, ducking through and all at the same time the light she saw enveloped her and she blinked open her eyes into the surroundings that she and the others pleasantly traveled. Her eyes rested on Percy as he moved his hands along the base of the ground as he looked for an opening straight to Captavia.

"It is strange," Percy said, "that I would have to say this, and not in pride, but for once I have no idea where the opening would be located, despite coming down these many passageways." Percy relayed this information while still trying to survey the area in which he felt sure of his search.

Gabriel, who had looked at the rock, pointed out with an observation, "There may be some that fill in the holes so that one would not find their way back in that area."

"Yes, I agree with you on that. They may have moved boulders in the area that one had once dug making it imperative that one finds the correct area to burrow through unless they become entrapped by the packed rocks." Percy warned the others of this possibility.

"Yes, but how do we find it?" Asher asked inquisitively while adding, "I admit I have never come to this level. We came out at the top of the cliff."

"We did come out of the top of the cliffs so I know you would not understand, but I remember it being down in this area," Percy continued on.

"But they may have filled it in," Asher added this to the conversation.

"Yes, let us try something else," Percy suggested this as they backed out of the area in which they stood and headed around the corner around another precipice of rock that could be seen from up above as tributaries of a river.

Going down the rock face, Percy glided his hand at the dead end of each passage and found no way of entrance. He felt the dirt of the ground to see if it gave way. Keeper's mind still illuminated an image of a green growing tree and as they reverted back from the previous passage they headed around the next bend. Keeper saw an image as though in a form of deja vu with a few dark trees spread around the opening and near the further end she saw a green tree with branches reaching onward with fully blooming leaves. The twisting roots could be seen with the knees of the roots jutting out around the base. On its front, a round knob could be seen swirling on the surface of the bark in which Keeper had envisioned herself, placing her hand on the surface. Like it happened many times before, she saw physically what had appeared in her visions. Keeper drew nearer down the passageway and rested her hand on the knob in which she had envisioned herself pushing on the tree as she had done in the vision. Unlike her thoughts of what should happen, she saw that her movement did nothing to open a passage into the tree as though guided by a sudden gleaming light, but she did recognize that at the base of the tree, the soil seemed soft and as though someone had pulled up the dirt into small piles. Someone had smoothed it back into its place.

"What have you found?" Percy came from behind and observed the bark of the tree in which Keeper's hand still rested. "I feel you will not find a passage through the wood of the tree, but—" Percy looked downward to where Keeper looked at the mushy ruffled ground at the base of the tree and near the edge of the valley. He looked back up at Keeper with a wide-eyed stare as his mouth spread into a wide smile.

"You know…" Percy did not finish his words, but

instead went to his hands and knees and began to feel the soil. With a fistful of sandy soil, he allowed it to flow gently from his hands as he observed it. He then began to grab handfuls of dirt and throw it swiftly to the side as he generated a suitable hole for the moment. Keeper realized what might be happening and sat on her knees next to the hole and began to dig as the Percy had just begun with just as much enthusiasm. Others began to come alongside and dig with them. One of the immediate challenges seemed to be the winding roots that grew out from the great green tree, but these did not hinder the area in which they excavated. It seemed quite nerve-wracking that they always had to go into the darkness of the ground, but most of the time it seemed like they always had each other and their own torches as lights. They knew they were led by the Holy One with the assurance that they traveled on their way to the completion of their mission.

As though one had hit the lever of a wheel to create movement, the dirt of the area fell through as the opening grew wider. From inside one could feel the movement of air as it blew through a cool hallway and hit their faces with a chill. The opening jutted downward and then lengthen out in a horizontal way to a long passage.

Moving back from turning dirt, Percy held Keeper's arm as if she would fall straight inside, but did not.

"Well, this seems to be a secure way in which to follow," He said, lowering his hand into the opening in order to see if there were rocks in which would dislodge themselves loose and fall onto them. He found none. Percy looked around to those who backed away from the hole and once again smiled. His chain ring shown in the sunlight.

"I think we are ready to go." Percy lowered himself down into the hole and looked back at Asher, Gabriel, and Keeper, sliding downward into the area. Asher had broken a few branches off the dead trees and used the charcoal that they had used while traveling in the cave that they had traversed earlier on. They used flint and steel in order to light the ends of the wood. They scuffed the flint and metal against each other for many times over until it sparked and lit the end of the wood as they put the pieces together in a group. The flint was used in the cave where they found the horses. Gabriel would collect items that were helpful and put them in his never ending bag.

The dirt of the passageway seemed solid enough to walk through and it was dark compared to the light that sparked and blazed from the makeshift torches.

They shuffled one after another through the scuffed floor which contained stones that they kicked periodically.

Keeper blinked as she looked around at the narrow surroundings of the tunnel, becoming uneasy.

"They are meant to meet us presently to help us rescue those in Captavia who rebelled against the system trying to be free." Percy's voice trailed off as everyone heard a sound like the rustling of rope that had suddenly been loosened. In a moment's time, Keeper looked down to see that an outstretched net was spread out underneath their feet. In a moment of time it was cinched tightly around the group, tightly pulling them above the ground so they hung, thrashing as they struggled to become free. Although this was the case, they could not get out.

"Hey, your hand is in my face, Percy." Asher voiced his discomfort and Percy tried his best to remove his hand and place it somewhere else. "I am sorry, dear fellow. I feel like there is not much room." As he heard the sounds of "Ouch," or "Please do not do that," as the rest of those present ached at the motion.

"How are we going to get out of this?" Keeper's voice contained the fear that they all presently felt.

Percy replied promptly with, "Well, those of the League were meant to come to help us and meet us near this spot, since the bird with the red ribbon on its leg was sent to fly over Captavia. It would show that we were coming to help free the prisoners. Something must have detained them, which would prevent them from coming."

Asher's heart began beating faster with uncertainty as Percy continued, "I am hoping they will come or else the Digstons will find us and the guards of Captavia."

Asher's fear of this place only increased for he had once been freed from this place with the help of Percy, but the thought of once again becoming entrapped created a claustrophobic feeling. What would happen if the guards of this place found them?

"You were freed for a purpose." Asher could hear and he heard the tall boots of the guards coming from another adjacent tunnel. The low chattering growls accompanied them so that a pack of Digstons came running toward them, teeth bared and snarling. They began jumping up to bite at the net in which they hung. The group could feel the net shift as one of the Digstons tore loose one of the ropes of the net that helped them stay suspended.

Everyone of the traveling group was slightly relieved as the guards rounded the corner calling with a loud, shrill whistle for the beasts to heal. They did, settling on their haunches, hungrily desiring to bite at the intruders.

"You are all trespassing." The guards came up close to Asher and Percy and realized something. "I have seen you before," they said, pointing at Asher. "You tried to rebel against the Pursuer." They held a sword to an opening of the net in which was closest to Asher so that he retreated as far back as possible. Asher did not speak to reply. The guard shook the net, grabbing onto it with a hand. "So you will not answer?"

The guard took the sword in which he carried and raised it up high to cut a slit at the top which made those on the inside fall out abruptly in a pile on the ground, with Gabriel's ankle stuck tangled among the net square rope. Asher sat up and helped Gabriel as he loosened his leg, sitting up gently on the ground. All of their things were taken from them.

The guards locked arms with the group of travelers forcibly pushing them down the tunnel so that they almost fell over.

They pulled Keeper back up, who tripped over slightly, and she winced. The guards with thick metal armor pulled the group through the tunnel so that they walked and began to sink downward slowly, deeper into the ground.

The Digstons came up beside them, nipping at their heels before the guards kicked them away so the group could continue walking.

Asher looked to see if the burrowed hole had been packed securely with dirt. It was the passage in which Asher and Percy had used to escape the previous time from Captavia. Asher turned his head away quickly so as to not draw attention to the patch of uneven dirt. Percy also looked at Asher, nodding upward to the hole and quickly turned forward again toward the direction they were being led. He too did not want to give interest to where they had escaped.

'If only we were not under the control of the guards and could find our way again from this place. Why come here again?' Even though Asher thought this, he knew the reason. 'We need to free those from this place.'

Asher, thinking of this, reflected on what Keeper has said about him. He pushed it away thinking he was alright, even though he had helped the Pursuer. In his heart, he could see that Keeper was right.

Asher had a sinking feeling inside of him as they were led by a row of steel bars lifted up and securely attached from the ceiling to the floor, to the dusty floor. All around had been packed tightly with the dirt of the opening.

The guards continued pulling them along the passageway.

The guard continued pulling them along the passageway, so that the torches that hung notched into a leather pouch on the wall became dimmer as they moved farther away from the light source. The cool bars knocked against their feet with soft clinks.

Asher peered into the cell to see many of the ill-fated prisoners with their torn tunics shivering profusely.

He looked for his Cabin Boy, but he was nowhere to be seen. The prisoners stared out with pinkish bloodshot eyes that sunk into their skulls. It looked as though they had not gotten any rest, tossing and turning as they lay clumped on the floor of their cell. There were places along their wrist where the shackles that held them seemed red and were swollen from trying to pull free.

Asher knew that they had been there for no one knew how long. They had been accused by Captavia and had resided there long before he had been taken there. They passed the opening of the courtroom, which contained intricate etchings with swirls wrapped around chain links. At the top was the symbol of a judge's measuring scale with two trays tilted that symbolized that someone was found guilty. On either side of the scale there was an image of coiled snakes that were arranged in an "S" shape of forest green. Their tongues slurped outwards toward the measuring scale, almost casting condemnation.

Keeper looked into Captavia Court where she saw where the judge's seat stood with a gavel. A witness sat in the witness seat beside the judge's stand. The jury was in a discussion where the traveling group could hear. "If he is guilty of one, he is guilty of all." There was a ringing sound as the judge let down the gavel for silence. The judge stood up and read from a long list on a scroll of everything they had done. The one on trial yelled out, "Please, I am a good person! Do not allow this to happen to me! I know of this lawless judging system. I will fight as long as there is breath in me!"

The group of travelers stood frozen at the doorway, peering in to hear this conversation. The guard seemed to allow them to do this, showing what may befall them. This could add to their sense of hopelessness.

"Good, you say. The very nature of humankind is evil. The heart is desperately wicked. You fight against this sentence, but there is no use. Still here in Captavia you are a captive and always shall be." The gavel crashed down, wood upon wood as the words can out, "guilty as charged. You have life."

Asher shuddered as he remembered being on trial where they brought up every one thing that he had done wrongly. Even if he had made a ruckus and uproar against those on the Forlorn Isle, they were still as trapped and as guilty for these things had been true. "If he is guilty of one, he is guilty of all." Asher repeated the words. It was their nature. How could they avoid it? Was there any hope?

"You all will have your trials tomorrow," the guard

chuckled hysterically, pulling out the pain and fear they must have felt, "bringing up everything one by one. Especially you…" He pushed Asher quickly and with a swift but hard blow he fell to the ground. Gabriel quickly knelt beside Asher, pulling him up and giving him support so Asher could stand again.

"A runaway prisoner can have the worst of the punishments." The guard did not offer an explanation, but Asher truly knew he was in grave danger and wished now that he had never come to this place again.

How were they even about to do any good to complete their mission if they could not save any of the prisoners or be met by Percy's League in order to aid them?

Asher could see as a witness was pulled from his seat and a pair of handcuffs that reflected the translucent chains were put around his wrists. Those guards who stood in the courtroom, guided the person to a dark opening in the back of the courtroom that led to a dimly-lit hallway. The boos and chatter of the shouts reverberated in Asher's ears and caused there to be great fear in his heart. He remembered the translucent chains around his hands and Keeper's concern for him to be rid of them. He knew for sure because of this he would be condemned while the others would have the covering of the Holy One.

The guards continued to pull them past the ruckus of Captavia Court into the dimly lit passageway that continued onward. They walked further and they could see that the condition of those in the cells only grew worse as the living conditions decreased. The passage began to slope downward as the ground began to feel damp.

"This is your cell—get comfy." A guard gruffly said, shoving each of them through the opening so that they landed in a pile on the ground, elbows jabbing into one another. The group of travelers pulled themselves off of the pile and gradually moved to the edge of the cell so that their backs rested against the cold bars of the cell. The guards individually chained them to the wall so that the chains did not run long.

The door shut and the rattling of the key could be heard as it clumped inside of the keyhole. After a few moments it was moved in the correct way, turning it vertically so that it was pulled from the keyhole. The guard placed the key on a ring securely on a belt.

They all looked at each other just wondering what they would do, why no one had been there to meet them, and how they were going to save the others and help them escape from this place.

They looked over at the other cell and tried to get their attention, but the prisoner did not make a sound or acknowledge their existence.

"How are we going to be able to help those here if they will not respond?" Keeper asked.

"I can hear you, but if I respond there may be more punishment for me. My trial is tomorrow and I cannot further ruin my chances." The prisoner had a sternness about him and they could see that he was trying his best to not make trouble for himself.

"I understand," Percy said softly and with a respectful tone. "We are here to help. We too have trials tomorrow as well, but we have some from the League who are coming to help. Then you and the rest will be saved and those who want can help us fight against the injustice of the Pursuer."

"Where is the League now?" the prisoner said with a sarcastic tone. "You are still imprisoned now. I do not even think the League is real. They have not been here to save. You know as well as myself."

"You have seen them," Percy waited and mentioned

with hushed breaths. "They have left notes in your food. I would say that you look for the signs."

The prisoner shrugged, thinking this was nonsense and he had never seen or heard of it, but was still open to the idea. He went back to his place, shutting his eyes as a guard came down the corridor. They handed each of the prisoners a pile of beige oat mush. As the guard slipped it under the metal bars onto the hard solid ground, he then walked away swiftly in another direction with the key attached to his belt.

Both of those in the cell with the group of travelers as well as the prisoner in the cell next to them dug into the slick substance so that they scraped the bottom of the bowl, but could not feel any parchment paper. They pulled their hands out covered in the grayish substance smeared on their fingers.

The prisoner shook his head since he was not able to find anything as well as the group of travelers.

They then decided to collectively eat their meal carefully in order to look through the substance. As their small meal progressed they picked at it carefully, but none were able to find anything. Seeing this, they truly were at the verge of having no hope of escape. They had been captured in Captavia Prison.

"I wish I still had my sword..." Keeper mused disappointedly.

Chapter 28

In the house where the Holy Spirit abided there were many rooms. Keeper felt as though she was growing in curiosity and understanding as she began to explore. Keeper opened the wooden door engraved in gold swirls, finding herself at the base of a steep staircase. Keeper, seeing that they seemed familiar, grabbed the railing as she made her ascent. The walls were covered with drawings of flowers and of sunrises, and at the top she saw a picture of a lion with deep eyes as though they saw right into her.

Keeper moved past this to a door at the head of the stairs. Keeper put her hand on the golden knob as she let herself into a room that felt as though it pulled her inside. There was railing encircling the inside of the room so she could look down on the first story. All along the sides were lined with hardback books with golden letters or others which were leather bound and looked much older.

Keeper's hand glided along the shelves, pulling out one book at a time.

There was an atlas with vibrant pages as it showed variations of maps of her world and some she did not recognize. Drawn in the blue areas that represented the sea were ships, tall masted and sails filled with wind. In the corner was drawn a key indicating the directions of the north, south, east, and west drawn in a star-like shape.

The map itself showed a great mountain range along the middle of the main island with more lush land up toward the northern area, and more of an arid and dangerous area near the south. In a corner there was drawn a round shape of an island which Keeper had seen on the map that Gabriel had carried as the Forlorn Isle.

As Keeper flipped through the pages there seemed to be some areas that she did not recognize and did not know how to pronounce.

Feeling she had learned as much as he could from this book, she placed it back on the shelf and scanned the spines to see a book with the title: True Stories of Battles and Adventures. Keeper saw this to be interesting as she opened up to see the contents of the pages. She found there to be rulers, perilous fights, and victories, which seemed to be a familiar structure she had seen before, but something about it caught her eyes. She saw a woman dressed in a white flowing dress, with a sword extended from her hands. In her eyes shone determination. "That is you," the Holy Spirit said. It seemed a strange sight, but Keeper had connected with the picture.

The Holy One took her hand as they walked from the still streams and lush green pastures to where there came a valley, all along of which was dark.

The jagged rocks shot up to easily trip her.

She could hear the faint echo of her footsteps , mirroring the emptiness and hopelessness that she felt.

She grabbed the Holy One's hand as he guided her along the way.

This by far had been the darkest and most hopeless part of the journey, one that she could barely fathom why there was so much darkness, as she straightened out her arms in the darkness trying to gather herself in order to find the light. As happenstance had it, there was no light for a long time. Rain dropped down as a storm gathered and the thunder clapped its hands in applause.

At last, the light of day came from an above entrance of the opening of rock.

Keeper's eyes glowed as she began to see that the Holy One had taken her out of the darkness.

Keeper opened her eyes as she looked around. She could see this moment as it reflected from reality. All her experiences of these dreams came from what really occurred inside of her as she went along the journey.

As she saw these different experiences, she could also see what would happen. Although she had been in this place, in reality it felt just as deep.

The Holy One gave her his hand and pointed around as they arose from the darkness of the pit. It had only been for a little while, but the harshness had been enough to make one fearful from then on, but she again reminded herself of the power she had and this fear that had been multiplied, still scared her.

"Do you see?" The Holy One said, going to the light. "Yes, even now you have a much clearer view of the world as you journey onward. Yes, you are ready to battle."

The Holy One's eyes shone brightly as a smile spread across his face. "This is the world in which I have given you the hope to become all that I have meant for you to do. Even so, do not trust in your own ability. You have seen part of who I am and I want to guide you even deeper. What you learn here will be helpful there, and not a retreat. Keep living in the real world."

The valley had opened up so that Keeper now found herself standing in a flattened greenish gray field as the grass stretched upward. She could see mountains that formed around her as though she stood in a bowl. The billows of clouds settled on the peaks. She knew she stood *not in reality, but in some other world, one with an ever closeness to the Holy One, ever-increasing in knowledge from glory to glory as it was revealed to those like her who are saints, who were chosen, and who did not walk like the world. In the moment of stillness, she breathed and released her fears in this cold brisk place right after the rain.*

Chapter 29

Asher woke up from a chill in the middle of the night as the light of the torches had burned low. Asher had been curled up against the cold floor with the hard breathing of Percy close by. He looked down at the shackles that held him. They were cold and reminded him of this unfeeling place and what was about to befall him. He thought that somehow if he helped the Pursuer this would not happen. He would find Cephas, they would be safe, but none of this was true. He felt the guilt of allowing the Pursuer into the city of Buffington in order to protect those who he thought best to protect. He realized those who would have helped the Pursuer probably ended up in the Forlorn Isle anyway. Then, he thought of the moment he was confronted by Keeper about how she said the chains that he contained were keeping him captured, but how could he be free of them?

Asher's knees rubbed up against the hard, blistering, cool floor. Asher looked up toward the ceiling and drops of water came rolling down his cheeks until they splashed in little droplets in the dirt.

Asher's voice was not heard out loud, but he was speaking loudly through his sobs.

"Holy One, I see what has happened around us. There is no sign of the League that Percy talked about that was meant to help us. I am one who will be condemned at Captavia." Asher looked again down at the chains that held him. "And these chains I have been shackled to are all that I have ever did wrong. There seems as though there is no way of escaping it. And..." Asher put a hand up to his mouth, trying to cover his sobs. It did not wake anyone up, but the pain was real. "I betrayed you by helping the Pursuer."

Asher at once could see the Holy One's face as he stepped into the cell, standing amidst those of the travelers who were sleeping. Asher could see the compassionate kindness that came from his eyes. A sincere hand stretched out for him to grab and Asher did, being pulled up right. In the Holy One's other hand was held the Spirit Sword that he had seen Keeper use. Asher was confused and asked, "Is that the same sword that Keeper had?"

The Holy One's face formed into a grin as he moved his arms slightly apart.

"Yes, and do you want to be able to be free this time? It is not the sword you know, but I who will free you." The Holy One's expression of total calm gave Asher some comfort, but in Asher there was still some hesitancy.

"There is so much that I have done wrong. I have not done enough right to deserve it." Asher's hesitancy showed a serious expression upon his face.

"You did one thing right, by calling out my name for help. Will you again call out my name to free you?" The Holy One lifted the glowing sword which shone with a blue crystalline hue. He pulled the sword upwards slightly as though motioning to continue. The Holy One replied, "Asher, you are justified, you have access to faith."

Asher put his face into his hands and sobbed. The Holy One drew close and they embraced. Asher then pulled back and looked at the Holy One. With a nod, he said, "Yes, I want to be free." Asher stood back with his arms outstretched before him, pulling the chain links as far back as they would go. The Holy One let down the sword upon the chains so that the links sparked and all at once the blue luminous light of the sword was all that could be seen because the chains had been dissolved.

Asher looked at the cuffs around his wrists, clenched his fists and opened it again so that his fingers lengthened out. He wondered how all at once the process of being free was long in waiting, but simple in action. He felt this freeness and joy as though the same chains were off his soul and his heart all at once. He breathed in deep, as a wind filled him and he felt a strange but wonderful peace.

The same Holy One who created the world had come to help him in his weak state.

"Where the Spirit of the Lord is there is liberty." The Holy One offered these words with the revealing sense of the power of what has just occurred.

"I have come because you called my name for help. You will continue on this journey and will have some hard and blessed times."

Asher, at this moment, thought about a major stressor in his life and why he had helped the Pursuer in order to get what he needed. "Please, will I find the Cabin Boy again?"

The Holy One's expression gave Asher the feeling that he might say yes which was imminent, but he was confused with the statement, "Yes, but not at this point."

Asher's face showed the concern which had grown inside of him, "so when are you talking about?"

"At the right time." The Holy One tried to offer as much of a comforting tone in his voice, but could still see that Asher was agitated. "You will, but at this point we are going to have to get you out of here."

"But where is the League?" Asher did not know how they would escape without their help.

"They are all among you," The Holy One replied and Asher looked over to see the prisoner in the cell next to them picking the lock with a device. The lock jammed and the man pulled it out with frustration and pain since he had gotten his hand caught and pulled it out quickly.

"Ouch," he muttered. He saw that Asher was awake and noticed that he was holding the glowing crystal blue of the Spirit Sword in both hands. "Hey, can you help me with that sword?" The man questioned.

Asher looked down to see that the Spirit Sword was in his hands, and the Holy One had disappeared. All that Asher knew was that he was thankful for the great immeasurable sacrifice of what the Holy One had done for him, and now using the Spirit Sword they had a way to escape.

"Yeah, you can use the sword. Let me open our door." Asher said, letting down the sword blade in between the metal bars and the door frame, coming straight down upon the lock so that it sparked and broke almost immediately. The door quietly creaked on its hinges as Asher used a hand to push it open. The sword was heavy for him, though to Keeper it seemed light. Asher went to the cell adjacent to their own, and he slashed the sword upon the lock so that it broke too and the prisoner was able to open the door.

"Are you from the League? How are you feeling?" Asher asked this carefully, not wanting to assume anything.

The prisoner was hesitant, but then offered an explanation in whispered tones, "Yes, but I am very new at being in the League. I would be considered an amateur Rockling part of the League since I was sent to meet your group, but got captured in the process. As you can see, I cannot even pick a lock correctly. You will have to forgive me for any inconveniences I may have caused you and those alongside you.

"I was even supposed to put a note in your food last night, but hopefully I can complete a mission next time around. The rest should be coming along shortly." The League member talked through his reasoning.

"A man in the town of Buffington named Frederick who is a League member tied a red ribbon to a bird's foot. The bird flew here to Captavia to alert the League, including you, that we were coming to free the prisoners. There is still hope for a successful mission. What is your name?"

"Yes, we received your message of the bird with the red ribbon, but I was captured in the process of meeting your group. Yes there is hope. And oh, my name is Darrin." He waved his hand so that it made a sliding motion where he then crossed his arms together.

"Good to meet you. Let me wake them and we shall make our escape."

Darrin put a hand on Asher's shoulder and with a serious tone relayed the words, "I will explain."

Asher was the first to be let into the trial in Captavia Court with a sack cloth cover around his head.

Pulling it from his eyes, Asher could see that he now sat in the witness seat at the front of the courtroom. There was a luminous crystal on the ceiling which he had seen as something similar to the crystals he had seen shimmering and clear in the cavern. It was the cavern where he had by happenstance ran into the dark figure of the Pursuer, and Asher sadly was willing to follow in the footsteps.

'They are going to read all about everything wrong on that scroll like my last visit to this place.'

Asher looked around and the trial had not yet started. There were several rows which were split down the middle of those who were there to gawk at those who were on trial. They were already at the point where they would mercilessly mock who was about to be sentenced.

On his left was a boxed sitting area in which those of the jury sat glaring suspiciously at Asher. Their light colored wigs were tied around their face in a part, tied at the back with a grayish green bow. They conversed among themselves as the time would soon start.

Hammering the gavel, the judge sat high upon his seat wearing a light-colored wig with many curls and coils standing lofty upon his head. He had no bows tied upon his wig, but wore a pair of thin wired silver spectacles that he would pull from his eyes once in a while in order to see at different distances. His face was wrinkled around the eyes and forehead so that he would furrow periodically, showing his stern features of anger that burned from within. Lovelessly giving the judgment, he continued to speak and others would respond afterwards. "We are here today."

"We are here today."

"We are here today."

The judge started the same way for each of their trials, as though it was a procedure. "To proclaim…"

"That the Spirit Keeper."

"That Percy."

"That Gabriel."

"That Asher."

The judge continued on, "and Darrin, have been found to have charges against them."

The judge was handed a scroll on which would appear everything that a person had done. He looked at the parchment paper and looked twice. There was nothing found on Keeper, nor Percy, and Gabriel's case. It was blank, for they had been covered by the Holy One. As far as the east is from the west, so far had he removed their transgressions from them.

Seeing this fact and knowing truly that they were found innocent, he continued on with a condemning accusation.

"I see that Keeper has dealt with crippling fear, and

does not trust the Holy One." One of the jury came up to whisper these things into the judge's ear, since they were somehow able to bring it up.

"Percy, you trust in the League more than you trust in the Holy One."

"Gabriel, you have been inadequate to lead this group of travelers in a successful mission."

"And Asher you have…" the judge listened to one of the jury say these condemning words and his eyes grew wide as the jury member mouthed the word "Pursuer".

The judge jolted in shock. The judge all at once tried to adjust his glasses so that he lost his grip on the scroll and it fell face up so that all the members of the court could clearly see the so-called list of faults.

It was completely blank. There was no so-called list of faults seen physically, but somehow there was a whole list of faults said against them.

'You have nothing against you.' Asher could hear the Holy One as he spoke the words. 'I have covered your faults. They are no more. Even if…'

The judge's voice was loud and irate as he repeated all that he had heard one of the jury members relate.

"Asher is a revolutionary who was brought from the Forlorn Isle to Captavia, but then escaped despite his prison sentence. He has also been a traitor against his own friends, serving the Pursuer."

The Holy One's voice reverberated, 'Even if others accuse you wrongly for your past, you are guiltless and free.'

Asher doubted so much that it showed on his face.

"Asher doubted that Cephas would be safe so that he

became a traitor and followed the Pursuer to get what he desired."

Those in the courtroom arose and heartily cheered in approval for those who were there to condemn him. Keeper and the rest who stood waiting for the court to end looked at each other and Asher with shock. They somehow felt like something of this nature was occurring, but not at this level.

Keeper had not understood the gravity of the situation. Asher felt the disappointment of their expressions and turned away. 'How will they continue on this mission with me?'

Keeper's features softened.

"But there was nothing written on the scrolls, does that mean there is actually no guilt toward him?" Keeper felt confused but considered these facts, as Gabriel leaned over and offered an explanation with his best knowledge.

"What appears on the scroll of faults is everything in which a person has done wrong, listing it in the order in which it occurred. This, as you have seen, does not apply to those who have blank scrolls with no mark of ink... It means that the Holy One has covered over their transgressions. That they are dispelled and not counted against you." Gabriel said in whispers that were shortened because of the guard who commanded them to be quiet.

Keeper was confused and looked closer to see if Asher still had those translucent chains. All she could see were the physical chains that he had now since they were captured, but no translucent chains to hold him. He was free.

"Did the Holy One free him last night?"

Percy leaned into the conversation and added the comment, "That may be so, but no one can know someone's heart."

Keeper was joyful at the thought, but knew that it was

a personal issue with someone's relationship with the Holy One. She was convicted of the ways she thought.

"Did we too have nothing on our scrolls?" Keeper asked this to both individuals standing beside her.

"I assume. If our hearts are really the Holy One's, then yes." Percy replied, sincerely giving his thoughts.

"Yes." Gabriel's eyes looked up toward where the sky would have been, if they were not under so many packed layers of dirt. "Yes, the Holy One does not accuse his chosen. This lot, however,"

Gabriel pointed to several of the individuals, "The one who is whispering to the judge is an Accuser of the brethren who comes up with many ways to bring up the past. And you see there the 'judge', his name is Unscrupulous or False Guilt, since he makes one feel guilty for crimes that are not. For the ones who have been set free there is no guilt involved, but to those who are not freed the guilt is rightly placed." The judge's mallet rattled.

"Darrin, you have been charged for being found as a part of the League, being a runaway, being a failure to your own people, distrust, self-loathing, and for the very act of talking to other prisoners."

The judge listed off a grand list of faults, some more outward, some were more personal.

"He has a list, sadly," Gabriel whispered these words and in a moment, he saw as Asher came walking to where they stood, overseen by a guard. Asher at once, snapped a finger and with a sudden elbow jab into the guard, forcefully with a backwards kick, sent the guard spiraling onto his back. In a moment, Darrin pulled out a sword and the hoods of the League members flew off as they revealed themselves in the crowd.

Darrin handed the sword to Asher and he had one handed secure grasp onto the hilt of the sword as he pulled

330

the sword out. In a few quick precise moments he pulled the sword out and turned his arm in a position so he forcefully sliced chains off his hands. Both hands freely held onto the sword.

All of the members of the group's eyes got large in amazement of what had just occurred.

"We have the sword back." Keeper was relieved that they would again be free and do what they had come for—to free the captives here in Captavia.

The League came with swords and also Darrin with swords and freed the travelers.

The guards immediately pulled their swords from their sheaths and began to jab at the League members dispersed among the wooden rows of seating. A guard swung his sword so it notched into the wooden back of the seats, splintered into his hand, notching deep so it was unable to be pulled out easily. The League member grabbed him by the shoulder and rammed his forehead into the guard's forehead so that the guard lost consciousness and fell limp between the rows. The League member walked over and came up to where Keeper and Percy blew out torches and used them to swing at the guard that came up toward them. They stood back to back since there were many guards who wanted to secure them into the cell.

A few moments later, Keeper and Asher at the same moment fought back to back as they warded away the guards. They kicked the guards away while back to back, slashing some of the guards with their swords.

"I got you," Asher yelled toward Keeper.

"I got this other side too," Keeper replied. "Watch your back," she said, swiping her sword.

"We got this," Asher replied as he fought another guard, keeping them away from attacking Keeper.

Keeper felt like she overextended her arm at some point from the old injury she had in the burning house when her family was taken by the Pursuer. She held her arm close and used the other one to fight.

Keeper and Asher were pulled away in the fight, but they felt as though they were on the same team.

Manachi was one who wore a ring that included chain links. It flashed on his finger and the group knew he was of the League. The League member quickly maneuvered himself into the tight-knit circle Gabriel had just joined and they warded off the enemy, despite only having wooden torches.

"I am Manachi, one of the League members." He ducked as a sword of the guard missed him. "I have come in order to help you and the other prisoners escape safely as directed by the League's recent Assembly meeting and with the help of the junior Rockling, Darrin."

Percy was relieved. "Thank you, my friend. I am happy that you have come." They both raised up their hand with the chain linked ring and bumped fists.

Swiftly, Manachi used his blade and guarded against the coming up swipe so that the sword of the guard came from his hand. Manachi kicked the guard's legs and at the same time grabbed the key ring that hung off his belt. The guard sat sprawled on the ground, holding his knee and not able to come after the group.

Manachi held up the key in shock so that the keys twinkled as they moved up against each other. "It is time, while the guards are trying to ward off the League members in this room, let us use this opportunity to free the rest of the prisoners."

"There's a—" The group yelled out.

He made a fist and jammed it in a backwards motion toward that guard who came up behind him suddenly.

The group tried to warn him, but he seemed to already sense the guard, who was holding his face in pain.

"Run…" Manachi replied in a hurried way as the guard began to use backward swings.

The group of travelers were closer to the opening with its carvings and fled all at once, breaking free from every attacker, one by one, warding them off as each took on an enemy. They made it to the door frame and were about to turn a corner when Gabriel realized a problem. "Where is Asher?"

The group wheeled around to see that Asher was in the middle of the fray, going for Darrin who was being held by the Accuser. Asher let the Spirit Sword face the underhanded jab of the guard. The sword was translucent as they could see inside power moving from the inside.

Asher tried to cause the opponent to make a mistake by feigning. At this point Asher was able to start attacking at the guard's arms, but arched in a different direction, attacking his legs so a jab made the guard completely debilitated. Again he kicked the guard so he lay on the ground. Asher sidestepped another enemy's blow and, at the same time deflecting another, was able to break free from him. He ran toward the seat at which the Accuser held Darrin as Asher had seen before, with the sword to his throat. Darrin's fear reflected in his eyes as all the flashbacks started to come in connection to Asher's own Cabin Boy.

"You will not escape with all. Give up to Captavia. Call it off or this one dies. This one truly is guilty," The Accuser sneered and held the sword dangerously close to Darrin's neck as he squirmed uncomfortably at the thought.

"Fight me." Asher's voice firmly called out the words and the Accuser shook his head. Asher felt sick for succumbing to the conditions of the Pursuer and those who would follow his ways. "I think you may be a match for the Spirit Sword." Asher was bluffing by creating in the Accuser a sense of pride in his ability.

"Even so, how can he be free even if the Spirit Sword is in his possession?" The Accuser presented the problem. "Oh yes, I will. I will take it from you," The Accuser shot back.

The Accuser let go of Darrin, removing the blade from his neck, but at the same time tied the rings of steel chain links that held Darrin to the chair cemented like stone into the ground. Darrin was held closely tied, laying his head up against the railings of the chair as both of the opponents faced each other. The Accuser stood upright with the sword, but he glared fiercely under dark brows that accompanied the dark robe in which revealed him.

The Accuser tried to grab the hilt of the sword, but was not able to and he retracted his hand.

The Accuser tripped on a chain on the ground and fell off the platform into the hard dirt packed floor.

It was a quick fight for sure and no match for the Spirit Sword. Asher came up to Darrin and realized the chains may not come off because he was guilty. Asher then decided to ask, "Do you want to be free, Darrin? Do you want to be rid of the guilt from your list of faults? Through the Holy One, you can."

"The Holy One... How can I be good enough for him when I have been a failure in my own way?" Darrin related his dilemma.

"Yes, you can Darrin, he forgives you for all. He can remove these chains of sin since you are incapable of your own."

Darrin's head went down and then back up again. "You know that I am ashamed to be the League member with that list. I thought I had done the right actions and fought for the right side. All of it for naught it seems.

"Yes, if what you have said is true then yes." Darrin looked up, "Holy One, please free me from these chains. I want to be forgiven. I am sorry for trusting in the League to be free; I trust in you."

Darrin for a moment could see the Holy One's face and could hear the words, "You are free in me, dear son." This was all that was heard, but this was all that Darrin needed.

"Are you ready?" Asher said these words after a few moments and Darrin understood the weight of it all.

"Yes, I know the Holy One has heard me," Darrin replied with confidence in his tone. Asher felt much awe in the moment and motioned for Darrin to spread his arms and the Spirit Sword fell down onto the chains, sparking and crackling as it had done with his. All at once, they dissipated and became naught.

Darrin's arms waved and he replied, "I feel like a great weight has come off my mind and off my soul."

"Yes, it is true. I felt the same way." Asher's eyes at once filled with tears at the thought of himself recently being freed and now his friend Darrin also being freed. It was overwhelming.

Darrin comforted Asher, "My friend, I know you are crying, but if we do not move along we may be trapped here." The room at this time was still raging with combat. "How are we going to make it over there?" To their relief, a League member came alongside them and warded off the recovering Accuser as Asher had used the Spirit Sword to free Darrin.

"Run," the League member suggested.

They dodged many blows and faced some head-long as a League member helped them across the room. It was nothing short of fierceness.

"Hurry, we are to shut the door so they will be trapped, but again, hurry to free the prisoners," The League member offered. "The court members have all gathered into Captavia Court. Just pray for our safety as we will pray for yours."

One of the League members handed the travelers the rest of their belongings that had been stolen by the guards, including the never ending bag owned by Gabriel. One could tell he was overjoyed.

Asher nodded and Darrin did the same thing as they dashed down the hallway where there were many cells that had to be opened. Asher brandished the Spirit Sword as it glowed and opened some of the locks, pulling some from the cells, coming to one that was unable to open. The one inside looked away for a moment, and the blade ignited the lock.

The group of travelers were found running quickly from the other direction with a group of many prisoners among them. Manachi, Darrin, Percy, Gabriel, and Keeper stood in the midst, Manachi holding the ring of keys.

"Asher you are safe," Percy cried. "See who we have freed. There are many, but there are some who will not, and that is their personal choice. It is a sad reality to still feel like you belong in captivity or do not want to receive freedom."

Asher looked over again at the man with the chains that would not open. "Do you want to be free?"

"No, you are also hypocritical. Saying one thing, but doing another. Even those who are 'good' have a list that is a mile long. I do not want to be a part of it."

The man's eyebrows furrowed and the hurt turned to bitter anger seeping out.

"Are you sure? This place has a way of thinking where there is no way of redemption," Asher again asked, but the man turned away without saying another word and looked downward while huddled in the darkest part of the cell.

Asher's heart sank at the thought of this man rejecting such a great gift, one that could change his way of life. Asher still wanted to help. "What is your name?"

"Ophil."

"Well, I will pray for you, Ophil. I hope we meet again."

The man only looked away once he met him and though he was upset, he felt touched. He did not say another thing and would not reach out as Asher hoped he would, but for some reason Asher had a feeling of hope of where he would end up.

Even so, Asher still looked around and even asked the others, but could not find Cephas.

Keeper looked around the dark area of the cells. Still, she searched through the area in order to find the possibility of seeing her parents and family. There was nothing. Her eyes went this way and that. Her heart fell as she rounded the last corner where the last empty cells stood. There was no one else. The hope felt like it dwindled and she was downtrodden, but knew that in a moment she would need to run. Where would they be if not here, if not in the Forlorn Isle?

The group found themselves digging through the opening of where Asher and Percy had escaped.

At that moment Asher saw an enemy and threw the Spirit Sword to Keeper. "Here, this is yours."

Keeper replied, looking into Asher's eyes, "I am trusting you more. It is all of ours. It is a tool that we wield." Keeper grabbed onto the hilt and slid it into the slot on her back. "I will keep hold of it, but you did make good use of it."

They then saw an enemy. She swung fully and guarded the way that was the entrance. Keeper's strokes mirrored her training, so they continued to show her skills as she and others warded off the enemy and ran.

The dirt crumbled away past the members as they made their way up a steep incline and into the first level of the cavern.

They helped those who were free through the opening and into the first level, shoveling dirt in an upwards way.

They stood on the level ground of the opening, with rocks dispersed in certain areas and they ran swiftly across the surface to the side of the wall where they began to again dig upward into the second level. They all at once pulled.

As the escapees dug through the dirt, there was still space where it was already open from where Asher had dug through in his escape before. The flashbacks continued to come, but now he was truly free.

The arm strength of Gabriel, Percy, Keeper, and Asher, Manachi, and Darrin allowed the many freed prisoners to shuffle and break free as they were pulled through.

Those who accompanied them finally came to the second level and for a moment they stood still. Percy and Asher looked around, but could not see an opening in the ceiling that seemed lower here and they moved their hands along the surface of the ceiling. In a moment, Percy felt the dirt crumble in an area and he moved his hand along the area, so that there was an opening of light that appeared as the dirt gave way to the blue sky.

"This is it!" Percy's voice showed excitement of this moment of hope for them.

They had covered over this area in their escape. Keeper was able to climb up on top in the outside world first, and then pulled up Gabriel, as they all eventually found themselves solidly on the ground of the outside world, above the world that was underneath. They had dug adjacent to a large boulder and now some helped fill in the opening solidly with fistfuls of dirt so that it solidly filled in the gap between them and the distant growling of the Digstons who were heard from underneath.

Some sat on a large boulder and others sat on the ground around it, breathing hard, taking in large gulps of air in order to relax themselves. They truly had been freed, and the prisoners who had not seen the light of day for many years stared, blinking their eyes at the brightness in the sun and the intense, vibrant blue of the sky as they scanned the horizon.

"We must get these prisoners to Buffington while some could come fight with us." Keeper allowed for this arrangement to be made.

"Yes," Manachi instructed. "I will take those who cannot or will not fight to Buffington for safekeeping. Who will fight?"

There was only Darrin that raised his timid hand out of the bunch, in addition to two others. Their names were Buck and Copper. "Aye, if you are going to fight we are coming with ya," They replied. "Yes, we are." Buck included.

Manachi continued, "Well, it is only good for those who are willing. I will come to you as soon as I have secured each of these freed people to a home in order to hide. I pray they will be safe, even though the Pursuer is roaming around." Asher shuddered and then quieted with peace.

Manachi explained, "I heard there was a break in Buffington. Even so, it is the safest place we have for now. Best of time to your travelers. I was glad we were able to aid your escape."

Manachi then began to lead them down a slope from the high ledge on which they stood on, going toward Buffington. They would go as swiftly as possible.

The group of travelers went down the rough, sandy ledge in the opposite direction, farther away from Buffington. They made their way down gingerly as they surveyed the landscape for guards and Digstons who would all at once come after them. Keeper looked to see a bird circling around, much closer to them as they had been in the valley below. The wind whipped their skin, as the dry air with the mixture of sand and dirt beat up against them. Keeper's mouth began to get dry, but she knew that getting water was far away.

They continued down the slope as the day dimmed and finally found themselves at the base, where they felt sheltered from the intense wind. "We did go back the same way Manachi went, but we passed by Buffington and took a separate trail through the mountain range," Asher and Percy explained their direction they took to arrive near Rockfirm.

"If we had taken the easier route through the mountains and maybe did not take so many divergent paths because the ledge on the mountain broke off, we would have gotten to this point easier," Percy sighed. "But we saw what we needed to see and did what we needed to do. It has been the right direction up till now."

Chapter 30

"The city of Buffington was taken down. It became open for me to take over," The Pursuer said. His carriage had rolled back into the town of Rockfirm. "Now on to the Forlorn Isle to fight these insurrectionists."

The Mayor and Messenger were present and heard these words. They felt the pain of those who had been taken and felt remorse for the situation. They knew of what had happened based on their actions of giving the Pursuer the idea to invade the city of Buffington with Asher's help, but not enough to go against the Pursuer.

Now the Pursuer continued with darker tones, "but the people of Captavia were attacked by the travelers with Keeper with them so some escaped and now… Asher is on the Holy One's side."

Suddenly the atmosphere changed to a darkness that was impenetrable. The Pursuer started to come toward the Mayor.

"Why are you doing this?"
There came the battering of the voice of the Mayor as his hand extended outward. The Purser held a chain with the shackle that he clamped securely and turned the key, that could lock doors but was not the key of sin and death.

"I have done everything that you have said," Mayor pleaded.
The Pursued ignored this pleading comment, and continued as he fastened the chain securely to the inside of the carriage wall.

The Pursuer pulled the Mayor up the extended stairs, before turning with a harsh jostle, and kicking him to the floor as his face rubbed up against the dirt crusted floor.

After a moment the Pursuer's raging tone came out with, "Yes, you do think that in obeying me you will be free. That somehow you are able to worm your way around what I commanded of you and this town, as though you have the upper hand. Everything you were banking on as leverage with you using your vision has been for naught. The enemy has been undermining my plans. Well, you will never have freedom under my dominion. Anyway, Asher did not complete his tasks as well as I liked. Not getting enough information from Keeper or changing course. You did help me to invade Buffington."

The Mayor unfeelingly mouthed the words and then spoke, "Oh my. Oh, what a shame." absolutely showing his lack of empathy for the situation.

The Pursuer pulled the rim of his collar so that the man stood on his toes and spoke these words, "Do not mock me. I know you rebel and even against me, a good quality, but even so, rebels will pay for their disrespect."

The Pursuer again let go of the Mayor's collar so that he again fell on the floor of the carriage that served a tall enough place to stand. His thick leather boots thudded as he stepped down the stairs, locking the door.

The Mayor cried out, "I still helped you. We were allies."

The Pursuer looked back, red eyes glinting brightly, as his tongue flicked as his temper rose and then fell. "I have no allies, nor foe that can rule over me."

Messenger watched from afar as he peered through

the window. He had much concern for his superior, and the punishment he would receive. What would happen if he intervened? Anyway, he felt as though he had not the strength. Inside, he knew that the Mayor deserved this sentence. Many would fear after the rumbling wheels of the rough road could be heard leading to the Forlorn Isle.

The Mayor had seemed aware of what occurred, but now seemed in a trance as he stared blankly at the bar doors of the carriage. The crack of the whip was again heard as the horse again took up a brisk gallop.

Chapter 31

They had descended into an area in front of them, level to the ground. There were many dark looking trees that looked as though they grew no leaves as though it was winter always in the Dark Forest. The group stepped under the overhanging branches and their feet began to feel unsteady. Below, the ground contrasted from the dry, grainy sand from the land above to the moist, uneven ground. It looked like an offshoot of the area of land they had traveled on before they had entered Captavia. Their feet congregated to lines of grass outcroppings and went around the more muddy areas.

With one slip of the foot, Gabriel had his foot covered in mud, but was able to pull it out quickly since his other leg solidly stood on the grassy patch. They solidly walked along the grassy patches and sometimes had to make a leap to the next destination.

"This swampy portion of the trip was always hard for those coming to Captavia." Buck recounted his memory of this place.

Copper added, "Aye, it is easy to lose men since—" Copper's voice quieted as he saw Darrin jump from one patch of grass to one that was a ways away, but at that moment Darrin's foot hit it and he fell straight into the dirt.

"Darrin—" Asher was concerned. "Are you all right?" Asher was close behind him and expected to reach out a hand and pull Darrin, who was timid with an inner strength, up from the mud onto a patch of grass. Darrin seemed to pull him down not intentionally, but because the dirt began to sink.

"Aye, because of the quicksand," Copper replied,

giving this last bit of information a little too late to help anyone.

Asher had been here before as well, but one had fallen in as they traveled from the Forlorn Isle to Captavia because of their rebellion. Somehow they just kept fighting against the Pullings and captivity.

Darrin sank deeper as the weight became heavy.

The dirt and sand began to sink deeper and Asher dangerously waved his arms as his face was being covered, and for Darrin it was up to his elbows.

Gabriel, Percy, and Keeper crossed over their arms as they grabbed onto Darrin, pulling him up steadily with his outstretched arm, with the other he grabbed onto Asher's arm which was flailing. They seemed to sink deeper, but there was a moment when Darrin came free and was able to drag Asher out with him. They stood breathless and exhausted, Asher gasping for any air available since his face was covered in mud and he had been underneath for a moment. Asher and Darrin rested on the patch of grass and gradually could lift themselves up. Keeper, Copper, Buck, Percy, and Gabriel were able to each help them along the tufts of grass. They watched as Darrin and Asher would jump to the next tuft of grass creating a sort of chain to pull them across. They at the same time tried to find ways of going that were not separated by the sinking mud puddles, but kept a continuous trail of swamp grass, weaving in and out.

They felt as though they continuously walked along this winding area. As they made their way along, the trees eventually began to weed out, so that there was only the sky above them. The mud patches on the swamp began to become clear with the murky water. The grass lengthened and there were sounds of crabs clicking their claws together in chattering noises. Open shells began to appear around and they smelled salt that came from the water that had gathered in puddles. The dark type of dirt aligned with the clumps of grass of the marsh. The many patches of water dotted the area and Keeper looked back to see the dark line of trees. Keeper could see a large crane as it flew across the area and landed, flapping its wings as it dived to retrieve a sleek silver minnow from the saltwater patches. It bent its head, pulling away the pieces.

Keeper continued to walk along the grassy splotches as they had widened so that several people could walk alongside each other. The brown and green sea grass lengthened and waved up against her knees as she walked along its shoots.

In front of them they could see in the distance the edge of the land where this marsh cut off. There was a scent of sea salt and mud, with a mix of freshly growing grass. The wind whipped into their faces as it had done when they had been exposed to the parched ground above Captavia.

Keeper pulled her hair from her face and saw the intense deep blue of the ocean. She felt amazed at the sight. She could see as the crests formed like billowy clouds in the sky. The group seemed a little more excited at the sight, knowing they were getting closer to the sea. There was much of the ecosystem that had changed as they traveled along the path that day. It felt like the terrain changed quickly and was confusing. Asher went to a water patch to wash off from falling into the mud in the Dark Forest and stepped back on the grass. Darrin did the same.

Asher looked out toward the horizon, where the edge of the water started. "I know of a boat we can board to make our way across to the Forlorn Isle."

Those around looked at each other. "I know I have been thinking about how we are to make our way across,"

Gabriel voiced his thoughts to the others. "But I have now just thought of it. You, Asher, I know you have been on the sea before and I am glad of your assistance." Gabriel came up to Asher and slapped him on the shoulder. "I am glad you are with us. I know there have been mishaps, but I know you are at the right place and with the right people."

"We support you," Keeper assured Asher, hopefully trying to make him feel accepted even if he followed the Pursuer. Now it was a known fact.

"Yes, I am glad for the chance again." Asher at once diverted the conversation. "I am going to buy us a boat once we are near the shore." He pointed to a little harbor that jutted outward toward the sea with several buildings for fishermen, identifying it as a fishing town.

The sun was lowering in the sky and the travelers knew that it must wait until the morning. They continued to walk forward, as the grass of solid ground began to converge so that there was no need to worry about falling in puddles of seawater.

The grass grew up in tall stalks mixed with some green small growth tilted and curled at the tip. The ground began to become sandy with miniscule, beige sand granules that were wet as mush from the water.

The wind continued to whip into their faces as they drew closer to the fishing town. The town was open so that there was not a gate. There was not any hindrance for the Pursuer who would pass through this area. "Many of the ships coming through the port are the Pursuer's," Asher's voice lowered, but had a confident tone all at once.

"We must abide by the restrictions put on by the Pursuer. Many residents' boats also cast off from this port and must succumb to his will," Asher continued on with his speech concernedly, but with a little hope.

"We must appear to be under guidelines. I will go into

town since I have an old friend who will let us borrow a ship. The rest of you," Asher advised understandably, "must search for supplies in the town. We will be on the sea for a while so I will create a list. Percy, Gabriel, and Darrin, you go to find what we need for the journey."

"What about us?" Copper and Buck asked concernedly. Keeper also asked this.

"You all come with me. I need your help," Asher instructed.

The first group of travelers met at the outskirts of the town, and Asher and his group went onward into the street of the square with wooden homes, with white paint that flashed from the sides of the panels. There was a mixture of sand and mud for the ground, and stones on the streets that lined the path.

The first group of travelers saw that on one side of the little outcropping of buildings was a few shops with wooden signs hanging out front. They had all the supplies so they stepped into a shop that had all types of fish laying out on top of ice: mackerel, sailfish, halibut, grouper, flounder, red fish, mahi mahi, tuna, and tilapia.

With the light of the lantern, it reflected the scales of the fish. As they pointed to the selection, a large, gruff shop owner cut the fish up into pieces and smothered it thoroughly with spices while packaging it in parchment paper with a piece of string. The prices were lower since everything had been caught recently by the fisherman off the port, among the others and general travelers that came through the port.

Carrying their parchments, they went one shop over in order to stock up on grain for dry biscuits, cheese, and vegetables at the different shops with fresh ingredients.

They also went into a store with defending weapons that they would need. They wrapped them in leather. With them Gabriel filled his never ending bag as they made a clanking sound, while carrying it lightly.

"Is that thing finally getting heavy, dear chap?" Percy joked.

Gabriel still lifted it up with not much effort. "Not in the slightest." Then he laughed heartily.

In another part of the city, Asher and his other group walked along the adjacent path, with stones tightly cemented together that broke off into wooden planks that lined the docks that extended into the water. Down the sides cretaceous creatures with shells grew up the lower portion of the pier legs.

Asher walked onto the boards as they creaked and flared up with brittle pieces of the wharf. They looked up at the large hulls of ships raised up from the water.

Many people bustled around the busy dock area and in the streets of the fishing town.

The crowd spoke loudly as many of the ships got ready to sail.

The group that had gone with Asher walked along the road toward the dock. For a moment Keeper addressed what she had seen in Captavia. She had previously realized something different, as though her Spirit Eyes could see something that she had not ever seen before. There were no chains—Asher had no chains upon his hands. She had noticed this though they went through the swamp and through the seagrass marsh. It was only now that she had time to talk to him of what had been revealed to her, maybe in the perfect time.

"Asher," Keeper did not know how to start. "Is there

something different about you?"

Asher almost felt shocked, but he smiled understandingly at the importance of what really happened in his life from this past time in Captavia. The other travelers, Copper and Buck, walked silently alongside them listening to the conversation.

Asher thought about it for a second before wanting to talk about what really happened. This was the first time Asher had actually verbalized his decision.

"I saw the Holy One," Asher started out.

Keeper replied, "Where did you see him?"

Asher answered, "I saw him while in Captavia. He delivered me." Asher said these words as they meant the world to him. He began to tear up and cough.

Keeper too began to tear up. "Really, that is wonderful." Keeper seemed overjoyed at the thought. Keeper could see it in the way he acted and in the way she could not see the chains on his wrists.

"Is he not wonderful?" were the words that came from Keeper's mouth and Asher had begun to understand what Keeper meant.

"Yes," he replied reflectively. "Even though I have done so much wrong in my life. Even though I tried to live in a good way, I always felt as though I lived in so much bondage. I even… I even served the Pursuer." In this moment Asher was truthful, letting the words come out clearly. "I thought I could get rid of it on my own, but as I came to the Holy One, he had the ability to break my bonds and set me free. There has been much done for us. He has done it all to set us free from bondage."

"Do you remember the old stories of how he set captives free?" Keeper asked, remembering the story.

"I heard the story and you have shown it through your example," Asher said back to Keeper.

"He did so in order that he could defeat sin and death, even though he died. He surely rose again and he is still living in those who believe in him."

"Yes, I believe," Asher answered back.

"And he will."

"And Keeper…" Asher stopped for a moment. "I have to admit something."

"What is it?"

"Well, I have been helping the Pursuer, but I have chosen not to help him anymore. I have been set free from that." Asher walked through the streets as it began to get crowded, but Keeper could still see the emotion.

"I am so happy for you. Thank you for confiding this information to me. I am sorry for ever doubting you," Keeper paused.

"It is alright Keeper," Asher responded. "You were concerned for my well being."

"Thank you for being understanding. Anyway, we are free, and all we can do is begin to walk righteously." Asher knew this to be true. It was a massive step in the right direction, but he knew with the Holy One guiding him and also his friends such as Keeper he would make it.

"Is that how it goes?" Asher asked expectantly.

"The Holy One said, 'My grace is sufficient for you, for my power is made perfect in weakness.'" Keeper tried to encourage him.

Keeper was so emotional at the words. Her friend, her fellow traveler, was finally able to see the light. She knew she was far from perfect, but that she hoped she was able to show him the hope she had been shown. She was able to experience the Holy One from a place of emptiness and depression of knowing no where else to turn, but he had a longer and heavier journey. But now they were on the same page. What could the Holy One do now? What hearts could be healed? The Holy One was working in all their lives outside of their own knowledge and control.

They reached the dock as the others who had traveled behind came close.

"I am going to help you guys find a boat." He turned to the group saying this. "I know of a captain of a ship."

They stepped over rigging of ropes tied in many elaborate knots that wound around a metal hook that kept the rope secure. Looking up at the wooden hull, they raised their eyes to the rigging. The rope ladder stretched up to the crow's nest. The ranges of rope were stacked one on top of another. There was a flag that had a blue background and a sun with rays.

Many of these types of ships lined the dock so that their masts stood tall, marking the area where they had been docked. The wind came to fill their sails and in every which way that it blew. Many sailors walked along the dock, some ready to cast off as one could see some tinkering with the rigging on board of some of the boats' main decks which are in the middle of the ship.

Asher went up to one individual. Those walking along the deck wore dark bandanas, with gold earring piercings in their ears. This individual had a dark sash used as a belt, tying a red button down shirt. He looked up immediately and recognized Asher, greeting him with, "Aye, my brother Asher. I have not seen you in many years." He came up close to Asher, slapping him hard on the back.

His teeth showed a mischievous smile. "I heard you had been taken over by the Pursuer's ship, and you and your crew had been taken by the Pursuer."

"Yes, but one is still lost."
"Well who?"

"The Cabin Boy, my best sailing partner while on the sea." Asher explained, but not without sadness in his voice.

"Aye... I have not seen him in the port. Must have truly gone missing." The man said this in a concerning way.

"More recently I have understood that the Pursuer has captured him again. You know I boarded the Pursuer's ship just so Cephas could be safe."

"Aye, it is unfortunate and understandable. Sometimes these tales become a bit mixed as a fisherman might talk about the size of their catch." The man winked an eye, but Asher did not understand the reason but instead went along with it. The fisherman pulled out a sword from his belt and pulled it toward the sky. "If the Pursuer hurts him, I will get him." he said this brandishing his sword.

Asher turned to introduce Keeper, Buck, and Copper to the man. Keeper felt untrustful of him as he said, "Aye, nice to meet ye. I am Sylvian."

"Well," Asher again began. "We have come here to borrow a boat if you have one, in hopes to protect those in the Forlorn Isle and maybe my Cabin Boy."

The man almost gasped, but contained himself. "That sure is a mission to go to the Forlorn Isle. It is a dangerous trek. Nevertheless I will help you." He said this, walking down the dock. "Anyway, do not speak so loudly, this is a dangerous place to mention such things, with so many that serve the Pursuer that are about." He walked along the boardwalk and turned right as the wharf jutted out to a row of ships that looked of a medium size. The man walked up to the boat which rose high above the others. Its flag was crimson.

"It has a wide deck stretching out to the captain's wheel," Asher observed.

"Here is *The Duchess*. I know you remember it," The man gave the name of the boat.

"Aye, I do remember."

It had a carving on the deck, stretching out like a curved wave. It came to a tip with an engraving of the name of the ship bolstered on the front.

They saw this ship among the others. "It's nothing like my old ship, *The Atticus*, but I feel like this will serve us well." Asher commented, reminiscing on the past of his old ship but still being appreciative of the ship at present.

"I agree, and I hope this ship serves you well. It is certainly an excellent vessel." The man raised his hand gesturing to the ship, with an explanation.

Asher tried to pull out something from a bag of coins to pay for renting out the ship, but the man placed a hand so that he closed Asher's hand into a fist with the coins gripped inside. The guards had taken their weapons while at Captavia, but had somehow missed his hidden pouch of money within his leather coat.

"No, I am allowing you to use this ship as long as you need," the man kindly offered. "Just as long as you take care of it."

Asher nodded and returned the coins into the leather pouch, returning it inside of his leather coat. "Yes, I will do my best. We are to travel tomorrow."

"Aye, sure to be good sailing, but you never know, these sea storms blow across in a hurry." The man tilted his hand and smiled. "See you early tomorrow," the man said walking back down the pier where he had first been standing, talking to some other sailors that discussed their adventures while on the sea.

Chapter 32

Before Keeper went to sleep she put in her journal some thoughts on those who had escaped from Captavia. She at that moment began to see something in her dreams.

Keeper could see something, but she did not know what. The vision became blurry as a deep gray mist went over everything. Out from that licked the water of the sea, spilling out onto dry land. Keeper could feel the wind as it blew away the mist so she recognized waves crashing. Keeper looked at the waves, but they seemed a distance away. She began walking closer to the water and began to wade into the surf, pulling her arms in front of her as she dove forward into the waves. Underneath she pushed through as the bubbles floated up to the surface of the glittering underwater. The sea was billowing up as though it was a tumultuous storm in her own life. There were many rough waves that were raging in her present life. Despite the waves raging, she knew the Holy One would get her through and calm the waves. It was dark for a moment, and she blinked her eyes open to see a light underneath, resting on the sandy floor. She rose up quickly, flapping her arms as she ascended from the water for air. She arrived on the surface of the rough sea. The waves began to crash over her from a large height, curling up and falling on top of her. She raised up several times in order to gain the breath that she needed, coughing out the water that had crashed into her mouth. She gained her breath and dived back into the deep, as the water surrounded her and she felt as though she could breathe and she could as she opened her mouth for air. She glided around in the water and felt an overwhelming sense of peace as though she dove into a sea of grace. It was abundant and deep, almost overwhelming. She descended deeper into the water, following the glowing substance at the bottom. Keeper came to the glowing sword, but the Holy One was holding it.

"Know that I have covered everything. My grace has abounded greatly over everything. Do not be afraid. Have peace. You are in the sea of grace." The Holy One had a calming voice, but Keeper felt fear of the situation and grabbed the Spirit Sword as water came down as the Holy One let it go. "Do you want me or the protection that the Spirit Sword provides in diminishing your fear of the Pursuer?"

Keeper could hear these words as she rose up from the water, hanging onto the sword.

She looked back at the Holy One, coming back to him as she took another breath. She swam down back into the glittering water as she returned the Spirit Sword. She could still breathe at this moment.

"I am sorry for trusting in the Spirit Sword." Keeper allowed her voice to reach the Holy One.

"You are forgiven. Know that the sword is only for protection. A tool to help others. Please trust in me." The Holy One extended a hand toward Keeper and she exchanged the sword back to him, grasping his hand as he pulled up from the water.

"But how will I fight?"

"Nothing you can do can save you. But only my grace can save you." These words came from the Holy One's mind and were revealed to Keeper as the foam and bubbles of the water gave way to the air.

All at once she found herself, jolting up from sleep.

356

The sheets of the bed came off as she sat up and looked around at the empty inn room.

'I have to be careful. I do not know what everything means in these dreams and visions, but at least the Holy One made himself known in the dream. I agree, and I want to do as he said.' Keeper thought through this realization. Overall, she found peace in the thoughts of the dream.

Her walk of faith gradually grew as it should have.

She felt alone with her thoughts, but knew she was in the presence of the Holy One. She peered out the window at the large opaque moon that reflected off the roofs of the few homely buildings. The same light reflected from the side of her bed, on the smooth wooden floorboards so that the Spirit Sword reflected and shimmered dimly as a blue mist moved floating along and inside of it.

Keeper grabbed the hilt and brought its blade in front of her. Her eyes reflected the light of the mist within as she studied the contents enclosed inside the object for protection.

"I do not trust this object too much and my visions and dreams for guidance." Keeper paused, laying the sword back down on to the cold floor and laying down to sleep once more. She meant the words she spoke.

"This time, I will trust the Holy One. Despite my fears. Despite the roads that I have traveled that have been tumultuous, I trust you."

Meanwhile in the distance she could hear the faint sound of chains rattling.

There was another clearing as Keeper walked along. Keeper began to feel cold as a shadow passed against the

group as a figure in a hood emerged from the woods. The fear that rose inside her was like she had just seen this being for the first time. He ran faster as she ran past the trees, almost tripping.

He did not turn his head like a dream of the past. The dark shadows glided as he walked toward the beginning lines of the field where there stood the dark horde of troops that had been set there for yet another battle. Their dark-clad armor reflected the light of the noonday sun as the clouds and rain had departed.

Keeper had anticipated this moment with dread, as the fear that she had once possessed so intensely filled her body. Everything felt shaky. She remembered how last time she ran from the Pursuer in battle. This time she would defeat him for sure, but there were so many enemies.

"How are we to fight this enemy?" Keeper seemed frantic, but she looked to the Holy One who understood her face.

"They are all around us," He said, pointing around the open area. "There are myriads of ones that are on the side of righteousness."

"I do not see anything," Keeper admitted.

The Holy One told her to close her eyes and she did so, shutting them tightly. It was completely dark, but Keeper felt as if she heard the noise of horses' hooves and metal rattling.

"Open them," the Holy One asked.

It was to Keeper's surprise, yet great relief that she saw the Holy One's army with long spears hoisted over the shoulders while others carried swords. The Holy One stood there in front as one of his troops, Jehovah Sabaoth, stood behind. She knew she was surrounded by the Holy One and that he was there with her.

Above flowed the flag Nissi, the banner which those of the Holy One stood under.

The messenger began to speak.

"Aye, they are still trying to reroute us, but we have almost surrounded the Pursuer. The only way out is toward the sea."

Keeper cringed at the thought of the Forlorn Isle in which the Pursuer continued to dominate. There needed to be a way in which to defeat them. Keeper then remembered the reality, 'We have almost completely surrounded him.' Keeper had this burning sensation to meet him once again in the middle. She had grown much stronger now and she carried the Spirit Sword beside her, knowing the power it contained. She could truly get rid of this fear. As she said this it was infused with blind strength and the fear that she may never be rid of this figure.

"He may have won the battle, but we have won the war." The Holy One reminded her of the time when she was afraid, adding with a great certainty, "Remember as I have told you that he was defeated a long time ago. You know he has no reign, but everyone must still turn to the Holy One to be saved."

Keeper asked something that had been gnawing at her for a long while. "But why does he still fight us?"

The Holy One sighed, but said in a low tone, "He knows if he can take over your mind, then you are his. Even those who are chosen still fight. This is called a battlefield, just like pillars being cracked through the middle as they made the whole stronghold collapse. This is when you stand firm just in my strength." Holy One guided a horse by the reins up to Keeper. He nodded and she reached her long sleeved arm and she got on. Keeper was heaved up the side of the horse, moving her leg over the top. The Holy One got onto a horse with a white velvety mane.

Keeper agreed with the words of the Holy One, but inside she felt weak as she looked at the sword. 'How does this have power?'

From the other side of the field, the attackers began a steady charge against Jehovah Sabaoth's horses, so they ran across the field marked with tall grass.

Far behind there was the extension of bluish mountains, covered with billows of clouds. From there the mountain range dipped down so that there was an opening to the sea.

They had almost gotten to that point as Jehovah Sabaoth had nearly surrounded them.

They had decided to attack so that the Holy One or mainly Jehovah Sabaoth would not follow them. They would have a cut short way to the sea to the Forlorn Isle. The Holy One would not have that.

The Holy One or Jehovah Sabaoth called to arms with a resonating sound made from blowing a ram's horn.

The soldiers all at once charged, being heavily clad in armor similar to ones that Keeper wore upon her.

Some came running, some on horseback. Jehovah Sabbath rode upon a white horse, pure as snow. The horseback riders came to the front with swords extended from the robe clad arms.

Keeper came up from behind as she rode on a dark brown horse of her own, and the fiery spirit of the horse reared up as it galloped along. Keeper could hear its hooves as it tore at the matted grass.

The Holy One rode in front as a protective guard. Those who held the spears flanked into individual small square-shaped groups, holding their shields boxed together as some extra protection.

As the horses ran with the riders atop, those with

swords clashed against the enemy with silver tipped axes with chips in them from much use. These clashed against the legs of some of the horses. Some included Keeper as they tumbled down, hitting the ground with great impact. These soldiers pulled the horses up swiftly and allowed the horse to walk in a slower manner.

Keeper, who was not a rider now, climbed to her feet in the middle of the fight and began swinging her sword against the attackers. The soldiers glared into the hateful eyes of the enemy, slashing at their shields. The attackers fell to their knees with pain. At the same moment another attacker came up with two swords drawn and swished them parallel in the same arm motion. "You are unworthy," The enemy taunted.

"I am chosen and in the beloved." Keeper held up her sword as she said these words.

These words made the sword glow every time she would say it out loud. It gave the sword its strength so that it skillfully deflected every sideways blow.

Keeper's arm became strong as she beat up against the parallel blades. The attacker pulled back for a moment and made a whipping motion with the blade. The attacker twirled it so it slashed as a wheel through the air as the attacker again grabbed the hilt in the air securely.

Keeper felt a bit intimidated at the moment while whipping the blade so the extra blade came out at right angles, but was able to straighten up and get into a fighting stance. Keeper mirrored her motion as she threw her sword into the air as it flipped, but she realized she could not catch the sharpened side of the sword that struck firmly into the ground. The matted piece of dirt and grass flew up.

Keeper at once felt afraid as she ran to grab her sword that had flown in front of her and the attacker just lifted a hand and pulled the blade from the ground. He held the lengthened blade in one hand and the Spirit Sword in the other, though it did not have the same power.

Keeper turned back to run away so that at the same moment she ran into the Holy One who came up from behind and handed her another silver weapon. "Here is this." Keeper grasped the weapon tightly as the Holy One gave it to her.

She observed as the Holy One drew his blade, which met the long blade so that the attacker used his might to push the Holy One off of him. The Holy One did not budge in his stance, but the attacker did, swinging with his overhand so that it once again deflected against the Holy One.

The Holy One motioned for Keeper to come to the other side to advance. The attacker once again spun the long sword as if the pistons of a wheel met the Holy One's blade as it clanked. Keeper at once came from the other side holding her blade up high so that it came down hard on the Spirit Sword so that it once again fell to the ground. Keeper again picked it up as the attacker had no way to advance in her direction. The long blade in which he held spun again wildly as the Holy One hit it so that it slashed at another attacker. At this point the one who came against them frantically turned and ran back into the fray, straining for the back of the line. Keeper was allowing the Holy One to fight and they began to win.

The Holy One sighed as there came a deep mist coming from one side of the field. It trailed behind another one's cape, so that it created a blockage in which one could see.

The Holy One did not seem anxious, since he never reacted in that way. He knew that this fight would still be one of many, but he knew of the strength, of what the power *that was already over the Pursuer.*

The Holy One stood still as Keeper too stood in a fighting stance. The Holy One encouraged her with these words, "Look to the hills. Where does my help come from? My help comes from the Holy One, the maker of heaven and earth."

The enemy came closer, but for once Keeper did not feel afraid. Maybe this time she had enough strength... She held the blade again and waved it in front of her, but suddenly saw the Holy One looking inquisitively. "Why are you trusting in a blade as though it had strength to save you? It is your faith in me that has saved you. I do what my Father has sent me to do. If you see me, you see my Father who is God. You have faith in me, the begotten Son of God."

These words showed her what to believe in and how to walk.

The Pursuer came closer, but Keeper began to flinch. She knew she needed to face him. This time she knew she could, she disregarded what the Holy One had said and dashed ahead with her sword raised above her head. Keeper let out a battle cry, which was not a wise thing to do, but she did it anyway as a way to seem stronger.

Chapter 33

The next morning the sun brightly shone on the horizon, with a red brushed sky painted across. The clouds wisped across with little puffs of gray.

The sound of the seagulls could be heard as the group of travelers arose from the inn, with burlap sacks and food in parchment paper placed in Gabriel's never ending bag. With supplies in hand, they had fully refreshing sleep to rejuvenate them on the journey.

"Aye, what a day," Percy exclaimed at the sight.

They arrived at the dock to find Sylvian, the man Asher had asked for the ship, and he helped them load everything on board that they would need for a journey in a storage space below deck.

The ship's sails pulled upward ready to set sail into the Derorian Sea. The deck stretched wide so that most of them stood on the main deck, guided by Asher in instruction of how to work all the different ropes.

The man also prepared the ship with the help of some other sailors. When he completed these tasks, Sylvian, who was Asher's friend, and the other helpers exited the ship.

From the deck, the group of the traveling members, including Asher, pulled up the anchor.

Asher waved a hand in salute to his head towards Sylvian who stood placidly surrounded by sailors scurried to and fro on the wharf, preparing for other voyages.

Asher could see a ship that held the flag of the Pursuer with the green winding snake with the dark backdrop of the flag's material.

It seemed a surprise and a relief that they had gotten through the town, without running into the Pursuer. It seemed he would have come during the night. Asher looked back to see that the ship had been ported and a chain gang had been led toward Captavia, stomping through the mud of the swamp.

It really was a relief that they had not noticed them, but Asher wanted to stay low, pulling the flag down so no one would recognize them or know who they associated with. He pulled the rope attached to the mast, pulling the red flag downward. He still felt scared to show his allegiance, but that would take time.

He turned around and did not see anyone following them. He stood at the captain's wheel controlling the rudder that could steer the ship through the water into any direction. Keeper could feel the sea breeze as it wafted up with the scent of salt. Flying fish could be seen jumping with their fins outstretched. They moved in schools like little puffs of smoke rising and falling into the sea. Keeper could also look up to see the seagulls sitting perched on the mast and flying high overhead. Their squawking cry seemed as though they spoke one to another.

The waves crashed up against the shore. The light cyan blue faded into the darker gray crests of the Derorian Sea. A group of pelicans flew above the sea water, with large bills, diving down into the waves to find fishes and coming up with scoops of water spilling from their beaks. They glided almost without flapping and as if they could glide as long as a dolphin could hold its breath. They traveled together in a triangular array, switching places for who led the group. The white foam of the sea road was like a myriad of white horses racing in a stampede, as they crashed and dissipated into the greenish, blue surf.

The boat's tip careened through the water. The sails of the boat were filled with the wind as though the Holy One created that very wind as a breath to propel the boat further along on its journey.

The waves crashed up against the shore.

Keeper watched all morning and afternoon. Near the evening, Keeper looked out to see the sights of the ship upon the water, but in a moment noticed some dark clouds billowing up, rising upward and pulling together.

Keeper's mind reverted back to her dream of last night of the untamed ocean as she sunk down into the breathable air. In this moment, it felt quiet, the light still waned but with enough to see. It would be there soon enough. She again went to help those on the deck, as each learned a new job. Asher instructed them how to tie knots and steer the ship in the correct direction. Some scrubbed the deck, others manned the sails, but it all depended on their shift. Asher used a directional tool that he looked through and it dropped down with two rods looking like a protractor.

"Come, let me show you how to tie this knot," Asher told Keeper as he demonstrated the over and through strokes of his hand with the rope. "Now you try." Keeper did and failed, but Asher laughed and said it would take practice and did another knot as she finished the knot correctly. "Wow, good job. You can always practice to do better."

Keeper replied, "Sure thing."

The rest of the crew drew close together and Gabriel retrieved the map, so that they observed the direction in which they headed to the Forlorn Isle.

The laughable Buck and Copper began to jig with arms folded as they twirled around at the thought of the path before then. They seemed either too naive of the trouble that might again befall them or without the absence of fear because of the Holy One guiding them with courage. Their song rang out so that the others began to follow along.

"Sea with billowing foamy white
We are here to sail all day and night
To free those whose shackles bind
Follow the Holy One both brave and kind
Ayo, we adventure to make it right."

Darrin started singing first and then all the others sang together.

"Ayo, we adventure to make it right."

A hearty laugh reverberated from the deck and reflected off the sea.

"Yes," Gabriel started. "We are close. We are almost to the Forlorn Isle, but the trials are far from over. Anyway, we do need to celebrate how far we have come."

"I agree," Keeper included. "There has been much that has occurred, by the time we are on the other side of this. We will not lose hope. The Holy One is working and he is still on our side." The warm wind at once began to pick up. It was summer and the weather could change quickly. The clouds Keeper had seen drew closer so that the sound of thunder could be heard rumbling.

"A storm is coming," Percy remarked, noting the approaching clouds.

From inside the clouds a purple flash began to spark, creating a curved light outlining the rounded portions of the cloud. There seemed a whole bright world on the inside. The light at once extended in streaks, jaggedly moving from the clouds to the sea. The light of the sun had disappeared because of the darkness of night, making the brightness of the lightning only intensified.

The waves appeared by the flashing light as they crashed up against the sides of the ship. Those on the ship barely slept that night, but they instead found themselves on the deck trying to steady the sails so that the wind carried in the correct direction and did not make them too far off track.

"Man overboard!" The call was spoken between intervals of the cracks of thunder. Darrin yelled it so that he called to the others who found themselves bashed up against the railing. Asher decided to do something he said he would never do again. He used a piece of wood and wedged it into the spaces between the spokes of the captain's wheel, hoping to steady the direction. The rest of the members of the ship had found themselves busy keeping the rigging from being tangled as they kept the sails steady, but Asher still called for backup. In a moment's time, the pressure of the waves up against the rudder caused the wood ledged into the captain's wheel to break, as it spun wildly, turning the ship around in an adjacent direction. Asher had already jumped into the dangerous torrent, as Keeper secured the wheel with much force, keeping it steady as she turned back into the correct direction. Gabriel came up behind to help her keep the wheel secure.

Asher at the same time found himself underneath the water, with a dark, moving surface, but underneath there seemed a wonderful calm, as it had been in Keeper's dream. He felt as though the second he pulled his arms around Copper and he safely pulled him from the water, it felt like it had become himself. He had once been drowning in an ocean of water, boiling up into a storm. The Holy One had been his savior and now he could help Copper, who flailed helplessly, but the waves grew larger as they crashed into him. The heat from the cracks of thunder created a warmth in the water. He at once feared for their safety as a round crest came on top of him, sending them back underneath the water. All at once he saw the Holy One, as if he was standing above Asher on the water with a hand outstretched underneath the surface. Asher reached for the hand that stretched into the water and then in a moment the Holy One lifted him from the water, while he grasped a lifeline of a rope that had been thrown overboard. Copper grabbed tightly onto Asher's shoulders, as Asher used one arm to secure Copper and the other to grasp the rope. It took a few straining moments, but Percy and Darrin had the ability to pull them over the edge and onto the deck, sopping wet and coughing.

Asher could hear as the Holy One replied, "Asher, you are no longer a slave to sin. For one who has died has been set free from sin."

Both lay there for a few moments before they sat up and Gabriel brought some blankets to cover them up.

"I thought you had been lost to the sea," Darrin continued. "How did you do that? The waves clobbered you two."

Asher blinked with sea water dripping from his hair.

"The Holy One…" Asher began. "I saw him again. I did not think I might see him this soon." As Asher said this he doubted it was him because when he arose from the water it had been because of the rope. 'It could not have been him. Could it?' He stood steady as though it was flat ground. Though he had seen these things and all that had happened, for some reason his rational mind questioned.

The Holy One did save him, but he was not ready to believe that much.

"At least I think it was him," Asher added as he thought further. Despite that, he had been relieved that he and Copper had been retrieved safely and still felt thankful for the Holy One.

The night storm raged on as they continued to keep the shift afterwards. Not one of them slept. The storm did not die down until the early morning as the sun rose over diminishing waves. As the yellow rays of the sunlight pierced their souls with hope, the sea seemed to calm considerably. The world became warmed by the sun and the morning. Those who saw the waves had dissipated, those who had been on shifts during the night, slept in the morning hours as one person kept steering the ship in the correct direction. Someone was designated to use the spyglass-looking protractor that Asher bought in town. They also used a map, but it would have been easier to follow the stars that aligned to the compass Asher once possessed, but the storm with the thick cloud cover proved that they could not find the stars to travel by. In any case, they kept to their own method and made their way along nicely.

Up ahead could be seen a strip of land that rose high with many dark rocks that jutted out and piled one on top of another. The storm had not diverted them enough to lose the course to the Forlorn Isle.

It looked as though a carved piece of rock on the side had a fixture of a snake. A sure sign of the Pursuer's rule. Everyone on board had been woken up by Darrin, who had taken the captain's wheel last and saw the sight of the snake upon the rocks of the isle. All that saw it shuddered at the fear and excitement of what this meant. They had made it to the Forlorn Isle through so many obstacles. They had planned on how to get into Captavia through the help of the League, but they had not discussed the plan for entering the Forlorn Isle itself.

"We should go onto the shore to attack on the inside,"

Percy urged.

Gabriel responded, "There needs to be surprise and the inside of the Forlorn Isle has too many to come against us. We need a way to divert them."

Asher opened his mouth to speak, but at this moment a ship of the Pursuer rounded the Isle, with the dark flag of the snake upon the mast. Those aboard at once saw the ship and fired as it made its way around the bend.

Those aboard the travelers' boat ducked instinctively as a cannonball flew past uncomfortably close around the starboard side of the ship. Everyone aboard winced.

"That is what I was thinking," Asher began the thought that he left off, now with more evidence, "now we distract them with our ship." Asher said this confidently as another shot fired but now quite close.

"Come up to the island after you have done that," Keeper said.

"Yes, I will try. Now get on it," Asher said, climbing onto the quarter deck where the captain's wheel stood. Turning the posts wildly in an opposite direction, he headed in a direction where he could drop the others off on the back side of the island. He quickly found himself away from the range of the canons of the Pursuer's ship.

It proved a risky move, but they could not turn back at this point. They had to get on the island as soon as possible.

"Are you sure this is safe?" Keeper asked, coming up onto the quarter deck. "Boarding the shore while being in pursuit?"

"Well..." Asher had a nervous laugh that seemed unsure. "There have been crazier things that have been done. Now to the lifeboats. I will meet you on shore."

Keeper nodded and at once said in approval, "I agree. We just need to do it."

Keeper pulled everyone together, asking them for help

to lower the lifeboats. They all pushed up against the spokes in the wheel, making the rope wind into coils so that they could lower the lifeboats into the surf of the beach.

The shots continued firing, and the shots found their way toward the ship. The lifeboat that they had been lowering into the water with the seat like pulley settled into the water.

They took the oars and began to row. In the same way, Asher turned the ship around so that it faced the pursuing boat. Asher's shot struck, cracking the top of a tall, wooden mast at the ship so that the flag shook from the impact as the smoke seemed to be his unforgiveness of the opponent.

Keeper, along with the others, quickly felt the boat scrape up against the gravel-like sand of the shore, and they jumped from the lifeboats into the waist-deep surf, pulling it hastily to the land. The boat hit the sand and scraped up against a rock in which Darrin tied a rope to keep it secure, tucking the oars on the inside.

They dashed across the sand, creating individual footprints. They began climbing up onto the ledges laden with piles of boulders so that they mounted one just to find another. They helped one another in order to pull those such as Copper and Buck securely up from the ground and onto the next boulder ledge. Asher stayed behind at the ship.

Keeper looked back to see as Asher continued to fire without ceasing so that the wooden bow at the front of the Pursuer's ship had been damaged. As Asher made these shots, the ship of the Pursuer's suddenly stopped firing. The ship turned the other way, making its way out to sea.

Asher seemed confused, but all of a sudden Keeper could hear Asher's voice as he whooped and hollered. "They are leaving, yeah!" Asher seemed to regret his loudness and quieted himself quickly.

Asher felt that it had become safe to anchor the ship in order to get onto the island. Asher did this looking back to see if the ship returned. It did not. 'It should be safe.' Asher's thoughts reflected his confidence.

He immediately anchored the boat and lowered the remaining lifeboat which he let drop into the water without a splash. Asher at once climbed down the side of the boat and landed in the hull of the lifeboat, rowing quickly as the others had. Securing the life boat onto the shore, he came up swiftly behind the others who had reached the full height of the island and now stood on the brown grass of the surface.

Asher yelled out, "Keeper, hold on! Are you alright? I am coming!" Asher knew this island to be dangerous. Although Keeper never heard Asher's words.

Asher had been climbing some of the boulders near the top ledge and passed in between two boulders that stretched much higher than him. He did not realize what happened until he already found himself pulled into the shadow between these two rocks. He immediately recognized the glowing red eyes of the Pursuer, as Asher stood face-to-face with him. Asher at once pushed back, drawing out the sword he had bought in the fishing town.

"Get back," Asher commanded. "I do not follow you anymore. You can not mess with us anymore."

The Pursuer glared and his tongue slithered quickly between his fang-like teeth. He laughed heartily at the advancement but did not seem concerned.

"I fear you are in more danger now than you would have imagined. See." He pointed toward the ocean and the ship that belonged to the Pursuer had returned from the outer sea and had come close to the island, aiming its cannons directly at the ship given to Asher.

Asher gasped and realized he made a grave mistake

by leaving the ship anchored on the shore while the enemy's ship could easily shoot it down.

Even so, he did not expect what the Pursuer said next, "You know my stand-in captain of my ship has excellent aim. He could blast those who are in the open field on the top of this island in an easy manner." He paused and added, "He could also easily blast your ship." He again paused while pulling out the compass that Asher had given to his Cabin Boy. "And you know I still have your Cabin Boy. Cephas, was that his name?"

Asher winced and knew he had once again been put into a difficult place, literally between two rocks. He knew he had been freed. The Holy One had done that for him. Asher knew this, but all at once felt that he had become trapped again as the Pursuer always seemed to use him for something of his own desire. Should he fight? How could he with everything stacked up against him, going up against the safety of the others?

"You know you should not fight. You should only cooperate so that the ship does not fire. Return to your ship. Do not get onto the ship and fight.

"My gunmen boast of their ability up and down. You are their greatest asset, but now there are only six present, not seven."

Asher had once realized this point and felt like he needed to follow along, despite all the good the Holy One had done.

Asher at once backed out from between the two boulders into the light, so that he looked and saw that the Pursuer disappeared among the mangled rocks.

Asher descended from the tall ledge of rocks thinking that he could have protected them with his actions, but instead they had gotten in a much worse situation than expected.

Keeper began to worry. "Where is Asher?" She said walking to an area in which she could see over the boulders with a full view of the beach. She saw Asher maneuvering down the faces of the boulders, away from the place he said he would come. "What is he doing?" These words just as soon came out her mouth as she was faced by guards emerging between boulders. 'Asher served the Pursuer before. Is he doing it now by deserting us?'

Keeper raised the Spirit Sword in defense of herself as several guards surrounded the outside ledge of the open area of the isle.

"Guys, I need help." Keeper backed up so that the others saw the threat. They brandished swords that they had gotten in town, which Gabriel pulled from his bag. Gabriel pulled out his walking rod for defense.

"I have an army in here too if you need a little extra help." Gabriel looked over seriously and then smiled.

Darrin held a crossbow that had been strapped onto his back, with a leather strap. He raised it up, pulling the arrow further back into the firing position.

The guards did not seem fazed at the sight. Even when Darrin let the bow loose, the arrow went toward one of the guards, but the guard swiftly pulled out a sword, swiping downward so that the arrow fell to the ground mid-air.

Other guards advanced from the central underground region of the island so they came toward them from another side. Keeper knew they had been surrounded. Keeper lifted the sword as she defended herself from the blows.

If Asher would have stayed, he would have seen the attack and how they increased in their vulnerability as the guards surrounded the group of travelers.

Keeper again raised her sword in defense, being able to guard against the attack. The guards all at once came from all sides. However, Gabriel could still defend himself and the others by knocking the sword from their hand and holding them, keeping their arms pinned behind their back with his walking rod.

Those that came to break free the guard who Gabriel had retained, could not make it through Buck and Copper, who fought with daggers so that they jabbed with down strokes as two of the guards fell onto their knees before laying on the ground.

"Quick, out to the field," Percy instructed, gesturing to the brown grass that covered a clearing. "They would have no place to hide in order to surprise us."

Those who Keeper and the others held up broke free from the advancing attack so they shifted positions to the open area.

All at the same time, the ground exploded upwards, where large pieces of dirt became unlodged by cannon fire. The shots came from the Pursuer's ship floating close to the island.

The cannonfire came frequently and forcefully. Keeper began to run as the shots landed near them as the explosions rumbled the ground. Buck and Copper still fell behind and Keeper came around them, grabbing their hands.

They tried their best to again gain cover among the scattered boulders, but they realized that more of the guards had arisen as though hidden holes had formed in the ground.

Asher, seeing as the Pursuer's ship had armed its cannons at his undefended friends on the exposed part of the island, became frightened.

He had drawn close to his ship and knew he had the ability to fight back with his ship's defense from his position.

Asher ran toward the lifeboat, but as he rowed there seemed an absence of sound. He thought he should be hearing the blasts of the cannon against the island and the reverberating movement, with a blast creating ripples in the water. Instead, Asher felt nothing but the tide pulling his boat toward the shore as he rowed against it with his oars.

Asher looked up and realized what had occurred. The ship belonging to the Pursuer had turned with the rudder so that its bow faced Asher's acquired vessel. The shots had ceased for a moment just as quickly as they started again. They fired directly at the lifeboat Asher sat inside, so that he jumped overboard before a cannonball split the hull in two. He held his breath as he stayed underwater, hoping to be shielded from the cannon strikes.

For a few moments, he raised his head to gulp in some air, finding the snake flag that seemed to taunt him as it fluttered while strikes came close to the ship. It missed the ship almost purposely, seeming only to warn them not to use its cannons as weapons.

Maybe the Pursuer knew that he had met his match as he desired only that they would turn back.

Asher understood the message and pulled the lifeboat that still floated capsized, to the shore. It took a bit of heaving to allow it to rest on the upside. The boat was cracked so a hole created a leak in the base, but there still rested another lifeboat on the shore which they could use. Asher at once knew what he should do. 'I need to get up there.' He clutched the sword suspended from his belt. Asher began to run across the beach, reaching the boulders quickly as his advance became interrupted by cannon shots toward the boulders piled along the ledges. They began to fall as Asher had once seen during the avalanche-type threat that presented itself as they climbed on the mountain range.

Asher instinctively ducked and dashed away from the first few boulders he climbed already. The boulders created deep indentations in the sand and Asher stood back far enough on the sandy shore, away from the danger and waited for the falling stones to subside.

They did after a few moments, but he could tell by the few wobbly stones that were ledged into the wall, that it would be unsafe to climb to the top to help the others.

For a few moments, the cannon turned again toward the others on top of the upper surface of the isle. Asher stayed by the ship and remained on the coast.

From the area above, the guards sent out arrows. The flames scorched the ground in areas in which they landed, barely missing Buck and Percy. Darrin shot several shots with his crossbow so that he injured some. He reloaded his bow several times, while also being mindful of how many arrows he possessed.

The group scattered, weaving in and out in order to prevent being targeted. The volley of arrows subsided and those ready to fight came out, putting their bows away because of the short range and retrieving their swords. Others came from behind the rocks to join the other guards. The group of journeyers reconvened as they stood back to back.

Asher stood by the ship on the coast because he still felt chained to the Pursuer's power, though he was not. Their weapons raised, Gabriel used a long staff, which he spun quickly so that it hit the jaw of the guard, making him fall back, but not without recovering. The guard's sword raised up and it struck into Gabriel's horizontal staff, pulling the blade from the guard's hands. Gabriel kneed the guard in the leg with a swift motion and whipped him horizontally across the chest so that he laid flat on the ground.

Buck and Copper had counter attacks as the guard mockingly said, "You think you are able to defeat me? You're all susceptible."

Buck roughly replied, "Yeah, it is true but when you know freedom, nothing can stop us." Copper came up from behind and kicked the back of his legs as Buck clashed with the guard's sword, knocking it to the ground. Before the guard could retrieve it, Copper had already come from behind to snatch it. The guard stood still, almost shaking with sword blades surrounding him from both Copper and Buck. He turned to run, and both of the travelers saw it as an acceptable action.

Percy found a competitor that had more energy in comparison to his middle-aged years. That still could not make a difference in contrast to Percy's years of training that came from the League.

The guard immediately ran toward Percy, both hands grasped on his blade's hilt as the sword pointed across in order to slash across Percy. Percy side-stepped, but he still turned at an angle where his blade met the guard's as the guard turned, as the guard was in shock.

Percy drew close so that the blades came closer together, but pulled away from the pressure as he quickly slashed against his leg in several quick strokes. They pushed so that one gained ground and then the other. The guard's forehead dripped of sweat as his hand's grip began to weaken from the quick strokes, but they still continued fighting.

Keeper, began to feel the paralyzing grip of fear as she saw a guard that seemed to know the crafts of the sword art. The sword at once clashed up against the opponents as it sparked and the inside moved as a mist. Keeper remembered her training and how she had prepared for this moment to fight, to free those who were captives. She extended her arm as much as she could with her injury so that she sometimes pushed too hard and had to back up. Keeper could hear the explosions of the cannons as they landed near those fighting, making her shake with fear.

Keeper could envision the dreams as she trained for this moment. She felt much closer to the goal when she gained the Spirit Sword, but something continued to nag at her. How were they going to free the others? There was the Pursuer in the way. She had the vision as she ran away from the flashing blade and had fallen into a bed near the beginning of the journey, but she felt as though nothing had changed—except now she knew the Holy One. She still possessed the fear that she had of the Pursuer and that she might never defeat him. How would she escape this unending cycle?

As she made several moves in defense of herself with the blade, both her and the guard's blade stood suspended as their faces came close.

"You think you can defeat the Pursuer? You think that your minds have enough defense to go against your very nature. You think you can, but you cannot—"

Keeper gasped as she saw from behind a tall rock near the ledge of the island, a figure appeared in a dark hood. The sense of fear again gripped her as she realized who this was.

Asher from the shore, spotted the Pursuer standing and in almost the same position at which he had seen him as they conversed. He watched the skirmishes. Asher at once realized that he needed to do something to intervene as he saw the Pursuer draw a spiked blade from his tunic. Asher again heard the loud rumbling of the ship's cannons firing, but this did not deter him from what he proposed to do next.

Running the length of the shore to the escape boat, he unroped it from the rock and he climbed inside, throwing the rows into the water. For some reason the ship did not aim in his direction so that it seemed as if its attention completely concentrated on something on land, which seemed a heavier attack on the travelers.

Asher arrived at the ship, using a lift to find his way up the hull, and he secured the row boat so that he could lift it into the deck for the moment.

Asher hurriedly moved to the quarter deck and, grasping onto the captain's wheel, turned in the direction of the other ship with the rudder. Going toward the cannons, he loaded a round heavy ball and with some gunpowder and a flint it began to hit directly at the ship's hull.

The water filled in and shouting was heard so that the cannon shots ceased from the other ship and, at least for now, those on the island were safe.

Asher's cannon shots from the ship flew at the Pursuer's guards near the rocks as the dirt exploded and many were injured.

Chapter 34

Keeper saw the Pursuer coming near them, closer to where they stood. He came as though gliding. Keeper held up her sword and was ready to fight, moving it toward the angle at which to strike. She had been waiting for that moment to defeat the Pursuer. Suddenly, the sword became heavier, and her fingers seemed not to be able to grip the side of it as it suddenly fell rattling on the ground. In that moment, she envisioned how she had seen it fall as she had been envisioning how the Holy One had cut off the chains that were on her arms.

Keeper felt entrapped.
She looked downward, reaching for the hilt of the sword as the Pursuer presently drew closer, with his tongue flicking in and out and Keeper seeing his red eyes created a sense of fear.
Keeper could feel nothing but the clump of the moist grass blades. What enveloped her was the sense that the sun was blotted out by a finger that stood from behind her out of view. In a moment of fear, she turned to face the foe, but as she did, the fear melted as a large smile and a sense of great relief overtook her.

The one who had haunted her dreams stood there. The one who had created the fear. If only she could be strong enough to defeat him. She brandished the sword that she held. She knew that it was important in order to defeat this fear, knowing that what Frederick had said was true. The sword would allow her to defeat him and free those who were enslaved underneath his power. She breathed hard as the Pursuer's blade cracked up against hers, and she could see as it glowed that it had power. Although it felt like this time would be different, that she should see a difference, that finally she could meet face-to-face. The warm, steady vision of every sword stroke already determined a victory was projected as a strike slid down her blade. Keeper pulled back, holding the blade horizontally across in front of her as the Pursuer's blade bore down on hers. She felt like the weight would pull her down.

"I will defeat you. You cannot win. Your gift is worth nothing. You are worth nothing. I will destroy like I should have done when I destroyed your family in the fire." The Pursuer's face was close to Keeper's face. "Why are you here?"

Keeper pulled away slightly from the slithering tongue that sent bits of spit into her face. She shut one eye and though she blinked to make the stinging go away, it never subsided. Pulling back, she wielded her sword around to clink against the Pursuer's as Keeper readjusted herself in a timely counter-attack. Keeper thought of the mention of Pursuer who had captured her family as horrid. The memory flooded her mind.

"I am here to defeat you. To free those who are captured by you. I will fight with everything in me. You may have tried to capture my family, but you will not capture me. The Holy One now helps me use my gift, and he has made me free." Keeper said between blade strikes, all the while keeping the Pursuer's gaze.

The Pursuer sneered, "You have to defeat me?" He paused as if laughing and Keeper could hear his throat rumble. "I am the one who will defeat you. You cannot win.

And for those who are captured, they are only doing what is in their nature. You may be free from me, but I will always taunt you."

"Well, I know who has the keys and that can be stopped. They will be saved. The Holy One will protect me and all those who will be saved. I will continue to fight."

"It is not by you. There was no one strong or worthy enough to take those keys. Someone who can really set free the mind. And that…" He took the tip of the sword against Keeper's and allowed himself to spin around, "Is…" Keeper's hand twisted in a contorted way, "Not…" Keeper's hand let go of the blade and it fell to the ground as though it was hard stone. "You."

Keeper drew back as far as she could, but the Pursuer's blade came close to her throat.

Keeper's vision of this moment and the Holy One's efforts in training her and the power that was instilled inside the sword was not as she imagined. In focusing on the fear of the Pursuer and thinking his power could undo her, she felt like she had to muster up enough courage, "I must defeat him. If only I could do enough. But I can…" She reached her hand down toward the blade, hoping that in grabbing the blade it would allow her to continue to fight, but at the moment she could not.

El Roi and Sabaoth fought brilliantly during the battle and came behind Keeper. Sabaoth's sword was strong, and his face was solid. He gave the signal to the men to charge and they went out in full force. El Roi continued to use his spyglass to see far away as well as near.

Jehovah Rapha came behind, picking up those who had been injured and pulling them away from the fray in order to aid them. The wounded were being revived as he tended to them.

As the battle increased, they fended off the darkness with light. They were filled with it; it was in their being. It dispelled everything that did not need to be there.

Keeper looked back at the darkness of the valley that faded but never really went away. She felt that she had traveled past it, but something inside of her felt shaken. As she passed by the calmly flowing river and felt the spryly growing grass, she sat down and knelt with her hands over her face as tears began to pour from her eyes. The sound of her sobs was quiet, but she felt a hand on her shoulder. She looked up at the Holy One sitting beside her. The tears came in a torrent as the volume of her sobs morphed into wailing. She had felt the darkness as she had sat in the cell in Captavia. It surely was darker than she fell as the hopelessness of not ever being able to escape creeped up into her being and consumed her.

"You do not understand that I worked while you slept?" The Holy One relayed this bit of hope, but Keeper blinked, trying to understand if he used a metaphor.

"I am not using a metaphor. While you slept I worked in your journeyman's lives. You do not have to feel alone. Even when you do not understand what is occurring, I am working."

Keeper saw the steadiness in the Holy One's eyes like the peaceful calm of the ocean. There always seemed a way to trust him in the moments that seemed uneasy. Keeper began to realize that trusting him in the hard portions of life caused her to become closer to him. This was her relationship with him, as he drew her close in a comforting hug in which she sobbed even more before she became quieted by his assuring words.

"He is close to the brokenhearted and those who are crushed in spirit." He rubbed her shoulder and Keeper quieted down and pulled away quickly. Keeper still felt fearful, especially for the well-being of those who journeyed with her.

"Will they be okay?"

"Yes, they will." The day reminded Keeper that something beautiful would happen.

Keeper continued to charge in her own strength. This was the only way she would defeat the enemy, this time for sure. "Why did you trust in yourself?" The Holy One yelled from a few yards back. She knew he could help her, but this was her fight. She had trained and this was what she hoped to defeat.

"I can do all things through the Holy One who strengthens me." Keeper felt in some way he might be able to strengthen her now.

She came close to where the Pursuer stood as the times she had faced him she always feared he may always defeat her. "If I was strong enough, if I were smart enough, maybe I could defeat him."

Keeper observed the glowing sword as it slashed forward and backwards as she ran. It would surely help her this time. She swung her sword and it opened up to the two blades, with one pointing outward.

The Pursuer came up quickly, eyes flashing as he slashed with his curved blade toward Keeper as she felt the wind fly past her face.

Keeper ducked and jerked backwards as she tried her best to make a skillful maneuver through the obstacle.

Keeper opened her mouth to say the words in defense with the blade, but none came back. She could think of none without the Holy One.

Instead Keeper came down upon the Pursuer's curved blade so that it became deflected easily and Keeper stepped back out of breath. It had done nothing. Keeper fought back, swinging around with a forceful kick so that the Pursuer moved back slightly, but Keeper had to move away quickly as his blade came down hitting the grass. Keeper stood back, feeling extremely powerless. She held her old injured arm from the force that she used to fight. She did not have much strength. The blade itself took on a dull grayish blue hue that she had not seen before, but she knew that this did not mean anything good.

Keeper began to retreat toward the lines in which the Holy One stood. The Pursuer at once came after her. It would not end like this. Not this time. Even though she knew it would not be the last.

"Come here," the Holy One called out. Keeper skidded beside him as they both turned around and faced the Pursuer with stoic faces.

The Pursuer stopped because he saw his opponent, and she raised her sword. The Holy One also raised his sword so they stood guard beside each other. The Holy One at once stepped forward as he in the Pursuer came against each other as they had done for ages.

The Holy One's experienced strokes seemed to intimidate the Pursuer as he continued to keep a placid, stern face. The Holy One seemed to keep him at bay as the Holy One slashed his blade as the swords continued to meet almost every second. The Pursuer shuffled back and forth. Both of their skills were greater than Keeper's but the Holy One's power was greater than all.

"Why do you even face me?" The Pursuer's voice

snapped as one could hear the hatred oozing out of his mouth.

"Because I am still the ruler, but you have been roaming around, seeking whom you may devour." The Holy One's voice was firm.

"Yesss." His tongue sounded more pronounced, reflecting the intense disdain he felt. "But you are here and I have the ability to beat you. They are still mine, even if you won over me before."

"Yes, but they now have the ability to come to me. That is the difference from before. I am here to defend my chosen ones who you torment, knowing full well that once they realize they are free that your power has nothing over them."

"Well, I will keep up with that." The Pursuer seemed determined, yet irritated at this point.

"But I have equipped those to fight," The Holy One said and Keeper stepped back as the Holy One moved away as the Holy One asked her to join in the fight.

Keeper looked at the Holy One and realized that this strength was what would help her. She had to trust in him in this endeavor as she faced the Pursuer's attacks. She had the strength and the faith in him to say, "We are more than conquerors through him who loved us." As she said these words out loud, she could see that the blade itself became more powerful, and as she swung from one side to hit the Pursuer's sword, he stepped back from the blow. The Holy One flew the opposite direction as the Pursuer again deflected the Holy One's attacks.

They both attacked at the same moment as the Pursuer fought whom he went against. He seemed skilled, but the endeavor seemed to be tiring him. Sweat came from his brow.

The Holy One kicked at the Pursuer so that he fell backward, steadying himself with his arms.

The enemy came all around them as Keeper and the Holy One stood back-to-back. Many of the enemy came with axes so that once they came against her with such force, she was pushed back against the Holy One.

The Holy One faced one with a long blade in which she slashed in quick steady motions. He too defended himself, never moving from the back-to-back stance of him and Keeper. They had found how to fight together. It looked beautiful and graceful as it had morphed from Keeper acting alone to them working together. A horn blew as a league of warriors with shields in front carrying spears came dashing across the field.

With the sound they knew they had come to the edge of a defeat.

They knew that their rule was almost over.

Jehovah Rapha, El Roi, and Sabaoth stood by the Holy One with smiles upon their faces. They knew of his power and had already seen much of it displayed. They knew that it was only the beginning of what could occur. The group huddled around, but they did not approach them but shared in the joy of the coming moment of this great victory, defeating a strong hold and the Pursuer. They looked at the Holy One and knew His power was much greater. They knew that even if a few battles were lost, that the Holy One had ultimately won the war.

"How will I fight in the real world?" Keeper asked hesitantly.

"You will. I am closer than you know," The Holy One kindly assured her.

Keeper looked this way and that.

"That did not work. Maybe I could tear down the stronghold again. Maybe I could fight another battle and defeat him." Keeper sat there for a moment in her thoughts. "I do not think I can do this."

"Keeper—" The Holy One held Keeper's shoulders and tried to calm her down. "There is nothing you can do. That is the point."

"The point?"

"Yes, sometimes you have to come to a place of brokenness. To a place where there are no other options than to look up."

"Look up?"

"Yes, to look up at me. Come to a place where you realize you are not able to fight alone. Sometimes I put you in those places so you can trust me." He repeated, "Do you trust me to fight the Pursuer for you? Do you trust that I am greater than your fear of your family being taken away by the Pursuer? Do you trust me beyond what makes sense or your crippling fear that controls you? Do you trust me?"

Keeper fell on her knees and cried. She had used the strength of the Spirit Sword, or her own strength, to try to defeat the Pursuer in this battle. She knew she'd had enough. That she had nothing left. That she had tried in herself to be strong. That even though she knew the Holy One that she experienced, she knew she still had fear and that it was something she was drawn to. Ultimately, she knew that this fear was not bigger than the Holy One. The Holy One was the only one to help her overcome her fear and to defeat the Pursuer.

Keeper still cried on her knees. "Holy One, I am sorry

for fearing. I want to trust you and let you do it this time. I know you are more powerful, and I want you to be my strength and my shield. I do not want to be guided by fear but by your perfect love. I trust you."

Keeper felt the overarching peace of the Holy One. She breathed, and he looked at her with his deep eyes. She sat there in the peace of the moment. It was like he had wings, and he was covering her to protect her.

The Holy One then reached out his hand. "Are you ready?"

Keeper reached out her hand in return and replied, "Ready for what?" She felt herself pulled along and found herself in the water of an ocean.

Keeper felt herself plunge into the water.

She rose up from the surf and felt as her feet glided along the top of the rough water, she saw the Holy One before her. He was there. His eyes were filled with the peace that Keeper felt on the inside. He came toward her and then they embraced. "Watch how I work," The Holy One said.

Her newfound peace did not mean that Keeper always had a clear mind. The more she thought about her family and their disappearance, the more she wanted to run. Her heart was filled with the pain of it all. She was filled with her past experiences. Her mind was saturated with the thought of losing everything around her. These new people around her were the only ones that she knew. She had lived alone for many years and had to take care of herself. It had been a hard time, but no matter what people said or how she felt, she knew she could give the pain to the Holy One.

The Pursuer ran after Keeper until she was sick of it.

Keeper realized that struggles in life did not equate being away from the Holy One. She felt a fight in her mind. Her fear was a real part of what she had to deal with—whether she liked it or not. The difference was being empty as opposed to being whole. It was the knowledge of being forgiven and asking forgiveness. It was the knowledge of the truth and continuing to chase after it. It was the truth that her mind was not always clear, but when she called on the name of the Holy One, a light would shine. It was when she was tested that she knew there was a way to overcome it.

All along, it was not about mustering up enough courage to fight, but it was about letting the Holy One fight her battles.

The waves of the storm had continued to rage until now.
At that moment, the sea was stilled so there was peace. The waves were calmed by the Holy One himself. She found herself dancing on the still waves as she held the Holy One's hand.

At that moment she saw the Pursuer run away.

Keeper's fear ran from her mind because it was being chased. The Holy One chased it, and it ran. It fell over the cliff and was plunged into the sea. The waves came, and it was dashed up against the rocks.
Keeper had reached her breaking point. She knew she had continued to let chaos roam in her life long enough. She had run away, let the Pursuer's sword chase her, let it run rampant, let the fear cause uncertainty and darkness, but

she was going to trust. Trust in the Holy One beyond everything she was anxious about. Fear was not bigger than the Holy One. It did not rule him and it would not rule her. In her mind, all she needed to do was make a choice, despite the unknown of what would happen.

Knowing she was able to feel what it really meant to be on the journey, she gave him control. She once began by saying that she trusted the Holy One. "I trust you Holy One. I trust you and put it into your hands. I believe you are true. I can fear about my past, or what has happened to me, but I choose trust. Fear has gone against me. It has made me doubt in your protection of me in your sovereignty, but it is what I will do because I know you are able and capable to do what you have said. In you only I will trust and give my fear."

She handed the Spirit Sword to the Holy One and he said with an hopeful expression, "All you needed to do is ask."

"But I still have control, and the fear will always come back." The Pursuer's eyes were taunting.

The Holy One confronted the Pursuer with flashing eyes, "You cannot plague my dear daughter with the lies of fear. You have no control over her. She is mine, and I will protect her to the end. I have prepared her for more than what you had planned for destruction. She is meant for light, and I am here and will always be by her side," The Holy One said. Keeper knew these words to be true, and they became soaked up into her being of how important and kind they were in changing her and filling her.

At this moment, the Pursuer began to run and the Holy One began to chase him.

Now the Holy One was at his heels. He ran, and Keeper knew he did not even stand a chance. The Holy One chased the Pursuer into the sea, and Keeper knew the fear *was gone and the strong hold the Pursuer had in his control had crumbled.*

The Holy One returned to her with the glowing sword.

She knew it was her choice to trust in the sovereignty of the Holy One and knew he had the power to change her.

As she had jumped into the water, she made a leap towards grasping more of what it was like to follow the Holy One. She was walking out the path that she was meant to follow. Even if fear did come back, she had the choice to trust in the Holy One. She knew he would be able to help her again, though she knew she would fall at times, he would always be there to pick her back up again.

Chapter 35

The great sword glittered in front of her eyes while her eyes glowed in a bright neon green. Her eyes shone brightly as the neon green lighted up as if there was something important that had been learned. The sword then began to glow and it began to dissipate as if it was melting away. "No!" Keeper cried. "Has it served its purpose?" she thought and at that moment she saw something from behind her—something blotting out the sun.

Her eyes widened as she turned around, unaware of the Pursuer so close at hand. There were different emotions coming through each. For the Pursuer it was fear. For Keeper it was peace.

It was the first time she had peace when she looked to the Holy One to fight the Pursuer in her dreams. The Holy One asked, "Why won't you allow me to help guard your thoughts and mind?" Keeper almost cried and said, "That place is too dangerous for you. I doubt even you can control it."

"Is nothing too impossible for me?"

Keeper nodded and as though a sense of darkness drifted away, she saw the Holy One walk in front of her. It was not the sun that shone but it was him. Standing there, he placed himself between her and the Pursuer. The mind is a battle ground that one cannot fight alone.

She looked into the Holy One's face as she noticed that he was holding a much greater blade than the one Keeper had handled.

He was dressed in a thick leather strap over his shoulder so that he was complete with a belt, shoes, and a shield. He had power in the sword. He had a connection to the sword because it was the Word, the *Bread of Life*. The sword is the Word and the Word is with the Holy One and the Word is the Holy One.

It was a moment when Keeper felt the understanding, "I cannot do it on my own." She saw the Holy One step quickly in front of her as she had imagined Asher to have done in his story as the Pursuer spouted between words.

"It is you…" His shock was apparent, but the Holy One came close as their blades clashed for several moments. "You think you can take away my control? Take away those who are captive and under my power?"

The Holy One's voice was firm when he said, "I have come to give freedom to the captives. He has sent me to heal the brokenhearted, to proclaim liberty to the captives, and the opening of the prison to those who are bound...

"They are those who are blind.

"I am anointed to proclaim good news to the poor." The Holy One defeated the Pursuer once and had the keys of sin and death to free people, but the Pursuer still was ruling over the strongholds to pull people away who did not know the Holy One. There was hope to still free them and save them from their sinful selves.

The Pursuer's eyes blazed as he cried out the words, "You have come. The one that I wanted to see. A worthy opponent. Do you think you can take away all that I own rightfully?" The Pursuer's voice tried to portray his perceived strength and laughingly said these words, but one could say he was terrified.

The Pursuer raised up his blade once again as the Holy One's blade gave a great blow onto the Pursuer's blade. The sword that the Holy One held glowed brightly. Keeper could see that the blade glowed because of the Holy

One's power. The sword that she had seen had dissolved so that all she saw was the Holy One.

He was all that stood there in front of the Pursuer, who looked in horror even if there was no one but the Holy One empty-handed. With a breath the Holy One breathed.

With a scream, the Pursuer was down but tried to get up quickly. So the Pursuer ran—he ran with all his might so that he was now retreating.

Just as the army tried to make a strike toward the other, the uneasiness of what was happening sent the rest of them sprawling as they knew their leader had retreated only moments before. All of the Pursuer's soldiers from the inside of the island emerged. However, when they saw the Holy One, they ran. Ran from what they had to face. Ran from the flashing blade. In a moment from the Holy One's breath, the enemy faded into nothing but dust, dissolved into the air.

There was a deep silence as Keeper could see each of the enemies fall away. They fell back in disbelief and looked around.

They looked around and saw that the stronghold of the Forlorn Isle was now in their possession. They could now free those captured there. It was a sweet relief, as they all collectively sighed.

Asher, who had stayed at the ship near the cliff's edge, was dazed at the thought that the others were free. He had seen from a distance as he had climbed up the cliff the face of the Holy One and the final breath of defeat that the Holy One had dealt to the Pursuer. He gazed on the Holy One and began to cry tears of remorse for not helping the Holy One and those with him in order to succeed, but at the same time he realized that the whole result of those who were captured was not up to him. For though he had authority and though he had aided the Pursuer's side, he saw the power of the Holy One and his ability to free the captives. From across the field, he ran over brush & blades of grass as he fell at the Holy One's feet as he had done at Captavia. The tears fell down and he bent his head toward the dirt, but the Holy One, with the compassion that he had, put a hand underneath his chin and raised his head so that they looked eye to eye. "I am sorry," Asher cried.

The Holy One's eyes gleamed with joy by his son's response. "I have forgiven you." The Holy One again looked at Asher, "Do not be afraid because you have fallen short—you will be used yet."

The Holy One lowered himself to his knees and wrapped his arms around Asher, who finally lifted his hands around the Holy One and they both cried. The Holy One used the edge of his sleeve to dry the tears from Asher's eyes. "You will have enough faith soon."

Keeper, who had been standing close enough to hear, was gestured over by the Holy One and the three hugged each other gladly. Percy and Gabriel came over as each began to give each other hugs and fist bumps. Darrin, Buck, and Copper whooped and hollered and embraced the others. Asher came close to Keeper as he said, "I am sorry that I stayed by the ship on the coast."

With that he received a forceful, but joking punch by Keeper. "Well, you could have ruined the plan, but I could not create a plan anyway. It was the Holy One's strength that saved us."

"Yes, but I am thankful for you believing in this cause even when I doubted it."

Keeper smirked and replied, "In spite of everything I

trust you now. We have all had our set of trouble. Thank the Holy One for having the power to break chains."

For a moment they both hugged each other and both pulled away.

"Well ,Keeper, deep down I have always trusted you." Asher's stern face turned into a smile. "It is time for us to go to the underground of the Forlorn Isle."

"Are their chains loose?"

"Yes, but they may need help being dragged out."

"So much dirt…" Keeper said and looked at those who were gathered around her. She had come to know them so deeply from the time they had first started their journey. They all had a place in her heart, and she knew that without all of them they would not have made it to the Forlorn Isle. She knew she needed to talk to someone before he would fade away. She went up to the Holy One and she could see that he still looked as if he had fought the battle. The Spirit Sword was lowered by his side. Keeper could see that his eyes were speaking before he said a word.

"Dear child,

"Know that I have been with you through the thick of the journey all the way to now. I have walked beside you. I have let you see me and what is to come. I ask of you this-that you would not trust in your own ability to see visions or understand what may happen to determine your life. For you know that you could not see the ending of the story, even though you saw a battle where you were the one to beat the Pursuer. I think that you see now that it is through me. Not even that Spirit Sword or your Spirit Eyes were the keys, but for you to say, 'I cannot do it, Holy One do it through me.' How can any be righteous? There is none righteous, no not one and even so I had traded your sin while you were captured so that you have the righteousness of the Holy One. Who else can free you from your chains? What else can be done? For it is by grace you have been saved by faith and it is not of yourselves; it is the gift of the Holy One. Not by works lest any man should boast—for we are his workmanship created in the Holy One for good works which the Holy One has prepared beforehand that we should walk in them. So now you are not slaves to sin, but slaves to righteousness.

"So there is nothing you could have done to free the chains, even if you had visions or did good. It is faith that frees the captives."

Keeper closed her eyes and opened them filled with a sense of completeness on hearing those words from the Holy One. She had joy of knowing him here presently before her, and he came and wrapped his arms around her as she buried her head into his cloak. She shed many tears of joy and relief with hope of the realization of the grace she had been given through faith.

"What about Cephas?" Asher asked the Holy One.

"You will find him, just not right now," The Holy One answered.

The group of fighters looked up across the gray landscape as it began to turn into a green field with many stacked stones around as it created a bowl in the clearing. They turned toward a hill of stacked stone. There were bits of grass peeking through the rock.

Looking back over her shoulder, Keeper could see the cliffs that lowered down to the sea with winding crevices. Keeper could still hear the sea as it crashed up against the sides of the rock face.

Keeper then turned again toward the scattered rocks that led upward. Each of the members scuffled over the stones and slid down the other side, their feet touching the newly growing grass.

The Holy One came along with them as they made their way up the hill. They came to a tree whose roots were set growing between the boulders. Keeper's mind again flashed in a vision that she had seen of a tree. Keeper came closer to put her hand up to the bark and this time the tree opened up as in her dream. She was able to see as the bark turned in on itself and opened up, and she could see a light. She stepped inside so somehow it transported her deeper and deeper into a long winding path with torches on either side. It descended and Keeper found herself standing on the ledge of an open area. She looked down to see dirt and those standing waist-deep were the many who she had seen in her dreams, digging their way to the depths. Keeper could see that they were dazed and looked around. They seemed unable to understand. At this time, Keeper did not see the chains that had bound them.

Were they real?

Everyone followed behind her.

They could not find Cephas.

The sand shifted from the wall in little crystalline granules. Looking down into the pit, Keeper could see the same types of granules of sand shifting as they began to dig deeper and it shifted as it came moving around them as an hourglass. It continually drained and no one was there to flip the contents over so that the granules could go the other direction.

Those who dug continued to grow more deeply entranced as they made their way to the central region of the hour glass. The hour glass shape of the walls was from a wide point in the ceiling to a narrow point near the ground where the sand continued to drain downward. They had created a deep pit which had grown deeper as the years had elapsed.

"Dig, dig. More to which it falters," was the chant that Keeper heard rising from the depths as she knew from her visions. With shock she saw the bitter toil of these persons which she had seen, almost recognizing some of their faces. The chains which had once held them were gone, but they still dug.

The Holy One looked around at those who were captured and shouted, "I proclaim freedom to the captives."

As if they had been in a daze, they looked up with blank faces, but after moments, their faces morphed gradually into beaming smiles as they looked down to see no chains holding them. Their minds were no longer trapped slaves by the Pursuer's power. They looked at each other and their dismal surroundings. Seeing the Holy One standing in front of them, they could see that he indeed was the one who had freed them.

Each let out a shout of joy that rose and with no restraint so that a musical quality was heard in the chant that Keeper had heard in the town of Buffington, "We are free!"

"Bless, Bless, Oh we give thanks to you
For Holy One your words are true.
You free the captive,
You break their chains,
You give them new life,
You provide safety,
You give yourself.
Hope, Hope, for we trust in you."

The sand slid beneath them as the granules shifted downwards while the group tried to help them.

The whole of the travelers let out a shout. "Praise the

Holy One!" Percy's eyes glistened as tears fell down his face, and he hugged Asher, slapping his back. "Our journey has led us to this moment, and see—the Holy One was standing here at the end of it all with his victory in hand."

"Yes, we are in his debt, and what he gave is priceless. There is no way to repay it but with praise." Gabriel's voice resounded through the cave.

"Now we must go to help them to the light of day," the Holy One offered. "For they need to see the world outside."

The Holy One then took off his outer garment and continued to tear the end into strips and tie into a chain which he lowered downward.

To Gabriel and Asher he said, "You stay at the top so we can be pulled up since the sand isn't stable." The Holy One then continued, climbing down the slope of sand toward the center valley.

He came up to someone who still had sand around his legs, and offered his assistance. Some took it, and he would allow them to put their feet into his hands as he hoisted them on his back. He continued up the slope with the individuals on his back, and they would grab the tethered sheet as they were pulled to the rock edge.

One person close by muttered as they gained consciousness, "Where am I?"

Keeper looked down and saw that some of them that received freedom did not have any chains that clasped unto their hands.

The Holy One spoke, "whom the son sets free is free indeed."

Keeper loved the words of the Holy One.

The Holy One continued to go to each person and pull them up toward hope. There were some that refused his help and continued to wallow in their sin. The Holy One took up those who had received his help as they ascended up the slope as he had become a bridge to safety for them.

"Those who have never been told of him will see, and those who have never heard will understand," The Holy One explained to them.

"What about the others?" Keeper had a concerned look on her face.

"If they do not receive me, then there is no ability to be rescued."

Keeper's heart broke at the thought of this, but she knew it to be true. Her cheeks became puffy and red because of the liquid that ran from her eyes. She looked toward the Holy One and could see he was crying as well with deep sadness for the ones that were not to be saved. There was still a way to be free, but still they fell deeper into the sand. Even though Keeper and those around her had not found themself in this stronghold, she had once been in the same state.

"I do not deserve this. I cannot come." One of the freed captives said honestly to the Holy One.

"That is why it is called grace. It is a gift." The Holy One's face was beaming as he said these words.

The woman looked up at Keeper, and Keeper saw this person as if she saw herself. She suddenly recognized the woman as the one who used to sell linen in Rockfirm and had disappeared. Keeper realized that the woman ended up here in the depths of the Forlorn Isle.

"Well then, please help me know you because I want to receive that salvation from your grace."

"You shall receive it…" the Holy One extended his hand, and she took it gladly this time. He hoisted her onto his shoulders so that her arms held on tightly around his neck. They maneuvered the shifting sand and they were able to help her grab the lifeline extended. "I receive that gift," she repeated, and her chains were broken.

Keeper recognized the Mayor, who looked down forlornly at his feet as he tried to step hastily through the sand. He used his arms in order to make strokes toward the ledge where the material stretched downwards, but he could not manage it.

"May I help you?" The Holy One asked this.

"I have done too many wrong things. I cannot come to you. I have not done enough good to be rescued."

"There are none righteousness, but that is why I am extending my hand—for you to see that I can bridge the gap for you since you could not." The Holy One again reached out his hand as he could grasp it securely, but the man swatted it away, feeling offended.

"So you are calling me a terrible person? I have done good things in my life, but no one could amount to the strictness of what you say. I can do it on my own, because there are many things that I have done that keep me from you. There is no way to be washed clean."

"Well, I can offer that to you. This will be my covenant with them when I take away their sins."

"No, I cannot come to you." The man again looked away and continued to dig with his arms through the sand and it again began to shift down around him. The Holy One, seeing that his outstretched arms were rejected, bowed his head in pain. A tear fell down from his eye and his insides ached with the pain of leaving this man behind. There was nothing he could do, nothing he could say to change this man's mind. If they never received his salvation, then how could he be able to help them? Keeper could see chains on the man as they began to appear around his ankles.

There were only those in which received the Holy One's help. He had created a way to be rescued from this place, but they had to receive it. Gabriel and Percy grabbed the hands of a young, curly-haired, green eyed boy who had climbed up the rope to safety. Asher did a double-take, thinking that this was Cephas. His heart sank as he did not recognize the boy's features.

Asher peered over the ledge, searching for Cephas anywhere about the sandy hourglass-shaped cavern. He saw some who he thought might be the same, but as the Holy One came up behind one of those in which he had rescued, Asher became concerned.

Keeper looked at the open expanse of the darkened sand of the Forlorn Isle. She looked around to find anyone she could. Her parents were not there. She did not know where they were, but she would keep searching.

The Spirit Keepers and guards from the town of Buffington were spotted and also received forgiveness. They were led up the ledge and to safety.

"Is there anyone left? Did you miss someone?"

The Holy One replied, "The only ones that are left are the ones that rejected my help."

Asher's face looked dejected, with thought, 'Did my Cabin Boy reject the Holy One?' In order to find out for sure if what he had suspected was for certain he asked, "Did you see my Cephas? Did he reject you?"

The Holy One's face had a peace about it when he said these words, "No, he is not here, and I know that he has not rejected me."

"But if he is not here captured, then where would he be?"

The Holy One replied, "He is free out of the Pursuer's grasp."

Asher felt immense comfort in hearing these words… Cephas was free and away from the Pursuer. These words were hope enough. Whether he would see him again was uncertain, but Asher's prayer was that he would. The Holy

One pulled up the rope and looked back at those who did not come and then turned toward the group. Those who had been saved hugged each other joyfully.

"There are still others who are waiting to be rescued. They too need freedom as all do. It is time that we go."

The group made their way through the tunnel, feeling the harder sand chunks along the walls. The light met them, and those who had been rescued blinked intensely at the sight of the bright day before them. The clouds had disappeared then the brightly-lit sun shone down on the world which the Holy One loved. Keeper made her way down, sliding across the rocks and looking toward the green battlefield and the cliffs. Keeper began to feel the wind as it wrapped across their faces and pulled them along.

They made their way, maneuvering above and across the rocks, coming to the green field in which many had dissolved into dust. They passed by them silently and those who were rescued knowingly observed the loss.

Those who were rescued began to skip and dance, and many began to run across the field as a sweet melody filled the air with thanks. Keeper joined along in the jubilee as well as Gabriel, Asher, Percy, Darrin, Buck, Copper, and the Holy One. There were no chains on them at all.

Their hearts were light as they went along. Coming to the edge of the field that Keeper had once been backed up against by the Pursuer in her dreams, she now looked at the water crashing beneath and smelled the deep salty air waft up in warm spurts. Keeper saw the edge along the cliff in which they had made their way. This ship still stood anchored in the surf as the many waves crashed against the sides. The lifeboat was securely attached to the shore near the edge of the cliff. Looking at how long of a trek it would take the group to make it toward the water, Keeper paused for a moment, holding her breath from the sea spray. Keeper then stepped backwards a few feet.

"What are you doing—" Asher started to speak with a bit of a joking tone. Keeper did not respond and began to run forward. "Keeper wait—" Asher exclaimed as Keeper leapt over the edge of the cliff, straightening her arms into a dive. The wind rushed past her as the water came closer. It was just as she had once envisioned herself jumping off the Waterfall of life and flying away.

And just as Gabriel had said, it clicked. And it had.

The others looked down and Percy laughed, "Well, that is one way to get to the ship."

Keeper splashed, but one could not hear the sound because the many crests of waves enveloped her. She felt the cool of the blue water and the foaming bubbles that gathered around her. She could see the deep depths of the water. Keeper propelled herself to the surface and was met with the air of the surf. She was cold, but she felt invigorated. She could hear the cheers of those up above as she made her way to a rope hanging off the side of the boat which she grasped to make her way to the railing. Keeper rounded her leg over the inside of the railing and sat on the deck watching as the others came down the walkway crevice of the cliff.

'Making that leap again…' she thought to herself as the boat swayed beneath her, secured to the anchor. 'This has been a good journey, one in which has turned out in a way more positive than not. There has to be more. There has to be more to come.'

Keeper delved into her thoughts about what adventures they may encounter yet to come. It took ten minutes and several trips of the life boat in order to give everyone safe passage onto the boat.

The Holy One and Asher were on the main deck of the ship while looking out across the ocean. "Where do we go?" Asher asked, thinking about all those aboard.

Percy, Gabriel, and Keeper came up from the lower deck laughing, "I guess you had enough of the dirt and sand that you had to wash it off somehow." Percy laughed, slapping Keeper on the back.

"Yes, you had to straighten up and jump into the ocean water," Gabriel replied laughingly.

The laughs reverberated across the group as they each breathed air in deeply to cool their laughing fit.

As it quieted, Asher repeated his question. "Where are we going?"

"We need a place where those once captured can live," The Holy One replied.

"Should we take them to Buffington?" This was Percy's suggestion.

The Holy One shook his head in disapproval. Gabriel came alongside him. "We need a place where they are in the world but not of the world." Gabriel had been discussing with the Holy One what should be done. "They will be a great example when they get to Rockfirm." The Holy One nodded in agreement.

"Rockfirm? Where I am from?" Keeper was disheartened at the thought. "It is such a dark place."

"Yes, but when there is more darkness, the light will shine brighter. You will be able to help them know me." The Holy One's eyes lit up.

"Aye," Percy agreed. "Though it's one of the hardest places to be, they will be more of a witness."

"Yes, even so…" Asher replied with a wave of his hand as he gave orders of the deck. "Time to man the ship. Get ready for another voyage which I think is not the last." The ship made its way over calm seas as they made their way toward the shore nearest to Rockfirm. The sun glowed with a soft warmth on the group's faces.

Chapter 36

A school of flying fish rose up from the water with their fins and tails flapping, reflected off their silver-flecked scales. They would let out nets in order to catch them for meals. Overhead were some gulls cawing at each other as though in a race to a misadventure and another day. They alighted noisily on the mast and from time to time would come down to meander along the deck. There were also a few dolphins which came up to the surface and Keeper would watch them as their dorsal fins rose above the sea line.

It took a day's time of smooth sailing and a group of travelers to make it to the shore nearest to Rockfirm.

It was a few hours' journey through the woods near Rockfirm as they continued to hear the screeches of creatures which used to make Asher frightened. The Holy One handed Asher a compass that Asher had given Cephas and smiled.

Keeper recognized the walls of Rockfirm through the bristles of fir trees and green leaves to the oak trees.

"Rockfirm," Keeper said to herself as a relief to see something familiar, even though it was a hard place to live because of its darkness. Those who walked beside her who had been rescued smiled as they heard those words. "We are about to find a place to stay."

Keeper led the group as they came up to the gate of the city. There were two guards standing below who looked stern but seemed to be aware that something had changed in the world.

"What is your business?" The guard wore a sword crossed on his back as Keeper had the Spirit Sword across on her own back. The guard saw the many people who had been rescued.

Keeper looked at the guard and simply replied, "I used to be the Spirit Keeper of this city of Rockfirm and I need a safe place for these new inhabitants."

The guard who inquired previously questioned, "Is this the Spirit Keeper?" He said this yelling upward towards someone on the wall. A brown-haired person with green eyes lifted his head above the gray stones of the rock wall and Asher gasped, holding onto the star-studded compass hanging around his neck.

The boy replied when he saw Keeper. "Yes, this was the Spirit Keeper before me who gave me this position."

The boy's eyes scanned the group, and both Asher and he locked eyes. "Is that you, Captain Asher?"

"Yes, hello there." Asher was overjoyed, but was having a hard time speaking.

The Cabin Boy at once looked at the wooden rungs of the ladder that scaled down the wall. "Open the gate," he called to the guards who, seeing that the former Spirit Keeper was with them, did so immediately. The silver of the sun broke through the widening door frame of the gate so that in a few moments the reflecting sun shone on the Cabin Boy who stood in the opening.

Asher blinked his eyes and was met with the embrace of the young boy who had now grown into a young man. He was taller than Asher remembered him to be as his head rested at the upper part of his chin.

"Cephas, my Cabin Boy." Asher choked out. "I thought that you had been captured by the Pursuer and captured in the Forlorn Isle." Asher looked toward his Cabin Boy and saw in his eyes that he seemed wiser, maybe beyond what was expected.

"Yes, but I was safe the whole time. You have no idea

of the journey it took to get to this city of Rockfirm and even knowing that I have Spirit Eyes."

"You have Spirit Eyes?" Asher took back his words in correction, "Yes of course. That is why you are a Spirit Keeper here."

Asher handed the compass which he had received from the Holy One's hands, who had retrieved it during the battle with the Pursuer, and Asher presented it to Cephas. The intricately engraved stars carved on the outer locket opened up to the shaking red needle of the compass enclosed in the glass. Its needle was pointing northwards as it usually did, following the stars.

"I was not able to use this on part of my journey here because the Pursuer tore it from me." Cephas fumbled with the broken chain, and he tied it into a makeshift knot around his neck. It would not stay tied and fell back into Cephas' hands. Asher cupped his hand onto it and slid the compass connected to the chain into his hands.

"I will fix its chain so that you will have many more times to make use of it," Asher assured him.

Cephas also came to Keeper and she asked, "Have you had any more visions?"

"Yes, I saw you and Captain Asher."

"You know Keeper?" Asher asked.

Keeper replied, "Yes, we met and he let me know that Gabriel was coming through the vision with his Spirit Eyes."

"Amazing," Asher replied.

"The Holy One was really taking care of everyone," Keeper assured him.

Asher turned to the Holy One and said, "I am sorry that I doubted you."

The Holy One looked toward him and said, "You are forgiven."

The Keeper's eyes flashed as it would often do when

her Spirit Eyes envisioned a vision or dream. She could see an old man in a cave, and she could see that something stood behind him that looked as if it had scales and guarding something. The man pointed to something behind a dragon. The Holy One who had been extremely quiet until now, looked at Keeper as she knew he comprehended the vision as well.

"What do you see?" the Holy One asked intently.

"I see someone." Keeper then again saw the white crests of the waves billowing on a rough sea. She at once saw the sand on which the waves crashed on an island in which much underbrush grew.

"Well," The Holy One looked at Keeper and asked her, "Do you want to do something to retrieve it? You are the ones I purchased—a pearl of great price. Whose souls will you catch?"

Keeper looked at the Holy One and her eyes glittered as she thought of what else may occur next in her life. What an amazing thing was it to have visions like these and for them to lead her in understanding what may happen. Keeper sighed and the Holy One could see that she was worn out.

"You do not have to leave right away. Maybe you should wait until I send for you again."

"Or more people join?" Asher asked.

"Yes, if many join, it will make the journey easier."

"Then I will," Asher agreed.

"So will I." Cephas raised his voice in the excitement of the moment.

"You all will go," The Holy One replied in an overjoyed way and all of the original group of travelers nodded.

One of the curly-haired boys who had been rescued inquired, "Can I go? I would serve as a bit of 'elp to ya." Both Copper and Buck echoed this.

The Holy One nodded and the rest agreed. "Let us rest up, for who knows what could be ahead," The Holy One replied.

The guards kept the gates wide as the group of travelers came to stay at Keeper's house. They sat around, talking about the many times in which they had traveled.

"Do you remember how hard it was to climb up the rocky mountain?" Percy inquired of the group.

"Do you understand how hard it was to spend those many years digging the sand as the Pursuer's workers?" One of those who had been freed explained.

"Remember how amazing it was to use the Spirit Sword and how the Holy One just appeared to use it to defeat the Pursuer?" Keeper could not get over the fact.

Chapter 37

Keeper walked through the door in one of the rooms in the house of her heart as she felt the sweat trickle down her back. Keeper looked through the clear panes of glass that lined the walls and ceiling of the greenhouse. Scattered along the ground and hanging from the ceiling there were plants in beige pots painted with light blue designs.

Keeper went up to one of the plants and rubbed her hand across the soil, so that her hands collected specks of dirt. Keeper moved her hands to the leaves of the green plants, feeling the smooth, waxy surface of the heart-shaped leaves.

Keeper heard the footsteps of the Holy Spirit as he shuffled onto the red tile of the enclosed windowed space.

"Do you see the growth?" The Holy Spirit said to her as she looked at the plants' vines.

"I do not know. I have never been in here to keep track."

"It was planted the day you came to know the Holy One. When you abide in the Holy One, it is like he is a vine of this plant and you are the branches. If you abide in him you will bear much fruit. The Father has loved the Holy One and he has loved you. Abide in his love."

Keeper looked at the small white flower blooming from the plant.

"So you love one another. No longer does he call you servant, for the servant does not know what his master is doing, but I have called you friends. For all that I have

heard from my Father I have made known to you."

She admired the growing plant and understood she was growing in the Holy One's love.

As Keeper came over to the larger book which stood upon a wooden carved pedestal, she asked, "Is this the scripture?" She said this paging through the leaves of the book, and she recognized a passage.

"Now there are also many other things that the Holy One did. Were every one of them to be written, I suppose that the world itself could not contain the amount of books that would be written."

Keeper looked around at the myriads of books stacked upon the bookshelves and imagined every collection of books in existence.

"Yes... He did much more," Keeper reasoned, understanding the greatness of all he had done.

The house of Keeper's heart had been built up in a beautiful home. It had once been a dilapidated house, but now through the help of the Holy One and the Holy Spirit it was now being built into something that the Holy One intended. It was painted, there were new shudders, and a new roof. When she came to know the Holy One, the Holy Spirit had come in to live and had cleaned out her heart, so it was made new. There were lessons learned in the rooms of the house. The house would continue to be built up until completion. It was fit for the Holy One to dwell in.

There was a door of the house of her heart and she

heard a knock from the outside. Keeper heard this and hesitantly went up to see who stood on the other side.

"Who is it?" Keeper asked, not knowing the important person standing on the other side.

"I stand at the door and knock... Let me come in so I can dine with you." Keeper, hearing this, understood who spoke to her. She let the Holy One in. She did not have anything ready at the moment, but they bustled around a boiling pot so that she seasoned it with spices and fresh vegetables, with pieces of meat. She ladled it out into bowls as they were placed on the table in a fancy dining room.

Keeper, the Holy One, and the Holy Spirit sat together before saying a blessing, "Our Father which art in heaven, hallowed be thy name. Thy kingdom come, thy will be done, on earth as it is in heaven. Give us this day our daily bread, and forgive us of our trespasses as we forgive those who have trespassed against us. And lead us not into temptation, but deliver us from evil, for thine is the kingdom and the power and the glory forever."

They looked at each other and smiled out of gratitude as they ate. There was much laughter and celebration of all that occurred so far. Keeper felt a great sense of comfort in understanding the closeness of the Holy One to her.

They continued this for many hours.

Keeper could see darkness and the things of the world in her mind. She could see her fear, doubt, and self-reliance. "What are you thinking about?" The Holy One asked.

Keeper turned away and then turned back to the Holy One. "I am just thinking about life, but maybe not the best things."

The Holy One spoke, "For those who live according

to the flesh set their minds on the things of the flesh, but those who live according to the Spirit set their minds on the things of the Spirit.

"If you live according to the flesh you will die, but if by the Spirit you put to death the deeds of the body, you will live."

"How will I do that?" Keeper asked, trying to understand how to act.

The Holy One replied, "Putting to death the flesh daily. You are not your old self. You on the other hand can be led by the Spirit of the Holy One as sons and daughters of the Holy One.

"Likewise the Spirit helps us in our weaknesses. For we did not know what to pray."

"Yes, I will begin to ask you for help in this area. I see that it is a daily walk to follow. I know you will give me strength," Keeper repeated.

"Yes, I will help you." The Holy One said as he held on to Keeper's hand. "I am always going to be with you in this battle."

Keeper looked up as she had heard the true account of the Holy One—how he had died and was able to defeat sin and death and then rose again. It was a miraculous story, one that he had done for all. It showed the immeasurable riches of his grace.

"Grace." Keeper had mouthed the word before.

The Holy One replied, "It is what you did not deserve. You could not earn it."

Metaphorically, Keeper could see a wall that she built in her mind of all her achievements.

"So none of these things matter?"

"It is not a result of your works. It is through faith. And I will again repeat it, none of the things you will accomplish allows you to be redeemed. It is calling on the name of the Holy One. Good works may follow after since faith without works is dead. The law of the spirit of life has set you free in the Holy One from the law of sin and death."
Keeper looked down at the stones of the wall in the backyard of the house as she built another room. This is what Keeper built. It was a wall she had begun to build herself in her own strength.

The Holy One replied, "I have many works planned for you to do. Now you know me, you can walk out in my strength to complete them."
Keeper looked down, nearly crying at the pile of things that she had tried to stack up before she was saved by the Holy One, but now she was saved. These were the works that came from him. She was bearing fruit as she abided in him.
She knew he was the chief cornerstone, and if she believed in him, she would not be disappointed.

Keeper walked through a densely filled forest, but stumbled upon a fallen tree. Keeper sat down on the tree, stretching her legs in front of her.

The Holy One stood in front of her and walked around for a moment before turning back to speak. Keeper had been reflecting on her life as she looked toward him in this personal moment.
"I do not want you to pity me. I want you to love me."
Keeper heard these words come from his mouth.

"Do you know that I love you?" The Holy One asked and Keeper began to see different emotions in his face.

"I understand it, but I guess I have not embraced it. I do want to understand it. I want to continue to follow you," Keeper said.

"If you understand that I love you, you will be able to love others. If you love me, you will keep my commandments."

"Please help me do that," Keeper pleaded.

The Holy One assured her, "I will. You are already seeing fruit."

Keeper stood up and began to twirl. There was still a certain calmness in the moment, so that the Holy Only took her hand and she turned around. She imagined herself in a white dress even though she wore a long sleeve shirt and skirt. They danced around for a moment, but suddenly she felt solemn, and she fell to her knees as she was talking to the Holy One. He knelt in front of her as she prayed.

"Holy One, I need your guidance in my life. I need to know in a deeper way. Please guide my life in the way it needs to go. I need to know how to talk to others about you. Please strengthen me on this journey of life. Please help me."

The Holy One's voice came clearly as he sat in front of her. "I will do it. And much more. Just have faith in me."

"What needs to be known is this…" The Holy One spoke.

"The Spirit Eyes that you have, Keeper, are the dreams you have. You continue to have these dreams, but they are different from the chaotic dreams of before. As you walk beside you, your steps will be guided along the way.

"You have visions of what will happen. Of insights of the future.

"You can see the things that are invisible, such as people's chains and the army all about. All of this makes up your Spirit Eyes. They are prophetic and help you to see." The Holy paused and continued.

"Also you need to know about the chains. The chains which are one's own sin, which one may not be aware of. One's own enslavement. Everyone has them from their sinful birth since Eden, where man sinned and that sin passed down to all mankind. They are what keeps one trapped. So that one goes back to their own sin. One does what they do not want. The sin keeps people captive. One is not worthy, but I am the one who is righteous. It is because I am without sin, I died for everyone. I died, breaking the bonds apart as I let a host of captives free as I went to Hell as I allowed everyone to be free from the punishment one deserved from one's sins. I then rose and defeated death completely. If one comes to a place where one needs me then, that one is sinful, that one cannot do it themselves, then I can break through the chains one has. I make one free. The invisible chains become visible as they are broken off and destroyed. One is then able to know me and one day live in Heaven with me. It is then one's job on Earth to tell others about this freedom. I have given one the power in my name to free others and tell others how I have saved them." The Holy One paused again.

"I also need to tell you about the Spirit Sword. Keeper, I am with you even if not physically. I show myself in the Spirit Sword which represents the Word of God, which is the Bread of Life. This is the fact that I was in the beginning, and in the beginning was the Word. And Word was with God and the Word was God.

"Keeper, when you say scripture the Spirit Sword has power so that it glows an icy blue with a mist floating on the

inside. You may see it as a power to go against the enemy, but in the end it is better to attain my power. It is used to break chains because of man's sin and it is done through my power and the Word of God. It is sharper than any two edged sword. It is used to break the chains apart through my power." The Holy One again told Keeper of more.

"There are also the waves. There were the waves that crashed that had been raging. The waves showed the storms of life. Despite these storms, I walked on them as those who follow me walk on them. These storms are sometimes too heavy. These may seem like one is sinking when one sees the storm. But in the midst of them I am able to calm them in one word. I am able to bring one back up from the waves and make one walk on them with one's eyes on me all the way. I calm the storms." The Holy One said these words, and Keeper listened intently, knowing how important they were and understanding what he had been teaching her. She would continue to listen to his words and learn from him.

Chapter 38

They stayed for many days conversing and getting up their strength for what was to come. Keeper would often take walks through the streets of the city of Rockfirm, sharing with others about the hope that she had found. There were many there who began to understand the Holy One to Keeper's great happiness. She had trouble containing sadness for those who would not receive it and continued to be slaves to sin. It was all a choice they had to make.

Messenger was asked to lead the town since the Mayor was no longer present. The town began to experience more life under his leadership.

Cephas had been training another Spirit Keeper and let him take control of the position of Keeper.

On one of the walking trips, Keeper roamed outside of the gates and into the pine forest where she felt the bark as it crumbled off the trees. She continued to walk and came out into a clearing which now grew small yellow daisies.

"You are here again," The Holy One said as he came up to her.

"Yes," Keeper said, looking at the wide expanse of the field surrounded by the dark green needles of the forest. It was where the Holy One had taken off her chains when she decided to follow him.

"This is the place where you freed me." Keeper's face glowed so that her eyes lit up, realizing the impact of her words. She had traveled far since that moment the chains had fallen from her hands.

"You have come far, and much has occurred, but I desire that you keep growing." The Holy One gave a hand to Keeper. She grabbed it as he raised her arms, and she was sent into a whirling spin. The edge of her tunic fluttered as she spun.

Keeper once again stood still, sliding down into the tall shoots of grass, pulling the stem of a yellow petaled daisy. The stem was fragile, and she twirled it gently between her fingers, seeing the petals turned around like spokes of a wheel rolling along a smooth road.

The Holy One sat beside her and they both observed this flower before the wind blew again so that the petals flew into the air one by one.

"Keeper, you know I will always be with you…"

"In this world you will have trouble, but behold—I have overcome the world. I have made a way for you to have a new life in a way you never knew possible. It is because you cannot free yourselves, but I can through my strength. You cannot change, and that is the point. It just means you need me." The Holy One paused, bringing Keeper back to the present and looking at the stem of the daisy that Keeper had laid down. "Will you keep trusting me?"

Keeper's eyes rested on the Holy One's, and there seemed to be a colorful shift that occurred within her pupils and spread like a storm cloud or a green forest or a wave. In the next moment she saw the sword, broken chains, and a wave. After a moment it settled down as her glowing neon green eyes turned back to their usual green hazel color.

"Yes," Keeper said, searching the eyes of the Holy One. "But I need you to give me the desire and strength." Keeper closed her eyes and opened them suddenly. "And please, will you help me to understand my Spirit Eyes and the Spirit Sword more?"

The Holy One only nodded and smiled in the kindest of ways.

"Even in that way, I have been doing something in you all along, helping you through the fears to help you overcome and become a slave to righteousness. I will continue to do this, and by my grace you receive it. After all, you live in the land of Deror, which means freedom." The Holy One said this while with her in the field near Rockfirm.

Keeper reflected on the Holy One's words. They stayed in the city of Rockfirm, regathering themselves, but knew that there was much more to be done. It was not long after that Keeper boarded the boat, *The Duchess*, with the other journeymen for the rest of the quest. They had decided to go further along the sea, to free more captives. Keeper looked back to see the looming cliffs, with the Waterfall of Life falling into the waves of Derorian Sea that moved below the boat. She gazed across and saw the foaming peaks of waves crashing up against the shoreline and then moving way out into the deep sea. She saw the rounded horizon with small islands scattered across. The mast had flapped with the flag attached securely. The wooden deck had swayed beneath her. All of those aboard had manned their stations.

The Holy One raised a hand as Keeper stood on a boat, and he stood on the shore, waving. "It is done, but it's not the end."

Keeper heard his words, but they were more than dreams this time. They were real.

www.ingramcontent.com/pod-product-compliance
Lightning Source LLC
Chambersburg PA
CBHW072336020726
47506CB00004B/902

* 9 7 9 8 9 9 9 4 6 5 1 7 0 4 *